PHANTOM HEARTS

A COLLECTION OF THREE DISTINCT SUPERNATURAL ROMANCE NOVELS

A.L. HAWKE

PHANTOM HEART, LLC

ISBN: 978-1-968775-52-0 (ebook)

ISBN: 978-1-968775-23-0 (paperback)

ISBN: 978-1-968775-07-0 (hardcover)

ISBN: 978-1-968775-10-0 (audiobook)

This is a work of fiction. It comes directly from the author's imagination. The book includes fictitious names, characters, places, and incidents. Any public names are used solely for creative purposes. Any resemblance to actual people, living or dead, or to companies, institutions, or locales is entirely coincidental or accidental. No artificial intelligence (AI) technology was used in the creation of this book's cover art or manuscripts.

Line edited by Stephanie Marshall Ward

Proofread by Alexa B., alexabooks.wixsite.com/authors &

by Faith Williams (Phantom Masquerade)

Series Collection Cover Design © 2026 by Brosedesignz

Phantom Masquerade & Haunting Joy cover © 2021 & 2025 by Mirella Santana

Shades cover Design © 2023 by Regina Wamba of MaeIDesign.com

Published by Phantom Heart, LLC

27702 Crown Valley Pkwy, Suite D4, #201

Ladera Ranch, CA 92694

Email correspondence: contact@alhawke.com

Printed and bound in the United States of America

First printing 2026

Learn more about A.L. Hawke at www.alhawke.com

Correspondence: contact@alhawke.com

❀ Formatted with Vellum

SHADES

On a road trip across the USA, while nearly being knocked off the highway, Amanda has a chance encounter with a shadowy man wearing shades. Amanda soon learns that devils from a biker gang won't stop pursuing her. Not before they steer her into more danger. There's trouble in store, all set as a trap to bring the man she's falling in love with closer to damnation.

1

ALMOST LIKE AN ANGEL

He shuffled his dusty boots along the mud and gravel. Yesterday it had rained, and there were still a few wisps of white and gray dispersed over an otherwise clear violet sky, but it was mostly clear now. This was his treasured spot. His sanctuary. On the infinite horizon, orange and red spread over vast distances of scattered weeds and shrubs, while behind him was darkness. He tore his eyes from the view and looked down at a drop of at least three hundred feet below. His fingers fidgeted in the pockets of his worn black leather jacket as he gazed down from the precipice. Then, as the sun rose, he removed his shades and stared out again.

"Angel down," said the voice on his cell phone. "Amanda. Twenty-two. A blond college graduate. English major. She's looking for a job in journalism. Born a Pisces. She's rooming in an apartment with an Asian student in Santa Monica. Now she's at the border by Arizona. Where are you at, John?"

"Not far from there."

He turned, facing the dark clouds of Los Angeles.

"The girl's off on some road trip, John. We have no idea where the hell she's going. Or why. Just intercept her. Get over there before Lilith does."

"Send me the location."

He turned back to the desert horizon. The yellow sun rose. It blinded his naked eyes, but he liked that. He withstood the pain from the burning light. He let the light wash over his face and body. Then a silhouette of a bird soared on the horizon, perhaps a few miles from where he stood. It was deep in the desert in the middle of nowhere. Like him, it seemed to wander without direction. Its wingtips touched wisps of the bright light of the sun, almost like an angel.

2

RESPLENDENT

"Guys, you know, I mean, what can I say? How can I describe this? Breathtaking? Check. Amazing? Check. Incredible? How 'bout resplendent? That's what the desert is. Resplendent." She laughed, remembering the word from an essay for her English Lit final. "I tell you guys, it's positively resplendent."

A perfect orange and red painted horizon opened up before her after she ascended an incline, while weeds and saguaros rushed by her, on both sides of her green VW, seemingly stretching forever in a stunning, endless desert vista. She pressed the record button on her old handheld recorder again.

"I wish you could be here with me. The sun's rising, the trees are gone, replaced by cacti the size of people, and behind me are LA's ugly rain clouds and smog, which I'm happy to be leaving behind. It's like nature's opening up and it's as excited as I am to be here. Hello, nature. Hello.

"The furthest I've ever driven in my life is Vegas and Portland, so everything is new. That's what I'm gonna bring to you. New. Fresh. And resplendent." She chuckled again. "I'm bringing resplendent to you all right now..." She leaned forward, gazing at the horizon. "God, it's beautiful. Spiny cactus. Yeah, spiny everywhere for miles. And the soil's changed too. It's getting red. Red! *Can you believe that!*

"So, Amanda?

"Hey, what's up?

"What's the first thing you're going to do after you graduate from college?

"Hmm… I don't know? How 'bout travel across the country?"

Like really travel.

Sunlight blinked between saguaros outside her window. Then, after another short incline, was the infinite desert horizon again.

"What do you hope to find a thousand miles away from home?"

"A tall, dark, and handsome man… Rest stops. Slushies."

She nodded, clicked the stop button, and stuffed the recorder back in her pants pocket. That was enough.

Then she tapped her fingers on the steering wheel, gazing over her green hood as the voice of Steve Perry sang "You Better Wait." The song seemed perfect for the start of her trip. She touched the glass. Chilly. Well, not for long. It was going to get hot later. Then she glanced at her sole companion, vibrating in the passenger seat—a small, prickly cactus in a clay planter she'd just bought at a gas station, her first souvenir. Then she accompanied Steve Perry like a total dork in a loud sing-along of "You Better Wait"—until her speakers were interrupted by the ringing of her cell phone.

"Mands," said a voice in her car speaker. "Hey Mands, you still alive out there?"

Amanda leaned forward again, watching a bird with wide-stretched wings soar over her car on the two-lane freeway. Behind its wings sprawled the vista of that orange-red streak. It was so much like a painting. So beautiful. The bird passed from view above the car.

"I just left, dummy," Amanda said. She looked down at the console. "Hey, guess what, Lu?"

"What's up?"

"I started my podcast."

"O-k-a-y."

"I thought you liked my podcasts?"

"Course I do. I'm your number one fan."

"Yeah. You know what I called the desert? Resplendent. Absolutely resplendent. Isn't *resplendent* a great word?"

"You're so freaky, Mands," she said with a laugh. "I love you."

"Love you too. So what's up?"

"Ben called." Luane laughed.

"That's early."

"Yeah, he said it's because he couldn't stop thinking 'bout me since last night. Can you believe that? I played it down. But I kept thinking of him standing over me, reaching down and gently touching my lips. God, Mands, Benji's so hot. He told me he was going to be working near Big Bear over the summer. I thought the mountains was all about skiing and snow. You know, it's the snow I love. He said he'll be running some sort of bike shop up there and he wanted me to come up. I thought we can visit together. If you don't get kidnapped in Texas or something."

Amanda headed down another incline but still, far off, she could see an infinite horizon with the rising yellow-red sun. She looked up, but her bird was gone.

"It gets really hot in the summer in the mountains," Amanda said.

"It gets hot everywhere in the summer. I sure hope so...'round Ben."

There it was. The large bird was hovering in the sky, easily visible now. It just floated. But it must have been gliding fast. Amanda was barreling down the highway at eighty-five miles per hour. She wondered if she was like this bird—like a bird flying without direction. That's what she was like this morning.

"Pretty."

"More like handsome," Luane said.

"Not Benji. It's just so pretty out here. I wish you could see it with me, Lu."

"I hate road trips. So here's the thing. If I go with Ben to the mountains, I won't be in LA. So—"

"How long will you be gone?"

"You don't get it. I want you to come with me, Mandi. Want to? It'd be so much fun! Benji said he has a few cabins up there that'll be free for us to use. We can spend some time up there free of charge and bike, you know."

"I don't know. I thought we'd hang by the beach."

"Well, the beach is expensive. I can get us a cabin for free for a few months until we're done interviewing. But I need to know, like, *now*. He said he's stalling and someone else wants it."

Amanda lost sight of her bird again. It had faded off the desert horizon.

"So? What do you say?"

"Big Bear?"

"Or Arrowhead. I'm not really sure. Something in that direction. Yeah."

"It wouldn't take me long to visit you even if I stayed in LA."

"Except you won't 'cause you're coming with me."

Amanda laughed. "Okay, let me think about it." She looked at the small cactus vibrating in her passenger seat. "Hey, whatever happens, I'm bringing you a new friend. He's smaller than Benji, but he's just as prickly."

"What do you mean?"

"It's a cactus. Your boyfriends are always prickly like that."

"That's my cue to tell you to go fuck off. Mandi, love ya and all, but I have to know. Can we stay up there or not?"

Amanda said nothing. She wickedly loved the silence, knowing it was driving her friend crazy. Then, instead of answering, she hung up the phone.

Steve Perry started blaring again, and she enjoyed his voice while gazing out at the desert horizon. The stunning morning view over the Arizona desert remained. And so did her soaring bird. Was it the same one?

Mountains? Biking? Is she joking? Lu never rides bikes. She gets into these flings. Benji? I mean, she practically just met him.

Her phone buzzed in her pants pocket. Amanda checked it. It read: "I need to know NOW. I know that wasn't the reception, bitch."

You'll have to leave Santa Monica eventually, Mandi...

A gust of wind was strong enough to push away any more thoughts. And it was so strong that it forced her to veer toward the opposite side of the highway. She felt terror rise in her chest as she struggled with the steering wheel, swerving the car back and forth, trying to merge back into her lane. Her VW Bug shook like crazy. Then her tires screeched as she slammed on her brakes. Her body was thrown back as her car stopped right before an incoming freeway barrier. Her hood missed a metal bar by inches. Or had she hit it? She wasn't sure. She looked down the road ahead, expecting to see a semi or something else huge that had pushed her. All she could make out was a black streak in the distance. A reflection? A mirage? It didn't look like a car, and it vanished after a few more seconds.

Then a larger streak of black flashed by her, shaking the car. She could make out this object more clearly. It looked like a dark orb racing at incredible speed into the distant horizon.

She unlatched her seat belt, threw her door open, and leaped out of her car. Then she placed her hand over her forehead, gazing down the freeway. There was nothing around for miles. She was completely alone out here. It was quiet, too quiet, as if nothing had happened.

She checked her car. There wasn't a scratch.

She took a deep breath and gazed at the view again. In the distance was that same gorgeous desert sunrise; vast saguaros, for as far as the eye could see, shone under golden light. She tried to calm herself by staring at the gorgeous view, but her hands still shook. Then she spotted that bird again. An eagle? A hawk? It was a huge bird soaring by the dunes and cacti as if watching her.

She turned at the sound of an approaching car. That was weird. There hadn't been anyone for miles a second ago. And when she had a better look at the car, that was a surprise too. It was a slick sports car, black as hell, with the windows completely tinted. The luxurious car pulled right behind her green VW.

The door opened and the first thing to come out were dusty black boots. This was followed by a tall man in black jeans and a black T-shirt. His dark hair was short, almost like a crew cut. He wasn't clean shaven, but his stubble was attractive. He was tanned, but his skin looked whiter with all the black clothes he wore. And he wore super dark opaque shades. In those sunglasses he reminded her of a cop.

"Are you all right, miss?" he asked. And he said that just like an officer too.

At first, he was expressionless behind his shades. But then, as Amanda turned to face him, he weirdly stepped back.

"I'm fine," Amanda said. "Fine." She took a deep breath and threw back her long blond hair. "Just shaken up, I guess. Some truck almost threw me off the road, I think."

He looked down at her chest. She followed his eyes and saw what had shocked him. Her white T-shirt was splashed with red. She reached up and touched her dripping nose. "Shit." She wiped blood from the back of her hand. Then she reached into her pants pocket for a tissue, but it was empty.

"I saw you lose control of your car," the stranger said, walking closer.

"Where'd you come from?" She laughed. Then she smeared more blood from her face on the back of her hand. "Did you see the truck that pushed me?"

"Your nose is bleeding. Here." He reached into a pocket for some tissue, dipping down his head and peering over his shades. *Holy shit!* His eyes were the most gorgeous blue Amanda had ever seen. What a crime to cover them! He handed her the tissue, closing her hand over it. And she almost died. Right then and there, it was almost all over. With her fatigue and near accident, and those eyes peering over his shades, she felt unsteady.

Get a hold of yourself, idiot!

"Are you okay?" he asked.

"Fine. Fine. I'm fine." She pushed away from him and laughed nervously. "Not used to driving this early in the morning, I suppose. And ... shook up, I guess."

"Well, I get it. You gave me quite a scare, miss. We're not far from Yuma. If you want, I can escort you to the border."

"Huh? Oh ... it's just a nosebleed. I'm fine." She nervously chuckled. Then she wiped her nose again with his tissue. She smiled at him. "Just looks terrible with all the blood. You some kind of cop, or something?"

His face went deadpan, just like it had when she had first seen him. He didn't respond. He just stared at her. Then he finally said, "That idiot on a bike almost hit you. I saw you swerve to avoid him. Guy was probably drunk."

"Oh."

Wait? Bike? How could a motorcycle have pushed my car!

He stood for a moment in silence just looking at her. It was like he was scrutinizing her, from her feet up to her face. He shook his head. "Well, have a nice day, ma'am. I'm glad you're safe."

And he headed back to his car.

She quickly blurted out, "Wait. Hey, what sort of car is that?"

He opened the door. Then he looked up and paused for a moment. "A client's. I'm delivering it from LA."

"Oh. I'm from LA."

"I figured that from your direction. Be careful out there, okay, Amanda?"

"Sure. Bye."

"Goodbye."

She held his handkerchief to her nose as she heard the roar of his engine. Then he drifted aggressively across the red desert sand, heading back onto the highway. She waved, watching him until she couldn't see his car anymore. Then she was alone on the desert highway again.

When she got back into her car, she put her hands on the steering wheel and tried to get a hold of herself. Her body was still shaking. She looked at her window and noticed blood on the beige cloth of her car door. "Shit." Then she looked at the passenger side. The cactus pot was broken on the floor. "Double shit."

Then she gasped. He had said "Amanda." "Amanda."

How did he know my name!

3

THE HERO

THE SOUND OF CLICKS AND BELLS AMID THE SMELL OF SMOKE FILLED THE large hall as John walked down a wide, red-carpeted walkway. It was early afternoon on a Saturday, but that didn't stop the casino from being loud. People were shouting by the craps tables beside the beeps, fake coin collections, and lever pulls. John wore his black leather jacket. Having been to Las Vegas enough times, he knew they loved overdoing the air conditioning in the casinos. It might be ninety outside, but it was usually sixty inside. And it was. He kept his shades on too. He didn't care to talk to anyone. He brooded. He couldn't stop thinking about the last mark. That last angel down looked so familiar. Too familiar. The whole meeting near Yuma was so weird.

Sherry? Could it be?

He thought of visiting Sherry's place and telling her about it. He considered it…but then thought better. He hadn't rested in days.

He was nearly done traversing the walkway toward the elevators. His thoughts of Amanda and Sherry left him as he passed a roulette table.

Sitting by the wheel was a captivating redhead, one of the most beautiful women he had ever seen. She sat perched on a stool wearing a sparkly white dress and a matching diamond purse. The sleeves elegantly flowed over her wrists, touching the backs of her hands. Her hair was long, soft, and strikingly dark red. She pushed it from her eyes as she looked around. But when she saw him walking toward the table, she quickly looked away. Yet he caught a glimpse of a smile as her dainty fingers glided over her bangs.

He wasn't the only one staring. Across from her was a group of sharply dressed kids, very young, talking way too loud and casting stray glances at her.

John sat on an empty seat right beside the redhead. Then he waited for the wheel to stop spinning. He reached into his jeans pocket and pulled out a hundred-dollar bill. He laid it on the table. The redhead faced him and smiled a beautiful smile with perfect white teeth. A dealer wearing a formal black pin-striped suit handed him four chips.

"Red," he said, placing all the chips on red. The redhead put a chip on black.

"Come on, man!" exclaimed one of the young idiots across from him. "Let's go! Let's make some money."

When the dealer finally turned to face John, she had way too big a grimace. It was Lilith. Lilith. The same Lilith riding the motorcycle he had chased near Yuma, who had nearly taken Amanda's life. But now Lilith was disguised. The devil wore a dark wig covering her white hair and contacts that made her eyes black. Lilith's natural eyes were pink. But she couldn't darken her pale white skin. And the wig was too curly to be attractive. Still, her facial features were pretty. Lilith had always been a pretty demon.

"Azracl," Lilith said, smirking at John. "Azrael, welcome to Sin City. How surprising to see you here."

She glared at him with those fake eyes and seemed to relish his recognition. From the corner of his eye, John caught the redhead biting her lip, and her hand holding her chips was shaking. The other guys, facing her, tapped their fingers impatiently on the green cloth table.

"Place your bets," Lilith said, finally breaking eye contact with him. "Place your bets."

Lilith moved her pale hand over the table. She threw a small white ball on the wheel. The ball rolled around and around. John looked over his shades as Lilith turned back, folding her arms and glaring at him, waiting for the ball to land. The ball hit black. Lilith frowned at John and smugly collected his chips.

"You know you can win a lot more by choosing a number," said a boy with greased-back hair across the table.

"Fuck off," John said, glowering at Lilith.

"What!" the boy said, jumping up, raising a fist. "What the hell did you say!"

"I'm talking to her," John said, nodding at Lilith.

Lilith smirked.

"Hey," said the redheaded stranger. John had almost forgotten about her. "That was a lot of money you lost, mister. I'm sorry."

"No problem," John said, gladly turning away from Lilith to the redhead. "But I see you won."

She nodded and smiled. The dealer handed her another red chip.

"What's your name?" John asked her.

"Her name is Bridgette," Lilith said.

"I was asking her."

"And I answered for her."

"Come on, let's go," said the kids across from John. One of the guys was still staring at John, but his buddy tugged at him. They left the gambling table. That left Bridgette and John alone with the devil.

"I was told to meet you," Bridgette said quietly. She waved her red hair back from her eyes. "Your name is John, right?"

"I think so."

"John, Bridgette," said Lilith, gesturing to them. "Bridgette, John. I hope she meets your expectations during this sanctuary, Azrael? She matches your taste. Does she not? She's quite lovely, isn't she?"

"I wasn't aware we were in sanctuary," John said. "It seems sanctuary is whatever the hell you and Samael call it. But she is pretty. Yes. Very."

"Always the best for Raphael's agents." Lilith turned to the rest of the table, but there was no one there. "Place your bets. Place your bets."

John reached into his wallet and took out ten more hundred-dollar bills.

"You think it'll be red this time?" John turned and leaned toward Bridgette. "I tell you what, if I win, I'll give you some of my winnings."

"I hope you win for your sake," she said, widening her large eyes. "That's a lot of money, mister. Good luck."

She had lovely eyes and perfect white teeth. An angelic smile.

"We've decided to kill Amanda tomorrow," Lilith said as the metal ball spun. "Unusual? Perhaps. But this mark is unusual, isn't she? Did you recognize her? I'd think you would. We made sure that this mark particularly interested you. Well, you might have won yesterday, but we've decided on another go on the road. What do you think?"

Bridgette put her hand on John's. He turned, surprised. Bridgette smiled uncomfortably. Her hand flapped a bit over his. She was doing a job, obviously.

"Go on," John said, looking at Bridgette. "What's the deal?"

"I shall tell you after you lose," Lilith said with a chuckle. "I shall tell you after you get used to losing. Life is like a bet, you know, and you have repeatedly picked the wrong side."

The white ball hit black.

"See?"

"It's all right." John pulled another hundred dollars out of his wallet and handed the cash to Bridgette.

"You said if you won?" Bridgette said, furrowing her brow.

"Who said I lost? When are we meeting?"

"Huh?" Bridgette asked, flustered. "Oh." Her face flushed almost as red as her hair.

"That's why Lilith introduced us, right?" John asked.

"Oh… I don't know. When?"

"Midnight," he said. "I'll see you then." He handed her his key card envelope with his room number and the spare key card. Bridgette nodded and tucked it in her purse. "Now, excuse us, but I need to have a word with your procurer."

John watched Bridgette leave. He couldn't help but stare at her legs under her sparkly dress. Lilith had done her job, indeed. She was perfect.

"Go on," John said, turning back.

"Life is a game of chance, is it not?" Lilith said, folding her arms over her suit. Then she showed her empty palms as if she were a magician. "Red or black? You never know. Is your allegiance to Michael? Gabriel? Raphael? Samael? Or… God?" She laughed. "Where does your soul lie?" She leaned forward. "Here's why we're meeting. From now on, I propose you and I converge in public in Las Vegas. I approach angels on the verge of ascension, you fuck them, and save their miserable lives by defiling them. They can then wait for perdition, like you. It will be as useful as your meddling with me on the road. Then we can stop the tiresome chase. It'll all be discreet and private, far more relaxing and satisfying for both you and me. You know we can't keep fighting in public like this. Eventually someone's going to be found. So how does that sound? Instead of the road?" And the bitch finished with a big smirk.

"Fuck you."

"You are Bridgette's guardian angel tonight," Lilith said with a laugh. "She's my gift. But I've marked her too. So you work for me tonight. If you don't guard her, I kill her. If you screw her, I *might* kill her… I *might* not. You never know. Place your bets. And then, after we've had our fun, tomorrow we meet for the real game. On the highway. For Amanda. Or…" She looked at him with disgustingly fake pity in her fake eyes. "*Was she Sherry?*"

John placed a hundred on the table. "Red."

"I'd say you're a masochist."

"I have a feeling the table's rigged. I want to prove it. Odds are I'll win on a third try."

"Odds are you will always lose without me." Lilith stroked his hand with her pale fingers. He jerked away. "Instead of the redhead tonight, you know, you…and I could be together? What do you think? After all, carnal pleasure can lead to the heart. Perhaps a taste of me will lead you finally along the right path. What do you say?"

"I'd rather be with the girl. She's prettier." He pushed the bill toward her again. "Red."

Lilith hissed at him. She grabbed his hundred-dollar bill and pushed a black chip on red. Then she hurled the white ball in the air. It landed perfectly on the spinning wheel.

"Red or black," she snapped. "Hmm, Azrael? What shall you be? Life is simply a game of chance. Nothing more, nothing less. You've been working for the wrong side. I offer pleasure, Raphael offers pain. When will you get this?" The ball landed on green. "Ah. See. Neither wins. But you still lose." The bitch laughed. "Perhaps this is the real Azrael. Destined to be green. A *John*? A drifter roaming roads saving people from peace and happiness? Work for me and all pain ends. All Samael and I offer you is pleasure. I shall demonstrate tonight."

"I save lives."

"I retire souls to heaven," Lilith said with a shrug. "Enjoy your prize. You deserve it for thwarting the death of the young Sherry yesterday. But tomorrow morning ends our sanctuary. We fight again on the road."

Bridgette stirred in bed. When she got up and stretched her arms, her breasts and perfect figure were silhouetted by the light emitted from the window. She yawned. Then he stared at her naked ass under her long red hair as she swayed to the floor-to-ceiling window. She pressed a button opening the drapes, and the lights of the city that never sleeps were unveiled before them. Now her knock-out nude body shone in the light.

"So pretty," she said with a yawn. "I love these rooms. Always working, I forget how breathtaking it is for the guests. You on vacation, hero?"

"Don't call me a hero."

She ran her fingers along the drapes and gazed down at the city lights. Then she yawned again. Her face, her stunning face, was silhouetted by the glow from the Las Vegas Strip.

"You want something to drink?" John asked.

"What do you have?"

"Fuck if I know. There's a fridge under the cabinet. Take whatever you want."

"Thanks," she said with a laugh.

She meandered over and then bent down, waving her ass before him as she searched the small refrigerator. He was sure she was doing that on purpose. Then she grabbed two palm-sized bottles of alcohol and closed the door.

"You best not be a cop," she said, cocking her head back. "Are you? I know you don't work for my contact."

"How do you know that?"

She sat beside him on the bed. She handed him one bottle and then unscrewed the other and drank it. He laid his on the nearby nightstand.

"You were fighting with her." She shrugged. "You seemed to hate each other."

"I'm not a cop."

"Hmm." She turned her back to him. "You kinda act like one."

"I'm not a cop."

"Can you scratch my back?" She turned her back to him again.

He ran his fingers along her neck and down her back, massaging deep into the skin.

"Ohhh," she said, closing her eyes, "you have such nice strong hands."

He pressed deeper and she bent forward. He ran his fingers over her nipples and his palms traced the curves of her breasts. She leaned back, shaking her hair out. Then she moaned. "That's it. Perfect."

"What should we do now?" she whispered. "You asked in the note that I wear black. Why?"

"Black is my color."

"Maybe you should have picked black when you put your money down."

"I didn't say it was my favorite color. Your hair's red."

"You're weird, you know that?" she said, cocking her head back. Then she laughed and put a hand up. "No offense. I mean, you're just weird. So were your friends. They were really weird too." She closed her eyes and relaxed again as he dug further with his fingers. "That feels so good."

Bridgette had lived all her life in Las Vegas, she had told him. She had wanted to be a teacher. But she didn't have money for school. So she whored. It didn't start that way. It started in a strip club. Now she wanted out of Sin City, just like John wanted out of his job. She wasn't happy. Neither was John.

Of course Lilith had picked the girl simply as a tease, a mockery of his job. A trap. Did he accept pleasure in pain? Either way, the damage was already done, and the prostitute's fate was inevitable. Like Amanda, this girl was marked. She would die. Just like Amanda.

"That feels so good." She drank more from the small bottle of alcohol. "You're really weird." She swallowed and put a hand up again. "Not in a bad way. Just weird. You don't seem to fit in. Ohhh... That feels so good, hero, keep rubbing like that..."

She turned and kissed his lips. Then she ran her long fingernails along his groin and touched the bulge in his underwear. She probed inside and touched his hard cock. Then she rubbed it up and down with one hand, while massaging his chest and stomach with the other hand, still holding the mini–liquor bottle.

"Perhaps we've had enough," John said, pulling away.

But he smelled her again. Roses. He wondered if she had added the scent after leaving the roulette wheel. Lilith knew he loved that scent. She probably gave it to Bridgette. She must have. Bridgette rubbed along his leg as she sucked on his lip. Then she entered his mouth and ran her tongue along his.

He'd let her in the room when she'd opened it with his key. Sure. To protect her, he had told himself. And then he'd let her kiss him. Sure, he'd let her do that. To keep the pretense. But that was it. At first…

She giggled and turned to him, staring into his eyes. It was dark but lit enough by the window to see her lovely profile. And her stunning eyes, opened wider in the dim light. They both froze. He felt hypnotized gazing at her. Then she ran her hand along the stubble of his cheek and over his short hair. For a moment, just a moment, he thought of lying down beside her and drifting to sleep. Not lying with her, but just lying beside her. That was enough to *protect* her.

"You want me now, hero?"

"Don't call me a hero," he snapped, lifting a finger. "Don't do that."

She snatched his raised finger with a laugh. Then, slowly, she sucked it. Up and down, as if she were sucking his cock. Gently, she pushed him on his back. "Relax," she said. She sat on her knees, bare breasted with the light from the window shadowing her perfect figure. Then she bent down and whispered in his ear, "I want to suck your cock and taste it. Then I want you inside me, lover. I'll be on top. Please. Let's do that. I want you to fuck me again. Okay? How about we do that, John?"

He could just see Lilith glowering at him now, those spooky, unnatural pink eyes, knowing full well that he suffered in her entanglement. Protect her and sleep on the couch? Yeah, right. He wasn't a hero, and he wasn't innocent either.

She gently touched her lips to his again. Ever so slightly. She smelled so nice. Behind the alcohol was that flowery aroma. He couldn't quite place it: Was it roses? Carnations? It didn't smell slutty. He liked that.

She pulled back for a moment and tipped her small bottle of alcohol into her mouth, downing the rest. Then she giggled and scooted on her knees to the foot of the bed.

"You don't like the word *hero*, huh?" she asked, looking up at him, pulling down his underwear to his ankles. "What should I call you then?"

"John."

"Is that really your name?"

"No."

"I didn't think so," she said with a laugh. "What's your real name?"

"Nothing."

"You want me to call you *Nothing*?"

He shrugged. She shook her head and pushed him flat on his back.

"You're not nothing, mister. Not with that cock."

And he lay still. And she sucked. He didn't move. She did. So everything was all right. *Right?* He leaned back, gazing up at the ceiling in darkness, trying to think of nothing. While she took his cock into her mouth and sucked him. Up and down. Up and down along his shaft.

Then she jumped up, surprising him. She straddled him.

"Sorry, Mr. Nothing, but I can't wait anymore," she said and laughed. "I want you inside me. Now."

She tore a condom packet open and rolled the condom on his dick —where she'd gotten it, he wasn't sure. Then she glided his cock inside her, bobbing up and down, running her hands along her breasts and then sucking his index finger while riding him.

She moaned as she gave him pleasure. Riding him. And this was it. This was his true sanctuary. He imagined Lilith's pink eyes staring into his, her mouth curled in a sinister, sardonic grin mocking his damned soul.

But he wouldn't give himself in to the pleasure. He wouldn't even move. Especially not now. He felt more miserable than ever. Of course Lilith had known he would. That's why she had arranged it.

Bridgette orgasmed, shaking over John's body. Then she fell to his side. He hadn't moved since she mounted him.

"Are you okay?" she asked, sounding confused. She ran her hand through his hair. "You're not done, baby."

"I'm fine," he said, turning his head from her.

"You're a nice guy," she said, nodding as if explaining it to herself. "Really nice. That's what you are. You're just a nice guy."

"I'm not a nice guy."

By morning her naked body lay sprawled on the white sheets of the bed. Her eyes were open, but glassy. She lay there on her back, in the spot where they'd had sex. He had stepped into the bathroom only for a moment. That had been enough time for them to break in quietly and suffocate her. But this would be easy for his enemies to cover up. Who'd care about a wandering prostitute?

She was dead. He had failed at protecting this wandering soul. To John, it didn't matter if they were pure or if they were prostitutes. A life was a life. Lilith knew that. The devil had won. She would either turn him or make him lose his mind.

On the other pillow one word was scratched on a note: *Colorado.*

4

MESA VERDE

Amanda leaned over a wood fence staring at the square stone structures way off in the distance. She let out a big sigh. Because she loved it. She had learned that around the thirteenth century, ancestral Pueblo Native Americans built their homes deep in the recesses of the hillside. No one knows why. Maybe for shelter? Then they were all strangely abandoned. Gazing at them from this lookout from so far away hardly did them justice. But really, Amanda wasn't looking just at them. She loved the views beyond the horizon even more. Ever since Albuquerque, the endless horizons had taken her breath away. The infinite horizon was like the shore by the beach, only this wasn't water. This was different, something she never saw in LA.

A gentle breeze blew against her cheek. It blew along her short white skirt too. The weather was just perfect.

She turned to the gentleman closest to her amid the crowd. He had parched, wrinkled dark skin and a cowboy hat and was enjoying the view too.

"Excuse me," Amanda said to him. "Can you take a picture of me?" She posed in front of the fence hoping she wouldn't block the ruins. He smiled. Then he handed her back the phone.

Happy enough. Check.

She turned around and leaned on the rail, staring out and sighing again.

Ancient pueblo village. Check.

Better move out now, Amanda, if you're gonna make it to Grand Junction before nightfall.

Then she snapped her fingers. She had almost forgotten her podcast! She pulled out her handheld recorder from her pants pocket.

"Guys, I'm here in front of Mesa Verde. Have you ever been? It's so incredible. There's this crack in the Earth and inside, pretty far away— it isn't a bear in a bear cave. No. No. It's an actual ancient city. I'm not kidding. A whole Pueblo town. They call it Step House. And they say it's a thousand years old. From here, it's kinda small. Like I can imagine a bear coming out and the houses just being rocks. But there's all these open square windows over the rocks too. So… I'm talking softly because a bunch of tourists are standing real close looking at the village but throwing a couple stray glances at me like I'm a total psycho. But I had to tell you about it live right now 'cause I'm right here right now, guys. If you're ever in West Colorado, you've got to check this out. You just got to."

She clicked the off button with a satisfied nod.

That's when she noticed a tall boy with a black T-shirt and jeans to her left. He was super pale and wearing shades. The boy was close enough to hear her recording. That must have been the source of his big grin.

"I have these if you want to try," he said, offering her binoculars.

He had a friend who was also wearing shades and really pale, but heavier. Behind the sunglasses, they had pink eyes.

"Thanks," Amanda said.

With the binoculars she could make out the individual holes in each square building. She saw stone steps and holes for firepits in the sand. And she saw people hiking around the ruins that she hadn't spotted with her naked eye.

"Have you checked out the petroglyphs?" the tall, pale guy asked.

"No," she said, not tearing her eyes from the view.

"We're backpacking tomorrow. I'm Charlie. We're hiking the whole area."

"My name's Amanda." But she was still looking through the binoculars. She spotted a couple climbing up steps into one of the rooms. And another, a bit ahead of them, walking through a crack in a stone wall.

"We just came back. We can go there again with you, Amanda, if you want to check it out?"

"It's too far," Amanda said, finally handing him back the binoculars. "I don't have time."

"The walk to the Step House is less than an hour."

"What brings you here?" asked Charlie's friend.

"Graduation present."

"Oh, are you with your parents?"

"No."

"Friends?"

She smiled and shook her head.

"So you're alone?" asked Charlie.

"Yeah. A gift to myself."

Charlie smiled again, but with a squint that meant he thought she seemed a little weird. He glanced at his friend.

"Well, bye," Amanda said, waving her hand. "And thanks. I gotta get going. It's gonna get dark and I've got a long drive." Honestly, they were creeping her out.

"Where're you heading?"

"Cross country."

"Where?" asked Charlie.

"Across the country."

That was enough. She wasn't going to tell these creepy guys another thing. And, anyway, she had to leave. She had spent too much time already trying to find Mesa Verde. Her hotel reservations were on the outskirts of Grand Junction, and she had a long drive yet.

She made her way back to the parking lot to her green VW Bug. But as she walked along the dirt walkway, she caught the two strangers trailing behind her. At first, she thought nothing of it because Charlie was nonchalantly drinking water from a straw in his backpack, gazing back at the cliffs, while the other guy just stared ahead with his hands in his pockets. But then, by a fork in the road heading to her car, they came right behind her.

But they turned the opposite direction in the parking lot and got in a beat-up white pickup truck. Thankfully, they just sat in their truck as she left the park.

She turned on the radio. It was the Eagles—the last song on her *Hotel California* album. A bit too mellow, so she switched the tune to her all-time favorite song on the album, "Try and Love Again."

Back on the road, it was just an empty desert—which she loved. She tapped her hand on the steering wheel to the music. But the song was interrupted by her phone ringing.

"Hey, babe!"

"What's up, Lu?"

"Finally got you. I texted you to call hours ago."

"God, you're like my mom. She hasn't even called yet." Amanda leaned forward and gazed between the trees as the horizon opened up again. The view seemed to go on forever. "Lu, I wish you could see what I see. The view is to die for."

"Take some pics and send them to me."

"It's not the same."

"Where's your next stop?"

"Denver. I was thinking of changing course to Mount Rushmore. But it's just so far, but my listeners would have loved it. Now I can check off Mesa Verde. Did you know Mesa Verde was the first national park in the US? It was so great."

"I really don't give a shit. Sorry, Mands."

Amanda laughed. "It's something you gotta see if you're driving across country."

"Well, I never heard of it."

"'Cause you've never traveled across country."

"Okay. But, ya know, I have been to the mountains. Speaking of such, have you decided?"

Amanda stopped listening to her. Not because she wanted to play mean again, but because she caught sight of a white pickup truck behind her. It was about a half mile back, but it seemed to be following her. And it was definitely the same truck those two strange boys got into when she was in the parking lot. Were they heading to Grand Junction too? Had they left the parking lot at exactly the same time she had?

Maybe. But didn't they tell her they were backpacking at the park tomorrow?

"Well?" asked Lu through her car speakers. "What do you say? How about it?"

"Huh?"

"What's the matter, Mandi?"

"Oh…nothing. I'm just wondering why these guys are following me."

"What! Amanda, I told you that you shouldn't be driving alone."

"Yeah. Well—" There were a few cars between them, but they were there. "They're two guys I met at the Pueblo village ruins. They didn't really seem dangerous, just nerdy."

"Sometimes the greatest serial killers are nerdy."

"Thanks a lot, Lu. You're making me feel a whole lot better."

Now they were at least a half mile behind her. She watched as they disappeared for a moment behind a hillside. Then they appeared again around a bend.

"You just came from a national park?" asked Luane. "Why not just turn around and talk to a park ranger?"

"I'm fine. There's only one highway out here."

"Well, you're scaring the shit out of me. Just pull over and see if they pass."

"I want to get to Grand Junction before it gets dark." But Luane's idea was, in fact, perfect.

Amanda pulled over.

"Gone?" Luane asked after a moment.

They drove by her car.

"Yeah." Amanda took a deep breath.

"Stop freaking me out!" Luane said with a sigh. "Shit. Call the minute you reach Grand Junction, okay?"

"Sure."

"And don't go to Mount Rushmore. Just do your cross-country thing, stay at Grand Junction, and then get your ass back home."

"But what about my fans?"

"Stop it, Mands."

"Okay," Amanda said with a laugh. "Bye, Lu."

"Wait, hey, what about—"

Amanda chuckled as she wickedly hung up the phone. She honestly didn't know yet where she wanted to spend her summer. If she lost the cabin, she lost the cabin.

She watched the white pickup travel past some trees up ahead and then disappear around another corner.

Now she only hoped that she'd arrive at her hotel before nightfall. It was getting late.

5

SHATTERED GLASS

There was no way Amanda was making it to Grand Junction before nightfall. It was already dark. Really dark. She had her brights on, but she saw so many shadows under the moon. That made her imagination race in fantasy. Because there were no other cars on the road. She was on a deserted highway with nothing out here, not even any radio reception. She kept playing old classic rock music, now listening to the band Asia, but her favorite oldies didn't stop her from feeling uneasy. Especially when a car's headlights started trailing her along the deserted highway, winding up a hill.

She estimated she had only another hour or so of driving, but she wasn't sure. The last sign had said Grand Junction in eighty-eight miles. Even at seventy-five miles an hour, that had been over half an hour ago.

She jumped as the car behind her turned. Under the moonlight, she saw a white pickup truck.

What! How?

She had lost them a hundred miles ago. It couldn't be the same car. Could it?

But then the vehicle came closer, swerving in and out of its lane. It didn't pass, it came right up alongside her car, close enough for Amanda to recognize the beat-up pickup truck. She touched the console and typed in Luane's number on speed dial. Nothing. There was no reception.

What's Luane gonna do for you anyway?

The passenger window rolled down and she recognized the guys from Mesa Verde. Yes, it was their same pale features visible by the dim lights of the truck cabin. And most weirdly, they were wearing shades. One of them was drinking from a bottle, the one Amanda recognized as Charlie. He was driving. They gestured for her to roll down her window.

She shook her head.

"Amanda, your back tire's flat."

"What?" Amanda asked, cupping her ear.

They both signaled for her to roll down the window again. Amanda shook her head.

"Your back tire," Charlie hollered, pointing to the back of her car. "It's flat. We can help."

"Forget it," Amanda shouted. She gestured with her hand for them to shoo. "Go away."

Charlie cupped his ear. They moved their pickup so close to her car that she swerved to avoid hitting them. Then she caught them laughing inside their car.

She sped up ahead, climbing a short incline. When she reached the top, she caught a flash of light behind trailing her from the valley below. At first, she figured it was a plane. It was traveling at a speed not possible for any car. But then she noticed it followed the turns of the road. Under moonlight, she recognized it in the far distance as a sleek black car; the same car she had seen near Yuma. Her stranger! Here? Hundreds of miles away? How? But somehow, he *was* here, and that made her less tense. But then the black car cut its headlights and disappeared.

She heard more drunken laughter. The truck was paralleling her again, this time on her right side.

"Hey, Amanda," Charlie cried, laughing. "Here! Maybe this will help."

Crash!

Glass fell all over her lap. She quickly brushed it off as if it was poison. Then she screamed. She grabbed the wheel as her car swerved out of the lane. She must have accidentally moved the steering wheel during the explosion. She gripped the wheel tight, bracing for another attack.

There was a crash, this one much louder, but it didn't come from her car. Wheels squealed. There was another bang. Looking behind through her rearview mirror the headlights of the pickup truck flickered and spun in darkness, blinking out beside the road. Had it rolled off the highway?

Lying on the passenger seat among all the pieces of broken glass was the source of her terror: a large stone the size of a brick.

Amanda pressed the gas pedal to the floor. The whoosh of wind and the sound of her car through her now open window were the only sounds she heard as she barreled down the empty highway. She brought her VW up to over one hundred and ten. Her foot was all the way down on the floor. It even hurt pressing down so hard. But all she cared about now was getting the hell out of here.

Her hand shook. She glanced through all her mirrors. She was alone. Alone again on this dark, empty highway.

She drove in solitude in complete darkness for another mile without looking back. Only forward. Her only goal was to get to Grand Junction. If her window had still been intact, she could have thought her terror had all been imagined. But there was still a rush of wind and road noise over her right shoulder.

Amanda didn't slow down. And in her excitement, she nearly crashed, losing control of the car on a sharp turn. The road straightened and she pressed as hard on the gas pedal as she could.

She jumped at the roar of an engine beside her. Headlights switched on the right shoulder of the highway. The truck? Were they back?! Amanda turned sharply, almost being thrown off the highway. But she discerned her stranger again driving right beside her, paralleling her car.

"Pull over," someone shouted.

In the darkness, Amanda made out a man, behind dim, multicolored lights, inside the car. He had opened his window. She recognized his voice. It was definitely her stranger from the desert near Yuma. The oddest thing was that the man was wearing, like those goons, shades at night.

"Pull over," the man said again. "You're driving too fast, Amanda."

"I won't," she shouted back into the wind. "I can't trust strangers."

"We've already met. Pull over."

"I already met them too!"

"I took care of them."

Took care of them? What the hell does that mean?

All she could see behind her was darkness. Then she turned back to her stranger. She quickly shook her head.

"All right," he said. "But slow down. You're driving too fast."

"I can take care of myself. I have mace." And that was an absolutely ridiculous thing to say.

"I'll go," he shouted back. "Just slow down for your safety. Please."

He sped ahead of her, pulled in front, and zoomed past, becoming a blur. The light disappeared over the horizon. It was so weird. She felt like she had witnessed a UFO.

Then all became quiet again as if nothing had happened. Only the sound of the wind blowing hard through her shattered window.

He said they were taken care of. What did her dark stranger do? *Kill them?*

She wouldn't tell anyone. She wouldn't tell Lu or her parents—God, she could never tell her parents. Her mom had insisted she not go alone on this trip. She'd cover the window in plastic and not tell a soul about the vandalism. Maybe she'd say a stone fell from a cliff or something. Nor would she tell a soul about her UFO.

Perhaps she was going mad? Perhaps it was all a dream created by driving in desolation on the dark deserted highway?

Your window was smashed by drunken idiots, Mands. Is that rush of air in the car a dream?

No, more like a nightmare.

The rest of her drive back to civilization was one of the most torturous drives she had ever had in her life.

Amanda got up when it was still dark, early in the morning, and wheeled her luggage back to the parking lot. On the far-off horizon, there was a red shine. The sun was rising. She was still tired. She hadn't slept all night. But she wanted to move on.

When she approached her car, she gasped. Her car had been washed. The broken window was repaired. She was so surprised that she touched the glass, thinking perhaps she was going crazy. But there it was. The glass was cold, but spotless. The inside of her car was clean too. The stone that had broken the window was gone, and, along with it, all the remnants of fast food, sauce packs and empty soda cups, left-over clothing bags, socks and hats, everything was neatly arranged over a freshly vacuumed interior. Her car had never been this clean. There was a note under her windshield wiper. She unfolded and read it:

Fly home. Avoid the roads. They're hunting you on the highway.

6

———

ANGEL DIVE

"I'M SORRY, JOHN."

John was back at a bar in a secluded café in the middle of the night. And Sherry was doing her usual thing, standing across the bar, fighting his wishes for more and more whiskey. It seemed they had been doing the same thing for years. And he cherished it. She smiled a rueful grin, gathering up the wrinkles on her face. Her long silvery hair flowed over her T-shirt and jeans. Old? Sure she was, but she was beautiful.

Angel Dive was an old-fashioned desert café, a dump really, but Sherry's dump. The most welcoming place in the world. The burgundy walls of the restaurant held the usual decorative bar things: a dart board, a pool table, and a stage for entertainment. In the corner, facing the lone parking lot, windows looked out on the desert. But the café was in the middle of nowhere, miles from any other establishment. Sherry seemed to like that. And she liked talking to drifters, like John. On Fridays, it'd be busy. Not tonight. Not now. Tonight there was only a couple at the opposite side of the place sitting at a wooden table.

"I'm sorry, John," Sherry said again with a rueful grin. She cleaned the counter around him with a towel. Then she peered deep into his eyes. She had lovely large eyes. The exact same eyes as Amanda. "Rick said you were almost done. Why are they torturing you like this? Why is it so hard for it all to be over?"

"It's always hard," he said, downing another glass of whiskey and slamming it on the corner. "There's always some test. It's never over."

"There shouldn't be. You're a good man."

"I'm not a good man," he said with a chuckle. "I'm not a good man at all. You know that."

"You're a good man, John."

"Do you know the last girl I fucked?"

"Not now," Sherry said, losing her smile. Then she looked around at the other customers. "The drinking's getting to your head."

He nodded and raised his finger. "Let me tell you about it."

Sherry leaned against a counter full of bottles and shook out her long gray hair in a huff. She folded her arms and rolled her eyes.

"I'll keep out the details of the sex," he said.

"Please."

"Lilith got me a hooker in Vegas."

"Jesus, John." Sherry rolled her eyes again. "And you took her?"

"It was a job," he said with a laugh. "Yeah, sort of." He tapped his glass. Sherry shook her head. John shook his head and tapped the glass harder. Sherry reached over for the bottle.

"You know what she called me, Sher?"

"Who?"

"The girl I fucked?"

"What? What did the whore call you? Like I care. I'm guessing, asshole?"

"She called me a hero."

"You are a hero, John."

"I'm not a fucking hero," he shouted, slamming the counter with his open palm.

The couple at the table looked over. Sherry, who rarely got angry over anything, looked pissed. "I warn you. I'll throw you out of my place if you go crazy here again. This is your last drink. Don't be acting like that around here."

"Our place," he said more quietly, staring at his glass. "It's our place, Sher. I'm not a hero."

"You are to me. You save lives. You're an angel, John. And you're my angel. You're a hero in my eyes. You always were, even before. You said you saved this Amanda. Why didn't it end? Why did they go back and hunt Amanda again?"

"They'll get her eventually. She's marked."

"I know. But the job's done. They always move on. Why'd they go back and attack her again? What did Rick say? If you save this last soul, will you ascend? Is this the last test? Is that why it's so hard? Please tell me." She shook her head and took a deep breath. "God, I don't want you to go, but I can't stand you like this. You're only getting worse."

"Does it matter?"

"Yeah, it could take your mind. Live or die, soul or eternal, you could lose a grasp of who you are."

"They already did that to me." Then he glared at her and pointed a finger. "You won't tell me my name."

"Shit, you're in such a mood tonight."

He stared at her. Her wrinkled face. He tried to place her. He tried to see if he could remember more than just his occasional memories. He searched her eyes. Her face. There was nothing right now. But he would see her young features again soon enough. It was just a matter of time before he was tortured once more. Was it torture? He liked being with her. He liked visions of her younger self. There was that in this hell of a world. Perhaps that was enough?

"I know you're hurting, John," Sherry said. "They're bringing it all back to you. But that doesn't mean you have to hurt me."

He was surprised to see a tear roll down her cheek. He reached for it.

"I've accepted our fate," Sherry said, shaking her head and swatting his hand. "You haven't. You're miserable because you won't accept the will of God."

"Oh come on, what is the will of God, Sher? Huh?" he asked, reaching over to touch her tear again on her wrinkled skin. She turned from him. "And what is this?"

"I'm crying for you, you jerk."

"Don't cry for me. I don't deserve it."

"I'll shed tears for you whenever I want. I still care about you."

"And I care about you," he said with a sigh. "I love you." He took her hand and ran his fingers along it. The wrinkles in her hands—he didn't care. He loved her hands. He loved her smile. He loved everything about her.

"I love you," John muttered. "Why do you think I'm here tonight?"

"This young girl, Amanda," she said with a sigh. "Tell me, John. She really looks like me?"

"Exactly like you." He downed another glass. "She's your double."

7

SANCTUARY

John felt the rumble of his engine and the slow drift of his car, almost hypnotic, as he sped across the desert. Multicolored light rushed past the edges of his windshield, splashing like colored raindrops and sparks. A mountain rose on the horizon. It left him behind as fast as it had appeared. Every inch his steering wheel turned was a sharp turn. He tracked the road following the lines lit by his headlights, cars passing over the deserted highway every few seconds, though they were miles apart. When he had first driven the car years ago, he had gripped the wheel tightly with the realization that an impact with anyone on the highway at this speed would be fatal—not for him but for anyone he collided with. Now, seasoned and worn, having wandered for years, he passed cars as if they were hills and valleys.

He pressed harder on the gas. The hills and horizon bent before his eyes. At this speed, every mile was a turn. This fast, the car itself aided him in impossible turns beyond his senses. He'd be invisible to the human eye now, visible only to, perhaps, spirits and specters of the dead stuck in this cesspool of a world, like him.

He felt desolation. Blessed loneliness. So he headed for his sanctuary.

Less than ten minutes from Arizona, he found himself in another desert. In Denver the temperature had been in the eighties during the day. Here in the Mojave Desert in the middle of the night, it was a nice seventy outside.

He slowed down as he approached his favorite spot. The drops of light stopped bouncing off the glass. The colors faded. Then he was in darkness in a canyon. But even if the sun were out, it'd be completely barren.

He turned on a dirt road only he knew about. In another moment, he was there.

Before him was a vast field of sand and salt. He shut off his headlights, and it was pitch black except the bright stars above. He got out of the car, and his black boots crackled along dry, caked dirt. Then he put his hands in his pockets and walked away from his car.

That's when the images came. Usually he turned from them. Not after seeing Amanda. The images always came to him more clearly when he was in the dark. He never slept because of them. Now he longed for them while awake. Now he could sift through them to try to make sense of the new mark. Amanda. To see if she really was who he thought she was. Perhaps he had only imagined the resemblance?

In a short time, a picture came to his mind as vivid as the stars.

He was on the beach in Southern California. It was afternoon. But just as now, he had his thumbs in the pockets of his jeans, was wearing shades, and was staring out at the sea.

"Where've you been?" asked a woman. Her voice was rough like Sherry's. It was exactly like Sherry's. It was her voice.

In his past images, he might have called her Sherry. But this woman, with her long, flowing blond hair, smooth skin, and bright energy, didn't look like Sherry. She looked like the recent mark he had saved. Amanda. Her blond hair was covered by a wide-brimmed white beach hat, and she was wearing a beach throw with a red bathing suit. Her body was perfect, her face beautiful under large sunglasses.

They were standing on a cliffside. He could smell the salt and hear the waves.

She wasn't angry when she asked him that. She seemed happier than ever to just be beside him. She smiled sweetly.

"Away," he answered. "I've been away." He turned back to the view of the shore and leaned on the railing. "On business. But I'm happy to be back now."

"Well, I'm sure happy to see you," she said, rubbing his back. There was a bark and she looked down and laughed. She kneeled down and ran her hand over the hide of a large dog. "Bear's happy to see you too. Aren't you, boy? Huh, Bear?"

Bear?

The dog jumped on John's leg and barked. John just looked down. He didn't recall having a dog.

"Don't get on grumpy's leg now," Amanda said. "He doesn't like it. Jeeze, you could pet him, at least. You haven't seen us in weeks."

John kneeled down and ran his hand over the dog's head and under his neck. Bear barked and seemed to love it. John couldn't place this memory. He didn't recall having a dog.

John stood up straight again, looking out at the sea.

"How long will you be off next?" she asked.

"I don't know. I just got back."

"What happened?" she asked, sounding grave. "Tell me. Tell me something."

She had always been there for him. His sanctuary. He remembered that now. Even back then. Perhaps that's why Sherry chose to work in a bar after he left. Surely she did the same for her patrons in Yuma. And she was his confidant. His listener.

He turned and saw the outline of a canyon. He remembered that he was still in Death Valley and that this vision wasn't real. But he liked this memory. He didn't want to be in the desert. He wanted to be back on the beach reliving this moment again.

"I can't tell you the details," John said, now talking to the valley walls. "It's just hard. The things I saw were——"

"It's gotta stop," Amanda said, shaking her head. She turned grave. "It's like you're a soldier, not a cop. And it's getting to your head. You should stop all this now."

He nodded. It was almost the same words Sherry had just told him in her restaurant. He turned to her and tipped his shades down. She shimmered. Although transparent, the outline of her white dress was yellow like the rays of the sun. But behind her, he could still see the dark desert canyon. "I have you."

"Aha." She took off her shades and kissed his lips. "There's me. You have me."

A slight ray of light was coming off the horizon. It was in the direction of his mirage of Amanda. It spread a violet tinge over the whole desert valley. The light awoke him from his dream, shining through the vision—this was the brightest light in this world. The sun.

But he still felt her. She leaned into him and tried to kiss him. His sunglasses hit her face. She laughed as she pulled back. "Why do you always wear these things?"

He shrugged.

"Well, now's as good a time as any," she said. "Time for some bad news. Tommy's in jail again."

"When is he ever not?" John asked with a laugh.

"He idolizes you. You're his brother."

"Cousin. He's an idiot. Tommy will always be an idiot."

"You know, when he's out, he's gonna end up dead."

"I don't think so. Why's he in jail this time?"

"You know he's got bad friends. It was the coke. He got involved with the wrong people and was framed. Can you spring him?"

"I'll see what I can do."

The vision faded. Amanda was gone.

John walked alone on the sand under the rising sun.

Then she appeared again, joyously laughing this time among grass and trees. And this time his young lover wore a white T-shirt and dark pants. But she had that same big white hat. Green trees and grass surrounded them. There was a towel on the grass where they had picnicked. And Bear was running around him, the dog he had forgotten. She was playing fetch with a squeeze toy.

John's phone rang.

"Yeah," John said in the darkness. The park faded. He was back in the desert valley.

"Angel down. Tori. She's nineteen, Black, with long hair. She goes to Boise State University. She's studying sociology. Born a Leo. She's going on a date downtown. That's their lead."

"Samael or Lilith?"

"Samael, we think. Lilith was last spotted closer to Nebraska. Where you at?"

"Not far from there."

"From what I hear from Michael, you're so close to earning your wings, man. Just hang in there. Don't let this last test tear you up."

"Why so young?"

"What?"

"You said nineteen. Why is the angel so young? They don't go after kids."

"Nineteen isn't a kid. And how the fuck should I know, John? Or give a shit? You gotten over being a budding journalist? The look-alike. It's not her. It's not Sherry. Can I trust you to be on the case, or are you going to go chase their trap?"

"Sure," he said, scuffing some of the salt under his boots. "Send me the location."

"Done. Listen, man, work on this new case, give it some time and you'll forget all about the last one. This could be it."

But as he hung up his phone, he saw a vision of a girl wearing a wide-brimmed hat. She was outlined in the distance, in the desert valley, under the rising sun. The borders of shimmering light illuminated Sherry's face, smiling sweetly. Sherry…younger? Or was it Amanda?

8

———

THE PAVILION

WALKING WAS A REFRESHING CHANGE FOR AMANDA'S BEHIND. AS MUCH as she loved driving the open road, she enjoyed this day of rest even more. Plus it was absolutely lovely outside. The blue sky was clear with just a few wisps of white, it was warm, and the air was still. She had even dressed in a summery outfit, with a wide-brimmed white hat, a white T-shirt, and leggings.

She had spent most of the early morning at the Denver zoo. Then she had headed to the botanical gardens. Now it was getting late and about time for her to head back to her hotel.

As she meandered along the grass, heading back to her car, she glanced with interest at a white-columned structure. The sun was dipping behind the horizon and it'd be dark soon. She'd have to return to her hotel, but the building was inviting. It was a Greek-columned structure. Amanda had always liked Greek architecture.

Inside a young couple was goofing off, pushing and pulling each other into their arms with their voices echoing. Otherwise it was vacant. They stopped their antics as soon as she walked up the steps. Then they ran off into the park.

She gazed back at the view of the grassy fields. Light over the horizon was turning a yellow hue. The view was perfect. She heaved a long sigh and took out her cell phone for a photo.

"The best view is in City Park."

Amanda gasped and whirled around. There was a man standing there wearing all black. He wore sunglasses and had a leather jacket draped over his shoulder. He was so still by one of the columns that she hadn't noticed him.

Holy shit. It's my dark stranger!

"I didn't mean to startle you."

"Are you following me?" She reached into her purse for her mace.

"The park's public. I come here for sunsets all the time. It's a pleasant view."

"Then why'd you say City Park is better?"

"It's an even better spot."

He came closer, but Amanda backed up. He seemed to take the cue and returned to his column. Then he nodded at the view. "I love this place." He dipped down his shades and glared at her. If it had been another man, she would have been frightened. Not him. Not with those angel eyes. "Wasn't it enough, Amanda, for you to nearly get into a car accident? Or have your window broken? Why didn't you go home like I warned?"

"How do you even know my name?"

"You told it to me."

"I never did. I'm sure I didn't."

She came closer. She didn't know why, but she did. Though he was intimidating, she felt safe with him.

"Do you live in Denver?" she asked.

"I live back where I saw you. But I travel a lot." Then he pointed at her. "You don't. You need to go home."

"Well, I shouldn't be talking to you then." She flashed a sly grin. "My mom told me to never talk to strangers."

"I'm hardly a stranger." Then he gestured to the park. "This park is haunted, you know. There's a thousand dead bodies under the ground. Sometimes when it rains, people claim to see skulls and bones. It used to be a cemetery. Did you know that?"

"You can be so creepy. Are you trying to scare me?" But she found herself closer to him. "I'm not afraid of you."

"Be afraid and go home, Amanda." He looked down at her, because she was right beside him and he was nearly a head taller. He looked at her through his shades, stern as hell. "Go home. Fly home."

"I won't," she said shaking her head, looking up. "Not until you tell me how you know my name."

"You said it to me when we first met."

"I didn't." She took her sunglasses off. She felt like taking her glasses off would get him to take off his so she could see those sea-blue gems. But he didn't. "I didn't. What's your name, anyway?"

"John."

Then, before she could say another word, he raised a finger. He touched his fingers, one at a time, as if counting. The light on the ceiling lit up. "I wish it didn't turn on so early."

"You're so weird, you know that?"

He nodded. "Yeah. Come on. Let's talk and walk—on the way back to your car."

"Why should I trust you?"

"Why are you alone in a city park? Did you know this place can be dangerous at night? I'd think you'd have learned about danger by now. Come." He pushed himself off the column. "Take a walk with me back to your car. If I were here to harm you, I could have done it last night."

"Gee, that makes me feel better."

"I'm not always good with words."

"Yeah, you don't seem to be the type that uses them."

He shrugged.

"I love words," Amanda said. "I'm a writer. I even have my own podcast. I want to be a journalist." She flashed a silly grin, then hated herself for it. It seemed so juvenile. He just nodded solemnly. Then he walked down the steps and turned. With his black leather jacket slung over one shoulder, he used his other hand to reach out for Amanda's. Amanda didn't take it. But she did walk down the steps with him.

"You said it was dangerous here at night," Amanda said.

"I told you you'd be safe with me."

"What about muggers?"

"Or ghosts? You'll be safe with me, Amanda. And after we talk, you can drive to the hotel, take a cab, and fly home."

But as they walked, the weirdest thing was he didn't say a word. With his shades and, at times, what appeared to be a scowl, he scanned the park. He had talked self-assuredly about them being safe, but he seemed to be looking everywhere for danger. He reminded her of a bodyguard or a secret agent or something. It was as if she were the president and he were a member of the secret service. He even gently put a hand on her back and guided her in the right direction on the walkway.

"Do you ever say anything, John?"

"No." But he added a hint of a smile. That made her laugh.

She actually didn't mind that she was walking with a quiet, handsome man. Not at all. Nor did she mind the direction the stranger was taking her. They were almost back to her car.

"Well, I kinda liked it when you talked in that Greek building," she said. "I'd rather you talk. I like that. Can you say something to me?"

"That building is called The Pavilion."

"Yeah… Okay, that's something. How about I ask you something?"

"Go ahead."

She chuckled because he was so deadpan. Then he resumed scanning their surroundings.

"Why, or I should ask how, the hell did you fix my window?"

"Those assholes had no right to smash it. If they had touched you, I would have smashed them."

"Didn't you? Didn't you *smash them?*"

"I disabled their vehicle."

"That was nice, and thanks, but—" She turned and he was looking right at her. Even through the shades, it made her pause for a moment. "But…how did you get my window fixed so fast? And how did you get into my car in the first place?"

"I know people who can do it. I like cars. And it's not hard to get into yours, Amanda."

"Okay, see, that's creepy again."

"You should rightfully be afraid of me," he said with a nod. He put his thumbs in his pockets. "Most people are. But you're not, are you?"

"I don't like how quiet you are. But no, I feel safe around you."

"You're not safe."

She stopped walking and put her head down. For some reason, that really bothered her. She felt protected whenever she was with him, but there was something so off. Something really frightening.

"What's the matter?" he asked.

"Who are you?" she said, looking down and shaking her head. "Please. Tell me. Not the window." She clenched her fists. "Not Denver. Tell me about your car. Tell me why you're following me. It'll make me feel better."

"Now or in Arizona?"

"Whenever!" she snapped, looking up at his gaze. "And take those fucking glasses off for a second, won't you!"

He removed his shades. He had the loveliest eyes she had ever seen. They were glowing light blue. Gentle, which was juxtaposed to his appearance. Then she thought she understood why he wore them. His countenance seemed sad. And he had bags under his eyes, as if he never slept.

"In Arizona, a messenger came down to take your soul, Amanda. She is a lamia. *Lamia* is an ancient name for a monster that eats children. She's that kind of evil. She is called Lilith. But taking babies is a myth. Lilith takes souls. I chased her from you. But she managed to nearly collide with your car in the process, on a bike on the highway. Ever since then, ever since Arizona, you've been marked. You're at most risk on the road. The longer I can keep you away from the highway, the more likely they will stop bothering you. But they love battling on the open road. That's why I told you to go home by plane after I fixed your car. Here, in Denver, I'm protecting you. Though it's unlikely they'll hunt you in the middle of a city, they don't like cities, but they could approach you even here. Then they could follow you, like they did in Mesa Verde."

"Jesus, that's a mouthful," she said, wide-eyed. *Maybe it was better when he didn't say anything.* "Messengers? What does that mean?"

"Messengers. Watchers. We've also been called angels."

"Angels? Like heaven and God angels?"

"Angels," he said with a nod.

"And you're stalking me 'cause an angel is chasing me?"

He nodded.

"You're nuts, aren't you?" she asked with a nod, trying to convince herself. Then she just resumed walking, though a little faster.

They were near the parking lot. When she made her way around a tree, she saw her car. But parked by her green VW was his super-expensive black sports car.

"How did you know my name, mister?" she asked, whirling around to face him again. "Hmm? And why are you following me?"

"Forget everything I said," he said in a too-measured voice. "You're right. I made all that shit up. I'm just some rich freak that's following you because I'm attracted to you. But I did scare off those guys near Grand Junction. Remember? I think that should allow me a little fun telling you my fantasy."

She squinted at him. Then she shook her head. No, he was quite serious about his "fantasy."

He put his shades back on. She didn't. The sun had fallen under the horizon.

"I have something to show you," he said. "I told you the view wasn't as great back there. I can show you better."

"What!" she snapped. She turned from him and looked down. Then she shook her head. "I'm sorry. I didn't mean to act angry with you."

"Why are you sorry?" he asked with a chuckle. He gently touched her chin. "Only you are kind enough to say sorry to a man causing you pain. Come on. I have something that will make seeing me again worth it. It's right near here. It'll be a better photo op. Believe me."

"Thought you said you were bringing that car to a client?" And she found herself smirking at him. Then he took his shades off again and she felt lost in those eyes.

"I lied."

He didn't explain any further. Instead he walked back to his luxury car. Amanda got in her VW Bug. That's when she noticed that his vehicle wasn't marked. There was no license plate.

Amanda shuffled in her pocket and brought out her recorder. She nearly dropped it.

"Guys, okay, I… I… I found that man I was talking about in Arizona again in Denver. I think he's following me. He's freaky, creepy, spooky—like, scary as hell, vampire-like shit or something. But he's hot. I mean, actually, he's really hot. And he's asking me to follow him… And he acts like he likes me. And I mean… so… should I? I mean, if he was following me, why would he ask me to follow *him*? Right?" Amanda watched him make his way slowly out of the parking lot. At the stop sign, he stopped his car. "Danger? Check. Well…if you don't hear from Caligirl gettingold24 again, it's been nice knowing all of you."

9

DENVER

They parked in an empty parking lot near a glass building not far from another city park. He reached out again for her hand. She still didn't take it. She walked close beside him though. This windowed building was the museum she had seen in the distance when she went to the zoo this morning.

The sound of two bicyclists made her jump as they rushed by. She was so on edge. Because he was so weird. She welcomed his presence, but there was this cringy unsettled feeling that brought back memories of the whole shattered-window-in-the-car thing.

In the distance was a gorgeous man-made lake with a waterfall. At this time, it was quiet and empty around the museum. She stopped to breathe it all in. And in the distance a lovely orange hue from the falling sun was beautifully shining over the water.

"Come on," John said, tugging her elbow. "It's better this way."

John took her to the front of the building, but he took a sharp left. He went around to the side. There he checked the handle to a glass door. It was unlocked. He opened it for her.

"Aren't we supposed to buy tickets or something?"

He shook his head. "EVS locks this door late every night. It'll be open for a couple hours."

"Aren't we gonna get arrested for trespassing?"

He shrugged.

Oh, that's reassuring.

"It'll be worth it. Trust me."

Trust him. Hmm. Well, I suppose if I hadn't trusted him I would never have followed him. Why do you trust him, anyway, Amanda? Is it his chiseled chin? His wonderfully short dark hair? His bulging chest and arms under his T-shirt. His bright blue eyes. Why does he hide them? What a crime.

Whoever or whatever this John was, he knew this Denver museum. He walked as if he were a tour guide, turning at just the right hallway and moseying his way down the dark corridors. He stopped at an elevator. It looked very plain, like a service elevator. They exited at the top floor. Then another walk through a hallway beside glass windows, and outside onto an outdoor patio. And then—

Holy shit!

Amanda ran to the ledge of a wide balcony. She felt giddy. The sun was down, but the rays shone behind the mountains, casting a gold hue over the buildings of downtown.

"What did I tell you?"

She looked at him and nodded. Then she fumbled in her jeans pocket for her old mini-recorder. She turned back to the view, leaned on the rail, and clicked the record button.

"Umm…so here I am before this view of downtown Denver, Colorado. There's birds chirping, it's quiet, nobody's out because it's late. But that stranger I told you guys about is with me now. Say hi, stranger." And she pointed the recorder at John. John furrowed his brow, gazing at Amanda, looking as if she was crazy. "Hmm?" Amanda said, pointing the recorder at his face again. "Go ahead. Don't be shy. Say hi."

"Hi," he said into the device.

"He says his name is John," she said into the recorder with a chuckle. "He's mysterious as hell. Nice though." She gazed at him from head to toe with a smile. He continued to look at her like she was nuts. That made her laugh again. "We're at the top of, like, this modern glass building in City Park, and I can see the buildings of the city. They've got all their lights shining. And it's so pretty. How can I describe it? The sun's gone, but rays are shining behind the mountains, casting a gorgeous gold hue over the high rises. Even the green grass below the park surrounding the lake is pretty, with an orange glow over the water beside a forest green. It's…breathtaking. I couldn't be at a better place anywhere. Or with—" Her gaze turned from the vista to John. He didn't smile. "It's…" Then she couldn't find the words. God, had she become tongue-tied? She'd never had that happen before. "It's…this is what my trip is all about, folks. And my new friend, John, showed it to me. But now I have to go, take a few pics of Denver, and thank him. I tell you, this is what cross-country trips are all about. This is what it's… Shit, I already said all that, didn't I?" She laughed. She took a deep breath and sighed. "Damn." Then she clicked off her recorder.

She leaned on the rail and took another deep breath.

"That's for my fans," she said, cocking her head back at him. She didn't look at him, but she chuckled remembering his deadpan expressions. "I run a podcast. That's why I went on this cross-country disaster. You know, log all the stuff for my listeners. I want to be a journalist. So I figured the best way to land a great job was to get out there and show people what I've got. Go on vacation and log all my unknowns to people. I mean, that's what news is. It's about telling people cool stuff in a cool way. Right? This whole cross-country thing is unknown to me. Obviously, not to you. So I thought, why not add something to my podcast? And you never know, I could make money off my little traveling show. I already spoke about amazing tortillas and enchiladas in Tucson, the cliffs at Mesa Verde, and the fricking Denver zoo. It's amazing, you know? Do you understand?"

He shrugged.

"Now I'm on to talking about you to my fans, the weirdest guy of all."

He didn't say a word. And she laughed at that. She turned back to the beautiful vista. "Why'd you take me here? Huh?"

"You liked the view at the Pavilion."

"Yeah." She nodded with a sigh. "But you're right. This is better."

"I come here a lot."

"That doesn't surprise me. You're a drifter. Like a yuppie drifter. Right? That's what you said. A rich guy with a pretty car that drives for the hell of it. Right?" She chuckled at his expressionless nod. Then she reached in her pocket for her cell phone. First she used it for her reflection to shake her long blond hair out and fix it for the shot. Then she turned the phone with an extended arm to get a good selfie.

"You want me to take a picture of you?" he asked.

"Oh, could you?"

He grabbed her cell phone and she posed by the rail.

"Hey, why don't we get one together?" she asked.

For some really weird reason, he hesitated. But then he nodded and stood beside her. He put an arm around her, and his fingers left tingles along her back.

Calm down, Amanda. You're acting like a man's never touched you.

She had him in the picture on her phone. But then she jerked away.

"Take your sunglasses off, weirdo!"

He obliged, but he didn't seem like he wanted to. Then he posed with her again. After a couple snaps, and a glance at their pictures on the phone, she turned back to him. "It's not..." she stammered, looking deep into his eyes. There was a hint of a smile on his face. "Why...why do you cover that?"

"Cover what?"

"Your eyes?" she asked, exploring them. "They're so nice. Why do you cover them?"

He didn't answer. Instead he did something far better. He leaned down and gently touched his lips to hers. Then he stroked her cheek with a single finger.

"Thank you," she breathed.

He chuckled. That made her laugh too.

"Got you to laugh. I knew I could!" She turned back to the view. "Oh, it's just so pretty here. Thank you, John. I love views. That's why I love driving so much. I'm from LA, you know, and my favorite thing is to drive where you can't see the end of the horizon. LA always has some hill or building in your way. I saw my first great view in the desert when I first met you. Then when I entered Colorado, it was flats till the mountains. But the Rockies here are pretty too. I love traveling and experiencing places I've never been. Even the smells—aside from your cologne—which I don't mind. I mean, it's nice. There's even a park smell here. You know, mainly the grass, I suppose. And there's a lovely gentle breeze. Do you feel it? It's nice. It's a lovely night."

"Yes, it is," he said, leaning on the rail. Then he put his sunglasses back on.

She furrowed her brow.

"So…you're in town," she said. "Have you eaten? I'm sure if you can show me this, you can point me somewhere good to eat for dinner? We could eat?"

He nodded. But he weirdly didn't answer her.

"You sure knew this place," she said. "Can I ask how many times you've been up here?"

"You don't want to know."

"Okay, that sounds weird."

"I know."

"'Cause you're some kind of protector of souls, protecting them from angels?" She looked back at the view but cocked her head back at him.

He nodded solemnly.

"I know you're not just a rich yuppie in a sports car. I get it. You just don't want to tell me what you're really doing. It just made me feel better when I said that."

He just nodded again.

Before she could inquire further, his phone rang. He gestured with a raised finger and crossed the walkway alone. She gazed back at the view but watched him from the corner of her eye. From his expression, she couldn't tell if he was ordering a pizza or talking about a friend dying in the hospital. Then he put the phone back in his jeans pocket.

"I have to go, Amanda," he said. She pouted and there was a hint of amusement on his lips. "I need you to do me a favor while I'm away."

"Anything, handsome."

"Go home." He walked right up to her. He removed his shades, looking grave. "Go. Please, by plane from Denver. Don't drive. Go now. That's why I came to see you again. You have to go home."

But she came right up to his face, stood on her tippy-toes, and planted her lips on the stubble of his cheek. Her lips glided down with more kisses until landing on his lips again. His arm curled around her back as she swooned.

"When will you be back?" she breathed.

"I can't," he said quietly. "I can't. Go. Please."

But then he leaned down and kissed her lips again.

"No," she said, shaking her head. "I don't want to leave."

She wouldn't let go of him. She kissed him again. She felt his tongue enter her mouth and run along hers. And for the longest time, they just kissed. His arms held her tighter. And she was lost. And she wanted to be lost in his embrace like this for good.

"Oh, John."

"Go home, please," he pleaded. He gently pushed away from her.

"Sorry, can't do that to my fans," she said with a giggle.

"It's not funny," he said, looking angry for the first time. "I'll take you back to your car and watch you get back to your hotel safely. Then I want you to fly home."

She looked down at his hand hesitantly. She slowly shook her head. Then she snatched his hand and came really close to him again and kissed him. She pressed herself into his arms.

"*Go!*" he shouted, pushing her angrily from him. "Go home!"

She jumped in reaction to his rage.

"Look, you seem like a cool guy, okay," Amanda snapped back, "but I'm not going to go buy a ticket and jump on a plane just because you say it's not safe to drive!"

"If you don't believe what I've told you, tell me why you've been in so much danger?"

"I've been told it can be dangerous to travel alone."

She smiled and then, as he remained stern, she laughed.

"Come on, John, a near accident and a couple drunk vandals?" She put her hand on her hips and shrugged. "No. Honestly, the only thing weirding me out on my trip is you."

She waited for a reply. Anything. After nothing but silence, she headed back to the elevator, with or without him.

She didn't want to. She wanted to jump in his arms before the view of downtown Denver again. Kissing him. She could have done that for another hour. But that moment seemed ruined.

He followed her inside the elevator without another word. Yet, as angry as he seemed, he stood close beside her. And she felt his hand brush against hers. And it was, again, weird. It was as if the closer she came to him, the more he was repelled. It was as if she were poison. But it seemed he wanted the poison as much as she did.

"Thanks for showing me the view."

10

THE MESSAGE

The first thing that John noticed as he entered the motel room was the rusty stench of iron mixed with excrement. Then he saw red. The beige motel carpet was riddled with crimson blotches that trailed all the way from the door to the bed. John's pale-skinned boss, Raphael, known simply as Rick, stood over the white sheets wearing shades just like John's. And he wore identical black clothes. The sheets were drenched in red. And in the middle of a bloody puddle a naked dark-skinned woman lay on her side. The head was mercifully turned away from the door. As John approached, he noticed her abdomen was split open, body curling around coils that looked like snakes. He recognized the crimson snakes as her intestines. The stomach had been splayed open. And her legs were severed at her thighs.

John made his way to the other side of the bed and saw blood still dripping from the woman's fingertips. Then he saw that her face, her profile, was no longer identifiable.

"Angel's down," Rick said bitterly. "Tori. She was nineteen, Black, with long black hair. She went to Boise University." Rick held her limp wrist. "She was studying sociology. Born a Leo. They opened her up. Filleted her."

"How long till the police come?"

"An hour or so. No one knows much about this except us. She

doesn't have family or many friends. She was ambushed on her way to her date on Interstate Eighty-Four." Rick touched her hand. Then he touched the dripping, bloody finger. "It was very recent." Rick ran his finger along one of the only white sections of the sheet to wipe off the blood. Then he looked up at John. "I had a case in Belize with Samael. I couldn't get here in time to save this angel. But you could have. You were close. After the initial call, I called you again. You ignored my messages. You didn't take my call until it was too late."

"I was detained."

"Bullshit." Rick finally faced John, shaking his head and looking pissed.

"I've answered every job for years."

"Well, you can fucking live with this one." Rick dug his finger into his chest. "Her death is on you."

Rick brooded for a moment. Then he walked back to the face and turned the head toward him—her eyes being the only thing recognizable on her face. All other features were too bloodied. Knife wounds running down from both cheeks splayed the opening of her mouth unnaturally wide. Even her nose was severed. "Look at her. Look at this face. She's dead because of you."

"Oh, fuck off, Raphael. If they die, perhaps they're in a better place than we are."

"You were so close, man!" Then he looked for more "clean" sheets to wipe his hand again. "So close. What the hell are you doing? Falling into their trap? This final test is your fault. You looked too deep into your past. End your interest in the girl. You're the best operative I've ever had. You want to fuck up when you're so damn close to being done? You think Michael's gonna let you ascend now? Don't you get it? That's precisely why this Amanda bitch was put on your path. You know she's a trap. Don't you care? If not for your soul, how about Amanda's? And these other ones you're ignoring? You don't get it. You don't do my job, you'll be doing theirs. There is no both ways. It's either me or them. Lilith knows she can use Amanda to draw you away from me."

"Lilith told me Amanda would be chased again in Colorado."

"So what? You think you're in love? Is that it, John? She's not Sherry. Fuck, she's not her. She's Amanda. Amanda's gonna be just like this body within a year whether you fucking help her or not. If they don't get her now, Lilith or Samael will get her later. Meanwhile as you're screwing around, more of these bodies are going to pile up in every seedy motel across the country." He used his pale hand to pick up her head again. "This girl. Look at her. Tori was her name. Damn it, look at her!"

John turned away.

"*Fucking look at her!* This girl, Tori was her name, could have lived, like your girlfriend, for another year or two. But you traded her life for a goddamn date!"

"I don't need this shit right now." John walked to the door. Rick touched his shoulder, and John raised his fist to him.

"John," Rick said, quickly raising a hand, "her body was filleted. Legs were severed. They didn't just kill her. This was a message. Usually it's a noose or throat cut. If you get personal, they'll use it to damn you. They're fucking with your head."

"How is this a message?"

"The mutilation damages her chance of a proper burial," he replied with a shrug.

"Oh come on."

"You can't bury a body in pieces properly, John."

"Ashes to ashes, dust to dust," John said, shaking his head. "This angel's soul will ascend."

"Well, you won't. The mutilation is a personal message for you." He came up to his face and pointed a finger at him. "Is Amanda really worth losing your soul? You're being judged. This is the toughest, but speaking as your chief and friend, you've gotta come around on this."

John turned. Rick touched his arm, and John yanked it off.

"John, the next one's name is Carly. She's forty-two with short black hair. She's driving to Miami tomorrow. She's a Virgo."

"Are you serious?" he asked, removing his shades and staring at him.

"Move on," Rick said with a stern nod. "Let Amanda go."

John grabbed the doorknob. "Fuck you."

"Fuck!" Rick cried, "I'm not even sure this has anything to do with Amanda! I think you're washed up, man. Lilith already got to your head in Vegas, didn't she? Both heads."

"Fine, consider me washed up."

"They're going to extend your time. No proper burial for her, no proper burial for you. No ascension. Your soul will be damned if you keep letting people die. Your soul will be forfeit. That's the message. Stop thinking of yourself and think of these victims."

"I got the message."

He headed for his car in the parking lot.

"If you don't answer your call, I'll be needing your keys," Rick cried out. "I warn you, if you're grounded, we're done. It isn't my decision. One more death like this, and you'll get even more time here on Earth. You'll be removed. I remember how you talked about Amanda. You're smitten with the girl version of your former lover. Lilith is mixing up your mind. I tell you, the broad's not Sherry. Leave Amanda. Leave her."

John opened the door to his car.

"The new angel down is Carly, John. She's forty-two with—"

John showed him his middle finger.

"Angel down, John!" Raphael yelled. "Miami. *Not fucking Kansas!*"

11

KANSAS

Amanda gazed through her windshield at the rising sun, the surrounding clouds splashing yellowish orange, as light rose over a short plateau off the horizon. The infinite vista was like water off the shore back home, only this wasn't the ocean. It was miles upon miles of farmland. Her land. She felt like a pioneer. She was the driver, and behind the wheel, the whole world was hers. She sipped her nitro brew reflecting on that. Then she put her clear plastic cup, filled with the wonderful elixir, back in her cup holder. But…she didn't like that. Before her window was broken, her cup holder had been full of gum wrappers and trash. The lack of clutter reminded her of her nightmare.

She had a flashback of glass shattering in the side window.

Turn on music. Get your mind off of it, Mandi.

So she did. She put on Journey. As she tapped on her steering wheel, Steve Perry's voice, and the now-bright sun over the lovely vista, made her feel better. Then her eyes fell on the passenger seat—her replacement cactus, her only companion. It was vibrating as she drove down the empty highway.

By the time she was on her third Journey album, it became overcast. That reminded her of all those documentaries she used to watch about tornadoes. She loved tornado hunter shows. But not now. She wouldn't mind seeing one far off in the distance though—in the very far distance, not beside her car.

She exited onto an off-ramp at a gas station. It was lunchtime. She pumped gas and then walked over to a small diner beside the gas station.

"What'll it be?" asked an overweight guy in suspenders by her table. He pointed to the small menu on the table and winked.

"Do you still serve breakfast? I'd love a bacon and cheese omelet."

"Sure." He nodded. "Where're you from?"

"Los Angeles."

"Los Angeles? I've got a sister in Malibu. You live out on the beach?"

"Santa Monica," she said, shaking her head. She chuckled. "I mean, it's close to the beach, I suppose."

"On vacation?"

She nodded.

"You'd like anything to drink with your eggs?"

"A cup of coffee would be nice."

"Cup of Joe. You betcha. I'll be back soon."

Cup of Joe. Cute.

He winked and headed for the kitchen. Most of the café booths were empty. So she pulled out her small recorder.

"Guys," she said quietly, "I'm at a diner in Kansas. Can you fucking believe that? The waiter is sooo nice. I'm gonna eat an omelet at one p.m. cause…why the hell not? I've got a view of wheat and grass fields. That's all there is. It's like a sea of green. And I'm already liking it. I mean, I had Steve Perry with me in the car."

She clicked the recorder off.

She looked over at the people pumping gas. That's when she noticed a very distinctive woman by one of the gas tanks wearing all black, too black, pumping gas with a black-gloved hand into a pitch-black motorcycle. She kept her helmet and opaque visor on, but she wore a white scarf around her neck that matched the long white hair trailing down her back—very white hair. As she waited to fill her tank, she stood folding her arms. Then she scared Amanda by gazing right in her direction.

The waiter brought over her cup of coffee. Amanda gladly looked away.

"You get tornadoes here?" she asked.

"Hope not," he said with a smirk. "I haven't seen a twister in these parts in a long while. Plenty of wind though. Watch what you wish for, miss."

"I figured it'd be like seeing surfers on the beach in California," she said with a chuckle.

"Only in the movies."

The biker was still staring at the diner. That was so weird. Especially because she must have been done pumping gas.

Is this the danger John was talking about?

But then she remembered the glass windows of the diner were tinted. The woman could just be staring at the restaurant, not at her. She did her best to ignore her.

After Amanda's omelet lunch and a second cup of coffee, the biker outside had, thankfully, disappeared. Amanda checked her phone. It was one-thirty. Her plan was to get to Kansas City, or at least Topeka, by nightfall.

Back behind the wheel, she enjoyed the open road again. It was pretty empty—except for the motorcycle. That black leather–clad biker had reappeared and was following her.

Two semis slowed down traffic, blocking both lanes. Amanda breathed a big sigh of relief when the biker quickly zoomed around her and between the two trucks. She zoomed off into the distance.

After another five miles in the clear, she leaned back in her seat and pulled out her tape recorder from her pocket, turned down the radio, took a deep breath, and—

"Guys, I'm loving this view. It's awesome. Or, resplendent. I'm a Caligirl, so when I'm driving off in the desert or plains looking at sunsets or zooming past hilltops with an endless horizon, my mouth is, like, totally dropping. The beach is great but the desert horizon is to-die-for. And as I'm getting into Kansas, I've got grasslands forever, which is just as good. It's like totally Dorothy. Honestly, I'm still glad I took this trip—even after that death-defying danger I told you about."

Amanda drove past another slow semi. She spotted the weird motorcyclist, in the distance, thankfully—a mile or so ahead now. It was hard to judge distance with the flat horizons. She clicked the recorder back on.

"Let's check off what I've seen so far, shall we—oh, and each comes with a photo on my website, of course:

Saguaros, check.

Speeding over a hundred miles an hour (maybe, but that'd be illegal (wink). You can just guess).

Sampling Starbucks in every state, check, check (lattes taste the same everywhere!)

Sunrises over the Great Basin, check.

Pueblo village in caves, check.

Dark handsome man with shades. Check.

Dark handsome man showing me a view of Denver at sunset. Check.

Dark handsome man kissing me over the view of Denver. Check. Check.

Dark handsome man holding me in his arms… Okay, you get the picture.

Danger?… Yep, a bit too much. Love? Check. Check. Check."

She pressed stop.

Amanda jumped when her music changed to a ringing phone. She touched the phone button on her console.

"Hey, Mands. Just checking in. I gave you a day off. How's your trip?"

"Fuck, you scared me, Lu."

"Sorry. How's the trip?"

"Great, Lu."

"Did you make a decision about next month?"

"What decision?"

"Come on! Cut it out. I have to know."

Amanda froze. As she had passed a bridge overpass, two more black bikes with black-leather riders had appeared behind her. Then the black bike ahead in the other lane had slowed, letting her pass. Now three bikes were trailing behind her.

"Well?" asked Luane. "Can we or not? Ben's ready to break up with me for waiting so long. Really babe, I have to know. He has to know so he can decide on renting the place or not."

"I don't know, Lu," Amanda muttered, staring at the bikes in her rearview mirror. "What if you break up with Benji and we're left out in the cold."

"That won't happen."

"You just said you were fighting." Amanda kept talking to stall. Because she didn't want to scare her again.

"The mountains aren't cold in the summer," Luane said. "You said that yourself. And we can buy a tent if the place doesn't work out. We won't get stranded."

"Okay, Luane. Fine."

"Okay? Really! Okay? Love you, babes! Hey…how many more days do you got driving around the world? When will you be back?"

"Just a few more. It's so pretty in Kansas. But the clouds are graying."

"As long as you don't drive through a tornado."

"This guy in a diner told me they don't have that many tornadoes here."

"There's like a hundred a year in Kansas, Mands. Oh, before I forget, I got more good news for you."

"What?"

The bikers were swaying back and forth, swerving pompously from lane to lane, in a pack behind her. Their bikes were so black that they stuck out on the two-lane highway. They reflected the sun like black jade. They were alone on the highway now. But that wasn't comforting. It reminded her of Colorado. What did they want? If they wanted to break her window, they would have done it already.

"Are you mad?" asked Luane.

"What? Mad about what?"

"Aren't you even listening to me, Mandi? I said, I opened your mail. I couldn't resist. You got an interview, babe."

"No way! Where?"

"Phoenix. They want you in Phoenix next week. Guess you'll be off driving again."

"No way!" Amanda said again. She stared at the console as if Luane were in the car. "Hey, wait a minute! What the hell were you doing opening my mail?"

"See. That's why I asked if you were mad."

"Oh, I thought you meant crazy, as in I'm insane."

"No, I already know you're crazy. I meant angry. But I saw the formal letter and I thought it was one of *my* applications."

"Phoenix. That'd be so awesome."

"I know, right? You won't be some spinster waiting on some hot guy to pay your rent."

"That's one of my top jobs, Lu."

"Mine too."

"Nothing for you, yet?"

"Nope."

One of the bikes approached Amanda's driver's side window. A man seemed to be studying her and her car through his tinted visor. He signaled something to the woman rider behind. Then he fell back with the other two bikers. Then the three bikes trailed close, too close, tailgating her car.

"You know…" Luane was still jibber-jabbering. "If I get a job there, we can room together again. I've got a lot of hopes in Phoenix. But even if I get something back here, we won't be that far apart. I say do your best. Take the job, whatever it takes, Mands. We'll see."

Amanda glanced at her rearview mirror. She couldn't believe her eyes. On the far horizon behind her, a black streak was approaching at an incredible speed. A car? John? Her heart sped in excitement; all morning she had been filled with dread over losing him. But somehow she'd known she'd see him again. Now she felt a queer mix of relief and fear. For it meant…

Shit. I'm in trouble again.

"I think I have to go, Lu."

"Oh. Okay. Thought you were bored in Kansas."

No. Not exactly bored.

It was her dark stranger for sure. His car had become definable about two miles back. And in another second, he was right behind the three bikes.

The female biker with white hair and a white scarf was in the center. She gave some hand signal to the other bikers. Two of the bikes split off and ended up beside Amanda's car. One was in the fast lane; the other was driving on the right shoulder. Then the ringleader-lady rode in front of Amanda's car and slammed on her brakes.

"*Shit!*"

Amanda pressed hard on her brakes, and her car swayed left to right, losing control for a moment. She came an inch away from hitting the biker in front of her. Then a bike on Amanda's left came dangerously close, forcing her to veer toward the shoulder. She thought she was going to hit the bike on her right, but that motorcycle had already fallen back again. Then John crashed his car into the white-haired woman biker. The biker lost balance for a moment, shaking like crazy, but then somehow, impossibly, recovered on the highway. Then all three bikes were back to riding behind her, swerving left to right, as if nothing had happened, seemingly taunting both her and John.

John crashed into the biker again. The impact was hard enough to throw the motorcycle in front of Amanda's car, and she had to swerve to avoid hitting it. But somehow the biker recovered, pulled back, and came right next to Amanda's passenger window. She pounded on the glass with a gloved fist and shouted something. Amanda couldn't understand the words because before the biker could hit her glass again, John hit her once more.

But then another biker came dangerously close to Amanda's driver's side. This one didn't bother with her window; he just rammed his bike into her car.

Amanda found herself pushed toward the shoulder. In front of her, John slammed on his brakes, and the motorcycle ramming Amanda was hurled back. Then her VW was hit by a third bike. She didn't see the collision coming. She felt it.

She lost control and her car spun off the highway, running right into the green wheat fields. She tried the brakes, but her car launched over a ditch and a dirt road. Then she came to a stop in the middle of the wheat field. One of the bikers was waiting. He leaped off his bike, still wearing his helmet, and ran toward her. Behind him, on the far-off horizon behind the freeway, John's black car was still battling the two motorcycles. As the biker moved closer to her hood, Amanda hit the gas, plowing into him. Then she pushed her car through the wheat, pressing her foot hard on the accelerator.

She merged onto a dirt road adjacent to the freeway. She looked back and her assailant was still lying on the ground near his bike in the wheat field. She might have run over him.

She speeded back onto the freeway. Then, like she had done in the middle of the night in Colorado, she drove at the fastest speed she could manage. And, luckily, her car wasn't damaged enough to stop her.

She rapidly passed a large truck. The trucker was wide-eyed with horror. But he wasn't paying any attention to her. He was watching the bedlam between John and the other two bikers ahead. They kept ramming each other.

She nearly caught up to John and the two bikes. That was because more cars were appearing up ahead, forcing them to slow down. She looked in her rearview mirror for the third biker. Thankfully, he was gone.

Then, perhaps the weirdest, most normal thing happened. A police car pulled up behind her. She saw red and blue lights flashing and then heard sirens. She would gladly pull over. The officer said something through a megaphone, but he only said a couple words. The remaining male biker rode full force into the police car, causing it to launch off the freeway like she had. But the impact made the biker ricochet into the central concrete barricade.

The motorcyclist started his bike again behind her.

How!

Then he came right behind Amanda again, doing that infernal leaning back and forth behind her. But the police officer was gone.

Traffic thickened. John and the demon lady had slowed down to a nearly normal freeway speed up ahead. They were heading into construction, and traffic in all the lanes were merging into a line of cars.

About a half mile ahead, the lady's bike squeezed beside John's car and rode on a thin shoulder. They approached a bridge. On the bridge, he squeezed his car on the thin shoulder behind her and slammed the girl biker hard. The crash was enough to send the biker over the concrete wall and into the river below.

Amanda's car was hit. The last biker had hit the back of her car.

She sped up but then had to slam on the brakes by the bridge. John turned his car around up ahead and drove backward along the right shoulder to catch up to her and the bike. He zoomed right past her passenger side.

When her car came to a stop by traffic on the bridge, the sole biker behind her got out of his bike. He brandished a gun and approached her passenger window. Then he pointed it at her. She screamed and covered her head.

Bang.

It was loud, but it wasn't a gunshot. A black blur on the shoulder rushed by the window. John must have collided full speed into her assailant's body.

After that, John pulled his car over where the construction ended. To wait for her?

The biker gang was gone. Her dark stranger had saved her again.

Amanda looked at her console. She gasped, remembering her friend.

Lu! God, are you still on the phone?

No, either she had hung up or Amanda, in the throes of chaos, had hung up on her.

Amanda waited for the traffic to open into two lanes. John's window was open. He gestured to talk to her. She didn't roll down hers. Instead, she weirdly drove with other cars at the speed limit—a "normal" speed again. John pulled up behind her VW and followed her.

There was a rest stop two miles ahead. John drove up to her side and pointed to it, but even as traffic cleared and the off-ramp was ahead, Amanda was too afraid to stop.

She drove for another half hour with John trailing her.

Soon they approached a small town. Amanda drove off one of the off-ramps by a gas station. John followed.

She pulled into the station, parked her car. Then she put her head in her hands. She was surprised that her eyes were wet. She had been crying. She didn't even know when the tears had fallen.

John pulled his black car into a space next to her. His door opened. She watched the dark man, his black pants and T-shirt and shades.

"Are they gone?" she asked. She realized she hadn't opened her car door or rolled down her window. He nodded, seeming to understand her.

"God, John, what's happening?" she asked, rolling down the window. "What's happening?"

"You're in shock," he said with a nod. "Come with me."

"I think I'd rather stay in my car."

He nodded.

Then he just put his fingers in his pants pockets and stared out onto the infinite horizon through his shades. He waited and she thought if she stayed in the car forever, he'd still be there waiting for her.

Slowly, she opened her door. When she stood up, she reached for him. He embraced her.

"It's over."

12

A FAMILIAR TRAIL

THEY WALKED. SHE HAD NO IDEA WHERE BUT, SOMEHOW, HER DARK stranger seemed to know the way. Just like at the museum, he seemed to know every direction, even down this trail in the middle of nowhere. She let him hold her hand this time and lead her through bushes and then down a small slope onto a dirt road. The dirt path was beside rows of wheat. Like the highway, this road went on for miles in both directions. It seemed to go on forever—which she loved. But clouds were out, so it was gloomy.

"Are you feeling better?"

"No." She turned to him and flashed a grin. "I'm terrified. But at least you're with me."

"You're marked," he said with a nod. He looked down at her shoes and she followed his eyes to her sandals.

"I didn't expect to go walking," she said with a shrug.

"I don't think you expected a lot of things. We don't have to walk far. Walking helps get my mind off things. I do it a lot. I thought it'd help you."

"I don't mind. Why won't they leave me alone?"

"I told you, you're marked. If Lilith or her messengers find you, they'll terminate you. They will do this until you return home. Big cities, like Los Angeles, are safe. Denver's safe too, the highways between aren't. Your home is your best hideout. They'd rather do their jobs outside your home, away from the city. When you're alone. That's why I told you to fly home."

"It's too unbelievable to believe."

He nodded.

"Why me?"

"You're pure. Pure souls are deemed worthy of an early release to heaven."

"Pure?" She laughed. Then she shook her head. "That's funny. I'm not pure, John. Sorry, but boy, you've got the wrong girl on that one."

He shook his head.

"So what do *you* have to do with all this?" She was examining his face. "Hmm?" But he was wearing his infernal sunglasses. She couldn't read him.

"I'm protecting you." He resumed walking beside her. "Usually after the first fight, they leave targets alone. Lilith wants to torment you."

"Why am I the lucky girl?"

"Because I've been doing this job for too long." He heaved a long sigh and turned from her, looking at the infinite fields of wheat. Nothing he said really made much sense. He was the most closed-book guy she had ever met. "It's difficult to explain," he said, still staring at the horizon. "I only needed to save a few more souls to ascend. But Lilith met me in Vegas and warned me that she'd be after you. While I protect you, others die. And the punishment is far greater than the rewards I've accrued. Every soul that dies is worth many times more than the souls I've saved. So every couple days means months and months more time here as I watch over you."

"Then watch over the others, John," she said, shaking her head and brushing her hand along his arm. He stared at her hand.

"The touch of an angel," he said quietly.

"I'm not, I tell you."

And she squeezed his hand. She felt him play with her fingers.

"We call the victims angels because of their purity," John said, gazing into her eyes through his shades. "Now that you're marked, you're an angel ready to ascend to heaven, like me, only sooner."

"Well, that really doesn't sound so bad."

"I realize it all sounds nuts. But certainly you believe me after everything that's happened to you?"

"Uh, yeah. I believe you."

"What else do you want to know? You deserve answers now."

"How old are you?"

He grew a smile. Finally. She loved that she could make him smile.

"I'd be twenty-eight."

"So you're alive?"

"Ah," he said, lifting an eyebrow. "I understand." But, of course, he didn't answer, and that was worse.

"Do you have a girlfriend?"

"No." And she was rewarded with a smile again.

"John, every question you answer leads to another. I don't get you. What's worse is you really don't say anything even when you talk. You just nod."

And he infernally nodded. Then he looked up at the sun behind a cloud. "It will be dark soon. Ask me anything you want. Then I can escort you to the next city and you can fly home and leave for good."

But she didn't want to say a thing after he said something dreadful like that.

They came upon water. It was probably a run-off for the crops, but it was about ten feet across. John let go of her hand and stepped onto a pipe crossing the water. Then, while balancing his body with outstretched arms, he walked midway across. He reached for her.

"Are you crazy! Oh, no. Do you have any idea how clumsy I am?"

"I'll catch you."

"Nuh-uh. I'm wearing flip-flops. And if I fall, I'm gonna have all this dirt on my white shorts."

But he didn't take no for an answer. He reached out for her. She grabbed his hand. Then she closed her eyes and screamed as she stepped on the pipe. He guided her, but as she adjusted her balance, it nearly threw him over. She somehow made it across and landed in his arms. He laughed. She looked up into his face. *OMG.* He was so close.

"Why... I have another question... Why do you wear those sunglasses?"

He took them off. That was far worse. She got lost in his eyes. He leaned down and kissed her again and held her in his arms. He smelled good. Like vanilla. She liked his cologne. She brushed her hand along the stubble on his cheek.

"You have lovely eyes," she said between touching his lips. "Why do you cover them?" She realized she had stupidly closed hers.

"The light can be blinding."

She let that go. Because it sounded like another riddle. She looked away, toward the fields. It was getting more dark and stormy. Then she shook her head and headed down the walkway again.

"I'm special?" she asked. "I'm pure and innocent?"

He nodded.

"That's really fucking dumb. And, by the way, I emphasize the word *fucking*. There. I cussed. Fuck, fuck, fuck. I tell you, you've got the wrong fucking girl. I'm not innocent. And I'm hardly an angel."

"Michael doesn't make mistakes."

"Who the fuck is Michael?"

He brushed his hand over the tips of some wheat. Then he put his thumbs in his pockets. "I don't know exactly. He's an overseer. He's not really a person. He determines who is damned and who ascends. This world is an in-between world. Michael watches over all of us. And the messengers decide who ascends and who falls."

"I think you mean God."

"No. I don't believe in God."

"You're an angel, but you don't believe in God?" Her eyes widened. She laughed heartily. "Are you kidding? That is the most ridiculous thing I've ever heard. I tell you, John, it's almost as ridiculous as you calling me innocent."

"Michael is not an all-powerful being like God. If he were, I don't think there would be so much suffering in this world. He's a judge. And he determined that you must already ascend as a good angel and be sent to the next realm. He wants you to ascend so you can go to heaven."

"You said I was an 'angel down.'"

"Yes. An angel on this Earth in trouble. Every being on this planet is born angelic. When close to death, we call them fallen. 'Angel down' is a code that means there is an angel that needs help. So far, Lilith has hunted you near the border. Then when I saved you, two angels near Grand Junction attacked you. Now in Kansas, angels, with Lilith in the lead, tried to kill you again. They hunt to kill you because you're marked to go to heaven early."

"What can I do to get unmarked?"

"You can't. Some live for a few more years. I need you to fly back before you ascend early." He turned from her and looked at the clouds. Then he stopped talking, which bothered her more. After a long silence, she said, "ascend?" Then she gesticulated with her hand for him to explain, but he didn't say anything. He looked away. "As in, *die*. Why? Why would I *ascend* early."

"Those souls," he explained, "that are too pure no longer need to be tested. The world we live in is a test. We are between the states of heaven and hell. In ancient times, it was called purgatory. It's up to you, in your lifetime, to either ascend to heaven or be brought down to hell. Those that are too pure are deemed ready to be taken immediately. Those souls, like you, are rare. But there's no more need to test them. Have you ever wondered why the most angelic people die so early? They are taken and killed by angels."

"So you're protecting me from angels trying to kill me? If they take me, I die and go to heaven?"

"So they say."

"What in the hell is wrong with that?" She looked at him. Really examined him. "And if they're angels, what does that make you?"

He didn't answer. He looked more serious than ever.

She stopped and gazed at his black T-shirt and pants. His boots. His dark shades. Emotionless. He had a presence about him. A power. But he also reminded her of shadows. A vampire. Or darkness... Death. Death... Yes, he was like death. It reminded her of that creepiness she felt when they met in Colorado. Like that first meeting, when she thought she had gotten into a car crash and was going to...die. No, worse, he was death itself. And that's what he said she was destined for. Angels were trying to kill her. And every time her life was threatened, her dark stranger, her so-called guardian angel, appeared... Every time she was near death. Like a grim reaper or something.

She felt a lump in her throat. For the first time since she met him, she shook before him. She felt like she was in the presence of a devil— an entity that could harm her. Her eyes grew wide. She became afraid, just like in the car chase.

He put his hand up and shook his head.

"You're *dark*…you're *evil*, John. If you're fighting angels, you're a bad one."

He nodded. He actually nodded.

What! What the hell?

"You're evil," she repeated, as if trying to explain it to herself. "You're evil, John."

"Wait—"

She turned from him.

"Let me explain."

She would run back to the car. Crossing the pipe, she slipped and her leg fell knee deep into the water, of course. She cursed and blamed him for her soaking muddy feet. But she didn't stop running. She continued down their trail back to the gas station.

"Amanda!"

Her bare legs now drenched in mud and water, her sandals caked in mud, she picked up her pace, tripped on the dusty trail, and rushed on.

"Amanda!"

He shouted a few more times. She wouldn't turn.

The weirdest thing was she believed him now. With his black car and clothes, his mysterious demeanor, with those fucking sunglasses she wanted to tear off his face, she believed he was darkness. He was some sort of angel of death. Everything had been too weird to believe anything else. But why was the grim reaper helping her? To stop her from going to heaven? Or to stop her from dying?

When she scrambled the shrubs and got back up to the gas station, she cringed at the sight of his pitch-black car next to hers. She looked back. He was reaching out to stop her.

"Don't touch me! Just stay away from me!"

"Amanda. Stop."

She stopped at her car door. Then she put her head in her hands and cried. It was like she was suddenly crying over everything, from the near accident near Yuma, to being attacked near Mesa Verde, to the recent chase. She was marked, he had said. So she would die. And he was some evil demon helping her? John, her guardian angel, was telling her she was going to die soon.

She felt so confused.

"I have to go, John," she whimpered. "Please, don't touch me."

"Amanda."

"Stay away from me. Stop trying to help me."

"All right."

She looked up and squinted into his eyes. He had his shades off and this time, instead of lovely alluring blue, all she saw was his weariness. For a flash, she felt bad for him. It was almost enough for her to stop running.

She opened her door. He gently opened it wider for her.

"You're more than dark," Amanda said. "There's something sad about you."

"I can't believe I'm trying to stop you, Sherry. Yes, get away from me. Run home. Please. Run as fast as you can from me. Fly home, Sherry."

She slammed the door on him…but she didn't want to. And as she drove for miles alone, she already missed him. Yet she was too scared to look back.

Then she thought of his last words. He had called her Sherry.

Who's Sherry?

13

—————

PROTECT HER

"I didn't expect to see you back so soon," Sherry said. "What'll it be, John?"

John gazed at her through his shades. Sherry. Or an older Amanda? There she stood, with wrinkles and long silvery hair, leaning over the bar with an angelic smile. Once her hair had been blond, at least according to his dreams. With the same face as the girl he had just saved in Kansas.

John had seen nightmares. In his line of work, he'd witnessed bodies torn in half, bleeding, mutilated, burned, and knifed. He had lived a living hell. But never in this purgatory had he felt his world turn so upside down as when he stared at the older Amanda while thinking of the younger one.

"Just give me the whole fucking bottle."

"That bad, huh?"

John nodded. He looked behind him. The bar was quiet. There were only three couples sitting at tables under dim lights. The windows looking out at the parking lot were dark. Sherry put the bottle down on the counter before him. "Free of charge."

"No shit," he said, unscrewing it. Then he guzzled down the bottle. A quarter way down, Sherry touched his arm. "Easy. Don't you have to drive?"

"Of course I do. I always have to drive, don't I?"

"Tell me what happened."

He drank a little more first. Then he wiped his mouth with the sleeve of his leather jacket.

"She found out who I am."

"A hero?" Sherry opened her eyes wide and quickly put up a hand. "It's just a joke."

"Why are you so chipper anyway, Sher? I haven't seen you this happy in a long time."

"My friends and I are planning a trip to Arrowhead in a month for the summer. I'm just looking forward to it, that's all. Not that I like the mountains, but they thought I needed a change. So we'll be heading to LA for a few weeks for the mountains. Which means, sorry, but your psychiatrist will be out of the office. You'll have to see a real shrink or do without the therapy. Can you handle that?"

"As long as I have this." He pointed to the bottle. "I'm happy for you."

"Thanks."

John drank some more. Then he looked back at the place again. "When are you closing tonight?"

"Does it matter? So, what did you tell her? Please don't tell me you told her that demon shit."

"I am a devil," he said with a shrug. "It's a fact." He picked up the bottle. He didn't drink from it though. Sherry was right. He had to be ready in case Amanda was in trouble again.

Why won't the girl just fly home?

"Why'd you tell her that, John?" She folded her arms and shook her head. "You're an angel. I wish I could talk to the girl and explain. You're messing with her head."

"How am I messing with her head?"

"You're letting her into yours."

He chuckled and then drank some more over that.

"Listen," she said, leaning forward. She rubbed his arm. "You said you're happy for me. I'm happy for you. This girl is making you happy."

"She's driving me crazy."

"That's familiar," Sherry said with a shrug.

"I'm here to protect her. That's all. The minute she gets back home, I'll stop. Only Rick's still giving me jobs. I've failed for the first time. That damages my chances of ever getting out of here."

"Trap or not, doesn't your boss get what you're going through?"

"What's there to get?"

"You're in love."

"What!" John asked. He pulled his shades off and stared at her. Sherry didn't flinch. She just flashed him a rueful smile and slowly nodded.

"You're in love, John. What did you expect? You've met me at your age again."

John rubbed his whole face with his hand. He picked up the bottle and drank more than ever. Then he hit the bottle hard on the counter, pointing at her. "I love *you*. I've told you that for the past few years. You're the one who pushes me away."

"I love you too. But I also recognize when you love someone else. Be honest with yourself and this will be easier. When's the last time you left a job? Shit, even before when you lived with me?"

He turned from her. He heard her walk around the counter. She walked up to him and embraced him.

"I love you, Sher," John said quietly in her ear.

"I know."

"Then why would you say that?"

"That girl is me. You said it yourself. You said she acts like me, looks like me, and has my voice." She stepped back. Then she ran her hand through his short hair. "You've gotta let *me* go. I don't mean the visiting —shit, I live for seeing you. I'll still be here. But you've gotta let me go *here*." She touched his chest. Then she sighed. "I understand. I've had decades to do this. You haven't, John." She touched his cheek and kissed his lips gently.

"We could try again," he said, looking down at the ground.

"It won't work," she said, shaking her head. "Take care of her like you would me. Guard her. Then love her like you once loved me. Not like now, like it once was for the two of us. Maybe this isn't a curse, John. Maybe it's a gift. Not from Lilith. Or Michael. Maybe it's a gift from God."

He took a deep breath and put on his shades.

"Whatever you decide, protect her. You're right to do that. The hell with Rick and the job."

14

ROADSIDE MOTEL

The rest of the day had been unpleasant for Amanda. She had tried to enjoy the road, like she always did, but she couldn't stop looking over her shoulder. Nor could she regret leaving John the way she did.

By the time she had reached Kansas City, it was late. And she was hungry. She ate at the busiest restaurant that she could find downtown —because busy felt safe. Then when she arrived at her motel room, she didn't like it because it was too quiet and she was alone. She had never felt afraid to be alone before.

She washed her face and prepared to take a much-needed warm shower. She felt the water with her hand and it was, of course, cold. Then she gazed at herself in the bathroom mirror. Her long blond hair was shaggy like a bird's nest. And her eyes reminded her of John's. She had those same thick bags under them.

"I think this can be checked off as a fucked up vacation day, Mands," she said to herself. Then she dug in her pocket for her recorder to talk to her audience instead of herself.

"Well, guys... Caligirl's a bit deflated." She sighed. She hesitated about what to say—which she never did—and then said, "Gettingold24 got into a car accident today. My green jewel still drives, but it has these huge dents along the side. It was pretty gnarly. But you know, it wasn't the car accident, it was the roads. That's what's still freaking me out.

There was a car chase, police and all, in the middle of Kansas. Yeah, I'm not kidding. A car chase. And I was in the middle of it. This is all for real. And, well… I guess I'm still breathing. Sort of. So that's good. I'm still alive. Just freaked out."

She clicked the off button for a moment. Then she ran her hand through her long, messy hair. She replaced her recorder with a comb. She'd shower, cold or not.

She slipped off her flip-flops and turned the water back on. Then she removed her pants. But before she finished undressing, she picked up the recorder again.

"I lost my dark stranger. We had a fight, our second I suppose. Now the last. I don't know, I suppose it was cool enough to meet a stranger on a road trip. Right? And I mean, shit happens on road trips. Right? That's why they call it an adventure. It can't all be roses. Move on, Cali-girl, move on.

"Should I just go home? Hmm. I'm over halfway to the Big Apple, but… I'm probably going to head back tomorrow. I'll let you guys know in the next entry. For now I'm signing off so I don't depress you any further. Tootles."

She removed her T-shirt.

That's when she heard a knock on the hotel room door. Who could that be? John? Would he have followed her? Of course he would. He was totally creepy like that. That's why, incredibly hot and attractive or not, she had run from him. But now she hated herself for feeling giddy that he was back. She quickly fastened the clasp on her bra and pulled on her T-shirt. It was a long enough shirt to cover her underwear. And she wouldn't open the door for him anyway.

No way. Right?

Well…depends. Maybe he's brought roses or something.

There was another knock. She laughed at her stupid joke.

"Shit," she said to herself, shaking her head.

Should I even bother to answer the door? Why won't he just leave me alone.

Fuck him. I can take care of myself. I have fucking mace.

She opened the door, but it was stopped by the chain.

"What!" Amanda cried. "Why don't you leave me the hell alone, John!"

There was a scream. It was her own voice. A figure was standing in the hallway with pitch-black clothes like John's, but it wasn't a man. It was a woman with long white hair and pink eyes, wearing a black leather jacket and white scarf over a motorcycle jumpsuit. There was another scream. From her own voice.

"Shut your hole and open the fucking door, Amanda."

"What do you want!"

"I want to talk to you," the lady said calmly. "Now open the door."

Amanda did the opposite. She threw her shoulder against it, but it didn't shut. Looking down she saw a boot in the crack of the door.

"Oww. That hurt. Unlatch the lock."

"Go away!"

"Calm the fuck down and undo the lock. I just want a word."

But she didn't. And the stranger didn't move her boot.

"What did he tell you?" she asked. "Did he say I want to kill you? If I'm an angel, why would I want to kill you, Amanda? If I'm good and he's bad, why do you listen to him? Did you ever think that maybe we're protecting you from *him*?"

Yeah. That's why she'd run from him. But she'd give anything for this woman to disappear and John to take her place right now.

"Go away!" She shoved her body against the door again.

"Oww! Fuck! If I wanted to kill you, Amanda, you'd already be dead. Now open the fucking door or I'll open it for you. I do breaking and entering for a living, and this is a goddamn chain lock."

"Help!" shouted Amanda. "Help!"

"Goddamn it," the woman said.

A white-gloved hand squeezed through the crack and ran a wire over the chain. The wire caught the chain and the door was pushed open. In a panic, Amanda launched her whole body at the door for a third time.

"You fucking bitch!" cried the woman as her foot was slammed.

Lilith threw the door open. Amanda fell on her back on the carpet. Her eyes bulged, staring at the motorcyclist now hovering over her. Then the woman shut the door behind her and, ironically, fastened the chain lock.

"Shut your dainty little cunt-voice," she said with a smirk. "'Kay?" She shook out her injured foot. "Just shut the fuck up."

The stranger was attractive but had pink, almost red eyes and pale skin. And the sight of her odd paleness made Amanda cry out again. Albino? Or one of these so-called pale angels? *Who knows anymore in this nightmare.* An assailant ready to rape or kill her? Yeah, that was more like it. Amanda quickly crawled backward toward the bed.

"Will you stop acting like a frightened little pussy?"

Amanda searched the room for something to strike her with. Her mace was in her bag.

She got up and ran for it, but before she could open her bag, her wrist was grabbed from behind. She was thrown against the bed. Amanda screamed again as Lilith twisted her arm hard. Then her other wrist was grabbed. Her wrists were quickly tied with rope. Then Amanda was thrown on the bed.

The woman let go of her and grabbed a desk chair.

"Let's talk," she said with a wicked smile. "Now you've been marked. And now you're bound because you're being an uncooperative little cunt. Calm the fuck down or all your fantasies of bad things will come true. Especially looking pretty and half naked as you are right now. I'd love to fuck that."

"Help!" Amanda cried again. "Help!"

"Shut up," the woman said, rolling her eyes. "Do I have to tape your mouth?"

Amanda shook her head.

"My name is Lilith. I am an archangel assigned by Samael to ascend you. I could have taken you in Arizona, had it not been for Azrael. We tried again on the road this afternoon. You know how that went."

"What do I—"

She raised a finger. "Don't talk unless I permit it or I'll tape your lips." Then she ran a finger along Amanda's bare arm. "It turns out, my lovely, that you arrived just in time. See, your friend is the best operative they've ever had. You're disabling him. That is more valuable than your ascension itself. For the first time, it's not really about you, angel. It's about him."

"What—"

She put her finger up again. "Shut up, Amanda, until I permit you to speak. I'm not done. Azrael and I have a long history together. Did he tell you?"

Amanda shook her head.

"You may speak," Lilith said with a smirk.

"He didn't tell me exactly what you guys were. He said angels, and then he just said I'm marked and I'm destined to die."

"Yes. That is so. You will die." She stroked Amanda's cheek with a white-gloved finger. Then she stared at her with her pink eyes. "My lovely, innocent girl, you will die. You're beautiful. Is that why he is breaking his pact? Or is he just tired?"

"I don't know about any of this." Then Amanda paused for a moment. Lilith was staring at her with this devilish sardonic smile. A grin that felt so evil, just as if the devil were here with her right now. "I don't know what's going on. I'm just driving a cross-country trip."

"Pretty, pretty," Lilith said. "Do you like my eyes?" She blinked them near Amanda's face.

"What?"

"Do you like my eyes? I was born with red eyes."

"Oh. I thought you—"

"Looked like all archangels?" Lilith asked with a laugh. She started going through Amanda's things. She even took out the mace bottle. She nodded and chuckled at that. "It's what Lilith looks like."

"It's nice."

Lilith nodded.

"What are you going to do with me?" Amanda asked.

"You mean?" she rummaged through Amanda's bag by the hotel desk. She looked at her compact and lipstick. "Am I going to have you ascend *now*?"

"Yeah."

"Not yet. You are his bait again. I told you…" She stopped going through Amanda's purse. "I was supposed to have you ascend in Arizona. Azrael saved you. Our spat earlier in the day was simply to prevent John from doing his job. You and he thought we lost. We didn't. The mission was a success. An angel died on his watch. And now, my dear, my hope is that capturing you will drive him completely crazy."

Lilith crossed her arms and just stared down at her. Then she walked across the room.

Amanda had to turn onto her side to watch her. She couldn't take her eyes off the woman. She was terrified of not seeing what she was up to.

Lilith went over to Amanda's spare bag and started rummaging through that too.

"What are you looking for?"

"Your goddamn phone."

"Why not just ask me?"

"I don't think you'll cooperate."

The phone wasn't in her bags. So she searched the room. It was lying on the counter near the TV. Lilith picked it up.

"What's the password, Amanda?"

"Why should I tell you?"

Lilith nodded and smirked. Then she walked around the bed. Amanda struggled to turn to her other side to watch her, but she couldn't turn fast enough. Then Lilith yanked her right hand from behind. "Let's see if you used your fingerprint." Lilith twisted her thumb and Amanda cried out in pain. She thought she was going to pull her finger off. Then she felt her phone against her thumb. Lilith grabbed another finger and bent it back hard.

"*Ow!*" Amanda heard herself whimper, but the bitch stopped bending it.

She couldn't cry. She couldn't appear weak. That's what this monster thought she was.

"You'll learn soon enough to not fight me," Lilith said, "or I'll just cause you more pain."

Amanda turned and saw Lilith scrolling through her phone.

"I don't believe it, you fuck him, but don't have his phone number? Is it a code? Like it's this Jeffrey or Kurt guy? Or do you actually not have his phone number?"

"I never fucked him. I barely know him. He's as creepy as you are. Only he doesn't tie me up."

"I'm not so sure about *that*. Watch your mouth. When you say *fuck* it really turns me on. Especially when you add *tie*. You keep up your attitude and I'll do to you what he's been wanting to do to you all along."

"Are you gay?" Amanda cringed. Lilith's voice had been sultry and now she wanted to throw up.

"I love anyone, male or female, anything, my dear, if it leads to pleasure. Especially pretty little things." Lilith hurled the phone at her. "You're my worm. Don't squirm. If you move, little worm, I will cut you to pieces." She leaned forward so her face was an inch away from Amanda's. Then she grew a sinister, nasty smile. "If you resist, I'll fillet you like I did a nice Black woman a day ago in Idaho. Cooperate or suffer, lovely, pretty girl." She laughed—Amanda guessed it was over her disgusted expression. "Don't worry. You're too pure for my taste. You're simply bait, my dear. Simply bait."

15

———

RETURN TO SANCTUARY

MULTICOLORED LIGHTS RUSHED PAST JOHN'S WINDSHIELD AS HE DROVE at tremendous speed across the plains toward the desert. Slight turns of his steering wheel averted crashes. But obstacles were rare this early in the morning. It was daybreak. He was close to the border between California and Arizona. It was fairly empty and one of his favorite drives. But closer to California, it had dips. He slowed down for these.

It was when he reached fields of saguaros—shrouded in shadows by the freeway—that John really slowed. He whooshed by another trucker then dropped down to a hundred and fifty miles an hour.

Then he came to his favorite spot.

In desolation, he walked along a cliffside. His sanctuary. But it was still dark with only a thin line of light off on the horizon. He removed his shades waiting for the sunrise. It was far too early, so in darkness, he followed a path down an incline along an infinite desert vista.

"What happens when you die?"

It was his "aunt's" voice that came to him. His adopted mother.

"I don't know."

"I think it gets brighter. The brightest light you've ever seen. Like staring at the sun. Then you're taken somewhere. Somewhere without pain. I fell once and hit my head. I remember such peace. It's when I woke up that I felt pain. I think it's like that. Tranquility away from our pain."

"I hope so."

"I hope I see your brother there."

"You will."

"Hold my hand, please."

"I'm already holding it, Mother."

"I'm scared. I'm scared."

He scuffed the red sand against his boot. He felt dread. This memory was a mix of feelings. He so wanted to hear the voice of his aunt, but not this memory. Not this pain.

As if it obeyed him, he felt her presence leave him.

The first rays of light brightened the horizon. Below the cliff was a vista of orange and red over the weeds and saguaros. Empty sand for miles. He caught a large bird overhead circling in the dark clouds. It was reflecting the rising sun.

Amanda finally knew what he was. He was a monster. That's why she ran. Why was he so surprised?

So why did it still upset him? Was Sherry right?

His phone rang.

"Angel down," Rick said. "A man. Benjamin. He's thirty, Asian, bald, an engineer. He keeps to himself. His sign is Leo. He's traveling out in the open, leaving Minneapolis. You near there?"

"Not that far from there," John said, turning around and looking into the dark clouds toward Los Angeles. "A man?"

"A man."

"Send me the location."

"Are you back on board? We just lost another soul in Florida because of your shit. I only have so many agents, Azrael. I've talked Michael into giving you this one last chance. But he said you'll pay for the two souls that passed."

He watched the bird circling above. Its shadow flew under the now dim stars. Right between the rising sun and the dark evening. That reminded him of himself. A wanderer in the shadows with just a glimpse of light. He remembered that, on her deathbed, his auntie had told him there'd be a bright light when he died. He yearned so much for that light now. He felt like Amanda had been a glimpse of it. The sun, even though it was blinding, was just a glimpse too. But he wore his shades to cover it all up…for the job.

"Send me the location," John repeated.

"I already have."

He nodded.

"John?"

"Yeah?"

"I'm going to tell you something as your friend. It goes against everything we do. But if I don't tell you, you'll never forgive me. Lilith's taken Amanda. She's getting off of Interstate Seventy near Columbia, Missouri, following her car. Intelligence says she stopped by the motel Amanda had checked into and now has her captive."

John gripped his free hand tightly. He pulled off his shades and stared at the rising sun.

"Send me her location."

"You need to go to the target in Minneapolis. Amanda is no longer your concern."

"I'm closer to Columbia, Missouri."

"John," Rick said, sounding uncharacteristically cautious, "listen to me carefully, man, for once in your life. Please. Listen. I just told you that we lost another soul. If you ignore the new target, this will make three failures. I might be able to work with Michael on the other two, but if I lose you this time and you do Lilith's bidding, your pact with us is broken. It's over between you and me and it's done for you. You'll essentially be viewed as working for them. We can't accept your attachment to someone they're using as a trap anymore… Damn it, John, is this one girl worth giving up your soul? You want to wander forever?"

John took a deep breath. It wasn't over indecision.

"Text me her location."

"This will be it between us. I'll send you two sets of coordinates. Follow the right one and I'll meet you back in Vegas tomorrow for a debriefing. Go for the wrong one and we're through."

"You would never have told me as a *friend* if you didn't know what I'm going to do."

"Then we're done. You're stranded. It's over. I'll be expecting your keys."

"And I'll meet you in hell, Raphael."

"Yeah? Try being careful around the police. Remember when we're through, you don't have my protection."

"Sure. And…thanks."
"Fuck off, John."

16

CINCINNATI

Amanda felt more helpless than she'd ever felt in her life. Although she wasn't tied up and was allowed to drive—she wasn't quite sure why—the white-haired demon followed close behind, haughtily swerving back and forth, like when they pursued her in Kansas. If Amanda wanted a cup of coffee, the bitch followed her into the gas station. If she wanted to relieve herself, the devil was there too. She had almost escaped near a mall in Columbia, Missouri. It was of no use. The wily woman let her run; then as Amanda got back on the road, she was back to swerving pompously behind her car.

At a stoplight, Amanda had rolled down her window and asked her pursuer where they were going. "Just keep driving," Lilith had said.

Now Amanda had time to worry. And yawn. She was so tired after driving all night. And unlike in the beautiful open desert, leafless trees had sprouted up everywhere in Missouri. It wasn't as pretty.

Then it turned urban.

Amanda drove by the famous Arch—a landmark she normally would be telling her listeners about. But she was hardly in the mood now. She slowed in traffic.

But soon traffic opened up, and they headed out of the city onto open roads again. And the demon signaled for her to keep driving.

It was the next city, Cincinnati, where she saw a black car streak past her on the other side of the highway. It traveled faster than any normal car. It had to be him! It just had to be. And before she could contemplate anything else, his sleek pitch-black car was nearly touching the back of Lilith's bike. Amanda felt safer now, until more black bikes appeared beside her car on the freeway. And there were more than ever before. Then she jumped as a few of them waved pistols at her and John.

Amanda slammed on the brakes and came to a stop, almost rear-ending a car in front of her. She hadn't been looking at the traffic up ahead. Then one of the pistol-waving bikers rode right alongside her driver's side window. He stopped and aimed the gun at her head. She ducked and screamed as glass came flying into the car.

Again!?

Amanda screamed. She sat crouched with her arms over her head, too afraid to sit up. Then she heard more metal crashing outside her now open window—and honking horns, and screams—this time from bystanders surrounding her.

Something was hurled into her car, hitting her leg. In the pandemonium she thought it was some kind of bomb. It hit the passenger floor mat. She bent down, but couldn't reach it.

"Amanda. Amanda."

She recognized that voice. It was John! Her guardian angel.

"Amanda!"

Somehow John's voice was inside her car. How?

"Get up. Sit up and hit the gas. Get the hell out of here! Now!"

She sat up. There was an opening in traffic in the right lane and she took it. Many cars were avoiding her. Why?

Gunfire. They heard gunfire. Anyone hearing that would do anything to get away.

"They're circling back," said John in a calmer voice. "Drive forward and stay to the right shoulder. Try to get off at the exit. I'm on my way behind you."

"John?"

"Yes."

"Where the hell are you?"

"I threw my cell phone in your car. I'm on speaker phone."

"Then how are you talking to me?"

"My car has another line."

Amanda's body was thrown forward and her head hit her steering wheel. Fortunately, she had a seat belt on and she didn't hit her head hard. It hurt though. From what? Most of the cars were staying as far from her as they could now. She glanced in her rearview mirror. It was one of the black bikes. But this guy wasn't brandishing a gun. Instead, he just kept ramming her rear bumper.

"One of them is right behind me."

"The right shoulder is open," John said. "Lose us. *All of us.* Lose us now. I don't think that dick has his gun. Hit the gas and run, Amanda!"

The guy was riding up to ram her yet again, but he missed. Because Amanda accelerated to the right as fast as she could just in time. She looked to her left and wished she hadn't. Lilith and three of her stooges were riding backward on the freeway near the center divider. Apparently, they had advanced between the cars ahead of them and were now circling back. And they were getting close.

The right lane blocked her again. But there was an off-ramp bridge leading off the freeway here.

"Take the exit now," John said.

"I can't. There's a line of cars in front of me."

"Drive on the shoulder again."

"What if I'm squeezed against the barrier and fall off the ramp!"

I mean, what the fuck!

"You don't have a choice," he said too calmly. "You have enough space. Trust me."

"How do you know? Where the fuck are you, anyway?" She leaned forward and searched ahead. Then she searched her rearview mirror. "I'm not innocent! Okay! I'm bad. Okay, John. Fuck, fuck, fuck. See! I cussed. *So get these fucking freaks off my tail!*"

"Lilith isn't after you," he said more calmly. "She's chasing me. She's using you to get to me. Take the shoulder. It's big enough for your car. I've scoped it out. If you drive fast and go, you'll make it."

She felt dizzy. Sick. But then she saw that bitch, Lilith, with her long, flowing white hair and scarf, only two car lengths from her side. It sure looked like she was chasing her. She was thrown forward again by a biker behind her. That was enough.

Amanda hit the gas and squeezed between the line of cars ahead of her and the rail of the highway to her right. The rail climbed more and more steeply, separating from the rest of the highway over a raised bridge. She was passing the bridge just like John had said she would. But then four, no all five, black bikes were right behind her. And the bikes had no problem squeezing between traffic either.

As the road started flattening, the shoulder became too narrow. She was forced to stop again.

She looked back through her rearview mirror. Then she jumped again. John's black car was airborne over an overpass. He must have launched off an adjacent freeway bridge. She thought he was going to collide with her car. He didn't. The black car landed short, crashing into her motorcycle pursuers. It smashed Lilith and another bike then rammed into a third, sending a fourth right over the off-ramp rail. Only one biker hadn't been hit. He stopped his bike behind her and rushed to Amanda's car.

John threw open his car door and tackled him.

Traffic moved again. That opened an exit.

Amanda did the same thing she had done on the bridge, quickly maneuvering around the cars surrounding her. After running a stoplight, and then another, she stared at her side mirror. Her pursuers were gone.

She was shocked to discover that she was alone in downtown Cincinnati. Then she looked down at John's cell phone. She reached down to grab it but jumped at the sound of a car horn. She was in the middle of a city street.

She drove another mile downtown until she found an indoor parking structure. She drove up to the next level, parked in a stall in darkness, and shut off her engine. The lot was lit only by slivers of daylight through a few holes in a concrete wall and a flickering light on the ceiling.

She heard panting. That was her breathing.

She looked down for John's phone, now in the shadows, but couldn't find it. It was too dark—and too eerily quiet. And John hadn't said anything since the freeway.

Did they kill him?

She looked at the passenger side mat. She couldn't see anything, so she turned on her cabin light. Dirt from another of Luane's cacti was all over the mat. And by the passenger door was John's phone. The screen was off.

She fumbled along the mat and picked it up.

"John?" she said quietly into the phone.

The screen was cracked too. But when she slid her finger over it, it lit up.

"John?"

The call hadn't been dropped. It was still ongoing. But there was only silence.

"John?" she said in a hushed whisper.

Shit. Is he hurt? Dead?

"John? John?"

17

THE PARKING LOT

John couldn't stop hitting the biker's face. Even after his foe fell unconscious, he kept slamming his bloody fist through the open visor into the guy's teeth. He heard yelling around him. Many people were sitting in their cars in traffic witnessing the fight. Some were shouting at him for wrecking their car with his crazed jump over traffic. Finally, he stopped bludgeoning the biker after noticing his own blood dripping from his fist.

He heard motorcycle engines. The other black riders were recovering. And they were weaving around cars, heading right his way.

"John," he heard through the car speakers as he jumped back in his car. "John. John." It was Amanda's voice. But she was talking almost in a whisper.

"Where are you, Amanda?" He closed the door.

"I don't know. It's…it's an indoor parking lot. Very dark. I thought they killed you. I'm so happy to hear your voice again."

"Where?"

"Where what?"

"Where are you?"

The minute John saw an opening in the traffic, he hit the gas. He got off the freeway and drove onto the city streets. Here the traffic thinned, and he was able to accelerate. He crossed two intersections. That's when he noticed silence in his car.

He wrapped his bloody right fist in a towel.

Why isn't she talking?

She's scared. The fuckers blew open her window again.

I should have put a hole in his head.

"Ditch your car, Amanda. I'll pick you up. You have your cell phone?"

"I can just use yours."

"No. Listen to me carefully. I'll text you the number to my car phone. Put that number in your cell and then call me the minute you get out of the parking lot. Then leave my phone in the car."

"What?"

"I'll text on the number to *my* phone. Copy it on yours and leave my phone in the car. Then get out of there."

"Why?"

They were right behind him. Five bikers with Lilith, the ringleader, in the center. As John felt a dip at the next cross-street, he watched all five of them drop down and jump a few feet up in the air. With all their visors down, he couldn't discern which biker was the man he had bludgeoned.

"What about my luggage?" Amanda asked.

"Leave your bag in the car with my phone. Hell, throw the phone in the bag. I can track the phone and we can get the car and your things later."

"I'm not leaving my belongings."

Are you kidding me? "I don't know how far you'll have to walk."

"I've got all my stuff in this bag," she said. "And it has rollers."

"We can get it later."

"No. I can't just leave it."

"Fine. Whatever. Take the bag."

"You don't have to sound upset."

"I'm not upset," he said with a sigh.

"I gotta tell you… I'd rather just stay put in this parking lot. It's dark and quiet. Why don't I just do that?"

"No. They'll find you."

"Okay, fine. I'll call you on my phone. Bye."

A block ahead was another line of cars. John steered sharply to the right, onto a quieter street. The bikers did the same. John passed a car, swerved around a pedestrian, and then hit the gas again.

That's when he heard a siren. A pair of police bikes with red and blue flashing lights rushed into the street, joining the chase. They were signaling for them to pull over.

John's phone rang. It was an unknown number—he figured Amanda's.

"John?" It was Amanda's voice.

"What are your cross streets?"

"Are those sirens? You got the cops after you?"

"Never mind. What's the cross streets? Quick. Get them for me."

She was breathing heavily. Then he heard the ding of an elevator door.

The road was blocked ahead. At the red light, he drifted right into oncoming traffic. He heard some horns. Then he swerved around two cars and continued down a narrower road.

John heard an explosion from behind. It was gunfire. The bikers were firing at the police. Another call came in on his phone.

"Amanda." No answer. "Amanda!"

John touched the dials on his console to put her on hold and take the other call. The contact on the monitor read "Hunter."

"I got a cop dead in downtown fucking Cincinnati, John!" cried Rick on the line. *"Give me one reason, one good reason, to not blow you off the goddamn road!"*

"One?"

"Yeah."

"You owe me."

A bicyclist was in the middle of the street. John swerved to avoid hitting him. But the force of the near collision blew the guy off his bike. This was bad because John's pursuers were right behind him, and one of the bikers ran over him.

"I owe you?" Raphael said with a sigh. "Sure. Sure. This one time. You've got three minutes before we disable your car. This warning makes us even. I won't stop them from hitting you after that. And avoid pedestrians. I saw that."

John bent forward, looking at the sky through his windshield.

"Where are you?"

Rick hung up.

John quickly flipped through his console searching for recent numbers. He called the last one.

"Hi," she said. "I think I lost you in the elevator."

"Cross streets?"

"Oh… Hold on. Let me get past the gate."

John pressed another button and searched the map on his screen. She couldn't be that far away.

"Cross streets. Now, Amanda."

Lilith caught up to his car. She banged on the side window. Then two other bikes behind her crashed into his car. They were trying to push him off the road. They couldn't damage his car, but they could disable it by driving him into a building. John had to move faster.

He accelerated but then slammed on the brakes as two cars crossed the next intersection. A biker rear-ended him hard. That launched his motorcycle over John's car, and he collided headlong into another vehicle. John looked back. The biker's body lay on the ground motionless. Dead.

Lilith and the other bikers passed him. About a block ahead, Lilith was signaling for them to circle back.

John hit the gas and turned down a different street.

"Now would be a good time, Amanda."

In his rearview mirror, John caught a police bike being struck by a black bike. That made two police "disabled" and an innocent bystander killed.

"Amanda?"

Any minute, the entire police force of Cincinnati would be chasing him, and he wouldn't be able to save her.

"Cross streets. Now."

"It's Chestergate, John. Chestergate and… Dawn Street I think."

"I'll be there in a second."

He quickly typed in the address while swerving around a bus and a semi. There was a busy street with a red light ahead. He was right about being close. But he realized a big problem. Lilith was on his tail again with her stooges. If he stopped to pick up Amanda, they'd simply kill her while she was getting into the car.

"Amanda, how far are you from the entrance to the parking lot?"

"It's right here."

"Go back inside the structure. I'll meet you right at the entrance. You'll be safer in my car, but stay inside the structure till my car's there."

"They're still trailing you?"

"Yeah."

"I don't hear sirens anymore."

John looked at the digital clock on his dash. Raphael had said three minutes. He had about thirty seconds left.

"Are you there now?" John asked, staring at the parking garage.

"Yeah."

John slammed on the brakes. A bike collided with his car from behind. But Lilith evaded collision with the other biker by swerving in front of him. John hit the gas and accelerated toward the parking structure. He skidded right into the building, landing about twenty yards inside. Amanda was standing there with her luggage by her side staring with wide eyes.

John leaned forward and threw open the passenger door.

"Give me the bag." He reached for it. "Hurry!"

She handed it to him and he hurled it into the back seat. Then he tugged her arm, pulling her into his car.

"Close the door."

She was thrown back in her seat as soon as the door closed. John accelerated. The screech of his tires and his engine echoed inside the dimly lit parking garage.

Bikers were colliding with the passenger side. One biker hit the door. Then another goon took out his pistol and fired right at Amanda's face. She screamed, but the bullet didn't crack the window.

John looked in his rearview mirror. A line of red and blue lights were about to enter the lot. He couldn't exit the way he came.

"Put your seat belt on."

John floored the gas pedal. Lights flickered along the windshield. Then he felt the impact. He drove straight through a wall at over a hundred miles an hour. Fortunately, the wall was thin enough to penetrate and led to an outside road.

John turned right and sped toward a freeway entrance.

"I can't see!" exclaimed Amanda. "I can't see!"

"It's temporary."

"God, John, I can't see!"

"Just wait a minute. It'll pass."

John looked at his side-view mirror. A plume of smoke followed him as the wind brushed off dust from the shattered wall. The motorcycles were trailing him, but now they were caked with the dust from John's car.

His phone rang. The console read "Hunter" again.

"Look up, John. Your time's up."

John leaned forward. There was an orange helicopter in the sky.

"That's not ours," John said.

"No, that's a news chopper. You've been spotted. Find a spot and jump. Do it now. Get the hell out of there. And take that pale bitch and her bikers with you *away from the city* or she wins."

"You're not blowing me up?"

"Get the fuck out of the city before it's not up to me anymore."

He hung up on him.

Amanda was brushing tears from her eyes. Was she crying or was it the blinding light?

"The effect will fade, Amanda. I promise."

She nodded. But she kept rubbing her eyes.

John leaned forward to look up. He had lost the helicopter. For now.

Meanwhile, Lilith was pompously swaying back and forth on her bike with the rest of them right behind her. John found the entrance to the freeway. He drove on the shoulder.

"Are you all right?" he asked Amanda.

"You asshole!" she said, hitting his shoulder. "What is this about! How did we just drive through a wall!"

"I didn't know you saw it. Can you see now?"

"Yes," she said, turning away from him at the window. "But it burns."

"I'm sorry, Amanda."

"It's not your fault," she said with a sigh. "I know… Sorry."

"Do you have your sunglasses?"

"No. I left them in my car."

He checked his scope. He had an opening on the shoulder alongside a straightaway for at least fifteen miles.

"I need you to dip your head into your hands. Cover your eyes and don't look up until I tell you. We're going to jump, and it'll blind you again if you open them."

"I have to?"

"If we're to get them off our tail. Yes."

Amanda squinted at her side mirror. "Guess you saved me again. Thanks."

"Cover your eyes with your hands, Amanda. Do it now."

Amanda obeyed and crouched with her head in her hands. John pressed down hard on the accelerator. The lights rushed along the windshield. He and Amanda were thrown against their seats. She didn't scream this time. Nor did she cry. She didn't say a word.

John drove as fast as he could to lose the motorcyclists and escape Cincinnati. He could outrun them. He could lose them.

At first, they continued to chase him. But soon they fell back, not able to keep up with his car.

After an hour of driving in Kentucky, Amanda still didn't say a word. At first, John caught her staring out at the fields. Then she curled up like a ball, facing away from him, and fell asleep.

John watched her sleep for hours. Her chest gently rose and fell. Occasionally she'd shift a little in her seat, but she didn't wake up. Of course, that bitch had probably dragged her across the highway all night without letting her rest.

Why had he risked everything for her? She was beautiful. Sure. Pure and innocent. Good. Yes. She was an angel, yes. But John had known many beautiful women, many good women, angels, that had fallen. His boss was right. Amanda might look like Sherry, but she wasn't her. So why lose everything for her? Because she was special to him… Why?

She's Sherry.

A little later on, Amanda asked quietly, with her eyes still closed, "Where are we going, John?"

"East somewhere. Somewhere across the country. To New York, I suppose."

"Good. That's the last place I have to go to finish my trip."

18

THE BIG APPLE

"DID YOU SEE THIS MIRROR, JOHN!" AMANDA CRIED. "OMG, I CAN'T believe it! It's like made of gold or something." John didn't answer. She really didn't expect him to. He didn't talk much.

They had checked into a hotel in Manhattan. It was the swankiest place she'd ever stayed in. There were these magnificent chandeliers by the entrance with vaulted ceilings, a large hallway, and an actual red carpet that led to grand elevators. It must have been over a hundred years old. And there was even an elevator operator with one of those cute bell-hop hats pressing the elevator buttons for guests. Amanda loved that. Now Amanda sat by the giant wall mirror fixing her long blond hair. It looked awful. It was frizzy again. And she still had bags under her eyes, like John always did.

She shrugged, removed her sandals, and enjoyed the feel of the swanky cool marble floor on her naked feet. They were filthy. She had thrown water over them in Kansas before she was kidnapped, but they were still dirty from when she ran from John yesterday. Yesterday seemed like a week ago—after driving all night.

She peeked through the crack in the door. She could just make out her guardian angel staring out the large hotel window—guarding them. From what? A bird? They were over thirty stories up.

"This place is amazing," she said.

He nodded, still staring outside.

"Whatcha doing?" She walked over. It was dark outside, but a thousand city lights twinkled from windows and the boulevard below. John was, of course, oddly still wearing his sunglasses.

"Lilith is still hunting you," he said darkly.

"By helicopter? Or does she walk on tightropes?"

He cocked his head, and there was a faint smile. "Why don't you get some sleep. My car was hardly a place to rest."

"I look that bad, huh?"

"No." He shook his head. "You look fine."

But then he was back to patrolling the window.

Amanda hopped on the bed. Then she pulled out her recorder from her pants pocket.

"Guys," Amanda said quietly, "I'm sitting on the thirty-fourth floor of a posh hotel before that dark stranger I was talking about. We're like two thousand feet up, and I feel like I'm in the fucking clouds. Can you believe that? It's a breathtaking view of downtown Manhattan. It's wonderful."

"Will you stop that?" John snapped.

"Shh." She said, gesturing for him to be quiet. She jumped up and stood by his side, looking at the ground. "The cars are just tiny lights from up here. And across the street, even in—like—the middle of the night, there are people walking along the sidewalk. But they're like ants. I mean, I'm on a top floor of an effing Manhattan penthouse. Can you believe that! And guess what that means? My mission to drive cross country is a success." She sighed. "Yep, thanks to tall, dark, and handsome standing to my left." She laughed as he shook his head. She guessed he was probably rolling his eyes, but she couldn't tell through his shades. "They're like insects down there walking to God knows where. As I put my forehead on the glass and…look straight down, I'm imagining just floating in the clouds over all these people. Where are they going? What are they doing? I don't know. So many. Just another day for them in the city, I guess. Not for me. It's…exciting. Thrilling."

John shook his head again. That made her laugh.

"Yeah, my guardian angel is back with me," she said, laughing and falling back on the bed. "He's back. Freaky as hell, I tell you, but kinda funny. He's the kind of guy who doesn't realize he's funny. He's wearing sunglasses *in* our hotel room. *Inside* the room. I'm not kidding. I mean, who the hell even does that? He says he's an angel—a dark angel. Doomed to walk this earth damning people by saving their lives." John stared at her. "Would you like to say anything to my listeners, fallen angel?" She held the microphone of her handheld recorder up to him.

"Delete that."

"Let me tell you what happened," she said into the microphone, looking back at the window.

"I told you to stop it," John said. "You can't say all that to the public."

"'Kay." She clicked the recorder off and smirked at him.

"You can't say anything about me. Or what happened."

Too late.

He stared at her in disbelief. Then he slowly turned back to the window.

She clicked her recorder back on. "Back in Cincinnati, my car got abandoned in a parking lot somewhere in the middle of no-fucking-where. Then this guy drove me across Kentucky in his sleek man-car. My VW was totaled. I know, I'm in total bereavement over losing my green baby. But I think I can get her back. There were red and blue lights and sirens and all sorts of crazy shit in another car chase. I know you probably don't believe me, but truly, it happened. And, well, this guy and I got the hell out. I mean, guys, so many things have happened on this trip. You can't even make this shit up. It was fun, but scary as hell."

There was a knock at the door. Amanda looked up. John was standing right over her looking like he was ready to crush her recorder. Now he quickly gestured with a finger over his lips and signaled for Amanda to go to the other side of the room.

He rushed to the door. He looked through the peephole and then undid two locks. It was a maintenance woman handing him linens and a pillow for the sleeper sofa.

After she left, he went over to the couch and worked on putting together a makeshift bed, not saying a damn word. Amanda sat cross-legged on the bed just watching him.

Boy, my guardian angel really has a stick up his ass.

"You do realize your life is in danger?" he asked, tucking in a sheet.

"I don't need my bed that tight. I kinda roll all over the place."

"I'm not making the couch up for you. This is for me. You can take the bed."

"The fuck I will, John. I'm already blown away by this hotel. You realize that couch is probably more comfortable than a motel bed?"

"You're taking the bed. And I'd appreciate it if you stopped swearing so much."

"No. Fuck, no. I told you, I'm not an angel. And I'm also not taking the bed, mister."

He turned to her. His brow wrinkled under his shades. She smirked again.

"I don't really like how you push me around," she said. She surprised herself with how angry that sounded. "If my life's in danger, fine, I'll listen, if it saves my life. I get that. But if it's over bedsheets, I mean, come on, I say go to hell. Or…go back there…or something."

"Who are you?" he asked, still holding a sheet.

Who the hell are you?

He sighed deeply and said, "Sleep wherever you want, Amanda. Fine." Then, after fluffing a pillow and throwing it back on the couch, he returned to being a sentry.

"Well, I was about to shower when that pale bitch took me hostage. What I'd really like to do is shower."

"Why don't you go shower?" he said with a nod, not turning.

"I'd prefer it if you tell me the reason why you're staring outside. We're pretty high up. Does this Lilith have Spiderman's ability to scale walls?"

"If I spot their bikes on the road, it means she knows we're here."

"How can you see her that far down?"

He pointed to his shades.

"Hmm." She let out a big sigh. "I also don't appreciate being told what I can say to my fans."

"There are secrets that we're not allowed to share with the public. You can't tell them anything about me."

"But you can give those secrets to me?"

"You already know enough. And I owe you the truth. But we keep ourselves secret from the public, Amanda."

"I said you could call me Mandi."

"Your people can't handle the realization that you're being watched. Everyone thinks they act with free will. They don't realize, or want to know, that there are forces outside of your control.

"We unveiled ourselves centuries ago. It led to darkness. Plague. An end to civilization. What would be the motivation for human advancement with a realization that everything is out of your control? We learned from that, until today. If it means stopping me, I think Lilith will do whatever it takes. Even unveil us here in an urban center—the largest of them all."

"Well, since you're yapping now, how about telling me how we made it from Cincinnati to New York in a couple hours *by car?*"

I mean, right? And, watch, he won't answer.

"I have a fast car."

See.

She laughed. It wasn't out of mirth. "Do you realize how irritating you are? Not only do you not say anything, every answer to my questions leads to a few more." He didn't answer that, of course. "When will I be safe? That's the best one of all."

"After you get some sleep."

He removed his shades and rubbed his eyes. She enjoyed catching a glimpse of his lovely blues. It made her chuckle again.

"I'm glad you're in a good mood."

"Who said I'm in a good mood, John? I know what's happening. My car's totaled. I was shot at, nearly blinded. I'm in a hotel room in a strange city. With a strange man. And my apparent guardian angel tells me he's a devil and that I'm doomed to die soon. Doesn't that about sum it up? But, sorry, I don't brood. I just don't do that."

He nodded. Then he returned to searching the roads below.

"Why New York?" she asked. "I'm happy to complete my drive across country, sure, but why here? Why didn't you just return me to LA?"

"You need rest," he replied, not turning. "I told you, they hate the cities and LA was too far. I doubt they'll come here tonight. But we have to go straight home tomorrow."

"So maybe we should just hide here for weeks? That'd be fun. Just you…and I."

She smiled at him smugly as he finally turned. It was fun playing with him because he was so serious.

"I don't have weeks. I have to get back to work. We're heading back to LA tomorrow. I can get you back tomorrow after we rest."

He took a deep breath and went back to scanning the ground. He pressed something on his glasses. Perhaps he was zeroing in on something?

"John?"

He shifted his gaze in another direction

"John?"

"Yeah?"

She shook her head. "Who are you?"

He furrowed his brow over that one.

Then she reached for the TV controller. She turned on the television and switched to an old movie. Then a Dodgers game. She left it at that. It was an LA team, after all, and that reminded her of home.

"How long are you going to stand there?" she asked.

He just nodded, not even listening. She turned the television off, sighed, and jumped up from the bed again. Then she stood beside him and gazed out at the gorgeous view with him.

"This is much better than television," she said. "It's so pretty out there."

He nodded.

She was going to say more, but she faltered as he turned and gazed at her face. Even with those cursed shades, he was so handsome. His stubble was like him—ever so unkempt, like his thin dark hair, but perfect in its imperfection. She searched his face. "You really think you're bad? How many lives have you saved?"

"Hundreds."

"You're good," she said quietly, shaking her head.

"Mandi, when you die, I'll have another angel to damn. And then another. All to keep them suffering here on Earth." He turned back to the window. "I know I'm bad."

"You're good for me," she said in a hushed voice. She wasn't even sure if he heard her.

You saved me.

She found herself just gazing at their amazing view of the

Manhattan skyline with him. She ran her fingers along his arm until she reached his hand. Then his fingers. She took his hand. He squeezed hers. Then she looked up at him. His profile. But he wouldn't turn. She reached up on her tippy-toes and kissed him on the cheek gently.

"Thank you," she breathed.

He nodded.

"John?"

"Yeah?"

"What're the chances you're going to find her down there? Even if she comes? Even with that gadget you're wearing?"

"What do you mean?"

"We're in Manhattan. There's millions of people downtown, even now at this time. I don't think you're guarding us. I think you're just trying to avoid me."

"What?" He quickly turned. Then he froze.

She giggled and stroked his fingers. Had she discovered his secret? He seemed uncomfortable enough to confirm it. Was that it? Was he just using his determination to defend them as a pretense to defend himself from his feelings for her?

He surprised her by embracing her tightly and leaning down and kissing her on the lips. They held each other before the window, kissing passionately. His hands drifted down to her waist. And he squeezed her closer. And they kept kissing. For the longest time. He didn't seem to care much about their defense now. Amanda wasn't even sure how long they kissed. But it was wonderful.

His hand touched her butt and she moaned. That embarrassed her. She moved back as he was still kissing her. Her face felt red hot.

"I… I think, John, I have to go shower."

He nodded, letting her go.

She laughed nervously and realized that, even outside his embrace, she still had his fingers in her hand. Seemingly a couple fingers at a time, he disengaged and she rushed to the bathroom.

She left the door ajar by a thin crack. Then she pulled down her shorts. She could see him, through the door, scrutinizing the city. And she knew that all he had to do was turn around to see her in her underwear.

"John? Have you seen this? I tell you, the bathroom is to-die-for."

That is not the best choice of words, stupid.

"I saw it," he muttered.

"I think…they used real gold. You should really check out the mirror. It's a nice view."

Just cut it out and shower.

But her heart was pounding. She watched him through the crack of the door. He turned and she saw his profile. He wore those shades and he kept pressing on them, looking in different directions. All he had to do was turn all the way around. But he was doing his job by the window again.

She pulled up her T-shirt. Then she unclasped her bra.

"You really should come here and see the marble floor. Come over."

"I already have."

She nodded and pulled down her panties. Then she felt her chest and face flush redder than ever at her embarrassment. She was naked before him. She stood there for a moment just waiting for him to turn.

"John? John?"

But he wouldn't turn. After waiting long enough, she gave a long sigh and walked into the shower. Of course the water was perfect. Hot. Welcoming. She hadn't showered in days.

She lifted her left arm and ran the bar of hotel soap along the curve of her breast and around her areola and nipple and, for a moment, she imagined he was washing her. Then she traced her body down to her waist, pressed her belly button, and cleaned her hips and waist—again, all the while imagining those strong hands she had just held. The hot water felt good and soon steamed up the bathroom mirror. She could see it through the clear shower curtain. No doubt he was still outside guarding her stupidly but in a romantic sort of way, because he was protecting her. She imagined him seeing her through the clear drape as she ran the water through her hair. It'd be foggy, but he'd see her profile clearly enough. All he had to do was turn. And he must have done that by now. Right?

She closed her eyes. She imagined him taking off his jacket and shirt, unveiling his ripped chest and abs, opening the curtain, and running those fingers through her long wet hair. She'd let him bathe her if he did that. Perhaps less erotically at first, soaping her back and her hair. But then the soap would flow over her ass and her private area. He'd orgasm her in the shower using the soap and water to lubricate his fingers. All the while he'd be making out with her again, kissing her just like he had at the window. Just as she imagined it, like heaven.

She was an angel, he had said. Innocent. Maybe she wouldn't be innocent anymore if he fucked her? And maybe that'd protect her.

God, maybe you should make the water cold, Mandi. Won't you stop it!

She reached down, took a dollop of conditioner in her palm, and ran it along her long hair. Then she cracked an eye open for a few stray glances at the door on the off chance that he was there. No luck. But the door was still ajar. Of course, he could hear her showering. All he had to do was turn.

Some of the conditioner dripped down the pale skin of her leg. She used the soap to brush it off her leg. Then she ran the bar up to her waist and toward the crack of her ass. Then along her pussy, washing there too.

She could walk out instead. Naked, hot, she could walk right out the door and just grab him. How could he resist? She knew from their kissing that he was attracted to her. And he was hardly innocent. What was his hesitation?

The water kept flowing over her naked body as she washed herself. As she kept just thinking of him. Thinking of his short hair and the stubble along his cheeks and chin. Now imagining his strong, hard body naked beside her, embracing her, then bringing her whole body against his naked skin. His cock now entering her.

She hadn't seen his skin, but she imagined his chest, from what she had seen in a T-shirt, to be rock hard. If he came in now, she'd run her hands along his strong muscles, his pecs and biceps. Then she'd touch his cock. She'd dip down on her knees and suck it while the warm water washed over them. Then she'd stand up and it'd be his turn to dip down. Then along her waist and over her pussy...

Enough!

She shut the water off. She wrung out her hair. Then she grabbed a towel.

She looked at her clothes draped over the vanity chair. She had forgotten to see if the hotel had a robe. And she had left most of her clothes in her luggage, still in his car. So she patted her hair and body and wrapped the towel around her chest, covering a little of her naked body. For a second, she considered covering only her hair.

She opened the door wide. Her sentinel still stood there staring down at the street.

"I mean," Amanda said, "I suppose I can take the bed if you're gonna stay the whole night in front of the window."

John turned. He had his stupid shades on. But he couldn't hide his look at what draped her body—or lack thereof.

"Do you know if the hotel provides robes, John? Hmm?" She grimaced wide. It was all she could do to not laugh at his expression. And she felt her skin, already red from the hot shower, grow warmer.

"I can check," he mumbled. As he rushed over to a closet, she couldn't suppress a laugh anymore. It was funny to see such a confident man get all flustered.

He brought out an elegant white robe on a hanger and handed it to her. But she didn't take it. Instead she gently removed his sunglasses with both her hands. "Why do you wear this all the time?"

"Driving. You saw the light nearly blind you."

"But…you're not always driving? Not now."

"Always ready." With his naked blue eyes staring into hers, he seemed hypnotized by her. And she got lost too.

"Can I…have it?"

"What?… Oh." He handed her the robe. "Here."

"Lilith assumed we had…you know…done it. Why is that?"

"Archangels are dirty," he said with disgust. "Even my allies. Most of us view humans as objects. Especially Lilith. She's a demon."

"Yes, I think your enemies are demons. Not angels. Whatever you say, John. You saved me. You didn't damn me by letting me live. I think that's ridiculous."

He nodded, but it was almost more of a shrug.

She embraced him again. She reached up and kissed him on the lips. "Thank you," she said quietly. "Thank you so much. You're my guardian angel."

Then they were back to it again, French kissing.

I owe you my life. She was not sure if she'd said that or thought it. If she'd said it, it had been between kisses. "But you seem…to be… repelled by me. Why is that, John?"

"I can't be repelled by you," he said, disengaging his lips for a moment. But she kissed him once more. "It's not possible."

"So, you find me attractive?"

Her towel fell from her body. No, it didn't fall. She dropped it intentionally. She was sure it was intentional, but he wasn't. He quickly reached down and grabbed it. Then he held it over her naked chest.

"It's okay," she said, kissing his lips again. "Forget it."

"No, it isn't."

"Why?" she whispered in his ear. "Why are you avoiding me?"

"I'm not."

She leaned her forehead on his chest and nodded. The towel was only covering her chest in front of him. He held her, but when his hand felt her back, it dropped over the wet crack of her ass. And his hand shook.

Nervous? How could a man with so much confidence be nervous around her?

"It's okay," she whispered in his ear.

"I'm not pure," he said.

"Neither am I," she said, this time pulling the towel away from her chest. She dropped the robe on the ground too. Then he looked down. Her breasts were pressed against his chest, and she entered his mouth with her tongue once more. "I'm not…happy…being pure… I'm only happy being with you."

They stopped kissing and John just stared at her chest. She felt herself blush again, but she didn't turn. She let him stare, his eyes drifting down to her legs. The light in the hotel was dim but seemed very bright with her nakedness. Then she helped him remove his leather jacket. And then his T-shirt, revealing his bare chest. Yes, his body was hard. And then…

Nothing was acquiesced. Nothing accepted. There was no contract of evil touching good, pure being soiled. No words. Only their hands touched each other. She let him stare again at her bare body. And she didn't blush anymore.

She helped him remove his jeans while he stared at her. It was as if he were taking a photograph of her to remember forever. She looked at his chest again—she had been right. He was well built. His muscles bulged. He was a warrior and his chest and abs showed it. She ran a finger along a scar. And then another. He had long scars along his arms and side. So many. Next his underwear came down. His legs and flanks were scarred too. She ran a finger along some of his scars, kissing along others. Then her fingers ran along the crack of his ass. All the while, they met each other's lips between glances at each other, now both naked in the dim hotel light. Finally Amanda tugged John's hand and led him to bed.

Amanda lay down on her back and John gently grabbed a pillow and put it under her head. He lay gently beside her. Then he leaned over, kissing her some more.

"If I am so good, John," Amanda said quietly between kisses, "take the good from me. Take me. Protect me from them. Make me bad. Make me impure and bad like you so they can't hurt me anymore. Make me be alive, like you… Fuck me. Fuck me now, John."

He pushed his cock inside her. At first, it hurt a little. Then immense pleasure. A burning pleasure that only got better with every push. His weight beside her was enough to drive her wild. She pushed her pelvis back against him. Then her lips met his again.

"Oh, God, John you feel so good."

Faster. He started moving faster into her.

She turned to the window. It was unchanged. Still the twinkling lights of the city. There was darkness amid this light. Only the light from the bathroom allowed her to see the man she lay with. They looked deep into each other's eyes as he continued to push into her. His angel eyes.

He moved on top, his whole body now thrusting over her. She felt all his weight. He moaned, and that took her closer to ecstasy. He thrust faster. She had had oral sex before, but never penetration. And he continued to gaze at her with his angelic eyes. It had never been like this. She moaned harder, shaking in his arms.

He looked away as if they were done, but she moved him on his back. Then, on top of him now, she ran one hand through his short hair while the other moved his cock, rubbing it up and down. Then she dipped down and kissed him. Her hand brushed along the stubble of his cheek. He moaned again. She straddled him. Then she felt his cock move inside her again. He fondled her breasts as she bounced over him.

She could hear their sex. The sound of smacking. It only made her bounce faster and harder.

John turned. This time he stared at the window too. To look for Lilith? Had he left his guard post? Or was it just the gorgeous view of the city?

She fell over him, grasping him so tight. He embraced her, almost hurting her. For so long, she had felt him pushing away. Now it felt like he clung to her, not ever wanting to lose her. And he was still inside her.

"I'm sorry," he said.

"I love you," she said, shaking her head. "I think… I love you… Yes. I love you, John. Fuck me. Oh, fuck me, John!"

Even faster. She pressed her pelvis against him so hard.

He threw her on her back. And then he thrust again on top of her. Their lips met for a moment, and she felt him squeeze her body so close to his.

"I love you," he said.

"Oh, yes, John."

She climaxed again. Then she sort of collapsed to his side.

But now that they were done, he seemed unhappy. And in the light, he looked awkward. Confused. Had it been a mistake to desire him?

"Is something wrong?"

"No," he said, shaking his head. But then he turned his head from her.

"I guess… I'm sorry."

"It's not because of you, Sherry. I love you."

Who in the hell is Sherry?

19

AFTER

After sleeping with her, she thought he'd open up. He didn't. He remained tight-lipped. In fact, he was back to being a sentry by the window. The whole night while she slept, he had been standing by that window. Maybe she was wrong about that? Maybe he really thought he could spot Lilith down below? She thought she might have seen him on the floor, leaning against the glass sleeping, at one point or even back on the bed, but by morning he was staring out the large window.

They grabbed coffee and food from a buffet at a restaurant. Then they were off early. She wasn't sure what the rush was, but John was very anxious to get back on the road.

Inside the car, she marveled again at his machine. The leather felt soft, almost like skin. It was a material she had never felt before. The black seats were ultra-comfortable, of course. The central console looked more like a cockpit with tons of multicolored lights. In the center was a computer that he constantly flipped through. It was primarily used to access a system of maps. But the maps seemed far more detailed than a normal navigation system.

He quickly merged onto the freeway. Even in early morning, they ran into traffic. The whole time, John scrutinized his side and rearview mirrors, just as he had done with the window at the hotel.

Amanda put her feet up on the dashboard and looked at him. He looked over and furrowed his brow.

"So?"

"So what?"

"I liked last night," she said.

"Last night was fun," he said with a nod.

"Can I give you a little bit of advice?"

"Sure."

"Smile." *I mean, he really has a stick up his ass, doesn't he?*

But he didn't smile like she wanted him to. That made her laugh. She was just teasing him.

He pulled out some sunglasses from the driver's side door and handed them to her.

"When did you get those?" she asked.

"When we were getting breakfast at the hotel. I need you to put them on. When the traffic clears, it's going to get blinding again. The effect will continue, but it will be bearable with sunglasses on. You still should close your eyes when the lights first appear. We'll be in LA in a few hours."

"A few hours? You're kidding me. It takes five hours to fly there."

"Five to drive in this car too."

"Hmm." She snatched the shades out of his hand. Then she laughed again. She didn't know why this time, she just did.

"You know, I didn't get to see Manhattan," she said. "We could have gone sightseeing. I've always wanted to see the Statue of Liberty. And the Empire State Building."

"There it is." And he actually pointed at the buildings off in the distance. "But right now, I need to get you home."

"'Kay… Can I ask you one more question?"

"Sure."

"What were you before you became a…well…a—"

"A devil?"

She laughed again.

"What's so funny?"

"You. You're so serious that you're funny. Yeah. A devil, if that's what my guardian angel wants to call himself. What were you before that?"

He didn't answer. That was okay because it gave her time to look out at the skyline receding from them. She leaned back in the passenger seat, pulled out her cell phone from her pants pocket, and took some snapshots. She had read about New York. She knew some of the buildings, like the Chrysler building. She couldn't see the Statue of Liberty. She saw a ton of bridges though. Along with a ton of cars.

"I was like you," he said finally. His response was so delayed that it took her a second to register what he was talking about. "I started out like you. Human."

"What'd my guardian angel do when he was human?"

"I'm not your guardian angel. Perhaps your guardian devil."

"Okay. What did my guardian devil do before he wandered the roads looking for pure angels to damn? And if you don't hurry with your responses, I warn you, John, I'm gonna bring out my recorder and ask you in front of my fans."

He turned and actually smiled at her. *Finally.*

"I was a cop."

"Well, that's predictable. You should have let me guess."

"I wasn't on duty all the time. When I wasn't on duty, I drove a car like this one. I was adopted. My aunt spoiled me. It was on a drive that I died, I think. Or my soul was taken between worlds and my new boss brought me back down to Earth."

"Did you have a girlfriend?"

He turned to her and she could just barely see him squinting through the shades. He was always acting like she was weird. And that was funny as hell too, considering what he was. In fact, she laughed in his face. She touched his forearm. She felt his strong muscle contract under his tanned skin from the touch of her fingers. Those same muscles she stroked last night.

"You don't have to answer."

And he didn't.

Then after a long silence. "Well, did you?"

"Yes."

"Oh, so you didn't just have sex with, like, every girl?"

"Why would you think that?"

"John, look at you."

"What about me? I had sex. Sure. But I fell in love with someone before I changed."

"What was her name?" Amanda asked, turning back to her window.

"Sherry."

There's that name again… So that's who Sherry is.

"That's… a nice name. What was she like?" Amanda put a hand out and John stiffened. "I mean you don't have to tell me…" She burst out laughing. She didn't know why, but being silly around this stiff board of a man was a lot of fun. And this time, he looked so serious.

"She grew old," he said gravely.

"There you go again," she said, rolling her eyes.

"There I go again with what?"

"What the hell does that mean? Your answers lead to more questions. What do you mean, she grew old? So? We all grow old."

"*Watch out!*"

John quickly passed between two cars. The move looked so dangerous that Amanda gasped, but he executed the maneuver as if he were simply passing a car. His car was only a few inches from the vehicle on Amanda's right.

"You nearly hit him!"

"Sorry," he said, looking at the side mirror. "When I turned into an angel, I was turned into an Azrael. Rick said the process of transferring one body from human to an angel takes decades. For immortals, time is insignificant. It wasn't for Sherry and me. After my transformation, Sherry had aged thirty years or more, while I was still the same age."

"I thought you told me you were twenty-eight?"

"In human years. But I lived in LA in the eighties at that age too."

"Okay, that's really weird."

He nodded. Then he pointed to an open road ahead. "When we merge, I'm phasing. That light's gonna come on again. I need you to keep your shades on. And you're not used to it. You might want to cover your eyes too."

"Sure."

"I'm sorry you're going through all of this, Amanda," he said with a sigh. "I really am."

"You can call me Mandi." Then she shrugged. "Remember? And I was looking for adventure."

John removed his shades for a moment and squinted at her. God, she loved that. Then he smiled. That was even better.

"Put your sunglasses on."

She fumbled with them. She noticed for the first time that her hands were shaking. And it wasn't just because she was in the presence of Mr. Handsome.

As the engine roared, she felt tremendous pressure pinning her into the seat. Light grew by the sides of the windshield. With shades, it was beautiful, like sparks of rainbows hitting the glass. Then the light spread, turning a bright white—as bright as the sun. She had to finally cover her eyes. John didn't. With his shades on, he stared right into it.

When they stopped accelerating but continued at a fast speed, it reminded her of being in an airplane. There wasn't much noise. It was mainly just his engine, which was probably quieter than a regular car.

"You all right?" he asked.

"Yeah."

"I'll have you home in a few hours, Mandi."

"Sure. Okay."

Guess no more talking.

But then…

"John, what did this Sherry girl look like? Was she pretty?"

He just stared at the road.

Okay. No more talking, I guess.

2 0

———

GONE

It was around eight o'clock at night when Amanda was dropped off alone on a hill back home. She told John he wouldn't be able to park there, especially with his fancy car. It would stick out among the college apartments. So he had to just stop and drop her off. Of course he stopped it in the middle of the road, ran around, opened the passenger door for one last quick embrace (between some honking). And then said bye. And that was it.

Now a few students rode by her nearly knocking her and her rolling suitcase over. It was Friday and students from college were heading for parties. When she looked back, his dark car was gone.

That's it. Gone forever. Well, Amanda, you wanted an adventure and he gave you one.

Under a passing streetlight, she pulled out her recorder and pressed the record button. She wasn't in the mood, but she had promised herself she'd say something the minute she got back home. She tried to put on her best smile.

"Well guys, what can I say? Trip's done. The whole thing was amazing. I saw spectacular open desert roads. I saw Denver, Pittsburgh, Phoenix, Cincinnati, and New York City. For a journalist like myself, I just had to see the country. And I did. I wouldn't have had it any other way. Even with all the danger."

122

She clicked the stop button. Then she ran across the busy street. She looked back at where John had dropped her off. Yeah, he was gone.

In darkness on the sidewalk, as she walked up the rest of the incline, she clicked her recorder on again. "They say that going on a trip across the country alone is dangerous. Sure it is. But it's something you guys should all do."

She nodded over that and clicked the stop button. She wouldn't tell them about John anymore. Of course, those who listened would wonder. But she had promised him she'd keep mum and even edit some of the angel stuff later. She'd keep the Denver interview on the top of the museum, though. That was just way too good.

She jingled her keys and opened the door. It smelled like tomato sauce. Luane was probably cooking. Seeing Lu was the only thing moving her legs now. But when she crossed the threshold, the apartment was empty. The lights were on, but it was way too quiet. She walked into her living room. Then she meandered over to the bedroom. "Lu?" And then the other bedroom. Empty.

Then Amanda felt sick. Dishes and food were strewn on the tile floor of the kitchen. The tomato smell was from spilled spaghetti. On the counter by the mess was a note.

"My dear fallen angel, we failed at taking your soul. He sullied you. So we shall now go for another. If you and Azrael want to ever see your roommate again, meet me and Samael in Bakersfield. There Azrael can have sanctuary and discuss payment. But he cannot go alone. I request the presence of you, Amanda. Azrael cannot go alone if you ever want to see your friend Luane again.

Everlastingly yours,

Lilith."

Amanda felt short of breath. She felt like the air weighed heavily on her. Then she felt sick.

She ran to the bathroom and threw up in the toilet. As hard as it all had been—through car chases and a kidnapping—there was nothing worse than this, nothing worse than worrying that something would happen to her friend. And this was her best friend.

"John!" she shouted. "John!"

She ran back to her purse and rummaged for her phone. She

looked for his number but couldn't find his contact on the list. Then she checked recent calls. There were no new numbers. Had he erased it?

That asshole!

She remembered he had told her they would never see each other again.

"John! John!"

21

SHERRY'S

"I'M SORRY, JOHN," SHERRY SAID WITH A RUEFUL SMILE, LEANING OVER the bar and touching his arm. "I'm so sorry."

Angel Dive was busy. It was Friday night, but Sherry had help and after seeing him walk in, being sensitive as always, she seemed to know something was wrong. She led John to the end of the bar, where they could talk. Now he felt like he was spilling too much of his problems, along with his whiskey.

"Life is unfair," Sherry added.

"This isn't life," John said with a nod. "Leaving her, I felt like I was losing you."

That seemed to upset Sherry. A lot. She looked away.

"Now *I'm* sorry," John said, touching her arm.

Sherry flashed him a fake grin. "How is the young girl holding up?"

"I practically threw her out of my car. But she understood. I'm not good at goodbyes, as you well know. And having her hang with me longer only would have been more painful."

John drank down another shot glass. Then he tapped a finger for another. Sherry shook her head.

"Why don't you stay sober tonight, John," Sherry suggested. "Stay with me tonight. You know, Rick could need you any minute. Or the girl could still be in trouble."

"I sullied her."

"God, John," she said putting a hand up, "I don't want to fucking hear about that."

"Then don't," he said with a nod. "But…" He removed his shades and looked down at his glass. He tapped the glass again.

She rolled her eyes and went behind her counter, grabbing a bottle. Then she poured him more whiskey. Someone asked for her help but she ignored him. Then she walked back and leaned over the counter.

"She really looks like me? Seriously?"

"Samael and Lilith did their homework," John said with a nod. Then he reached across the counter and touched Sherry's cheek. Wrinkles and all, Sherry was the most beautiful woman he had ever known. So was Amanda…

Sherry pulled back and shook her head. "Life goes on. As long as you're here, move on."

"I'm here."

John's phone rang. The bar was a bit busy, so he got even closer to the wall to hear. The contact read "Hunter."

"We're still talking?" John asked.

"Angel down. Luane." It was Rick, but he wasn't sounding like his usual self. Instead of sounding characteristically indifferent, now he sounded grave. "Luane is twenty-two, Asian, long dark hair, just graduated an English major, looking for a job in journalism. Born a Virgo. She's rooming in an apartment with a girl named Amanda in Santa Monica. Amanda. *Your* Amanda, John. This is Amanda's best friend and roommate." Raphael dispensed with his usual banter, but the silence was worse. For a moment, John wondered if his boss had hung up. He heard laughter across the bar amid all the talking. "I'm sorry, John. It's her friend. You finally did everything right getting the girl home, but—"

"Where?" he snapped. "Did they get her yet?"

"They have her. Lilith wants to talk to you privately for an exchange. She's asking for sanctuary. She probably wants to speak with you to turn you. Then maybe she'll give back the girl. But you know how this works. She'll offer anything you want, I'm sure. You know the price. But the girl dies if you don't go."

"I'll fucking talk to her. Where is she? Send me the location."

"Listen, John, you know as well as I do that Luane's days are numbered now. This isn't about snaring you. You saved Amanda. This is payback. Most likely, they will kill the girl, if they haven't already. Let Luane go and forget this. Don't get caught up—"

"You really should stop fucking trying to convince me not to do something you know very well I'm going to do."

"I'm your friend." There was silence. "Amanda won't understand any of this, you know. If you see her again, you're going to give that girl false hope."

"Then I won't see her."

"You have to. They've requested her presence with you in sanctuary or they will kill Luane."

"Text me the location," John said.

"Where are you at?"

"Sherry's."

"Give her my regards."

"Fuck you and text me the location."

"Already done."

"I'm doing a job this time. Can you help?"

"I think so. But I'm far south—outside the United States, near Mexico City. If you're in Arizona, it's gonna take you a lot less time than me."

"Where did they take her? What city?"

"Bakersfield."

"I'll see you in Bakersfield."

"Sure, John. Sure."

John hung up the phone.

"What's wrong?" asked Sherry. He hadn't realized till now that she was watching him.

"They took her best friend."

"Oh, God. This has to end!"

"Goodbye. And thanks, Sher." He jumped up and headed to the door.

"Hey, John. Be careful... I love you."

2 2

BACK IN LA

Amanda sat on her couch with all the lights turned off, in the middle of the night, just staring at a wall. She didn't know what to do. Her car was still in Cincinnati. Her best friend's car was missing. She was desperate for help, but that bitch Lilith hadn't even told her where to find her. Bakersfield? Where? And John…how could he just leave her without his number?

'Cause he thinks he's a devil.

The nut. That sorrowful shadowy sullen nutjob.

Oh, what she'd do to see him now.

God, she was so worried about Lu. And now it was the middle of the night. And it still smelled like old spaghetti. She hadn't bothered to clean up the mess in the kitchen.

She could rent a car? Tomorrow morning. Nothing was open now.

There was a knock at the door. Amanda rushed over, nearly tripping on herself, and unlocked and threw open the door.

"Don't you look through your peephole?" John asked.

"Where were you!" Amanda hit his chest a few times with her fists. "How could you leave me home and erase your number! You're such an asshole! I told you not to do that! Didn't you think maybe I'd still be in trouble?"

"We have to go now, Mandi."

"What? Now? Really? Oh… I know. I know. But…it took you long enough!"

She ran over to a table in the dark and grabbed her purse. She hadn't even changed. She was still wearing the same T-shirt and jeans as when they left the hotel in New York. John hadn't changed either. He probably never changed, for that matter. He had on the same leather jacket, black shirt, and black pants. And shades, of course, even though it was dark outside. But he smelled good. He always wore fresh cologne.

Before Amanda knew it, he was running, dragging her behind him, to his super car. They hadn't said another word. He hadn't even objected to being hit in the chest, though she didn't hit him that hard.

"Sorry," Amanda said.

"For what?"

"For hitting you."

He laughed. Then he looked across the street. Seeing his super car across the street in a neighborhood of apartment-dwelling college students with their cheap cars was pretty weird. It was parked in front of a driveway. There was no other spot on the street even at this hour.

"At least I can still make you laugh."

"Yes, Amanda."

"I need your phone number again. And don't you dare erase it. You know, since I met you weird things keep happening—like a crazed demon-bitch friend of yours kidnapping my friends. It would have been nice to have your phone number, John. I need it and you're not going to say no."

"All right."

"Right."

She loved it when he opened the passenger door for her. But she held his arm before he closed the door. "Your phone number. What is it?"

"Now's hardly the time."

"I won't let you go and we can't save my friend until you give it to me. What is it? Now that we know each other better. And…you…you know—last night." She pulled him to her and kissed him on the lips. "Give it to me. Give it to me now."

He reached for her phone. Then he went to contacts and typed in a number. He handed it back to her.

"Lilith said you dirtied me. She wrote the word *sullied*."

"I did."

"Thanks for doing that." She put an arm around his neck and clung to him by the passenger door. "I'm scared, John. Will you do everything to help save my friend?"

"Yes."

But she didn't let go of him. "Promise."

"I promise. We have to go."

2 3

THE TALK

"We need to talk," John said.

That's a first.

She turned to him. They were both wearing sunglasses. They were moving at an incredible speed down the highway with shadowed hills and valleys rushing past the windows, and they could because the roads were clear and it was the middle of the night. Red, green, yellow, and blue lights bounced along the edges of the windshield and the side windows like rain.

"John, you never say a thing."

"I need to now," he said sternly with a nod. "There's a lot riding on this. Lilith might be with Samael this time."

"Who's Samuel?"

"Not Samuel. *Sam-a-el.* Samael is the devil. It's an ancient name. He's also known as Satan."

"Oh," she said with a nod. "That Samael."

She looked out the passenger window. She thought she was in the desert, but she could barely tell, it was so dark. Ever so often, a building would speed past. And John frequently inched the steering wheel in different directions, quickly passing cars and trucks on the road.

He laughed.

"There's another first," Amanda said. "You're laughing. I don't

131

think seeing Satan is very funny, John. Can you do me a favor? Just lay it on me. Tell me everything. When you feed me a little surprise here and there, you freak me out more."

"I laughed because you went silent."

"So Satan and Lilith are meeting us in Bakersfield? Great. I don't know. Yeah, it sounds kind of funny in a twisted way. Are there any good angels, aside from you, John, that will be there too?"

"I'm not good."

"Let's not go through that again."

He was so focused on the road. The landscape was whizzing by. She touched his arm. "Now you're claiming Satan is here to help bring the innocent to heaven? And what about Luane? John, I might have been a virgin before I met you, but Lu absolutely, most definitely, is not virginal. She's a certifiable liar, gluttonous, envious, and a cheat. That's why I love her so much. She's fun. I really think you guys aren't playing by the right rules. Your demons are good and your enemies are angels. But you insist that you're fallen and damned. Look, even when you were out protecting me, I wasn't *that* pure."

"Amanda," he said, quickly shaking his head. He turned to gaze at her. "It doesn't matter. I have to warn you. Your friend's in grave danger. I'm not sure I can save her."

"I'm always in grave danger around you. And you saved *me*."

"They won. By delaying me, she turned you. And while I helped you, she killed another two souls. Now there's no reason for them to keep Luane alive."

"We have to try." She glanced at the road again and nodded. Her nod was more to herself.

The shadows of mountains rushed by her like buildings do on the freeway. And those weird colored sparks occasionally scattered around the passenger window. She didn't dare look at the speedometer. At last glance it was over four hundred miles per hour.

Oh, Lu, I'm so worried. We just have to try. It's my fault. I should have just let these freaks kill me.

"We have to do everything we can," she said. "Do you hear me? Everything, John."

"I will."

She turned to the window again. She felt tired.

"Where are we?" she asked.

"Near Grapevine. We'll be there in a few minutes."

"What's this "sanctuary" thing mean? Lilith wrote that in the note. What does "sanctuary" mean? Are we meeting in a temple or something?"

"Sanctuary is a pact. It means both sides, good and bad, have agreed to come together and not fight. It's how we make agreements. If she keeps to her word and holds sanctuary, then your friend will be safe. Until sanctuary ends."

"And when do you agree for it to begin or end?"

He looked in the rearview mirror. Then he effortlessly passed a group of cars by driving onto the shoulder.

"When it's mutually agreed."

"So…have we agreed?"

"Not until we talk."

"And is that possible?"

"What?" he asked, turning to her.

"Talking? You don't ever talk."

"Yeah."

"I've made a decision," she said with a sigh. Then she kicked her feet onto the dashboard and scooted back again.

"What's that?"

"This isn't just about Lu. You're never leaving me ever again, mister. Do you hear me? Never."

He looked at her. She gave him a big grimace and chuckled. He didn't smile. He just stared back at the road.

24

BAKERSFIELD

THE YELLOW AND RED RISING SUN WAS BREATHTAKING AS ALWAYS FOR Amanda. It had first shown its majestic beauty rising slowly above a dark hill. Then after they had wound down a valley, it had reappeared along a long stretch of highway. She could see empty land for miles now. Still, few cars were on the road this early in the morning.

Amanda knew they were entering Bakersfield as they whooshed under an overpass. Indeed, they would be there in minutes. Amanda couldn't believe how fast they'd gotten there. Then the car decelerated and the color splashing on the windshield ceased. John touched his central monitor and dragged his finger across maps, shuffling through them.

A bird soared above the car. It seemed to be following them. She watched it through her shades as it passed over the car. The bird was so beautiful, so majestic. It wasn't all that different from John. No home. Their only purpose was seemingly to hunt.

"They're not moving," John said. "They're waiting for us."

For a moment, she caught red and blue flashing lights. John glanced at his side mirror, but then returned to checking his monitor. The digital speedometer still read one hundred and seventy five.

"We're slowing down to normal speeds."

"Thank god," she said. "What about the cop?"

"We've already lost him."

The sun rose and she could see buildings as they approached the city. And even this early, traffic was thickening. John was swerving around more cars.

"You okay?" he asked.

"Just a little car sick. And…no. I'm not okay. I'm worried."

"I can slow down more."

"For Lu, no. Don't slow down."

He nodded.

"Why do you keep staring at that map?"

"I'm calibrating their location. But…it's strange. I was tracking them. Now, if this is right, we should be driving right up their ass."

"How can you see it in the dark, anyway? It's so dim." She removed her sunglasses and pointed to them.

"Special lenses," he said, turning to her. "I can see you too."

Then he was back to his map vigil.

"How do you get all this stuff?"

"Hmm? What stuff?"

"The car. What is this machine anyway?"

"It's an old car."

She laughed and rolled her eyes. "There you go again."

"It is. It's an adapted GT40. I had one in my past life. This is military grade. CIA stuff." He was still counting. "We get this from the government."

"The government supports devils?"

He nodded. Well, that wasn't so hard to understand.

"I don't know all the odds and ends, really. Don't really care, Amanda." He started mouthing what seemed like numbers.

"Why are you counting?"

"I'm figuring out their exact location from these coordinates. It's about thirty more seconds."

The rising sun shone over a bridge about a mile ahead. Whereas before, they would have already passed it, traffic was slowing them down. That's when Amanda saw them. On the bridge were a motorcycle and two people.

"Oh my God, look!" Amanda said. "There she is!"

John looked up from his monitor.

It was Luane, her hands tied behind her back. And it looked like her mouth was covered with tape. She was wearing just a white T-shirt and shorts. The person beside her was in a black leather motorcycle jumpsuit, and long white hair trailed from her helmet.

"Oh no," she said.

The words came out of her mouth almost before the sight registered in her brain.

Crack.

It was so loud that it almost sounded like it came from inside the car. Luane's body fell on the sidewalk of the bridge.

Amanda heard a scream. It was from a nearby car. Or was it her?

"Lu! Lu! Oh my God!"

Light filled the car as Amanda was thrown back in her seat. She clutched her head as her eyes burned in pain. She was blinded again. Then she heard some grunts from John. It was gibberish. She looked and, after her eyes burned, she saw only a shadow of him. He had done it again. He had launched his car after she had taken her sunglasses off.

Then as quickly as she fell back in her seat, she was launched forward. The seat belt hurt her shoulder and chest as it stopped her from being thrown into the dashboard. The force was so hard that the belt dug into her skin. She was pushed against the car door. She worried that the force would throw her out. She was pushed violently back against the seat again. Then she was thrown forward once more.

The car screeched to a halt.

John's seat belt clicked. Then his shadow reached over her. He was opening the glove compartment. He pulled out a bag and threw open his door. Then she heard gunfire. The noise mixed with her burning eyes was horrible. She covered her whole head.

Then she thought of Luane.

Oh my God! Lu!

The realization was cloudy in her mind. Between the constant explosions from John's gun and her blind eyes, she didn't know what was happening. She was trying to accept the fact that she had just witnessed the execution of her friend. But she still couldn't even see.

The driver's side door slammed shut.

I can't see! Damn it, I can't see!

I have to see. I have to see if Luane's all right!

How can she be all right? She was shot in the head.

The pistol fire continued. It wasn't just John. There was another gun firing further off. They were in a shoot-out. A stray bullet ricocheted off the windshield. And a shadow of a man ran toward a motorcycle on the empty bridge. She could only see John's halo of light in the darkness. Her guardian. Her angel. He was brazenly rushing toward the motorcycle, holding his pistol with two hands, firing like crazy. He'd run out of ammo and reloaded from the bag he was carrying. And then he was firing again. He didn't even bother to seek cover.

As her eyes adjusted, she saw Lilith firing back behind a bullet-ridden parked car. A few stray bullets bounced off the windshield driver's side window again. Amanda could now make out the features of the motorcyclist. It was Lilith with her stupid white scarf for sure. But John was firing so crazily that she couldn't safely get back to her bike. She tried a few times, but it looked like the demon was limping. He must have hit her.

Finally, the bitch managed to hobble to her motorcycle. She got on, spun around a bit on the now empty bridge, and sped off.

John sprinted back to the car. He paused for a moment looking at the opposite side of the bridge. Before Amanda could turn, she heard them. She saw red and blue flashing lights approaching their car behind them.

John swung open the door. "Get out, Amanda! You'll be safe in the police's custody. Get out. Now!"

She shook her head.

"I'm chasing her!" He pulled his shades off and stared into her eyes. She looked into his blues. They weren't sweet now. His eyes were bulging. His tanned skin had reddened. "Get out of the car now!"

"She's already dead, John. Forget it."

His mouth clenched. "I can go after her. I can get back at her. Now get the fuck out of my car!"

Amanda stepped out. John jumped into the driver's seat. He hit the gas so fast that she hadn't even completely closed the door. It shut after the car flew forward. She watched his car shimmy and drift across the bridge and drive toward the motorcycle. Then it went at an unnatural speed, disappearing in the distance like a black blur.

A body still lay on the empty bridge.

Luane.

Oh, God.

Amanda ran across the bridge but halted at the sound of two approaching squad cars.

"Put your hands up!" she heard from a megaphone. "Put your hands up now!"

She raised her hands. She stood like that for what seemed like forever. Then some force, at first she thought it was wind, knocked her down. An officer had tackled her. She got up on her knees and saw a red flash of light. It came so close that she and the man who had apprehended her were thrown back on the asphalt. This red car, similar to John's black one, sped after John and Lilith.

Soon a whole squad of police cars filled the bridge.

Amanda looked at Luane. Her vision was still blurry, but she could see her friend clearly enough, lying motionless. Lu's eyes were closed. There was blood beside her head on the sidewalk.

Someone lifted Amanda from behind. Her arms were yanked back, and she felt metal handcuffs.

"You have the right to—"

"*Go help her!*" Amanda shouted.

25

STILL GREEN?

IT DIDN'T TAKE LONG FOR JOHN TO CATCH UP TO THE MOTORCYCLE. That didn't surprise him. They were maneuverable, but his car was faster. But the red streak behind him was a surprise. His phone rang through his speakers. The contact on his monitor read "Hunter."

John answered it.

"Don't do anything stupid," Rick said.

"I was told I was going to meet Lilith and Samael in sanctuary," John said. "They asked me—"

"I know. I know. I know the whole thing, John."

"I'm not done. They asked me to bring Amanda. They then proceeded to knock off her best friend execution style, in broad daylight, on a highway bridge in front of us. They brought Amanda to watch. She was already sullied, according to the bitch, by me. Why did they ask her to be there, Rick? What was the point?"

"You're talking about Lilith, John."

John took a deep breath. He looked out his window. He rarely drove this fast, especially during the day. The multicolored lights were splashing against the sides of his car, and he was thrusting up hills and back down like a rocket, so fast that he felt airborne a few times. But he was closing in on the bike.

"Azrael—"

"Don't fucking call me Azrael! Don't ever call me Azrael again. I'm done. I played by your rules. I saved your lives. Now it's clear that we've done things all wrong. We should have gone after the people killing the angels all along." He looked at his console thinking his boss had hung up. There was silence. "Clear the road," John added. "I'm going to do everything I can for justice. Maybe I'll shoot her in the head too. Clear the road."

"I think you're running out of bullets. And it wouldn't do any good anyway."

"Then I'll run over her."

"You can do that. Okay. You can do that, John. But what's going to happen to you after?"

"Why'd she do that to Amanda?"

"She's Lilith."

"What's her game?"

"Look what it's doing to you. Just like Vegas, she's confusing you and—"

"It ends this morning."

"You've nearly run over two cars since I've been chasing you. You're driving too fast and about ready to kill innocent people downtown."

"*She's* driving fast! I'm following her. Do the rules about killing the innocent not apply to her?"

"I have drone footage showing that you shot her in the chest while she was off the bike. She's hurt. She'll likely die. Stop the chase now. Let her go," Raphael said with a sigh. "Please, man. You've done enough."

"Was Samael there?"

"No. He's in Mexico. That's why I was down South."

"Of course. That was a lie too. I'm going to end this now."

"John," Raphael said sternly and slowly, "listen to me very carefully. This isn't going to *ever* end. You can't kill Lilith. Or Samael. Another devil will take their place. Just like if they kill you, there'll be another soul replacing Azrael. It's about saving lives when people need us. It's about your soul's salvation. You can't change the system."

"Lilith just executed Amanda's friend on a bridge in front of her eyes. And for no reason other than to fuck with her head. Was that part of your system? *Now clear the fucking road!*"

He was passing Valencia into Los Angeles. They had traveled hundreds of miles in minutes. Now traffic was getting thick.

"She's driving you into the city. You might want to kill her, but she's goading you. She still wants you terminated, and getting you angry is her plan. You asked me why she did what she did, this is it. You kill her, she'll kill you. You have no backing from us in the city. Drop the chase now."

"Clear the road."

"Oh, for fuck's sake! I can't clear all the police from downtown Los Angeles! If they see your car speeding, they'll go after you. Turn your car around or we'll stop you. Do you understand? We'll stop you. Friend or—"

John hung up on him.

Lilith was swerving left and right, merging between cars, taunting him. If she was hurt, she hardly showed it. As the traffic got heavier, she showed him the middle finger as she squeezed between more vehicles.

John drove to the right shoulder and hit the gas. Traffic rushed by him to his left. One car was turning into the outside lane, and John rammed right into him, spinning his car into the stop-and-go traffic. It wouldn't damage his car, but it would make everyone notice him now—including the police. Of course, Rick was right. She was provoking him to get him into the city. But how could Lilith have had Amanda watch that!

Lilith was now far behind him, squeezing between cars. Raphael's red sports car was nowhere in sight. He had passed her and his boss.

He had to get her on the open road. If he could knock her off the bike, she'd be vulnerable. Then he could run over the bitch. But he was way ahead of her. He had to goad *her*.

He got out of his car.

"You fucking dick!" cried a truck driver, lifting his arm out the window. "What the hell are you doing?" A few others shouted at him. That all ended when he brandished his pistol. Of course, Rick's observation was right. But he wasn't only running out of bullets, he was out. But Lilith wouldn't know that.

Cars were at a standstill as he ran to the middle lane. He pointed his pistol at the incoming motorcyclist. He was surprised she didn't pull out her gun. Maybe she had lost it, or it was out of bullets too? Then the bitch flipped him off again. She swerved between cars toward the outer right lane. She couldn't take the left shoulder as it ran right into a concrete barrier.

When she passed him, he sprinted back to his car. He jumped in and pursued her. She had likely bought his bluff, thinking he could still shoot her, and decided to get off the highway at the off-ramp.

Then they were back to the chase, only now they were driving down Van Nuys Boulevard running stoplights and avoiding near collisions.

And that's when he heard sirens. But they were driving too fast for the police to keep up.

He wasn't worried about cars. He was looking up at the sky. Straight overhead now, probably following him since his car accident on the highway, was a police helicopter. But that wasn't what he was afraid of either.

The light at the intersection ahead turned red. Lilith ran through the red light, coming an inch from hitting a car. She struggled to regain control of her bike, then a car in the other lane collided into her full speed. At this speed, the impact was tremendous and sent her bike spinning. She was ejected across the road.

John hit the brakes hard, trying to avoid oncoming traffic, right beside Lilith's bike.

Lilith was on the ground crawling. She was trying to get back on her motorcycle and ride off. John could run over her. All he had to do was hit the gas and run over her body.

He didn't. He threw his car door open. Then he ran to her before she could touch her cycle. He grabbed her. He pulled off her helmet and raised a fist to strike her. Her eyes were shut. She fell unconscious in his arms. Blood dripped from cuts along her face; worse, it was flowing from her chest.

There was the sound of metal smashing and horns honking around him. More accidents. John had stopped his car right in the middle of the road, and he was a sitting duck. Indeed, a car rode past nearly running them over. Then came sirens again, flashing red and blue, surrounding him.

John looked down at Lilith. She cracked open an eye.

"Fun," Lilith muttered with a laugh. She spit out blood. "That was fun, Azrael... Red or black? I've made my choice...have you? You and your twin bitch still green?" She chuckled a little as blood dripped from her lips. Then she closed her eyes and fell limp in his arms.

"Put your hands up!" cried an officer by megaphone.

John heard guns cock. He looked around him. He was surrounded.

"I said, put your hands up!" cried another officer. "Do it now!"

26

INTERROGATION

Amanda wasn't one to feel claustrophobic. But sitting in a room with lime green walls, the size of a walk-in closet, across from one cop after the other was grating on her nerves. Especially since they had confiscated her phone and she had no idea what time it was. It smelled like cardboard. She could run her finger over a line of dust on the table. And it was quiet—too quiet. The walls were obviously soundproof. The only other piece of furniture in the empty room was a large single mirror against the wall. She suspected it was double sided, like in the movies.

Did John know that she didn't blame him? She had cried for what, she figured, hours? She hated John's enemies. But she didn't hate him. Yet somehow knowing him, his sternness, his intensity, knowing the man he was, she just knew he'd blame himself for her friend's death—if he had survived. Because he really was her guardian angel.

The doorknob moved. But no one opened the door.

She turned, looking at the green wall, and saw an image of Luane's body falling on an overpass bridge. The visions kept replaying over and over in her head.

An older man, dark-skinned and bald with a mustache, finally entered. He sat down across from her, put a laptop on the table, and folded his hands before her.

"Amanda, my name's Officer Raymond. I'm the chief of police. We've questioned you all night. Now it's morning. Want some coffee?"

"No."

"We're hardly done."

"I told you everything I know," she said with a sigh, brushing back her hair. "Everything. My best friend's dead, okay? My friend's gone. And I don't know the woman who shot Luane. That answers every question you've asked, no matter how many times you guys ask me."

"You know what your friend did? Aside from complete mayhem for hundreds of Angelenos in their morning commute? His car was clocked by an officer around Wheeler Ridge driving over five hundred miles an hour. Do you know how fast a commuter jet flies? Around four hundred and fifty."

She shrugged.

"All my officers questioned you. I really have only one question. Who the hell is your friend?"

She turned from him. Again? *Seriously!*

"Amanda, who is he? I've never even heard of a car that drives like that. But I have over a hundred witnesses yesterday saying it did."

"I told you, but you don't believe me."

He ran his hand over his eyes. What, *he's tired? Really!* He opened his laptop. He waited for it to turn on, he typed something, then he looked up from the screen. "Angels. Like… Los Angeles?" he laughed. "Is this a joke?"

"I told you, but you don't believe me."

He leaned back in his chair, squinted at her, and typed something else. Coming from the computer, she recognized her voice.

"Yeah, my guardian angel is back with me. He's back. Freaky as hell, I tell you, but kinda funny. He's the kind of guy who doesn't realize he's funny. He's wearing sunglasses in our hotel room. Inside the room. I'm not kidding. I mean, who the hell even does that? He says he's an angel—a dark angel. Doomed to walk this earth damning people by saving their lives. Would you like to say anything to my listeners, fallen angel?"

"Delete that."

"Why did he want you to stop and delete that?"

"So you're not keeping me here because you suspect I was involved in the murder of my best friend?" she said, glaring at him. "You're keeping me here to find out secrets about the guy I was with?"

Amanda was fed up. Exhausted. She had never even talked back to an officer before, but these guys were relentless. And it was about the death of her best friend!

"A fallen angel?" the officer asked. Then he leaned back. "I almost believe it. That chase was something I've never seen before."

Just then the door opened again. A man in a black leather jacket and pants wearing shades walked in. At first, she thought it was John. But this man's skin was white as a ghost.

"What's the meaning of this?" the officer asked, jumping up.

"She's mine now," the man said. "This isn't your jurisdiction. She's mine to question."

"More questioning?" Amanda asked with a long sigh.

Fuck!

It was a very pale version of the man Amanda had fallen in love with. But his skin was so white. He handed the chief of police a few papers. The officer read them, stood up, and nodded to Amanda.

"Nice meeting you," the police officer said. "I wish you could share more of your story."

Then he walked out.

And Amanda was alone with the creepy ghost version of her boyfriend. He sat down across the table like every other interrogator before him. But then he said offhand, "Of course, you're free."

"The others said it'd be only after paying bail."

"I paid it," the stranger said, flashing a grin. The grin was weird on a man wearing John's clothes. John never smiled like that. Then he reached out a hand to shake hers. She didn't touch it. "My name's Rick. Raphael in the language of your friend. I've been directing his work. How much did you tell them, Amanda?"

"Everything. That is, everything I know—which isn't much."

He laughed and leaned back in the plastic chair. "Honest to a fault, angel. Luckily, no one ever believes it."

"You guys are the angels."

"John would never have met you if you weren't an angel. But you weren't just pure. You were special to him. And John's enemies used that against him."

"Is he all right?"

"Yes. But he's in custody like you."

"He chased Lilith?"

"Lilith is dead."

"How?" Amanda asked, furrowing her brow. "I figured she was immortal or something."

"Only when she was on the bike. The archangels are immortal in their essence, but they take on a different soul in every life. One dies and another is reborn. The Lilith that you knew is dead."

"Well, that doesn't make a whole lot of sense. And you don't have to worry about me saying much to the cops because I can't understand most of what you guys tell me." She leaned her head in her hands for a moment. She was so tired.

"You know John means a lot to me," Rick said. "You could almost say we're like brothers. There are few archangels and we work hard at what we do."

She looked up at him. He removed his shades. He had the same pink eyes as Lilith, and that creeped her out. He quickly put his shades back on. "I forget sometimes. Pardon me."

"You're albino?"

"No. All archangels have pale skin. The good and bad. But the similarity helps us a great deal as cover. Except Azraels. Azraels are closest to humans in appearance. White is divine. It represents the shining light of God. But evil is the twist and mockery of such purity. So even our enemies are pale."

"John's darkness seems closer to God than any of you."

"Hmm." He paused and stared at her from behind his shades. "Did John explain to you why he took a special interest in you?"

"No."

"He was instructed to save you in Arizona. That was all. Michael spared John from death from his past life and chose him to be the next Azrael. But he had a life before he was an archangel. They all do. He lived here in Los Angeles. The transformation from human to messenger took three decades for him. Even though he did not die, he might as well have been dead. When he returned everyone he had known was either old or had passed. His aunt, who had raised him, was long gone. So was his brother. Everyone in his family had left him.

"I was his one connection with his past world. You know what we do is secret. John could not confide in anyone other than me.

"Well, I warned him to never visit people from his past. We get flashbacks and images, but we don't hold enough memories of our former lives to make a whole lot of sense of it. But if you're smart, like my Azrael, you can put pieces of the puzzle together."

"What are you getting at?" asked Amanda. She yawned. "I'm so tired." She shook her head. "I just want to go home."

"Do you know why John took a special interest in you, Amanda?" he asked again. "He had only just met you, but he guarded you with his life. Why? Why would he do that?" Rick chuckled. "Too innocent, he told me. He claimed you were too innocent." He shook his head. "I met up with John in a bar in Yuma a couple years ago. He was doing precisely what I suggested he never do—he was seeking someone from his past. I walked into the bar and met one of his dearest friends from his past. Her name was Sherry."

Sherry. That name again.

He nodded, as if understanding her recognition.

"Unbeknownst to me, Samael had followed us. So had Lilith. John saw them in time to run out and fight them outside the bar. Our arch-enemy did not see John's connection with Sherry... Or at least, that's what we thought at the time.

"Well, years later, John stopped Lilith from crashing her bike into your car and killing you in a car crash. That's when he met *you*. Sherry number two. The trap was set.

"They say everyone has a doppelgänger in the world. An identical twin. The job of our enemies is to stop us from saving the lives of pure souls. The best way to do that is to stop Azrael, or any of my other operatives, from doing their job. What better way than showing him an exact mirror image of his former lover and then threatening her life?" He gestured to her with a finger. "You, Amanda."

"Are you saying I look like John's former girlfriend?"

"No," Rick said, shaking his head. "No, that's not what I'm saying. You don't look like her. You are a mirror image of her. You look exactly like her. He probably would have married Sherry had he not been taken from his former life. Do you understand what I'm saying, Amanda?"

He doesn't love me. He loves Sherry.

And now she felt more tired than ever. Maybe more tired than she had ever felt in her life. Deflated. Her best friend had died. And now her new lover only liked her because of a person she reminded him of.

"I'm sorry," Rick said.

"I don't know what else could go wrong," Amanda said, looking away. "Why are you telling me this?"

"John's alive. He'll get out of jail with my help. Then he'll seek you out. It's inevitable. You needed to know the truth." He smirked and looked right into her eyes. "For his sake, you need to stay away from him."

She looked at Rick suspiciously. "Wait a second. You want him back to work with you. And you want me out of the way."

"Amanda," he said, "going back to—"

"I don't care if I look like her," Amanda snapped. "I felt something with him. And I know he does with me. And I also don't care if it messes up your little arrangement of fucking over angels from going to heaven."

She stood up.

"Michael will have his Azrael," Rick snapped, jumping up too. "You can't stop John from doing what he was put on this Earth to do."

"I thought you were here to help me," she said, shaking her head. "I can't figure out which of you is good or evil. You seem like a sadistic devil right now. You said he was your friend? What would he think about you telling me to stay away from him?"

"I do care about him."

"But not his happiness, I think." She looked at the door. "Can I leave? You said I was free to go."

He shook his head. "I have to tell you one more thing."

"To hurt me?" she snapped.

"No. Good news. Your friend, Luane, survived the gunshot. She's in critical condition in the ICU, but she's alive. And the doctors there think she'll probably survive."

Then Amanda felt the most foreign thing she had felt in twenty-four hours of questioning: a smile.

"Believe me or not, I didn't come here to hurt you, Amanda. I came to free you. But, yes, you're smart like John. I want my operative back."

"That's not up to me or you. That's up to John."

He gestured for her to exit through the door. Then he shook his head. "Actually, it's up to you. If you show up in his life again, as the young version of his lover, you only torture him. And endanger both of you. I tell you, you have to stay away from him."

27

MICHAEL

JOHN SAT IN AN UNCOMFORTABLE GREEN PLASTIC CHAIR AGAINST THE wall of a small interrogation room. The walls were beige. The wood table before him had a sheet of white dust. He had been alone for hours, perhaps a day. When the cell door opened, he expected to see another cop. It wasn't. It was Michael.

Michael was the calmest being John had ever encountered. His face seemed incapable of trouble. His pale face and pink eyes were the warmest and kindest he had ever known. Whereas Samael and Lilith were monsters, Michael's countenance was the definition of peace. And as he approached, he even seemed to glide more than walk.

When John had first met Michael, he had seemed like a vision. He had long white feathery wings and wore a white cloth that seemed to blend with his skin. Not today. Today, Michael wore a black suit.

He sat down in the chair across from John.

"I always liked you," Michael said. "In an eternity of souls, yours brooded, but shone forth the most. And I always wondered why you hid your shining light? Perhaps the light that lies in your heart is too strong and must be darkened?"

"I've done everything you asked," John replied. "You said that if I saved enough angels, I could pass peacefully. I think the hundreds I saved would have been enough by now. Now this is where I am destined to be? I ask for what you promised."

"Those that serve God never ask how much good they need to do, John," Michael said, raising a finger. "They just do it. You've also been asked to kneel. You have yet to do that."

John leaned forward. "Fuck you."

"I'm here to explain," Michael continued, unperturbed. "Giving you a position as Azrael enabled you to purify your heart. Samael gambled with God over your soul. He found you the likeness of your lover. He did this for two reasons. To lure you away from being a guardian messenger. The other was far more insidious. Personal. You were told that if you saved enough souls you'd be brought to the gates of heaven. Yes, I told you that. Well, what if I told you that if you hadn't sacrificed for Amanda, *that* would have destined you to wander? Forever, driving you to perdition? Your heart chose Amanda. That was the correct choice."

"Why play games with me?"

"Why ask *me*?" Michael smiled. Then he shook his head. "I don't make the rules. What makes you think that you're the only Azrael? Perhaps everyone on the edge of death must be tested?"

"So these past years were just another test? If it's an illusion, what makes you any less evil than Lilith or Samael?"

"Evil is merely the shadow of light. There is only love. But there is blindness. That is all that lies within Adamah."

"Fuck off," John said, standing up and rubbing his eyes. "Don't play with my head with words. Why are you even here?"

"To give truth." And he smiled back. "Now sit down. I'm about to tell you good news."

"Give it to me and then leave me alone."

John didn't sit. He thought of Amanda. He thought of how he had failed in saving her best friend. He should never have given her even the pretense of victory. The rescue was doomed from the start. Although he had told her that, he felt like he had failed to convince her.

"Your name is not John," Michael said. "You know nothing of your past. Everything you know comes from Sherry."

"I've seen images."

"Fleeting. You were a good field officer before you died. I stress *good*." Michael leaned forward, looking up. "John, you were never a fallen angel. You weren't a demon. Azrael stands at the border between life and death. If you were destined for hell, God wouldn't have tested you at all." He leaned back in his chair. "Everyone who dies goes through judgment. Theirs is based on their past. You were an agent. So we watched you do your job. But others who die are tested differently. Now, because you chose Amanda and her friend, you are free. You can ascend." Michael grinned. It was a genuine smile, but it didn't make John feel any better. "You acted selflessly. You risked your soul for hers. For the height of such sacrifice, you may ascend." He raised a finger to the ceiling. "If that is your wish."

"Why wouldn't it be? And how do you know I didn't choose her because of her looks? Her similarity to Sherry?"

"That's Samael talking. You didn't help Amanda because of her looks, did you?" Michael shook his head and smiled. "Look behind you, brother, if looks are what you desire."

John turned. He was blinded by light. He missed not having his shades to block it from his eyes. But then he felt a release. All his fears and pain seemed to leave his body as he squinted before the brilliant light. It was the most pleasurable brilliance he had ever known, as bright as the sun. Perhaps brighter. The strange thing is he had seen this light before. He hadn't recalled this until now. When Michael had met him upon death, he had seen Michael in this light.

"All you need to do is walk through now."

John got up and walked to the wall, now an open portal. But his arm was grabbed from behind. John turned back and felt sick just looking behind him. He saw the dark shade of Michael still in the jail cell. Michael always shone light, but now the archangel seemed dark.

"Know this, brother," said Michael. "If you leave, you won't be able to help those you leave behind. Samael now plans to take the life of your lover. It is in retribution for the death of his love, Lilith. Every action in your past world has consequences. You have this last choice. You may either ascend or drop back down and help her." Michael touched his shoulder. "Angel down, John. This time it's her. But you are free. I suggest you head to the light. Your job as Azrael is over."

John hesitated. Then he blurted out, almost in a shout, "another test!"

"Think carefully," Michael said with a nod. "The consequence of going back and trying to save her is returning to purgatory. Even saving and good constitute desire. In purgatory, the fight remains. It is a world of darkness and pain. And God shall judge you. I suggest you walk through the light."

"Open the door."

"Which one? Gabriel gives you this gnosis. I told him it's cruel. Only the light is the right decision, John. Retire and end this. End this now."

"Before I leave, Michael," John asked, "tell me why the pure are taken before all others? Amanda reminded me, and I never understood. Why would devils take the innocent?"

"You and Raphael save the virtuous angels on Earth from death. But if peace will reign upon death, why does God not simply permit suicide? Or will it? Why keep anyone alive at all? Why not retire all souls to heaven? And why do I call you good for keeping the pure from ascending to God?"

"I was asking you."

"And yet you make your choice. It seems you already know."

THE HOSPITAL

LUANE BLINKED HER EYES AND SQUINTED UNDER THE LIGHT AS AMANDA squeezed her hand. This wasn't the first time she had opened her eyes, but it was the first time she'd had that awful tube out of her mouth. It seemed like Amanda had tried to talk to her for hours. Now Amanda had just returned from the hospital cafeteria.

Then Luane did what Amanda had waited for all night. She smiled.

"I won't ask you how you're feeling," Amanda said.

Luane groaned.

"Like shit, huh?"

Amanda put down another garland of daisies she had bought for her friend at the gift shop. Daisies were Luane's favorite. Then she sat by the bedside, brushed Luane's hair from her eyes, and took her hand. "I'm so happy you're all right, you don't even know."

"I don't feel all right, Mands."

Amanda tried to smile. Then she fought with herself not to cry. She wanted to be strong for her friend.

"At least you can speak," Amanda said, patting her hand.

Luane nodded. But then she didn't say anything. She turned and closed her eyes again. After a little while, she muttered quietly, "Who was she, Mands? She kept naming you with such hatred."

"Who?"

"You know," Luane said, rolling her eyes. Yeah, she was back to being the Lu Amanda loved.

"Someone I met on my trip," Amanda said. "If I told you who she is, you wouldn't believe me. But my friend got revenge. So you can be happy about that. With all your pain, she felt more, I'm sure."

"I never would have thought *I'd* be in trouble from your stupid road trip." Then she winced. "Fuck, my head feels like it's ready to explode."

"Do you know the chances of that bullet not blowing up all the important stuff between your ears? The doctor told me you're a miracle." Amanda chuckled. "Hmm, a miracle. Yeah, maybe my friend had something to do with that too. I'm just so happy you're alive."

"I don't think I really want to meet your friends."

Amanda nodded. Then she got up and gestured to a small table by the bed and showed her the flowers. "Got you daisies."

Luane turned slowly. "Thanks, babe."

"I still owe you your cactus. It was destroyed twice."

"When I'm better, I want to hear all about your adventures, okay? Just…not now. Fuck, it hurts, so bad."

"You want me to tell the nurse?"

"I'm maxed out on morphine," she said, shaking her head. Then she feebly lifted a handheld wire with a button.

"Well, you can just listen to my podcast later. It's live."

"Okay, Amanda," she said with a laugh. "But stop. Stop being you."

"You want me to let you sleep?"

Luane shook her head. Then she touched her hand. "I want you to be here."

And that did it. That made the tears finally come. She couldn't control it.

"What's wrong?" Luane asked.

"Nothing. Everything. God, I thought I lost you."

"It's okay. The doctors think I'll be better soon. It's just gonna take time. Come here." And Lu reached out her arms. Amanda hugged her gently.

And they both cried together.

"Crying's okay if it's joyful, right?" Amanda whispered in Luane's ear. "I'm crying because you're alive."

"Everything's going to be okay."

"Yes. But it's all my fault."

"Well," she said, pushing her back. Luane smiled. "I really can't wait to hear how it's your fault."

"It's on my podcast."

"Shut up." But then she laughed again. She laughed a little too hard and it made her clutch her head in pain. "We're gonna be okay," she said, squeezing Amanda's hand again. "You and I. Everything is going to be okay now."

Hmm… Not if I tell her where I'm going next weekend.

29

———

THE HUNTER

THAT OFFICER NAMED RICK HAD TOLD AMANDA THAT JOHN WAS IN Yuma. She remembered him saying Yuma. So Amanda figured all she had to do was drive near Yuma. It wasn't that far from LA. And it wasn't a big town. Of course, she had asked John for his number. He had typed it in her phone. The contact was fake, of course.

Maybe he never wanted to keep contact with you. But then why did he keep saving me? Why risk his job, his life, his soul, to help me? Of course he cares about me. He does. He fucking loves me. And, well, I love him.

She'd head exactly in the same direction she had when she began her dangerous adventure, only she had to rent a car. And she had to make sure not to tell Luane. Or her parents. Or anyone. But, whereas witnessing the desert had been breathtaking before, *resplendent*, now it reminded her of all the horrors of her recent trip. And although Luane was blessedly, fantastically, wonderfully feeling better, Amanda couldn't keep getting visions of her being shot on that bridge. She had never hated overpasses as much as she did now.

She shook her head and took out her recorder to get her mind off that.

"Guys, I want to say a huuugge THANK YOU to all of you for supporting me this past week over the recovery of my friend. You heard my unbelievable story. So many of you came to me with support

158

regarding the assault. Well, with that, it's with beyond *ecstaticness"—Is ecstaticness a word? Oh well, it should be—*"It's with ecstaticness that I tell you that Luane is feeling better. Yeah! Ain't that amazing! She's gonna make it out of this alive. And, aside from a headache, without much of a scratch. Still beautiful. Still Lu. I really couldn't be happier. God's shining over us with this miracle. I feel blessed. And I'm... I'm so happy.

"So...whatcha doing now, Amanda?"

"Driving.

"Where?

"You know I fell in love with that guy in Colorado, right?" She laughed. "Well, I'm gonna go find him. So, although it's with fucking-nail-biting-white-fisted-terror that I'm driving back to where it all started, I'm back on the highway in Arizona. Do you remember? Arizona. Yeah, I'm heading back to where there's red sand and cacti the size of people everywhere. I know, crazy right? I heard he lives in a small city out here. Yuma." She bent forward for a better view of the desert in every direction along the horizon. "Somewhere. Well, if he does, I'll find him. I'm just glad he doesn't live in Manhattan."

Click. *That's enough.* Then she sighed.

Shit, but what if I can't find him?

So she clicked her recorder back on.

"Okay, I lied...sort of. I always told you guys I'd be honest. Well, Caligirl gettingold24 also has an interview to go to in Phoenix. Can you believe that! It was delayed because of the horror that befell my friend, but they still want to interview me for a newspaper. How fucking exciting is that?! So, win or lose, I'll come home with something. A job? Maybe. How about a hot tall dark stranger? You never know. Maybe both. We'll see if I can get everything I desire—Lu back to her crazy self, a new job, and that hunk of a man. What do you guys think?"

Click. She laughed again. Then she nodded, satisfied at her work. That was a far better ending.

The beauty of the Arizona desert unfolded again, as she rode over a red summit, with those same saguaros on red soil by the shoulder of the highway and the bright yellow sun rising on the horizon. Then a large bird soared above, just like before. Seeing the bird somehow made her think he'd be here. She leaned forward for a better look at the majestic bird. Then she looked back at an infinite dark horizon behind her. All she saw was the desert and an incoming semi-truck riding far behind. She had slowed down on her lookout, driving near the speed limit. The truck passed and left open road behind her. Then…nothing. Just open desert with the rising sun.

She tapped on her steering wheel to the music of the band GTR.

Stupid. This is stupid. So you see a bird and you think your stranger will be here?

Well, maybe birds herald angels?

Don't be stupid. There's a lot of birds out in the desert.

Not mine. That one looks like mine.

She jumped as her cell phone vibrated in her pocket. She reached forward and hit speaker mode on her Bluetooth console.

"Hey, babe," said Luane. She sounded so weak.

"How are you feeling?"

"Like shit. The pain comes in waves. I was shot in the head, you know. I was hoping you could bring over my air pods. I want to listen to some music and kinda escape."

"Oh, good. You must be feeling better then, Lu. But listen, I can't come today. I'll try to be back tomorrow night to get it for you."

"Where'd you run off to?"

"My interview."

"Oh yeah. Oh yeah. You heading to LAX now? Good luck, babe. Forget the music. I'll get Ben to bring them over. I so hope you get that job. You deserve it. And have a great flight. I'm… I'm gonna go back to sleep."

"Okay, Lu. Love you."

"Bye, babe."

There's no way she'd tell her where she was now. It wasn't the airport, that was for sure. She leaned forward and searched for her bird again.

Okay, Guardian Angel, where in heaven are you?

The soaring bird hovered over her again. With yellow rays now lighting the surrounding vista, the bird sort of glowed.

But then the bird darted away. It seemed something had scared it off.

In her rearview mirror, she spotted the reason. A shiny black motorcycle was rapidly approaching. Too rapid. It was riding at incredible speed, vanishing down a dip in the road and then popping up again, seemingly riding a mile a minute. She hadn't seen the motorcycle behind her before. It had just appeared. Worse, it looked like the shiny black bikes that had followed her in Kansas and Cincinnati. The biker's clothes and helmet were the same pitch black. The only good thing she noticed as it approached was that the biker didn't have long white hair.

When close to the rear of her white rental car, the biker started doing that leaning back and forth aggressive stupid thing that Lilith used to do. Then the bike accelerated right beside her window. With a gloved hand, he hit the driver's window hard and pointed for her to pull over.

Not this time.

Amanda drove right into him. The bike swerved a little then recovered on the road. Amanda turned sharply into the bike again. But the stranger's bike just kept bouncing off her car.

The biker rode in front of her and slammed on his brakes. Amanda hit the gas. She had sworn to herself that if she landed in danger again, she wouldn't be intimidated. She'd go headlong into it. So that's what she did now. She *literally* drove into it. Finally, by the impact, the biker was thrown like a billiard ball to the opposite side of the highway. But somehow it shook and regained control again. Then he shot in front of her, pumping the brakes again. And so, yet again, Amanda braced for impact. She had searched for her angel in the desert but had found a devil instead.

Amanda looked at her speedometer. Although she kept colliding into the bike, her speed was dropping. He was succeeding in slowing her down. What would he do when he stopped her car?

Kill me.

There was no barrier by this part of the highway. So Amanda turned her car sharply and floored it. She slid over gravel and sand with the bike still in front of her. She saw the biker turn around to chase her. Then she drifted all over the place, performing an extremely dangerous three-sixty in the middle of the highway. Her maneuver was so sharp that she worried her rental would roll over. After swerving back and forth on the opposite side of the highway, she finally recovered. Then she caught a red flash in her rearview mirror. She initially thought it was just glare from the rising sun. It wasn't. It was a bright red flash and, when it was close enough, it materialized into a car behind her: a sleek red sports car, like a Ferrari. Not John's black one. Was it John? Was he driving a red car now?

The sports car rammed the biker behind her, but unlike Amanda's collisions, it hit the biker at great speed. The biker recovered and tried to ram into Amanda's passenger side, but then the red car hit it again. This time, the red car didn't relent, pushing the bike all the way onto the shoulder. The biker slid off the freeway as the car ran over him.

Looking in her rearview mirror, Amanda saw the driver, wearing black clothes and shades like John's, jump out of the car. It wasn't John. His skin was pale and his hair was short and white. He pulled out a pistol and shot the biker dead.

Amanda accelerated, pushing her rental car as fast as it could go. That's when she noticed a large piece of metal jutting from her hood. The car drove a bit wobbly too. But at this point she didn't fucking care.

The red car soon trailed her again. Then it flashed red and blue lights, as if it were a police car. But the police don't execute bikers. So she didn't stop.

Quickly, seemingly impatiently, the red car zoomed up to her driver's side. The dark passenger side window rolled down. The guy cried out, "Pull your car over. Now!"

Amanda recognized him. It was Rick, that officer she had met in the interrogation room.

She pulled over.

He jumped out of his car and ran to her. "What are you doing here!" he cried. He was so loud, she heard him through her closed windows.

She rolled down the window.

"I'm driving on my way to an interview."

Rick took his shades off. Then he glared at her with his pink eyes, as if she were absolutely crazy. Well, maybe she was. "Your interview is in Phoenix, Amanda."

"How do you know that?"

He leaned into her window. With the red and blue lights behind her, for a second, she felt like reaching in her purse and handing him her driver's license.

"How the hell do you know about my interview?" Amanda asked again.

"Amanda, what are you doing here on Interstate Eight? Phoenix is off of Interstate Ten."

"A detour."

He didn't let up, staring at her with his pink eyes.

"Okay, fine," Amanda said, rolling her eyes and laughing. "You got me. I'm looking for him. I thought maybe he'd be around here. But it's still on the way."

"Why don't you step out of the car. Come take a look."

"Is it safe?"

He nodded. Then he looked back at the highway in the direction of their chase.

She didn't want to get out, but she reached over to open the driver's side door. She couldn't open it. The car door was jammed. Rick sighed and heaved her door open.

The first thing she did was stand up straight and look at herself. She checked her shorts and T-shirt. No blood this time from her nose. She wasn't damaged.

Her car was. There were large gray metal gashes all over the side and front of the car. The white paint had been sheared off. One of the rear doors was completely dented in. Her door might have been jammed, but the passenger door was caved in. The front hood was bent. That's why there was a piece of metal jutting out.

She laughed and shrugged. "Good thing I gave them my credit card. The car's covered with my insurance."

"Amanda, go home," Rick said. He put his shades back on.

"Not sure I can now," she said with another chuckle. "Don't know if it's drivable. But I think I'm getting used to danger around you guys."

He gazed up at the rising sun. He reminded her so much of John. He wore the same black jacket with jeans. He was a good-looking man. And his red car was amazing. Of course, there was no sign of any damage to his car.

"We only delayed them," he said.

"Where's John?"

"I don't know," he said, shaking his head. "I've been looking for him too. Maybe he's ascended? We put out code bulletins when angels fall.

We sent one to him. He's not answering. I haven't heard from him since he was arrested."

"Can you give me his number? I can try to get a hold of him."

"Amanda, stop." He finally turned to her. "This is serious. If he wanted you to contact him, he would have given it to you."

She felt her curled lip turn to a frown.

"You're so much like her," Rick said, shaking his head. Then he looked out at the horizon.

"What'd ya mean, he might have ascended?"

"I've heard his care for you was looked on positively by Michael and Gabriel. It seems his compassion for you might have been enough to finally free his soul. I don't know." Rick looked back toward the rising sun. "I hope so for his sake." Then he looked back at her car and shook his head. "You need help after this wreck. Just—"

"I'll call triple A."

"Then you'll be dead by nightfall. You think that was the only angel out here? He was a scout. Come into my car. I'll drive you back to LA."

"I think I'll take my chances and call triple A."

He grabbed her arm.

"Don't fucking touch me!" Amanda snapped, looking at his hand. "Don't you ever do that!"

"Amanda, you need protection. I'll take you back to LA."

"And I told you, I have an interview."

"Forget the interview." Then he squinted at her. She could just make it out behind the sunglasses. He seemed to scrutinize her. "I tell you what. I'm heading where John would be, if he's here. It's close enough. If you came here to find John, I'll take you to the one place where he *might* be. You can be safe there before you head back home. Is that enough for you to come with me?"

"Maybe. Where?"

"Sherry's. I need to scope out her place too and make sure she's okay. It'll be a quick stop. It's right near here. But then I'm driving you back. It's up to you. I think you need to speak to her, anyway. She might knock some sense into you."

"You got a deal, mister. I'll hitch a ride in that little thing of yours. Interview's not till tomorrow anyway." She smirked. Then she walked over to her trunk. The trunk was fine. It was the only part of the car not dented. Then she took out her large suitcase. "You sure you'll have room in that little car?"

"Do you have sunglasses in your bag?" he asked.

That was enough to erase her smugness. She found herself shaking. Rick chuckled. "Yeah. Don't worry."

3 0

____

INFIDEL

JOHN STOOD OVER A CLIFFSIDE WATCHING THE RISING YELLOW AND RED rays brighten the valley, which was sandy and filled with weeds. He had his sunglasses off and he waited as the yellow rays slowly rose over this blessed place, this sanctuary. He let the rays blind him. The sun reminded him of the light Michael had shown him in that interrogation room, but it was dimmer and without peace, only providing warmth to his body. He didn't avert his gaze, wouldn't avert it, despite the risk of harm. Like in the myth of Phaeton, he stared at it and let warmth wash over him. But unlike the light Michael had shown him, this one only gave him pain and worry.

He looked down at the ravine. It was nearly a three-hundred-foot drop.

He tried his phone again. He called the code name "Hunter." Again, there was no answer.

Then he turned at the sound of a bird. It had landed on his hood and was fluttering its wings over his black car.

∼

"She's in the living room," said a voice to his left.

John turned around. There was a bright vision of Sherry, transparent but glowing before the view of the desert valley. She was smiling sadly. A younger version of Sherry. Amanda.

"She needs you now." She hugged him. A tear ran down her cheek.

"There's nothing I can do."

"Just be here. That's all she needs."

Rooms appeared beyond a grand foyer. They were familiar. It was dark inside. He remembered now that his aunt had always kept the lights off in her mansion. Now she sat on a couch and just stared out into the void, not saying a thing. She didn't even seem to recognize him as he walked inside. But then, as he sat on the old fluffy couch beside her, she leaned her head on his shoulder and wept.

"I missed you," his aunt said.

"I'm sorry it took me so long to be back."

"We know," she said. She forced a swallow and turned to him, patting his hand. Then she reached for his shades, but he didn't let her take them. "Stay with me. He was your brother."

"He was my cousin."

"He was your brother. But all is well now that I see you here and safe. And he will be in a better place in heaven. Will you say words at the ceremony?"

"If that is what you want."

"Of course it is." She turned to him and examined his face. "Take your glasses off." He obliged. Then she examined his eyes. "What's the matter? What are you feeling, son?"

"Anger. Anger for him getting involved with the jerks he did. I told you and I warned him to stay away. Anger for the pain it's causing you."

"But what good is anger?" She reached for his hand, but he pulled away this time. She forced a smile. Then she brushed her hand over his short hair. "Let it go. This isn't one of the enemies you can beat. I have you. And I have Sherry. All will be well now."

"Nothing will be well anymore."

"Through prayer, I have learned that there is no end. Only light in darkness. Let that gem of a woman you found be your light. She is such a treasure. Let her light your way, like God."

"I don't believe in God."

"It would make you less angry." She took his hand gently and he sat beside her again. Then she said softly, leaning on his arm, "He was your brother. And I love him. Just as I love you, my son."

Then she cried again.

He heard crying from someone else too. Not just from his aunt on his shoulder. It was from the younger Sherry, who was still standing in the other room by the front door, close enough for him to hear her weeping.

John put his shades back on.

"I have you. And I have Sherry," she said again. "All will be well now."

There was a shriek from a large bird. The bird fluttered its wings and took off from the hood of his black car. He remembered that memory of his mother now. He watched the bird soar the hundreds of feet down into the desert and disappear into the light of the sun. And John put on his shades once more, just as he had in the vision.

Then he got back in his car. He listened to a voicemail message sent by his organization and forwarded to him during the night. It was Gabriel's voice.

"Angel down. Sherry. White. Sixty-two. Born a Pisces. Working near Yuma at Angel Dive. Exercise extreme caution. Marked by Samael. If you're still around, we need you, Azrael."

Usually the APB was put out by Rick. What had happened to his boss?

He called Rick again.

No answer.

John looked back at the bright sun.

Let it go. This isn't one of your enemies you can beat. I have you. And I have Sherry. All will be well now.

"All is not well now, Mother."

He reversed his car. Then he hit the gas, drifted across the sand along the cliffside, and re-entered the highway.

THE DEVIL'S SERMON

Amanda found Sherry's place to be secluded, miles from downtown. Amid desert shrubs and sand stood a one-story building. The walls were windowed, kind of reminding Amanda of the diner in Kansas. To her left, if she looked hard enough with binoculars, she could probably find downtown Yuma on the two-lane road. The structure was simple and clean, its wood exterior painted red. There were hubcaps hung on wood columns by the entrance and old metal garage signs advertising gas and oil products. The automobile motif was a perfect fit for John. But Rick's red luxury car hardly fit the place's simplicity.

It looked deserted. Even though it was midday, their cars and an old blue pickup were the only vehicles parked on a dusty, broken-up asphalt parking lot.

Rick opened the front door. Then Amanda was instantly engulfed in smoke from inside. It wasn't cigarettes. It smelled like the place had been lit on fire. The light was dim and country music was playing, but they were the only ones there. The walls were painted burgundy, almost auburn, and decorated with lots of silly stuff like antlers, dart boards, and sports jerseys. And at the far end, through the smoke, was a large wooden bar. It was there that the wall was blackened. The charred wall was emanating all the smoke. There was an empty stage in another corner, empty except for an acoustic guitar leaning on a stool. Wooden tables with matching wooden chairs were vacant. But a few chairs were lying on the ground with their legs in pieces. And broken glass was strewn along the floor near the bar.

Amanda gasped. A shadow moved through the smoke near the counter. Rick noticed it too and touched his gun holster, slung over his T-shirt under his jacket. He pulled out the pistol. Then Amanda jumped when she saw the stranger—a woman with long white hair in a tight black leather motorcycle suit. Lilith.

How?!

"Took you long enough, Hunter," Lilith said. "But I expected Azrael. Well, you and she will do."

"Where's Sherry?" Rick asked.

"Right beside you," Lilith said with a chuckle.

"I thought you died?" Amanda asked.

"I thought I captured you," Lilith said with a shrug. "This is all very confusing, Sherry." She walked around the counter and approached them. Rick pointed his gun at the devil.

"It's Samael," Rick said, cocking his head back to Amanda.

"I thought Samael was a man?" Amanda said.

"I can take any shape I please, darling," said Lilith. "And, until I restore the beloved lamia you helped slay, I shall pay my respects by using her form. And now that I have you, I can kill both you *and* your older self."

She walked up close to Rick. Amanda felt her skin crawl when the woman's pink eyes flashed red as she glared at him. "Put the gun down, Raphael, or she dies. There's no need to break my body. I will simply take another."

"What's your game, Samael?" Rick asked. "What are you doing to my friend?"

"*We all have friends, don't we!*" she shouted in his face. But the shout wasn't what made Amanda jump. It was her voice. Her voice had turned deep, like a man's. "I lost Lilith! Now I have both the old and the young Sherry. If I'm lucky, they'll both pass away right before Azrael's fucking eyes!"

"You brought Amanda into John's life long before he killed Lilith," Rick said.

"I did, didn't I?" she said, her voice calming and returning to female. "I did." Then she walked up to Amanda. "So I did. Well, we had to test our Azrael, didn't we?"

"You shot my friend in the head!" snapped Amanda.

"Such courage," Lilith said with a nod. "The devil stands before you, but you hold yourself with pride. Bravery? Or is it stupidity? So like your older self."

"Where is she?" repeated Rick, raising the gun to Lilith's head.

"Right in front of you," Lilith quipped. "Does it matter? To humans, if the body is there and there is a glimmer of a resemblance, it's all the same. No one looks further than the face. Isn't that right, Amanda? What lies underneath is really of no consequence."

"The only thing stopping me from pulling the trigger, Samael," Rick said, "is your information. I need you to tell me where Sherry is. Where's the *older* one?"

"Transmutable, undeniable, manifested in God's glory right before your very eyes, Raphael, Sherry stands before you. Younger, but still the same vessel." Lilith raised a finger, and then she looked deep into Amanda's eyes with fiery bright red ones. "When you were younger, Sherry, you wanted to be a journalist. It was 1984. But you fell in love with an officer and during heroic duty on a secret mission, the man you loved died. Distraught, but with the funds left to you from the death of your well-to-do man, you decided to create this..." She gestured to the room. "This dump, instead of furthering your writing career. Azrael influenced you even then. You built this restaurant for sinful drifters, loners and alcoholics, because it reminded you of him. Angel Dive. And I reveled in it. I think it was because it was a place to remember the greatest drifter of all. Your guardian. My Azrael. That nothing. That zero. John."

Amanda was trembling in shock. Lilith's long hair shortened. Her jawbone hardened. Her brows moved out. Her skin dried. And she grew a beard. Lilith's beauty was transformed into a pale male version of herself.

"Not all is what it appears," the demon said now with a low male voice. "You may chase me through the firmament, Hunter, but I will never stop. Shoot me down, I return. So put your gun down. Because *I* can kill *you*."

"Where's the angel down?" asked Rick again. "Where's Sherry?"

"Sherry is hardly an angel down," Samael said with a laugh. "The only angel here was Amanda, before he fucked her." Then he raised a finger. "Or was she?"

He walked right up to Amanda and gazed upon her face again. Then he purred before her as she lurched back.

"Tell me now, Samael," warned Rick.

"Tell you what? Look behind you, idiot," Samael said, cocking his head back. "Let me finish my sermon or you'll never speak another goddamn word again."

The empty parking lot behind the windows was now filled with black motorcycles. The weirdest thing was that Amanda hadn't heard them approach outside.

"What makes a vessel pure, Amanda?" Samael asked. "Hmm? That is the question for the eons. The answer, I tell you, will open the door to heaven to you. Would you like to know? Would you like me to tell you?" He touched her cheek with a black-gloved finger. She lurched back. "I don't enjoy speaking with him. You're softer."

Rick cocked his gun and pressed it close to Samael's head.

"Zero," Samael said with a chuckle to Amanda. "Nothing. Absolutely nothing can purify you. There is no struggle on Adamah. I've already won. None of you will approach the purity of your so-called God. There is no return to the garden, just as there are no angels. That is the answer that all of you animals run from.

"It makes not a difference in the world what a cock fucks. It makes not a difference in the world what neighbor is strangled. It makes not a difference under the firmament if you worship God, graven images, swear, say the lord's name in vain, never go to church, kill your mother, fuck her or your neighbor, break her dog's neck, steal the clothes on her back." His eyes widened and shone red at Amanda. "It matters not. It makes no difference at all! For there are no angels. No angels, just as there is no God. There is nothing. Zero!" He stopped his tirade for a moment to catch a breath. "Oh, you can pray. You can do that. Ask forgiveness for your sins from your so-called lord with the vain hope of protection. But behold my occult. When you are alone in the dark, you won't find God. Oh, no. You'll find me. Nothing. Just as there is a man with no name called John. There is nothing. Absolutely nothing, Sherry!" The beast smirked at her. She cringed as his eyes glowed red. "You shall suffer eternally for my gnosis. That is my commandment for you and your kin. Your only recourse is to worship my rising star. For I will rise, as surely as dawn falls."

"So pretty—" The devil's voice eerily returned to Lilith's. "So pretty." He reached for her face with his gloved fingers again, but she backed away. "You're very pretty, pretty, Sherry. I see what he once saw in you."

"Are you finished?" asked Rick.

"Oh, I haven't begun," Samael said with his low voice returning. "He comes. Let us play his cops and robbers game, shall we? I bring *hers*. The damage Azrael shall cause in the name of love you may only blame on yourselves. Gabriel heralded him onto Adamah once more, rather than Michael ascend him. So comes choice. Love. And for this vapid thing called love, the greatest desire of all, I shall greet him with pain." Samael looked outside over Rick's shoulder. He lifted a gloved hand over his head and then closed it. "He works for me now."

Amanda heard a few cracks and then a crash of glass from a window. It was gunfire. Before she knew it, Rick fell to the ground. Shot dead? She couldn't tell. It was so fast. But she hadn't even seen Samael brandish a weapon.

She fell to the floor and shook Rick's shoulders, but his eyes were closed and he was unresponsive. From the corner of her eye, she saw Samael rush past her through the front door.

"Take the girl," he ordered.

She was grabbed. Amanda kicked and shouted, trying to swing at the person holding her, but whoever held her, held her tight. No, it was several people. She made out a few of the bikers in black jumpsuits clutching her. They dragged her through the dusty parking lot to the blue pickup. There they tied her hands and gagged her. Then they threw her in the back of the truck.

Lying on her side, she saw another woman with hands tied behind her back. Then the stranger stared at her probably with as much disbelief as she felt. It was her twin, only so much older than she was.

Bikers closed the pickup door. And the car drove off, drifting, hardly being easy on her body as she hit the metal sides on turns.

Lying on her side, Amanda couldn't see anything over the truck, only her older self. And her older self, with long gray hair, seemed to be trying to smile under her taped mouth. It was as if her twin was trying to say something. It was as if Sherry was trying to comfort her.

3 2

MIRROR

THE RIDE WAS BUMPY AS HELL EVEN THOUGH AMANDA FIGURED SHE WAS being driven on the highway. Her shoulder and back kept banging against the metal back of the pickup. And there was a lot of noise from the wind and motorcycles revving, but she couldn't see a thing above Sherry's head. The old woman was oddly squirming like crazy, lurching her back up and grunting for some reason. Maybe she was sick. The whole drive was nauseating.

Amanda turned her body and stared for a moment at the vibrating metal wheel hub, to look for something, anything, to calm her stomach. But that was more sickening. So she swung back and gazed at her granny look-alike. That's when she finally realized what her companion was doing. She was working the ropes over her wrists. And she was almost free! The rope was dangling on one arm. Then she was back to squirming until she freed a hand. Then she rolled onto her knees and yanked the tape off her mouth.

"Be quiet," Sherry said. "And stay down."

What the hell do you think I'm going to do? I can barely move.

Sherry was pulling at the ropes around Amanda's wrists.

"Next time you get tied up," Sherry said right in Amanda's ear, "press your hands together, keep your wrists apart, and tighten your muscles. That'll keep it loose. Shit, this is tight."

Amanda felt a hand get free.

"Stay still!" Sherry said in a forced whisper. "And keep down." Then she reached for her face. "This is gonna hurt. Sorry. No yells, 'kay?"

Amanda nodded. Then…rip, the tape was torn off her face.

Oww!

But she didn't say a word. Sherry smiled and nodded.

"Thank you." Amanda nodded. "How'd you know how to do that?"

"You think this is the first time that big oaf got me captured? Let me tell you something, hanging 'round John is always trouble." She smiled again, though a bit more morosely. Then she examined Amanda's face. And that was weird because it felt like she was staring in the mirror. "Now I get it. Damn, I forgot how good I used to look. You're very beautiful, Amanda. Or I was."

"Thanks a lot, I think. So, do we like just jump for it?"

"No." Sherry shook her head. "We have to time this just right. Those jerks will shoot you. Keep your head down and hold the rope close by your wrists so if they glance over, it'll look like you're still tied up." She looked up, squinting at the sun. "I'm not worried about us. I'm worried about him."

"They're trapping him again?"

She nodded.

"This isn't the first time they've used me to get to him," Amanda said. "Where are they taking us?"

Sherry put a finger over her lips. She gazed up at the shaking metal wall. She was listening for something. But all Amanda heard was the sound of revving motorcycles and the rush of the road.

"I'm not sure," Sherry finally answered. Then she furrowed her brow. "Why are you here, anyway? John said he took you home."

They must be close. How would she even know that?

"I get it," Sherry said with a nod. "Don't answer. I get why."

"Do you still love him?" Amanda asked.

Sherry turned away and nodded. Then she squinted up against the sun over the truck walls again. The truck was so bumpy it was killing Amanda's side.

"Next stop," Sherry said, still trying to gaze over the metal wall. But she didn't dare sit up. "We make a run for it."

"I thought you said they'll gun us down?"

"Do we have a choice? I'll tape your mouth back and you can just hold your hands together. Then I'll jump out and scream and holler to get lots of attention. While they're chasing me, you can quietly run."

"No way. I'm not letting you take the fall."

"One of us has to, Amanda."

She reached for Amanda's face. Amanda turned. "I'll tape you and you'll pretend to still be tied. I'll make such a fuss that it will distract them from you."

"No." Amanda batted her hand away. "I won't let you sacrifice yourself."

"Don't fight me!"

"I won't," Amanda said, shaking her head. "We either both run or we don't go at all."

Sherry reached for her face again. Amanda hit her arm.

Sherry tackled her, trying to pin her. Amanda elbowed the old woman in the ribs. Then she butted her head against hers. It hurt…*real* bad. They both groaned. Amanda thought that was it. But then Sherry leaped at her again, threw her against the wall of the truck, and pinned her, trying to press the tape against her lips. Amanda couldn't believe they were in a fight. The oddest thing was Sherry was trying not to make any noise. Worse, this was her way of helping her!

That gave Amanda an idea. Amanda cried out as loud as she could.

"*Fuck!*" Sherry said in a forced whisper. "*Shut the hell up! You idiot!*"

"Let go of me or I'll make more noise," Amanda warned.

Sherry rolled back toward the other side of the truck. She ran her hand through her long gray hair and rolled her eyes. Then she sat there panting. "You don't get it. Only one of us can get out of here. Whatever good you think you're doing."

"Both of us or neither," Amanda said, shaking her head.

Sherry looked up, more worried than ever, after Amanda's shout. But there was still the same rush of air with the occasional revving of the surrounding bikes. Sherry shrugged. "We can both die then."

"Fine. Just don't ever touch me like that again."

"Hmm," Sherry quipped with a smirk, staring at Amanda. "Well, keep your guard up, young-me, or I'll tie you up yet."

"Why don't we work together instead?"

Sherry looked up at the sky again, worried as hell. Then she shook her head. "I should have left you tied."

Amanda's eyes wandered around the truck bed. She was beginning to hate her twin. She'd look anywhere but at her. But eventually her eyes fell back on Sherry's face. She was surprised to see that same reassuring rueful grin she had glimpsed when she first landed in the truck. Sherry was nice as hell. Sherry wasn't fighting to hurt her, she was fighting to save her life.

Well, Amanda wouldn't let her. "Together," Amanda insisted.

Sherry looked away. She hesitantly nodded.

33

RED OR BLACK

THE TIRES SCREECHED AND THE TRUCK LURCHED TO THE SIDE. THE turn was so violent that it rolled Sherry over Amanda. Then Amanda felt the cabin shimmy back and forth, struggling to maintain control. At one point, she felt like she was going to be launched over the wall. There was shouting. It wasn't just her screams. Then there was gunfire.

"Stay down!" Sherry said.

The floor swerved again, turning very sharply and pressing her against the wall of the truck. A biker rode so close that Amanda could see his helmet. He was looking in.

Amanda was dying to get up and see what was going on, but Sherry kept pressing her body down.

"Are we just going to stay inside?" shouted Amanda.

More gunshots. They came so close that Amanda covered her head. So did Sherry. And the truck wasn't slowing down—it felt like it was speeding up.

Sherry rose onto her knees and looked outside.

What a hypocrite!

"John!" Sherry shouted. "John!"

More bullets, this time hitting the inside of the truck. A few stray shots bounced inside the cabin. And this time, Amanda was the one to yank Sherry back down.

"I thought you said to stay down!" Amanda said.

"Couldn't resist," Sherry said with a shrug. "Sorry."

"How far is—"

One of the motorcyclists leaped inside the truck bed. He managed to land right on Amanda's left leg, blinding her with pain for a moment. Then he reached for Sherry. As he leaned down to grab her, he was thrown against the front of the truck bed. His helmet cracked the small tinted window. Then his body was pelted by gunfire. He shook from bullets riddling his chest. Then the man, now quite dead, collapsed over them.

"How far is he from us?" cried Amanda.

"He's right behind us."

"How does he even know we're here?"

"We're the only car in the pack."

Her leg stung and hurt like hell. Sherry rose to her knees and shoved the fallen man off them. Then, gruesomely, she pushed him to the wall and over the side.

More shots quickly got her to duck again.

"Should we jump?" Amanda asked.

"We're driving a hundred miles an hour."

"Then what do we do?"

Sherry didn't have time to answer. They were both rammed hard against the front of the truck and then rolled over each other again. The truck was turning sharply. She wondered what was going on. Were they turning around at a break in the divider on the highway? It felt like that.

No. They were slowing down. Maybe she could jump out now? But before she could rise, the side of the truck was hit. She heard a squeal and felt the truck unnaturally drag sideways. For a second, she feared it would flip over. That would kill them for sure.

"He's ramming us!" Sherry said.

The truck slid sideways across the road and came to a standstill. Sherry tugged Amanda up. Amanda could now witness the mayhem. It wasn't just the biker gang surrounding them, she was surprised to see —though it was early in the morning with light traffic. Cars were strewn all over the highway, many overturned, others on their sides, some even aflame. And behind the cavalcade of black bikes were police cars. Red and blue was flashing behind the field of overturned cars.

Amanda recognized their location from a quick glance at a hill. White windmills. That meant they were near Palm Springs. All of this was processed in seconds because Sherry and Amanda were ducking bullets again.

John swung open his car and started shooting like crazy at the nearby bikes. Sherry helped Amanda off the pickup. Amanda landed, hampered by her injured leg, in a low crouched position. Then she groaned due to the pain in her leg. She found herself limping toward John's car despite the gunfire. Sherry was beside her.

Sherry threw the passenger door of John's car open and helped Amanda get in. Then John shut his driver's side door. That's when, aside from stray bullets cracking and intense pain, Amanda suddenly remembered in horror that John's car had only two seats.

"*No!*"

But Sherry had already shut the door. Amanda cried out for Sherry —she'd have her sit on top of her if she had to—but it was too late. Through the side mirror, Amanda saw a biker grab Sherry. She recognized that dreaded white scarf. It was their ringleader, Samael. Then, oddly, the other bikers started tying Sherry to the back of his motorcycle with rope.

Amanda was thrown against the seat as the car accelerated forward.

"John, we have to go back!" Amanda cried. "We have to go back for Sherry!"

John stared ahead, deadpan. Emotionless.

"John! Go back! We have to save her!"

But he wasn't ignoring her. He was turning the car around on the opposite side of the highway. A police officer barreled forward and slammed into the passenger side. John quickly turned his wheel and rammed the police car out of his way. Then they came about an inch from a headlong collision with a disabled truck.

Sherry sat behind Samael, roped to him and his motorcycle as Samael re-entered the highway.

"Open the glove compartment and put your shades on," John said.

Amanda quickly pressed the glove compartment button and snatched her shades.

"And put your fucking seat belt on."

"I'm sorry, John."

He furrowed his brow and glanced at her. Then he looked down at her pants and up at her shirt. "Are you hurt?"

She shook her head. She wasn't going to tell him about her leg. She didn't care right now. He nodded and gazed forward. Then he continued to mow down any black bike in his way, while swerving around innocent trucks and cars, heading for Samael. But the demon finally took off like a flash of light between two cars. Multicolored light gathered across John's windshield as Amanda was pushed back in her seat during the pursuit.

"Where…" she muttered. "Do you know where Samael's taking her?"

"Los Angeles."

3 4

THEIR MORNING COMMUTE

THE RELIEF OF BEING SAFE IN JOHN'S SUPER CAR SOON TRANSFORMED into sheer terror. There were constant collisions with fenders and doors, horns honking, people shouting. It reminded Amanda of bumper cars, as metallic objects crashed and slid along the passenger side window. John was chasing the motorcycle gang. Samael, with his white scarf and Sherry behind him, was front and center, leading the pack. But zooming around cars was not as bad as the flashes of light. Every time the bikers zoomed into rays of light, she was thrown back in her seat and, even with sunglasses, burned by the bright light. And the obstacles were only getting harder to dodge. Some vehicles ricocheted off John's car and went spinning out of control. Then came bullets raining down from the bikers shooting at them. Tragically, a few stray shots hit bystanders' windshields. One windshield was splashed with red.

John kept looking up at the sky. She didn't understand why, until she spotted a helicopter and copter-like black objects overhead. The squad cars couldn't possibly catch up, and even when they did, the bikers simply rammed them out of the chase. Not so with the objects in the sky. The sky ahead teemed with more and more black flying machines. And even with the jumps in speed, these pursuers could keep up with them.

"What are they doing?" Amanda asked.

He didn't answer. Instead, he tapped hard on the car console. He scrolled down to a contact named "Hunter."

"Rick was shot, John."

John avoided hitting a flipped big rig on the highway. He squeezed through smoky bent metal. The car shook, running over debris. Many cars were pulling over on the shoulder. But even with people trying to avoid the violence, traffic was thickening.

The phone rang. And rang.

"He was shot, John," Amanda repeated quietly.

"Yeah," said a man warily on the other end of the phone line.

"I need support now," John said.

"Are you okay, Rick?" Amanda cried, staring at the console.

"No… " Rick said on the other line. "And no…John. I'm lying on the fucking floor."

"Put me in contact with someone who can, then," John said.

"Fuck, that asshole hit me in the back." He groaned. "What a cheap shot. Sounds like you have her with you now. Is that Amanda? Or Sherry?"

"Amanda," she said.

"Well, isn't that enough? Turn around and give up the chase."

"I need support now." John looked up at the sky. "If you can't do it, send me their number and I'll call them off." Amanda glanced in her side mirror. Red and blue lights were flashing. This time, it was a whole army of police. But the police were busy dodging obstacles on the highway left by the collisions too. John didn't seem to care. He kept looking up at the sky.

In the distance, Amanda caught the LA skyline. But seeing all those high rises now was bizarre. They had just been in Palm Springs, normally two hours away.

"They won't listen to you even if I give it," Rick muttered.

"They're tearing up the city. Before you die, call in support."

"You're such an asshole, John," Rick said. "What do you see in him, Amanda?"

"I'll call an ambulance to the café," Amanda said. She wasn't sure why she hadn't before.

Because you were in the middle of a chase with devils.

"Look out, John!" cried Amanda.

They rammed right into two cars. At their speed, both cars were hurled into the sides of his car. In front of him, Samael slammed on the brakes. John didn't stop. His car rammed into him, pinning Sherry. Amanda screamed. But somehow, after Samael rode ahead, Sherry didn't even seem to have been touched by the impact. The police fell back. Samael's slamming on his brakes had worked.

Then the demon took off again, speeding along the shoulder of the highway. John followed right behind. There were less police but now, up ahead, there was a line of red lights: cars motionless in traffic.

"Rick?" John asked. There was no response. "Rick!"

"Shit," John said. He hit his steering wheel and pressed a button, hanging up the phone.

"This is it," John said, gesturing to the traffic. He took a deep breath. "They have to stop. They won't get through that line of cars."

There was an accident blocking traffic on the freeway. Even the shoulders were blocked. The median was too narrow for a motorcycle. And police were directing all the jammed cars into an immobile line of cars along the right shoulder, John and the gang's frequent escape route.

Samael gave a few hand signals to his biker gang. Then, instead of braking, he sped up toward the red lights. All the gang's motorcycles turned into a blur of light running headlong into the stalled traffic. The impact at this speed was as if a fiery bowling ball had been thrown down the center of the highway. Cars were thrown high in the air, and others were torn in half or exploded. It was so destructive that the damage tunneled a corridor of mangled and fiery broken metal through the center of traffic.

"*Jesus!*" John exclaimed.

Amanda was thrown forward against her belt as John slammed on the brakes. He stopped right at the entrance of the demon corridor.

People were jumping out of their cars. One woman was bleeding, trying to force the back door of her SUV open. Her poor kids were banging on the windows. And her face was covered in blood. Then an explosion erupted from another auto with a man standing by it. The fire raged and engulfed him in flames. Amanda could hear cries of others nearby, despite the quiet insulation of John's super car.

"Why are you stopping?" Amanda asked. "What's wrong?" She gestured at the fiery corridor. "Go chase after them."

"The car can't fit."

"Make it wider. Push the cars to the side."

"I can't do that, Amanda."

"Why?"

This was so weird. It was quiet in his soundproof car with just the occasional muffled scream. But they were surrounded by smoke, fire, and rubble. She felt like she was parked before a battle scene.

Meanwhile, the red and blue lights were getting bright in her side mirror. She was going to be arrested again.

"Why not, John?" Amanda repeated more quietly.

He didn't answer. He just sat staring from behind his shades at the narrow corridor.

Far in the distance now, another car was thrown airborne. The bikes were still plowing through cars miles ahead.

"You care about these people? Is that it?" she asked, staring at him. It seemed like such a simple question, but she felt like it meant the whole world. "You're not bad, John," she said, shaking her head. "You're good."

He finally turned and stared at her. Then he wrapped his arm around the back of her seat, turned, and looked out the back window.

"I'm not good."

She was thrown toward the door and then the windshield. Her seat belt was the only thing keeping her in her seat as John raced backward through oncoming traffic. At first, it was thick. But after another half mile, it thinned out. The police had cleared a lot of the highway.

He rushed by the army of police cars. One slid past the passenger door. The siren blared in her ears as the squad car was hit and rammed into a nearby truck. Then came a swarm of more red and blue rushing by the windows. Another was hit on John's side. But most swerved out of his way. None of it stopped him. But it seemed like, unlike the bikers, he was doing everything he could to avoid the cars on the road.

After passing the police, he continued driving backward at over a hundred miles an hour. Stray cars, many turned over by the earlier violence, now flew by the window. She couldn't believe John could maneuver like this.

"I think I'm going to be sick," Amanda said.

She pressed the window switch and rolled down the window. As she was tossed back and forth in her seat, she grasped for the handlebar above. Clutching it, she vomited on whatever passed by. After a few more heaves, breathing heavily, she sat back and put her head in her hands. She noticed car horns and shouting, police sirens, and a rush of wind from the now open window.

John shut her window.

"Are you all right?" he asked, glancing over.

"I think some of it came in," Amanda said. "I'm sorry."

She couldn't believe he was still racing backward.

Mercifully, the path soon straightened. Then he seemed to hug the median.

"I don't care about the fucking car," John said. "Are you okay, Mandi? Are you all right?"

She quietly nodded, wiping her mouth. Then she said very quietly, more to herself, "I really love you."

The route became mercifully straight.

Police cars, with their red and blue lights flashing, were heading straight at them now, or behind them, but they still couldn't stop his car. A few tried to ram the sides, but that just led to more crashing. Even a few stray bullets bounced off the glass.

"Hold on," John said.

Shit, that doesn't sound good.

She was thrown against the door as John turned and drove through an opening in the median. The car drifted a hundred and eighty degrees onto the other side of the freeway. They missed the concrete median by inches. As John straightened, his car nearly came to a standstill. Then they were launched forward again. This time, thankfully, driving on the right side of the freeway.

John touched the console. He started searching maps. Then he touched another button, causing a phone to ring.

"Where are you going?" she asked.

"Away from the city."

"That will be away from Sherry." *Shut up, Mandi. He knows that.*

He worked the console again. Then he leaned forward and looked up at the sky .

"What's up there?" Amanda asked.

"I'm waiting for them to hit us," he said, staring at the machines above. "That's why we have to run."

"Hit us? With what?"

"Bombs. After what they just did, it's just a matter of time before they knock us all off the road."

"Will the car survive?"

He shook his head.

Traffic got worse. She realized it must be because they had passed the area the police had cleared. But now they were entering morning traffic. And every time he had a long opening, he did that irritating blinding-light-exploding thing.

Then Amanda caught an explosion in her rearview mirror. It looked like a plume of smoke but it seemed so far away.

"That them?" Amanda asked.

He nodded.

The phone just kept ringing.

Then John hit his steering wheel. He started searching the maps while passing more cars. Amanda gazed at the speedometer. She wished she hadn't. It read one hundred and eighty. He was driving at that speed while flipping through maps again.

"Something I can do to help?" she said.

He stopped on a map with a red dot.

"What are you doing?" Amanda asked. She almost didn't want to ask.

"Trying to track that explosion."

"So, if one of those bombs hits her—"

"She dies."

"So does Samael."

"I don't care about Samael, Sherry."

"Amanda," she corrected, though quietly. "Amanda. My name's Amanda, John."

Another red dot beeped on the map. Then a yellow one.

"That them?" she asked.

"That's another explosion."

"The yellow?"

"That's them jumping."

"So we can find them."

He nodded. "We can track them." Then he looked up. "Maybe Rick did help us. They haven't fired on us yet."

"John, it looks like this yellow dot is further from downtown." She leaned forward and spread her fingers on the screen. John was about to grab her, but she managed to enlarge the area on the map. "He's leaving LA and heading back out. Look, this area of the map reads 'Pasadena'."

"His plan to lure me failed. Now he's running, like us. But he still wants to lure me. He knows we will follow if—"

The car tires suddenly squealed as he turned the wheel so sharply it threw Amanda against the door. Then in a split second she was thrown back just as hard. She felt intense pain from the seat belt. John had avoided hitting a stalled vehicle on the shoulder. His super car quickly corrected, moving straight as if nothing had happened.

"I think they haven't shot us down yet," he said, ignoring the near collision, "because we're leaving. I don't think Rick did a thing."

"He was shot, John." *Why do you keep telling him that?*

"I know, *Amanda*," he said with a quick glance at her and a rare smile. He stared at her for a moment. She smiled.

"The morning traffic's only getting worse," he said. "Hopefully, you're right and they're leaving LA."

"Can we slow down, then?" *Please!* He didn't answer. She really didn't expect him to. So she asked something else on her mind. "Has it ever gotten this bad?"

He shook his head.

35

ANGELS DOWN

THEY RUSHED THROUGH A NAUSEATING ORDEAL OF HIGH, ROLLING HILLS. They zoomed so fast it seemed the car was leaping over them. Then, at their immense speed, the flat desert sand, bushes, and weeds rapidly sprawled out before them for as far as the eye could see. The hills were gone. And so, again, she was out in that infinite horizon she loved. The sky was clear. The sun was out. If she hadn't been stuck in the middle of a car chase, it could have been beautiful. Only it wasn't a view to enjoy right now.

Because John wasn't slowing down. He was rapidly closing in on his target, following that yellow light on his monitor.

"We've almost caught up," John said. He'd been quiet ever since passing Palm Springs again. He pointed at another yellow dot that had just appeared on the map. It looked close to the center. "The car's faster than the motorcycles."

"But why's he taking her into the desert?" asked Amanda. "I thought he wanted you in the city?"

John pointed up. Pitch-black machines were hovering overhead. "He wants me dead. He doesn't care how."

"Why weren't those black things popping up before?"

"They were probably hoping the police could handle the chase."

"Those aren't the police?"

He shook his head. "He'll probably either disappear jumping full speed," John added, studying the map on the console again, "or give up and turn around."

"What do you mean *full speed?*"

That doesn't sound good.

John abruptly turned the wheel ever so slightly, just an inch. If he hadn't, they would have driven through a truck. At this speed, it took only slight shifting of the wheel to avoid obstacles. He was constantly doing it, even while talking. But it seemed like the car helped him. There were times when it looked like he needed to turn more sharply and the car corrected his steering.

A very small metallic flying object rushed right by Amanda's window. With metallic wings, it reminded her of a bug.

"There's little hope for Sherry," John said, gazing at the object in his rearview mirror. "Just like there was little hope when they marked your friend Luane."

"Or me," Amanda said, touching his arm. "But you saved me."

"Well, I should drop you off now."

Amanda looked at the clock on the console. It read 9:40. During their chase through hell, it had been a little before eight. How? Then in Palm Springs she thought it read a little after eight-fifteen. That was so weird.

"Well, I'm not leaving, John. I'm not leaving until we help her."

"Amanda," he said, glancing at her. "How are you helping her? You didn't come for her, you came for me."

"No, I came for my interview." She gave a nervous chuckle.

"You came for me. That was stupid. All that did was bring you into danger again. I told you to stay in LA. You're still marked."

"Well, I really do have an interview."

"Your friend just died and—"

"Luane's alive," Amanda snapped. "Okay. She didn't die. She's in the hospital."

"Oh…" he looked at her and furrowed his brow for a moment. She felt the car quickly sway to the left and saw a car blur across her passenger window. "Good. Then you should be caring for her, not chasing cars on the highway with me."

"Well, yeah, Lu's alive. And her getting shot was my fault. So? I get

all that. Her danger, I get, was on me. But my danger's my business."
She folded her arms. "Anyway, seems like this devil is leading you to
where I was going anyway. *My interview*, John. It's in Phoenix. We're on
Interstate Ten. So it all works out real convenient."

He frowned. "Next rest stop, I'm dropping you off."

"The fuck you are." She flapped a finger at the map. "You… you…
you drop me off and she'll be long gone."

He fell silent. Because she was right. All she heard was the constant
hum of the engine, like being on an airplane.

He took a deep breath while staring at the road.

She scooted back and threw her feet up on the dash. "Afraid you're
stuck with me. Till you get me to my interview. It's in Scottsdale, by the
way. Just a quick one-second detour for your rocket car. This seat is
more comfortable than an airplane, anyway. I'll just scoot back, let you
do your demon chase shit, enjoy the view, and wait to help you get back
your older me. Your older-*Amanda*, John. Amanda. Not Sherry."

She winked at him. He laughed. That made her laugh too.

But then the smile she loved vanished from his face. She was thrown
against her seat again. It took a few seconds to figure out why they were
racing faster. John had found his prey.

She saw only two black bikes now, each taking up one lane in front
of them. Had the rest been destroyed?

The demon still held Sherry on his back. He was riding in the right
lane; the other biker was in the left. She could tell it was Sherry by her
long gray hair. She wasn't wearing a helmet. But she didn't look back
because her head crouched tightly into the beast's back. Amanda shud-
dered imagining what it must feel like for poor Sherry zooming at these
incredible speeds on a motorcycle just hanging on to his back.

The other black-clad biker looked back. Then he dropped back by
the driver's side of the car, took out some sort of club, and swung it at
the window. He missed. And that made him lose control of his bike. He
spun onto the opposite side of the highway.

John drove right up to Samael's motorcycle, nearly touching Samael
and Sherry.

"Be careful," Amanda cried.

She fell back in her seat as he accelerated right into them. Amanda
screamed.

"She's protected by the bike," John said.

He was right. She hadn't been harmed. But the bike headed toward the shoulder.

"But she'll fall off!"

He knows. He knows.

Amanda flew forward again, feeling pain in her chest from the belt as John slammed on the brakes. Samael stopped too. Sand kicked up and covered the windows. Amanda wasn't sure why they had both come to a complete stop. Until she saw this huge black flying machine with bright lights hovering over Samael's bike and their car. It reminded her of a UFO. There were some words from a megaphone. But as Samael skidded his bike along the freeway, swerving around the huge metallic onyx structure, John rocketed forward chasing him. And whatever words were being said by the flying machine, the sound stretched and faded as the chase resumed.

When the freeway horizon became flat, Samael's bike blurred. Amanda was pressed against her seat again. At this speed, the valleys and turns rushed by faster than Amanda had ever seen.

Amanda was thrown against her passenger door by a sudden turn. John was avoiding wreckage from a semi-truck that had been torn in half by the impact of Samael's bike. Then the other biker, the one that had spun out off the freeway, appeared again. It rode through the wreckage but then collided with a van up ahead.

There was an explosion. Sand and dirt blew over their windshield. Amanda felt the car bounce over rough road, and dust covered her window. Her ears rang from the noise. Then there was a plume of sand in the desert off to the side. And another geyser exploded right by her window. As she looked in her rearview mirror, desert sand mixed with flames lighting the dust as more explosions engulfed the highway behind them. Soon dust filled the sky and occluded the sun, making it dark.

John swerved around an SUV.

Another blast exploded ahead. This one rattled Samael's bike. The bike shook and looked like it was going to turn sideways. Samael recovered. Then he blurred into lights again, moving faster than ever. Way faster. John was losing them.

"We have to stop this now," John said. He searched the sky.

Far into the dusty sky Amanda spotted another black object.

"Hold on."

Oh, no. Not again.

John sped the car up even faster. The dust quickly cleared and the blue sky was suddenly completely clear. But mountains and valleys now passed her like cars. And in the midst of the mayhem, she wasn't sure why, she gazed down at the console. Then she stared at it. The digital clock read 3:45 in the afternoon. How! A few seconds later, it read 4:11. It had been nine in the morning just a minute ago.

A bridge that looked miles ahead blurred by in seconds. In the sunlight it was a quick flicker. At this speed, hills moved like cars, but the copter bombing stopped. They must have lost them. So why hadn't Samael done this before?

But then, even more oddly, the bike chase slowed. The colored lights faded. John's speedometer quickly dropped to only one-hundred-and-ninety miles an hour.

Samael was slowing down. Then, and this was really bizarre, Samael reached back with a knife and started cutting the ropes holding Sherry behind him. John gripped the wheel and his jaw clenched.

John rammed them. Samael was thrown like a cue ball, shimmying along the desert highway. But he recovered. Then he was back to cutting ropes behind him.

"Oh, no," Amanda said.

Sherry down, indeed. Samael was cutting her to let her go. Without a helmet and at this speed, Sherry would just die. And the devil wanted John to see it, just as Lilith had wanted her to see her friend shot in the head on the bridge.

The only thing merciful was the lack of traffic on the highway. But this was weird because more buildings were cropping up. It seemed like they were now approaching Phoenix.

Amanda saw a red streak appear by the driver's side window.

John's phone rang. The contact read "Hunter."

"Fall back, John," Rick said weakly on the car speakers. "Now. This is enough."

"She'll die if you knock him off," John said. "If you kill him now, she'll die."

"She's dead anyway. Fall back."

"No." John looked up again, searching the skies. "Tell them to leave."

A rope was cut. That left just one more holding Sherry to the bike. She clung to her jailor's back more tightly than ever. Her whole body now twisted and turned on the bike, struggling to stay on. John sped to the right shoulder and moved in front of Samael, slamming on the brakes. Samael simply swerved, now with Sherry barely holding on. John fell behind him again.

"She's gone," Rick said. "Forget it. Look up."

Amanda crouched forward and looked through the windshield. There seemed to be a swarm of black flying machines above.

"We're all dead anyway, then," John said.

"They won't let him get to Phoenix," Rick said. "After everything that happened in LA, they're not gonna let it go on today. I came to stop them from shooting you down. Now fall back, John. Fall back so you and Amanda don't die too."

Samael cut the last rope. Sherry's body was flapping against his bike. She was clutching as best she could to her kidnapper. The only thing allowing her to stay on was their slowing speed.

A bomb fell. This time it landed right in front of Samael. It forced him to swerve his bike, skidding along the road almost to a stop.

"Fall back now! Now, John!"

Amanda saw Rick's car grind to a halt, and his red car rushed backward.

Amanda was flung forward against her seat belt. There was a flash of light. Then she was thrown to the side. Then came a gust of wind and smoke against all the windows. Amanda felt the car spin, turn over, and start rolling. The earth and sky seemed to switch positions. Gusts of smoke and dirt covered the glass, but she saw the ground. It was flipping repeatedly around her. The car was rolling. Then more dust and smoke filled the windows until it grew dark. And then…silence.

She looked over at John. Behind him, through a dusty window, she saw the sky below them. The car was turned over upside down. He was closing his eyes tight. His shades were on the floor—or the ceiling. He looked unharmed. She looked at herself. No scratch on her either. And the car? There wasn't even a dent and the glass hadn't even cracked.

"Are you okay?" he asked.

For the first time in the chase, without the sunglasses, she saw his eyes. There was water around those bags. And his angel eyes were bloodshot. Behind his shades, he had been crying.

"Are you all right, Amanda? Amanda? Are you okay?"

Amanda couldn't answer.

John threw off his seat belt, curled up in a ball, and fell to the ground-ceiling. Then he threw the door open. She watched him, backward. He put a hand over his forehead and stared through the dirt and smoke. He stood there for the longest time, just staring, until the cloud of dust cleared. He was motionless, staring with naked eyes because…

Sherry was dead.

36

HE JUST NODDED

John drove Amanda home. After a crew of his secret police friends in black heaved his super car over, he just drove her home. Initially, he had gotten back on the highway and driven toward Phoenix, but then, per Amanda's request—the only time she said anything—he turned his car around. He was actually still going to take her to Scottsdale despite everything that had happened. She had just said three words. "Take me home."

She had never come for the interview. John had been right. She had come for him. Now solemn as hell, her guardian weirdly drove the speed of traffic on the freeway. That was so strange. But no one driving by thought anything was amiss. His car was filthy though, caked in dust. But there wasn't even a scratch.

Heading back to LA, he veered south and soon merged with Interstate Eight. She nodded to herself at that coincidence. This was near the place they had met.

She had seen his tears. But now, after finding his shades in the wreck, he was his usual self. Probably more so. Deadpan. Opaque.

"Rick said…" She was surprised at how loud her voice seemed. "He said you were going to ascend, but instead you came back for her. Why?"

He was fixed on the highway and didn't even turn. She expected to see him clench the wheel, the way she had seen him do so many times before when upset. He didn't. He just drove.

"Why? Why'd you do that, John? When you knew…she wouldn't make it?"

"I didn't know it would be Sherry. I thought it could be you."

She nodded and stared out the window. A car drove by along the desert freeway. Just a lady wearing sunglasses driving her white SUV on the freeway. Two kids were sitting in the back. Nothing special. They were just normal people driving on the highway.

That's what people do, right?

"I had to try," he added.

She squeezed his right hand, which was leaning on the arm rest. "I'm sorry."

"When you take me back," she said, shaking her long hair back, "you don't have to give me your number. Just take me home. Take me back to my friend Luane. You were right. I need to take care of my friend."

His eyebrows furrowed. But then he just nodded.

And then she cried. She turned to the car door, rolled up in a ball, stared at the infinite horizon of sands and weeds she so adored, and faced them. And just cried. She hated herself for it; the last thing she wanted was his sympathy, so she faced the window. But she couldn't stop. And she cried for him because she knew he wouldn't.

"I'm…sorry," she said. "I'm so sorry."

More silence. All she heard was the rumble of the engine.

"I'll give you my number," he said.

"I don't care, John. I'm not crying about that. I'm crying for you and Sherry."

He just nodded.

DONE WITH ROAD TRIPS

LUANE SLOWLY OPENED AN EYELID A CRACK AS AMANDA LAID A SMALL cactus on a table beside her bed. She intended to just sit in a recliner and let her sleep, but her friend stirred. Then she groaned. She had all those wires out of her face, but she still looked awful. And there was still a plastic wire connected to her arm.

It was bright in the room. The sun shone through the window.

Luane turned and gave a faint smile. "You're back. How'd your interview go, babe?"

"It didn't."

"Huh?" She opened her eyes wider. She tried to sit up, and Amanda rushed over to help her.

"Don't worry about me."

"What happened?"

"Got into a car accident."

"Another one! Oh my God, are you okay, Mands?"

"I'm fine." Amanda nodded. Then she pulled up a chair and sat down. "Don't worry. I finally got you a cactus." She forced a smile. "This one's from a gas station. The first one was so easy to come by, I don't know why. Now I had to get you this replacement. Anyway, while you don't have any men warming you, the spikes can remind you of Ben."

"Bitch," she said with a smile. "What happened, babe? You were so looking forward to your interview. Are you all right?"

"I'm fine. There'll be others. I told them what happened and they'll see if they can accommodate, but they've already rescheduled, you know. Anyway, don't worry, Lu. I wanted to come back for you. You're most important."

She squeezed Luane's hand and smiled again. But she couldn't help but feel like her grin was fake. She felt nothing happy about seeing her friend like this. Or thinking of everything that had happened.

"The doctor said you won't be here much longer," Amanda said. "And when you go home, you're gonna need someone to help you around our place."

Luane patted Amanda's hand.

"I love ya, babe," Lu said, nodding. "But I'll be able to take care of myself. Did you check our mail? Any news for me?"

"Nothing more yet."

"Maybe I'll get lucky like you. I just hope if I land one, it's nearby and not across the country. I don't want to go anywhere near a freeway after everything you've been telling me about."

"Me neither," Amanda said, dropping back into her chair. "I'm so done with road trips."

3 8

THE MAN WITH NO NAME

"WELL, WHAT CAN I SAY, GUYS? I'M AT IT AGAIN. ANOTHER ROAD TRIP." Amanda laughed. "You know Caligirl gettingold24 could only stay home for so long, guys. I fucking love the open road. Just now, I passed the familiar buildings of the Los Angeles skyline, heading into the empty highway, where the only company is an occasional ground squirrel or bird fluttering in the sparse bushes and trees. Not like home. No mountains, skyscrapers, or beachy sand. Actually, we just passed *a lot* of sand. I wanted to slide down it, it was a dune like snow, but grumpy wasn't in the mood.

"It's desolate as hell out here, and… I absolutely adore that. You know I'm freaky like that. Oh look. I just passed a tree. That was like the only tree for four miles, guys.

"How can I describe to you what I'm seeing? Let's give it a try… There's an ugly cream-colored one-story building with a red roof behind a gate. It's not long, so hold on a minute… There. It's gone. Now I'm rushing by a fence, and beyond are fluffy bushes scattered along dirt. Lots of that. These mangy dog-hairs along the sand are everywhere. Just scattered bushes like a mangy dog. I absolutely adore it.

"Here's what else I love. Comments to my show. I've got to thank my listeners…" She tore her eyes from the passenger window and reached into a pocket. She unfolded a sheet of paper. "DirkyJ. You said I have a sweet voice. You said you listen every time for a new show. Thanks, Dirk! Or Dirky. I'm so happy when one of my listeners likes my show. Jerrybutt12 said I'm a lot of fun. Well, I'm really not. But I like to talk a whole lot. I'm kinda boring, really—sans the death-defying road trips. Brittany501 said she loved the story about that shadow man in Colorado. She asked, "Did you find that shadow man again in Arizona?" Well, as a matter of fact—"

John turned from the road and stared at her through his shades. She held the microphone toward him. He shook his head.

Then she pushed her note back into her jeans pocket, undid her lap belt, threw her feet up on the dash, and laughed. When John turned but didn't say anything—'cause she knew he'd die if he was recorded—she laughed even harder.

"I haven't got my car back yet, you know, Brittany. It's still in a parking lot in Cincinnati. But, you know, someone had to drive me to my interview. Yeah, they rescheduled me. How fucking amazingly great is that? Right! And you guys know Luane is still recovering at home. Thank God, she's feeling better. So a lot of stuff is going well. But my new rental was totally totaled. So, how's a girl supposed to get to Phoenix? Hmm…John? What do you think?"

And he glared at her. "Erase that."

She clicked her recorder off and frowned.

"And put your seat belt on."

"No."

"You know you can't have people know about me," he said, staring back at the road. They were driving at a "normal" speed. That's why she had dared to take her seat belt off. Well that, and because she knew she could get a rise out of him.

"I told you in New York I don't like being told what to do," Amanda said.

"I'm not telling you what to do. This is for your safety."

"It's my life."

"Well, unveiling my name—"

"John, do you have any idea how many people are named John?"

"You can be so irritating," he said, shaking his head.

"Not as irritating as Sherry, I bet?"

Oops. That was so stupid. Why mention her? Idiot!

"I didn't mean that, John. Sorry."

"Just put your belt on," he said. And he actually smiled. "Actually, you're acting just like her. If anything, that's annoying me more."

"It still hurts. I know. Sorry." She rubbed his hand. "You sure you're up to stopping by her place?"

"I don't like the fact that no one's been looking after it. And it's really not her place. It's ours. It's owned under my name. I let her run it. I was happy for her to keep it and run it for us. She named the place, you know. It's called Angel Dive."

"Angel Dive?" Amanda said with a guffaw. "Are you joking? Angel Dive? That is so funny!"

He shook his head.

"That's really good," she said. "I love it. I love it a lot. It's funny, but true. *Angel Dive.*"

"Sherry was good with words like you, Amanda. You two were a lot alike. A bit too alike."

"So…" Amanda turned back to the window and stared at those bushes she'd called "soft" to her listeners. They weren't soft. They were soft from a distance but thorny as hell, like a cactus. Kind of the opposite of her lover. "So… You sure you're up to this? You could just drive North to Scottsdale and forget about it."

"If you're willing, I'd rather make a quick stop, Mandi. You and Rick said the place was a mess."

"I don't mind at all," she lied. She kept having images of Samael flash in her mind.

She kicked her feet over the dash again. One foot touched John's windshield. Of course, the inside of his car was immaculate and he noticed.

"Put your seat belt on," he said.

She fell back in the car seat. "Sorry. Didn't mean to touch your precious—"

"Forget it. Put your belt on for your safety. And wear your shades, please."

She reached for her belt. But when she thought of sunglasses, she felt her hand shake. "You don't think I'll need sunglasses again?"

"You're marked. You'll be marked the rest of your life. Lilith's and

Samael's vessels were destroyed, but they weren't. They'll be back, Amanda. I've killed them before. You can't kill evil. Unlike—"

He stopped talking and looked back at the road. She knew he was going to say *Sherry*. Then his hands gripped the wheel tight, like he used to when he was upset. She heard the click of her belt. She reached down for her bag, by her legs, and pulled out a pair of sunglasses. Then she rubbed John's arm again.

He went silent. John was always silent. Sometimes she hated it. Other times, she liked it, because it meant she was with him. Silence and mystery *was* John.

She pressed the play button of her small handheld recorder, hearing her voice… "*So, how's a girl supposed to get to Phoenix.*"

Click.

"There." She turned to him and said, "Erased."

"Thank you."

But she pressed record.

"What's his name. He's a man with no name. He doesn't want to be named, sorry. Nor does he want attention, unlike yours truly. He lurks in the shadows. Not scary, but in shadows. He's like a shade. To me, he's my protector. Anyway, I'm with him now, Brittany. Yeah. And I could never be happier.

"Brittany501, let me tell you 'bout him. He's…" She turned, studying him. "Dark, mysterious. He wears opaque sunglasses. You can't see behind them, like he's always trying to hide something. He's got on a matching black T-shirt and pants. Very dark. But he's got bulging muscles on his biceps." She laughed. "And strong pecs. Strong as hell. That's him. His hair is dark and short, but nicely groomed. Perfect. Handsome. His jaw and face are hard. He's got stubble. He's shaven, but he leaves it sort of unshaved across his face. And the five o'clock shadow is…perfect. But you can't see his eyes. You can't see them, and that's the greatest crime of all, even worse than the not-talking thing he does. Not blabbering is annoying enough to a girl like me, but not nearly as annoying as not looking into those eyes of his. He has the bluest, most lovely eyes on the planet. They're the opposite of his outer shell. They're the eyes of an angel."

Click.

Damn, that's so good.

"Amanda?"

"Yeah?" She took a big sigh. "What's up?"

"Erase that. That's worse than saying my name. You just described me."

She laughed. "God, I hate you, John."

He nodded and just kept driving.

"The hell I'm erasing that," she said. "No way. Sorry. It's way too good. But…thanks again for taking me to my interview."

"You're welcome."

"And I'm kissing you the minute we stop the car."

"Suit yourself."

"I don't think you'd let me do it while you're on duty, mister. You know, on the road. I really want to, but I don't think you'll let me do it when you're driving. So I won't try now."

"You never know. You could try."

Oh—okay.

39

ANGEL DIVE RETURN

As John turned into the parking lot, Amanda felt butterflies in her stomach. She didn't want to be here. She couldn't get images of that she-he devil out of her head. But she'd be there for John. She couldn't refuse him. He was driving her to her interview, after all. John seemed nervous too. She knew because she saw him gripping the wheel tightly again.

When he stopped the car in the dirt parking lot, she felt more dread than ever. The lot was vacant. Most of the windows were boarded up. And the roof on the left side was still charred from the fire. John sat for a moment and stared. Then he unlatched his belt, threw his car door open, as if he was fighting to get out, and came around the car to open the door for Amanda.

"Thanks," she said. He closed the door, staring again at the small one-story building.

He couldn't open the front door. So he heaved his shoulder into it. After a few crashes, the door flew open.

There was a gasp. It was Amanda's voice. The place was so clean. Not just clean, immaculate. Unlike last time, all the broken glass was gone. The walls were as she remembered, burgundy with pictures and silly stuff, but in perfect order. Nothing was damaged or even hung crooked. The empty stage was devoid of dust. And at the far end was the bar. In the dark, it was still charred, but all the glass had been taken off the counter and the floor had been swept. And all the wooden tables had the chairs turned over sitting neatly on them.

"What the hell," said a woman's voice behind the bar in the dark. "I'd love to know how the hell you got through that door. It's jammed. Anyway, scram. Place is closed." Then she gasped. "Oh my God. *John?*"

Amanda turned around and saw a light switch. She switched it on and the whole place lit up. And there Sherry stood, in a white T-shirt and jeans, behind the bar. But her wrinkled skin was parched and sunburned. Her eyes were bulging, staring at them.

She ran to him. They embraced tightly, kissing each other's lips.

"How are you here?" Amanda asked.

She looked at Amanda over his arms. It was so weird. It was as if Amanda were staring at herself in a mirror seeing John and herself in the future. She had the same long hair, but it was gray. Her skin was wrinkled. And with John's shades on, he could hide his age. It was exactly how she thought they'd look in a few decades.

"You brought him to me?" Sherry asked with a kind smile. "Thank you."

Amanda shook her head. Then she shut her mouth, realizing it was gaping open.

"How are you alive?" Amanda asked.

"After the explosion," she said, slowly moving out of John's embrace, "I was thrown from the bike."

"You didn't have a helmet."

"But the jerk slowed down to cut the ropes. Remember? I was traveling fast, but not fast enough. Apparently. I was thrown from the bike and away from the explosion. I mean, the accident was gnarly, but no broken bones."

"Rick didn't tell me," said John.

"He didn't know," Amanda said. Her voice echoed. It had been said at exactly the same time by Sherry. With the same voice.

"I figured you'd come by soon enough, John," Sherry said. "I was going to look for you, but you know you never gave me a way to contact you."

"I thought I was the only lucky girl with that problem," Amanda said.

"It's for safety," John explained to Amanda. Then he turned to Sherry. "Both of yours."

"Well, I've had time to get the place back in order," Sherry continued, looking around. Then everyone turned completely silent. They all looked at the diner together in uncomfortable silence.

"The place looks good, Sher," John finally said. He had lost his smile and Amanda almost laughed at his usual sternness.

"It damn well better," Sherry said, looking around again with a satisfied nod. "It took a lot of work. I don't know about the fire damage, though."

"I can get a crew to work on it," John said.

"Sure, John." Then Sherry gestured to Amanda. "Sure. Why's she here? I thought she was supposed to be safe in LA?"

"I have an interview," Amanda said.

Sherry squinted and nodded slowly.

Then there was more silence. And John, who had run into Sherry's embrace a second ago, was back to being Mr. Cool, standing back holding his hands in his jacket pockets. That almost made Amanda laugh.

"Let me have a word with her alone," Sherry said to John. "Please." Sherry gently hugged John again and kissed his cheek. "I've missed you."

"Thank God you're all right," John said, patting her back. "I'll be outside."

The two of them watched John leave.

After he closed the broken door behind him, Amanda could just see his silhouette in the parking lot through a broken board in the window. He stood there, kicking dust with his boot and looking out on the horizon toward Yuma.

Sherry's alive. So what does that mean for me?

Well, relationship is over, obviously, dummy.

Amanda felt sluggish. Slow. The air seemed to weigh down on her.

"What will it be, young-me?" Sherry asked behind the bar counter.

"Huh?"

Sherry picked up an empty beer glass and smirked at Amanda.

"I made my place a bar, Amanda," she said. "I love talking to patrons, serving them drinks and just talking. I love this place. So, come on. This time, I'll have a drink and talk to you."

Amanda walked to the counter and sat on a stool. Everything still felt slow.

Will we fight?

"I'd like—"

"Wait," Sherry said, closing her eyes and raising a finger. "Let me guess. Cider. Right? That's your favorite?"

"Yeah."

"Mine too."

Sherry filled a glass at the tap.

As Amanda waited, she felt more uneasy. She was beginning to hate this place. Seeing herself was creepy enough, but feeling creepy reminded her of the last time she was in this dump with Rick and Samael. Maybe that's who this lady had been all along? What if she was going to change into Samael and then start shooting at them? She handed her a drink with a smile. *No, not with that sweet smile.*

"I've been thinking," Amanda said, sipping the drink, "you know, since the kidnapping, that I wished we could talk. I think I was more upset, when we thought we had lost you, at the possibility that it would never happen. I'm glad we can do that now."

"Me too." Sherry raised her glass. Amanda clinked it with hers. Sherry sipped the drink staring at Amanda. "Cheers. This is prime stuff. Organic, with a touch of cinnamon. Right off the tap."

Amanda drank and smiled back.

Sherry pointed to John in the parking lot. They both looked over.

"He loves you."

"No, he loves you."

"He loves you. When I awoke in the sand realizing I was alive, I had a lot of walking in the desert heat to do. I thought about you and him. And us. That's why I want to talk to you now before I go."

"Where are you going?"

"He sleeps on his side. Do him a favor, keep something under the bed to cushion his fall or at least yank him to the center. He falls off the bed all the time, Amanda. And he won't brush his teeth. I know, it's really gross, but he just won't do it. So every night, lay the toothbrush by the sink. Hell, even put the damn toothpaste on it. He'll be away a lot. But he'll care for you to death. And go get him a dog. A nice furry brown one. It's not only for him. He will fight you to hell and back again on getting a dog, but I tell you now, get him one. He doesn't know how much he loves them until he has them. Our favorite dog was named Bear."

"Why are you telling me all this?"

"He can't be with me. We tried. Maybe I'm too damned old. Or I'm too old to put up with his shit. But really, it wasn't the same. I mean we love each other, but not in a romantic way anymore. All he has is fleeting memories of our love. You're not. You and he are real."

Amanda shook her head.

"He's been in love with you ever since he met you," Sherry said. "I can tell from the way he talked about you. When I was young, I was rash, quick tempered, but energetic like you. Fun. Alive. I was you. You're what I've wanted for John all along since he's been back. You're what we lost. And, whatever you want to call it, whatever you say, young-me, the only arrangement that will work with a twenty-something man is you."

Amanda shook her head again, harder.

"Don't screw this up," Sherry said, sipping some cider. "Not if you love him as much as I do. He needs the young version of me. I'm a fleeting memory, you're real and now. And you don't only love him, he loves you. Me? I'm family. You, he's in love with you, Amanda."

"You can't keep sacrificing like this!" Amanda cried, jumping up from the stool. She surprised herself with her rage. "You and he keep doing this! That was the other thing I was going to say. You had no right to throw me in the car! He loves *you*. Not me. Look at the way you just kissed each other."

"Only one person could fit in his cursed car. I told you in my truck only one of us would make it. He didn't protect you across the country for nothing. He's not a nice guy, Amanda. He did it for you. Not me."

"Call me Mandi. And you know him far better than I do. You just told me all his secrets."

"Not all of them."

"I don't want this," Amanda snapped, shaking her head and pushing the drink across the counter. "I'm sorry, I'll let him drive me to my interview. Then I'm done. I can fly back home. He can come back to you."

"Who's sacrificing now?"

Shit, we are fighting.

But Sherry seemed to realize it too. She heaved a sigh, drank some cider, and looked away from Amanda, just staring at the empty stage. Then she nodded. Amanda stared at a red wall.

"Okay," Sherry finally said, "I'll try it another way. What interview are you going to, Mandi? Is it a job for a newspaper? I wanted to be a reporter too. I was working on that path right before I lost him."

"So?" Amanda put her hands on her hips, fuming.

Sherry frowned. Then she lifted an eyebrow and repeated, "So. We are the same person. And I think I know why."

"Yeah? Why?"

"Maybe I should get you another drink."

"Just tell me."

"Who's your parents?" Sherry asked.

"I was adopted."

Sherry shrugged.

"So?"

"Why don't you sit down?"

With the hand holding her drink, Sherry pointed outside, through cracks in the boards, at John. "John and I didn't connect only once after the accident. We connected twice. One time was shortly after he died—or I thought he had died. When he became an archangel. Did he tell you why he didn't see me until I'd aged so much?"

"Rick said something about it taking that long for him to return to Earth as an archangel."

Sherry shook her head. "It was instant. When he was first changed, I saw him a week or two later in LA. I had searched for him. I shouldn't have, but I did. Only he didn't remember who I was. It took a while for him to recall. The minute he changed, his past was erased. He had only fleeting memories, like he does now. So I did what you did. I hung out with him on my own little adventures. With his new position, like you, it put my life in jeopardy. Then I ended up on one of those cursed chases.

In that damned magic car. And it was that cursed car that took my John from me."

"I don't understand."

"Do you know what happens when you travel fast?" Sherry asked. "I mean, really, really fast? Einstein stuff?"

Amanda shook her head. But she recalled the clock in the car.

"John had to accelerate to a speed that pushed his car to the limit during that last chase. He had to do it in order to save me. I remember. It was horrible. But I also remember the car rocketing across the country in seconds. The car went so fast that John couldn't control it. I had escaped the crash—or so I thought, until John talked about you. When I saw him reappear, it was a few years ago. Decades later since the accident. I had lost him." She shook her head and took a deep breath. Then she gazed at him through the window again. "I waited so long." She shook her head. "Here." She smiled ruefully at Amanda. "I never expected him to return. But, more so, I never expected you to appear too. We must have been split. One of me remained behind at the accident, the other traveled into the future. But...it's just a theory."

"I don't get it."

"Or you don't want to. You're me. You know it. But you're me decades ago. We were split by the car's jump. That's what I think happened."

"That's nuts. That would mean...all sorts of things I remember never happened in my life. But they did. I remember everything about when I was a little girl."

"Who knows from the jump," Sherry said with a shrug. "You might have somehow lived a regular life. Or the angels covered things up in your mind. There's so much we don't understand about any of their mysteries. Shit, John doesn't even know half the stuff he does as an angel. He doesn't get how that car does the stuff it does. He just knows that what he does is good."

"He thinks what he does is bad."

"He is bad." Sherry laughed. "He's real bad, Amanda. You know that. That's why you love him so much, like I do."

"He's an angel," Amanda said, shaking her head.

"He's that too." She heaved a sigh. Then she shook out her long gray hair and gestured to him. "Maybe that makes him the greatest angel of all."

"You believe John is an angel?"

She nodded.

"No, I mean, a *real* angel?"

Sherry paused. She drank some cider and looked up at the ceiling. Amanda had just wanted a quick yes or no.

"He's told me their theory. Actually, it's beautiful. The idea that we're all angels and that some are bound for heaven early. It kinda makes everyone and everything good. Even if it's not that way, even if it's somehow something else, I believe what's really out there is beautiful like that."

"I'm not so sure." Amanda sat on the bar stool. She picked up her cider again.

"Yes, I believe in angels," Sherry said with a wink. "You know why? When John made that final jump, I thought I was going to die. When we crashed, I saw a light. It shone brighter than the sun—much brighter than the light from the jumps—flooding the car, shadowing John and blotting out everything through the window. I thought it meant death. At first, it terrified me. But it was more than just light. It was brighter than the sun. And with it came a sense of such calm and ease. A feeling that no matter what's happening in this world, there will always be peace. That's beautiful too. It means that even the demons John chases are not important. It means even the devils and their evil is nothing. Even death itself is meaningless. This ride we call life ends in a chase and departure from our world, I think, a departure into that wonderful light." She shrugged. "So ever since then, yeah, I've believed very strongly in angels and God. That's the good I got from all the pain of losing him. I only see that light. All the bad does is shade us from the light of God."

And Sherry raised her glass to that and drank some more. Then she laughed. "How about you? Do you believe in angels?"

"How can I not after all that's happened."

Sherry laughed and nodded. And Amanda laughed with her.

Sherry gestured to him again. "Go to him. He won't smile. He won't nod. He'll brood. Because he's John. But inside, he's got a bigger heart than both of us. And you'll make him happy."

"It's up to him."

"Hmm, it's really not." She sipped some cider. Then she looked right into Amanda's eyes. "It's up to you. I made my decision after our recent fight in the desert. John did when he met you. Believe me, I know him." Sherry smiled. "But it will make me happy. 'Cause, Mandi, you're finally gonna make *our* John happy."

40

MY REAL NAME

"Tony," John said, his hands deep in his jeans pockets. His eyes behind shades. He had been staring out toward the empty horizon on the desert. With his usual expressionless face. She wasn't even sure he knew she was walking up to him. "Tony's my real name, Amanda. I saw it in the deed for our place from her will."

"You want me to call you Tony, John?"

John shook his head. He turned away from Yuma and looked at her through his shades.

"She wants you to leave her for me," Amanda said.

John shook his head again. He gently took her in his arms. But then John looked over her shoulder toward Angel Dive.

Amanda turned.

Sherry stood leaning against the doorway and folding her arms, just watching them. That reminded Amanda of when she'd watched the two of them embrace when they had first entered the diner. Then she remembered the jealousy. That made her step back. But she still held his hand. And she felt him squeeze her hand tighter.

"The name's Tony," John hollered. "I saw it in the deed, Sher. Tony Lorenziano. I didn't know I was Italian."

Sherry just shrugged. Then she leaned back against the doorway.

"She never tells me a thing," John said quietly to Amanda. He removed his sunglasses and turned to her with those angel eyes. "Not a single thing. She was worried the past would hurt me because I couldn't go back. She was right. It does. I don't like being here. But I can't stay away."

"You're going with her after leaving this joint," Sherry cried out. "But the agreement includes visiting rights, John. You don't want to give me your fucking number, you better visit."

"Are you doing okay?" he asked Amanda.

"You're always asking me that."

"Are you?"

"She just told me I'm her," Amanda said with a shrug. "I *almost* believe her."

"Yeah," John said. "I've been trying to deal with it since we first met. But you act, look, and sound exactly like her." He ran a finger along her cheek. "I think she's right. I think you are her."

"She's wrong," Amanda said, shaking her head. "I remember everything from my entire life. I'm not her. What about Luane? And others I know? Hell, Mom and Dad. My entire childhood. I've known it all for years."

"They say there's a twin somewhere in this world for everyone. I don't know."

"Yeah, well, I…don't believe it." She sighed. Then she looked down. "What are we going to do?"

He gently lifted her chin and gazed at her with his naked eyes. "You've got an interview."

"Why don't you lovebirds fucking kiss each other and then get the fuck out of here!" cried Sherry, laughing heartily. "Don't worry, I'll see you back in another week, John. Don't think you won't need your next counseling session, especially hanging with me."

"Fuck off, Sher."

He put on his shades. Then he turned to Amanda and said more quietly, "Let's go."

But Amanda let go of John's hand and ran back to the diner. Sherry flashed that tranquil smile she always gave Amanda as she approached. Then she hugged her.

"Goodbye, older-me," Amanda said.

"Goodbye, Mandi. Take care of him, okay? Take care of him for me. And take care of yourself."

"I love him."

"I love him too."

CONSUMMATE SANCTUARY

JOHN GAZED AT A BIRD SOARING HIGH AND HOVERING OVER HIM OUT ON the horizon. It flew down three hundred feet and quickly glided over a basin of rocks and bushes toward the horizon. The horizon was splashed a red violet as the sun was dipping down. He gazed out enjoying the view of red and violet. Beautiful.

"Angel Down," said Rick through his cell phone. "Faith. Twenty-four. An English major. Born Scorpio. She lives in Little Rock. She's traveling to a funeral in El Paso. Where you at?"

"Not far from there."

"You're still on leave," Rick said on the other end. "Intelligence tells us you've got another day before Lilith intercepts her. Leave's over."

"I'll be there."

"Hi, Rick!"

John jumped back and glared at Amanda through his shades. Amanda laughed. And seeing how serious he looked, she couldn't stop laughing.

"What the hell?" asked Rick on the line. "Is that Sherry? Or… Amanda! Who the fuck is that? What's she doing with you?"

"I'm taking Amanda to her interview."

"Oh, fuck off, John. That's the same bullshit excuse she gave me."

"Are you feeling better?" Amanda asked, leaning over the phone.

John jerked his cell phone from her again. Then he walked to the far side of the cliff. He put the phone back against his ear. But Amanda was right behind him.

"Take her home, John," Rick said with a sigh.

"Sure."

"I mean it."

"After her interview."

"Fuck the interview. Now that Sherry's back and things are back to normal, you can get back to work."

"You said tomorrow. She'll drive me in the car to Scottsdale tonight. Then I'll help her get back home to LA after her interview. *Then* I'll take care of the one who's marked."

"Fine. Just get rid of her."

"We can't get rid of Lilith."

"I'm not talking about Lilith. Hey, wait a minute! What the hell do you mean, *she'll drive the car*."

John hung up the phone.

He was surprised to feel Amanda take him into her arms. He turned and they kissed. He felt her body close. Their tongues danced. Then they both turned to the amazing view of the valley. The sun fell below the horizon and twilight shone forth.

"You're right, John," Amanda said, leaning on his shoulder. "This place is breathtaking."

"More breathtaking with you."

THE END

HAUNTING JOY

Alec thought he had found peace in a secluded haunted manor, but instead, he discovered Joy, a woman tied to a tragic past. As they uncover dark secrets, the couple faces choices that could save or destroy their future together.

1

PLYMOUTH CREST

A LEC FELT A LIGHTER STEP TO HIS STRIDE THAT HE HARDLY RECOGNIZED —it was not the cadence of his stride that felt new, but the feeling that went with it, deep inside. A feeling in his chest that he hadn't felt in such a long, long time. As he walked up the narrow path on the woodsy hillside, the tree trunks surrounded in lovely green thrush, he cherished this sensation. Chip, his best friend and realtor, walked beside him. Despite wearing a pressed navy-blue suit and carrying a leather brief-case, Chip seemed relaxed too. Because they knew what this feeling was all about. After months of searching, they had finally found the house.

The façade of the large structure had wood siding, painted white, and grand glass cottage windows. An ultra-modern roof was constructed at a single slope. Between big windows were assorted black and gray granite stones. And a concrete path, meandering amid leaves and bushes and more towering, thick-trunked trees, rose from the large dirt driveway. Weeds grew through the cracks in the pavement, particu-larly in the steps leading to the front door. The house was old. No matter. This was the same dream house he had seen in pictures on his computer. Here under the glistening bright sunrays, it felt so inviting. And looking back over his shoulder, he had the perfect view of the lake down the woodsy hillside.

Chip jostled keys by the front door.

"It was built in the nineties," Chip said with a shrug. "I know you wanted something new, Alec, but this is a very modern home, ahead of its time—despite the window frames. Windows are everywhere, and you told me how important that open feeling was to you. Honestly, the builder seemed to have the same taste as you. You could always remodel the windows and replace all the walls with glass, I suppose."

"It's all wonderful. Exactly as I pictured it."

"Yeah, well," Chip said with a chuckle, opening the door, "wait till you see inside, man."

"You said the owner was a filmmaker?"

"The original owner. He was some producer, or Hollywood agent, or something like that. Richer than *sh*…well you know. He had to be to build this mansion. But no one has lived in the house for years."

"You can say *richer than shit* to me, Chip."

"Not today, man," he said, hitting Alec's shoulder. "Today I'm your realtor."

"But I found the listing."

Chip frowned. But then he managed to regain his smile as he opened the door. He turned on a light switch and then gestured with a sweeping arm. They stood together in awe, gawking. The polished alabaster stone flooring blended into white carpet, heralding the true masterpiece of the house: a super spacious central living room. Alec ran his fingers through his dark beard, shaking his head. It was devoid of furniture, making an already expansive area seem huge.

Alec walked into the living room and gazed up. Here, an indoor balcony circled around upstairs. It was a grand design he had seen in hotels and restaurants, but never in a home. The effect in this central room with a tall, vaulted ceiling over an indoor balcony was one of elegance and opulence, something very different from the surrounding forest. But the strangest thing was that, though it was evidently designed to feel open, groups of maple trees with thick trunks and full green foliage came close to the windows, creating a confined feeling. But that was wonderful too, because it made the home feel cozy. He could already imagine starting up the central fireplace, sipping some tea, and writing as it snowed outside.

"Large enough for a party," Alec quipped.

"That's the last thing I thought you'd say," Chip said with a laugh. "I thought you were looking for peace and quiet?"

"Just saying."

"Too bad it wasn't available back in the days, huh, Alec?"

Alec nodded. He took a deep breath and shook his head. A cold gust blew across his cheek from the still-open door, but something felt a little strange about it. For some reason, when he turned, he almost expected to see someone standing by the door watching them.

"Come on," Chip said. "Let me show you around. You've gotta see the kitchen. It looks brand new, immaculate, like it was hardly ever used."

"It's better than this?"

"Look, you can just sign the papers now if you want to," Chip quipped with a laugh. "Don't act so desperate, man. We still have to get you a good deal."

"How come everything is so clean? You said it's been unoccupied for years? I hardly see any dust."

"The owner's probably been looking over the place from time to time. All the old ratty furniture was recently sold, I hear. They probably cleaned the place up for us for the sale. It's an investment."

Alec followed Chip across the living room, under the mezzanine, and into a kitchen. The kitchen was empty, but there were silver stoves and ovens with a large central island. Expensive looking appliances, of course—no doubt the reason his friend wanted to show him.

"Viking stoves," Chip said. "Stainless steel ovens. Subzero fridge. Not sure it'll do much for your bachelor-self, but it's pretty top rate."

"My daughter cooks. She can use all of this when she visits. As long as I have a toaster, I can make do." Then Alec shook his head. "Wow. But…yeah, this kitchen doesn't look used at all. None of the place looks like it was ever used."

"I'm thinking it was constructed and then forgotten. You know, there's not many *yous* looking to live in the middle of nowhere—like totally in the middle of nowhere, man. When was the last time we saw someone on the road? If quiet is what you were asking for, this is the place. Come on. I got one more thing to show you that will blow your mind. Wait till you see this. When I saw it, all I was thinking is that this is what you were asking for in your early retirement home, you old fart."

"I'm the same age as you, Chip."

"Sure, well, some of us ain't lucky enough to enjoy retirement before fifty."

As they walked across the second-story balcony, Alec ran his hand along the wooden rail. Again, no dust. That was unsettling. Despite no furniture, the place looked like it was in pristine condition. Sure, Chip had said it was probably cleaned up after the furniture was moved, but Chip had also told Alec that it was cleaned out over nine months ago. Everything in the home was totally immaculate, a mystery his best friend, an all-too-inexperienced realtor, wasn't too concerned about. No, his friend seemed way too excited to really be concerned about anything.

As they approached the stairs, Alec felt another chill in the air. The source seemed to be the front door, but now the door was closed.

There was a Spanish feel to the hallways. It wasn't just the indoor balcony, the hallways were arched. Still, all the walls were painted colonial white.

They walked around the upstairs floor as Alec gazed down at the expansive room below. Then they surveyed four bedrooms and two bathrooms that felt extraordinarily ordinary. There was nothing wrong with that. The rooms were large with decent closets and, again, all were very clean.

"Enough of the small stuff," Chip said. "You have got to see this."

Alec followed Chip past a glass window overlooking the woodsy outdoors, and then into the largest room in the house. This was the master bedroom, spanning the entire front of the home. It was a huge room with a fireplace, a small sunken section in a corner, and, of course, walled by windows. But Chip ignored all of that, walking straight across the room to a glass door.

Alec trailed his friend outside onto a very large cement terrace. The outdoor balcony was similar to the indoor, spanning the front yard and then continuing over the side yard. It was spacious and very wide, but also a little unnerving with only a shallow wall separating a ledge from a sheer drop down the hillside. The side yard, to his right, was full of more trees surrounding a small cement patio. But it was the over-look in the front that his friend had, no doubt, wanted him to see. Far down the woodsy hillside was a gorgeous view of the lake. And now, with clear skies, yellow light sparkled golden on the large body of water.

Alec took a deep breath, taking in the fresh nutty and woodsy scent of the surrounding maple trees. He gazed up, and a hawk hovered amongst wisps of white clouds in an otherwise clear azure sky. He followed the large bird as it swooped down, passing over the green foliage. Then he lost the bird in the trees near the shore.

He was surprised to spot a stranger standing by the water. She wore a draping black shawl that hung down almost to her feet. The lady crouched down on her knees by the water, seemingly staring down at her own reflection. When she rose, she picked up a stone and tossed it into the water. Then she just cradled herself in her arms, looking out at the lake, seemingly in as much wonder as he was.

"So, what'dya think?"

"Huh?" Alec whirled around. "Oh. Yeah." He nodded to his friend, who stood near the short cement wall, admiring the lake too.

"Figured you could write here," Chip said.

"I bet you did," Alec said with a laugh. "So…what's the catch?"

"Well, it's the most expensive place I've shown you. And you asked for a place in the woods, but not this far from town. This is very, very, very far from nowhere. There's just a gas station and store along the road. That's about a five-minute drive down the hill. Your hill. The closest real town around here is called Badger. We drove past Badger too. I doubt you noticed. It was like two blocks long and is about twenty minutes south of here. I caught a few buildings and a Walmart. Not much else. So, I guess, if you don't mind stocking up and truly living like a hermit in frigid snow, this place should suit you fine."

"What's the deal with the place being vacant for so many years?"

"I don't know, but I wouldn't worry. If you like the place, its past vacancy shouldn't be a problem. Take it as an added bonus. Nobody lives here, Alec. Nobody. That's why it's priced so low, I figure."

"It's the best place we've seen. But a bit too nice and affordable."

"You're always suspicious. Don't worry, man. I'll dot the i's and cross the t's before we enter escrow. That is…*if* you want me to start escrow?"

"I'll take it," Alec said. But then he shook his head. "If the seller keeps the asking price. I can't afford what this place is probably really worth. I love it, but…something feels off. Maybe it's too good to be true?"

"Because you always worry," Chip said with a larger grin. Then he put an arm on his shoulder. "I'll get you the deal, maybe even slash a bit off the selling price. You wanted a place to rest by a lake. Right? To write? Even added a nice view, didn't I? Well, voilà, your Shangri-la awaits, sir."

"I found the place, Chip."

Chip lost his smile.

"Of course, I love it," Alec said with a chuckle, hitting his friend's shoulder. "Make the deal and I'm in."

Chip regained his grin. Then he gazed back out at the view, shaking his head.

Alec felt a cold breeze brush over his shoulder again. It seemed to be coming from the lake. The stranger far below in her shawl was still kneeling over the water. It was like she was still gazing at her own reflection, and under the sunlight reflected off the lake, her whole body seemed to shimmer.

"It sure is a nice view," said Chip.

Alec smirked at his friend. But then he startled when he gazed back down. The lady by the lake had disappeared.

2

IT WAS PRETTY ENOUGH GREEN

ALEC SPENT HIS FIRST DAY WALKING DOWN THE HILLSIDE, SKIDDING THIS way and that over leaves and mud, around thick tree trunks, all the way down until he landed by a two-lane road. Although the leaves were everywhere, the trees were sparse enough for him to move around them and use the trunks as breaks in his descent. And he hadn't been the first to do this. There were lines and gaps between the bushes likely made by prior hikers. His descent took about forty minutes. He could have made it down a lot faster—maybe in twenty—walking down a larger manmade trail, but he preferred taking his time scaling down the less trodden paths.

The lake was across the two-lane road by the base of the hill. But Alec wasn't heading to the lake, he wanted to visit Plymouth Hill. Beside him, along the road, a sign read "Plymouth Hill, two miles." No matter, he'd enjoy continuing to walk.

What a walk it was. There was that wonderful maple tree scent. And so little noise. Not a car passed. That was probably because the only turn toward the main road ended at the top of the hill by his house. Still, this two-lane road was considered a state "highway." All he heard was an occasional bird chirping or squirrel rustling in the leaves. Chip had told him that the best time of year was fall, when all the leaves would turn red and yellow. It was pretty enough green.

After passing a canopy of trees arching over the main road like a tunnel of green, he finally saw the "town." But, just as his friend had said, Plymouth Hill was just a few buildings with wood shingle roofs along the road.

Alec headed to the largest building, across from the gas station. Over a red wood-paneled wall read "Corner Store."

As he opened the screen door, the bell jingled. At the sales counter, a middle-aged woman with long, curly red hair, wearing a very long, baggy dress, thumbed through her cellphone. She had a distinctive black half-circle symbol on her forehead.

"Morning," the woman said. "Vacationing? There's a small supply shop for boats and oars down the street—for the lake. Just ask Knoll at the gas station if you're here to go rowing or fishing. You can rent boats and oars from him. He even has fishing rods if you're an angler."

"I'm not vacationing. I'm staying."

Alec browsed a food aisle. There were various chips, candy, and gum. Not a whole lot of stuff other than snacks. He should have stocked up more food before his move.

At the far back of the store was a weird, eclectic section. This area was the most unique, reminding him of a magic shop. Here a large dark blue cloth with stars and moons was draped on the wall. And on two tables against the wall were various crystals, candles, and books.

"Stranger turning native?" the cashier asked. "You kiddin' me? I don't believe it. You know, there's only like ten of us in this whole damned town." She laughed. "Where you from?"

"L.A."

"L.A.? You went two thousand miles to live in the middle of nowhere?"

Alec returned to the food aisle and snatched a bag of salami, checking the expiration date. He shrugged.

"You're really moving here?"

"Yep. Up the hill."

"You're shacking up on Plymouth Crest!" she asked, laughing more than ever. He couldn't help but laugh too. "You're joking, right? That place has been vacant all my life."

"It's a great house."

"I thought maybe you were moving to Badger. You're really living up on Plymouth Crest? I don't believe it."

Alec nodded. He picked up a bag of plastic plates. It was then he realized there weren't any baskets, so he stacked the salami and a bag of chips on paper plates and laid it on the main counter

"Your store's close enough," he said with a grin.

But her mouth still gaped open, staring at him. That made him laugh again.

"My house is called Plymouth Crest?" he asked.

"The hill is called Plymouth Crest. Your house is called an abomination. It doesn't fit. Kind of like you." She raised a hand. "No offense. I just mean it's misplaced, you know. The house is as if some owner built a home in a city and plopped it down on our hill. People like climbing to the top just to dare themselves to go inside. They're afraid, 'cause it's said to be haunted, but they dare themselves to venture in anyway. I've been inside a few times. The house is beautiful, of course, but all the stuff inside looks spooky—chairs, tables—they're all ratty and decayed. Last time I was there, the lights turned on fine. Me and my friends were so impressed, being the place is so old. But watch out. People, especially kids from out of town, love to camp around there just to dare themselves to go in. Just to dare, you know. So don't freak out if drifters end up on your doorstep."

"That's creepy. You've been inside?"

"Sure…" She suddenly looked guilty. "Years ago. When the doors aren't locked. Everyone in town has been inside Plymouth Crest. It's open to visitors more often than you'd think. But you seem normal enough. A tall, dark, and handsome man from Hollywood, huh?" She smirked. "Short dark hair, blue eyes. You're cute."

"Thanks," Alec said, feeling taken aback. "But I'm not from Hollywood. I lived in the valley."

"Same thing. Can I help you get settled in? Most supplies around here are from Badger, but I've got a lot more here than it looks like. And I can order things too. It's about time someone decided to live up on that hill. No one's lived there for years."

"I just need food. I thought there'd be a market here."

"*A market in Plymouth Hill!?*" she said, slapping the counter with her palm, laughing harder than ever. "*A market?* You're funny, mister. Well, meet Plymouth Hill's market. Me. There's a Walmart in Badger. But I get plenty of business from drifters thinking the same thing you just did. And the main road here brings plenty of strangers. I thought you were just driving by like them. So…what do you do for a living, if you don't mind me asking? And what's your name?"

"I'm a writer," he said, grabbing a box of toothpicks by the front counter. "Name's Alec."

"A writer? But writers do other stuff, don't they?"

"I used to work as an accountant. I wrote on the side and then retired. Came here for peace and quiet."

That sent her barreling into laughter all over again.

"What's so funny?" he asked, chuckling too.

"Quiet? We sure have quiet. Sure have that: no people, but loads of quiet. You know, there's just a handful of homes across the street. I live here. Well, I suppose we're neighbors now. Wow. Pleasure to meet you, Alec. Far out. And you're living up on Plymouth Crest? I don't believe it. If you need anything, anything, just holler. We all help each other in this boring town, especially 'round winter."

"I heard winters can get rough."

"They sure can. The elevation is high up here in the mountains. You can get snowed in with more than ten feet of snow for a week or two during a rough storm. Ever see *The Shining*? A few people go nutso like that. That's probably what keeps your place vacant. At least I'm by the road, so I talk to people vacationing around here all the time. A while ago, I knew a gentleman who lived at that house for only a few months. He left the place once the snow arrived. I've always guessed he got cabin fever. But don't worry. Cabin fever is all in the mind. No need to worry if you're sane. But also pretty cold winds can whip up, particularly around your house. Well, welcome, Alec. Welcome. Welcome to our quaint town of Plymouth Hill. You've come to the right place, I guess, if you were looking for nothing to do."

She put everything in a paper bag and handed it to him.

"Thanks."

"Hey, you want me to help you bring the stuff up to your house?" she asked, raising her brow. "I haven't been up to Plymouth Crest in so long. We can send it by 'Daisie's delivery service.'"

"What's 'Daisie's delivery service'?"

"That's my name. I'm Daisie."

"That's okay," Alec said with a laugh. "What's that symbol on your forehead?"

"It's a half-moon. Do you like it?"

He shrugged.

"I'm a witch. Don't worry, I'm a good witch. I'd be more worried about ghosts. And our winters. And cabin fever. But it didn't stop you from buying the place, did it? A woman died up there almost two decades ago, you know. She was from Hollywood too. Her name was —" Daisie put a finger to her chin and looked up for a moment. Then she shook her head. "Can't remember. She was some singer star turned actress that even made a few movies before moving here. Maybe trying to retire in peace and quiet? She and her lover probably went looney. Well, it's an old story I heard about when my parents moved here when I was, like, twelve. Me and my friends went up there quite often when I went to school in Badger. We wanted to see the ghost. Not much to do around Badger otherwise, as you can imagine. The haunting didn't stop you from buying the place?"

"Nope."

"I really love that, Alec. I really do. You're gutsy. You'd make a good warlock. Maybe I'll show you some magic one day. We can meet up in that house and do some rituals." And she winked.

"I don't believe in witches," he said with a chuckle.

"Yeah? But you believe in ghosts?"

3

THE APPLE THIEF

With the sun's rays shining between the green leaves of the trees surrounding the windows of his glass house, Plymouth Crest was enchanting. Gilded light shone through the leaves and branches creating yellow prism-like effects. And with all the green moss and thrush, it was enchanting—as if Alec lived in an English fae forest or Camelot, which he loved as a writer.

That was what happened during the day. But upon nightfall, all those large windows turned black. And then those same leaves and branches that covered the sunrays blocked moonlight. Then his house became very dark.

But not so quiet…

By the second week, he started hearing noises. At first, it was just stray creaks and cracks from the wood, and Alec figured it was simply the sound of an old foundation. But as time passed, he heard unexplainable things. Stray shouts and screams that sounded as if they were coming from the terrace outside. Doors opening and slamming shut downstairs. Kitchen cabinets left open. Plates and glasses being rearranged on the kitchen table. Doors left open all night. One morning, he even found the couch in the living room had been moved a couple feet. That was the creepiest. On yet another night, he awoke shivering. The glass balcony door of his bedroom was wide open. He was certain he had locked it.

As days passed, the noises only grew louder. One night a wooden chair tipped over downstairs in the dining room. Then another night, a plant was thrown from one of his tall cabinets in the foyer into the living room.

He began to not sleep. He didn't believe in ghosts, but he couldn't deny the noises.

Tonight, for hours, he had just stared at the white ceiling over his bed in silence. He had stared long enough for his eyes to adjust to the darkness. And after a while, the darkness made the faint moonlight that shone through openings in his dark mahogany velvet curtains seem bright.

His body jumped. His muscles reacted mechanically before he recognized the noise. It was glass shattering. Something had broken into pieces downstairs. It was so loud that he leapt out of bed and his hands scrambled along the walls to switch on the light. But the light wouldn't switch on. That was weird because his old clock on the nightstand still read one-thirty-two in red digital letters, and the clock didn't have back-up power. Electricity was another quirky thing about his house.

He opened the drawer in his nightstand by the bed. In his old house, he had always left a small flashlight by the bed. But the flashlight wasn't there. It was probably still in one of the boxes in the garage. And he had left his cellphone downstairs.

There was more opening and closing of cabinets and drawers. This time, it wasn't just stray noises, it seemed to be every few seconds. This didn't sound like the usual cracks and creaks of some phantom haunting his place. He was worried there was an actual intruder.

He rushed along the inner balcony. Most of his downstairs could be seen from here, but his furniture—his couch, end table, and chairs—were cast in shadows by moonlight.

"Who's down there?" Alec cried. "Show yourself."

He was answered by another crash. That made him move faster, darting across his dark, empty living room and running straight to the source of the noise—in the kitchen.

He was wearing only underwear and felt a breeze before seeing the open kitchen door. After doors being left open frequently over the past week, he was sure he had checked the lock on this door before going to bed. He rushed over to shut it.

"Sorry, I didn't realize anyone was home."

Alec whirled around. That made the intruder on the other side of the kitchen island cover her mouth and snicker.

He rushed over to turn on the kitchen light switch, but, oddly, it did not just turn on the kitchen lights, it switched on the digital display on the oven and the toaster and re-started a hum from the refrigerator. It's as if the light switch restarted the power in the whole house. And under the bright kitchen lights, Alec could now clearly discern a young lady, in her mid-twenties, leaning against the island. She had long dark hair and almond-shaped eyes. Her face was strikingly pretty. Beside her bare feet was a shattered glass cup—the glass that she must have broken. Being shoeless under her navy blue snow coat with a fur-lined collar was strange. And she held a red apple in her hand—which she had stolen from his grocery bag, no doubt. Her mouth was curled in an amused smirk.

They stared at one another. Then she drew the apple up to her nose.

"What are you doing here?" Alec snapped.

"Eating an apple."

"No, what are you doing in my house?"

"Door was open," she said with a shrug. "Sorry about the glass." And then she chuckled again, looking down at the shattered glass by her toes. "Have to be careful where I step now, I guess."

"Miss, this is private property."

She furrowed her brow and stared again, seeming to study him. Then her lips curled into that same amused smile. He wasn't sure what was so funny.

"Do I need to call the police?"

"Sheriff Denson?" she asked, bursting into laughter. "Are you fricken' kiddin' me? Denson can barely keep his pants on without suspenders. Speaking of pants."

She pointed an index finger at his body. It was then he remembered he was only wearing underwear. That made him angrier.

"I live here, miss! You're trespassing in my house."

"Aha," she said and turned her back on him. But she cocked her head back to catch a glimpse of his body.

"Gee-whiz," she said, sniffing her apple again, "I mean, I didn't think anybody stopped by this place anymore. I never had to worry about strangers before. I'm here all the time." She shrugged her shoulders. "You know, I roam—"

"In the middle of the night!"

"Hey, watch your tone, mister. I think you need to calm the hell down."

"Calm down? You're breaking into my house!"

"I'm not breaking into your house. There's never anyone here, I tell you. And the door was open. Okay already?"

She carefully stepped around the shards of broken glass. Then she roamed about the kitchen, picking up a decorative tray on the island and then a fake flower assortment. Examining everything. It was like she was inspecting the room. Then she opened a drawer and picked up a silver fork and knife. She opened a cabinet over one of the stoves and thumbed through more glasses.

"I sure like what you've done with the place," she said. "Not much different than what I would have done, I'd bet. You have really good taste."

"You scared the hell out of me."

"Man, I said sorry. You scared me too. Okay?"

She turned and faced him. They locked eyes again, and with her smirk, Alec had the sense that she was going to laugh in his face again.

"This is my house. You have to leave. Get the hell out or I'm calling the cops."

"Wow, you sure can be rude," she said, raising her hand. "Fine. Like I said, I didn't—"

Alec rushed her, hopping over the crushed glass and chasing her around the island. When she reached the glass again, she slowed and carefully hopped over it. He went to snatch her by the arm, but she burst into laughter as if they were playing chase and took off again, running another circle around the island before being chased out the door.

The game ended after Alec slammed the glass door on her face.

She scowled. Then she lifted her red apple over her head and intentionally dropped it on his mat outside. He answered by locking the door and fastening a chain lock.

When she oddly kept standing there, staring at him, he shouted, *"Go away!"*

The lights in the house switched off again.

Alec lay on his back in bed staring at the ceiling in the dark again. Now how could he get rest? Funny thing was, the creaking of the house had stopped. Still, every slide of a branch against the walls, or rustle of leaves by his bedroom window, made him stir.

The lady hadn't felt threatening, but her actions were. She had strutted around as if she owned the place.

He turned and gazed at the nightstand. His clock read four-twelve in the morning. The clock made him even more uneasy. The electricity was still out in the house. All the power wasn't working, except his clock. How? His digital clock had no backup power.

His cellphone buzzed on his nightstand. He rolled over to the side of the bed and picked up his phone. There were a few texts. One from his daughter, Rachel. It'd be around one o'clock in the morning in California. That one just read "call when u can." Another text was from Chip. But a third text, the most recent, was from an unknown caller. He figured the unknown caller was spam.

As he went to delete the message, he read in all caps, *"GO AWAY!"*

All the lights in his room switched on.

4

―――――

A FLASHLIGHT

It was drizzling. Something not too unfamiliar in Plymouth Hill, according to Daisie, but it dampened Alec's plans to hike down to her Corner Store in the morning. So he drove his gray Lexus SUV down the winding road to her store. After he parked in the muddy dirt lot, he opened the screen door. And, as always, she stood behind her sales counter, now reading a small black book with stars on the cover.

Daisie was becoming a good friend. There weren't many people to talk to in town, but there was always Daisie. And Daisie was a lot of fun. On some days, he spent hours at a time just talking to her about weather, politics, movies, and all sorts of random stuff. Not just because the woman was easy to converse with, but because she was the only person to talk to.

"Raining in July, huh?" asked Alec, shaking his head.

"Raining in July." Daisie put down her book. She heaved a sigh. "Raining in August. Raining in September. Raining in October. Raining in November. I told you about rain here. Wait till it snows, Alec. Then it'll be snowing in December, January, February, March, April, and maybe May. If you're lucky, you'll get clear skies in June. When does it ever not fucking rain or snow in Plymouth Hill?"

He chuckled.

"It's good to see you," she said with a smile. "Life alone on the top of your hill giving you cabin fever yet?"

"No, I love it."

"Hmm. How do you spend all your boring time? Oh yeah, writing."

"Well, not getting as much writing done as I dreamed. But trying."

Daisie walked around the counter and over to his aisle. She was wearing another draping dress. This one was lime green. It was striking with her red hair. And, as usual, she had a moon drawn on her forehead.

"What'cha looking for?" she asked with hands on hips. "I'll give you Daisie's special service."

"A flashlight."

"Whatcha need a flashlight for?"

"The power keeps going out at the house."

"Huh…hey, I've got an amazing one in the back. Hold on. I got one that can light up an entire baseball field. You want that one? You could probably go hunting with it. Do you hunt? People from the city come here to hunt all the time. Aside from fishing on the lake, that's what our boring town's all about. I'd rather sell you a flashlight in the back than one of these stupid small plastic thingies, Alec. But doesn't your cellphone have a flashlight?"

"I just need a simple light at night."

"Why not just use your cellphone?"

"I don't like carrying my phone around everywhere."

"Oh yeah. Your house is huge." But she slowly nodded, looking at him as if he were crazy. With the moon drawn on her head. He laughed. "I suggest you change your habits and just carry your cellphone in a pocket everywhere you go, Alec."

"You're not trying hard to sell me stuff."

"Well, I don't often sell flashlights," she said with a shrug. "Who the hell buys a flashlight these days? That's like buying cameras. Unless you get one of them special ones, like I've got in the back."

"The lights keep going out." That made him shudder. Because it reminded him of the intruder. "That reminds me. I wanted to ask you something. One of those bohemians you were talking about came by the house in the middle of the night a few days ago. She was so brazen that she walked right into my kitchen, stole one of my apples, and started eating it in front of my face. I couldn't believe it. I almost called the police, but I was able to just chase her out."

"I told you drifters are all over Plymouth Hill. That won't be the last. But Sheriff Denson wouldn't have done anything. Did you catch the apple thief's name? Maybe she's local and I'd recognize her name."

"No," he said with a chuckle. "I was too busy throwing her out. But she must live around here. She mentioned the sheriff's name."

"Like I said, lots of weird people live around Badger. Look at me."

"I threw her out. But…" He debated whether to tell her.

"But what?"

"She texted me. Or I think she texted me. It really was disturbing… I got a message after she left, on my phone, saying, '*Go away.*' My phone read an unlisted number, but the text came to me right after seeing her."

"Why would the words '*go away*' freak you out? If she was some stalker, it would have said something like '*I'm coming after you.*'"

"Because I shouted those exact words at her when I locked the door on her. It was all too weird to be a coincidence. But how did she get my phone number?"

Daisie grimaced.

"Honestly, Alec, I can't believe you're still up there on that hill. I would have wagered you'd be flying back home in a month. I told you, people go bonkers up here. Wait till winter. Maybe you saw your ghost? Just…just you wait a minute. Let me show you the amazing flashlight I've got stored in the back. You've gotta see it. It's such a beauty. I won't feel bad selling it to you, not as much as one of those small plastic thingies. I tell you, this thing can light up your whole hilltop. Just don't shine it directly into your eyeballs. It probably could blind you too." She laughed. "Hey, come to think of it, you could use it as a weapon to blind the next apple thief."

"Okay, sure," he said with a chuckle.

"Be back in a jiffy," she said with a wink. Then she walked around the counter and passed through a wooden door at the back of her store.

"You don't think it's weird that an unlisted number texted me the last words I said to the stranger?" he hollered.

He heard her in the other room rummaging through boxes.

"There's nothing special about the words '*go away*'," she said from the other room. "It's probably a coincidence."

"Just the whole thing was so strange. She acted like…eating that apple in my kitchen, she was acting like, I don't know, as if it was her house."

"I told you people are strange around here. Or maybe you saw your ghost, Alec. Yeah, maybe it was the ghost. Just because you don't believe in ghosts doesn't mean they don't exist." She laughed, still rummaging through things in the adjacent room. "You live in a haunted house. Remember? Yeah, maybe it wasn't a drifter? Maybe it was the ghost. A ghost that likes apples."

"You really think she was the ghost? I thought about that, but I can't believe it. She was too real, Daisie. I tell you, she was flesh and blood, right in front of me, just like you are."

"No, she was probably one of those drifters camping out around your house. Your house is not only a beauty, it's at the top of the woods with a magnificent view. Keep all your windows and doors locked. Maybe get a watchdog. Or install some cameras—hey, I might be able to get you some of those for real cheap too. I got an Alec-Daisie sale going on all week." She chuckled. "And then just… *fuck!* Give me one second. Where the hell did I leave that box? Tells you how strange it is to ask for flashlights. Geeze, I really like you, Alec. You're so weird. I like that a lot. You're not a usual guy, you know. Like I'm not your usual gal…goddamn it, where did I leave that thing? I tell you, this flashlight can burn a hole in your intruder's eyeball. It's like a light saber."

"Okay," he said with another chuckle.

"Nope," she muttered, walking back into the store. "Alec, sorry, it's not back with my supplies."

Then she stood behind the counter and dug her fingers through her long red hair. When she raised her head, she looked into his eyes and grinned.

"Hey, are you going to Badger for the fireworks show next weekend?"

"I didn't know about it."

"It's our Fourth of July fireworks show, Alec. It's a real special get-together for everybody around here. You want to go with me?"

5

IT'S REALLY NOT YOURS

ALEC SAT ON HIS LEATHER COUCH, GAZING OUT HIS LIVING ROOM window at the forest in his backyard. It was early in the morning, and a thin mist fogged the surrounding trees and thick green foliage along the grounds. Morning fog was something else he was starting to get accustomed to on Plymouth Crest, another beautiful thing about the house. If he had been able to see the lake, he might have seen what looked like wisps of smoke skating along the surface of the water. It was all breathtaking. But that made him feel worse. Because it was a view that, apparently, he couldn't have.

"You can't close escrow?" Alec snapped, leaning his head in his hands and rubbing his eyes. "I can't believe this."

Chip and his guest looked miserable too, sitting across from the sofa in matching black leather lounge chairs. His best friend wore a formal navy blue suit with his dark hair perfectly combed. The young kid, probably not much older than twenty, had a shaved head, tattoos running along his neck and right cheek, and a distinctive ring in his right eyebrow. He looked young enough to be Chip's son.

"You told me everything was done, Chip," Alec said, running his hand through his thin hair. "I never would have moved all my stuff in had I known about this."

"Calm down, man," Chip said, raising his hand. "We can still close. It's just a formality."

"Dad never signed the property over to me, that's all," said the kid with a chuckle. "But the law should give me the property, right?"

"You're asking me?" Alec asked, leaning forward. "You're the one who put the house up for sale."

"You don't have ownership, Robin," Chip said, shaking his head. "You told me you had full title and then you signed documents, but it means nothing if you don't hold the deed."

"But the house had to go to Dad after the owner's death. And I've been selling Dad's stuff for years. I sold all his furniture in the house without any problems."

"How can you enter escrow without looking into all this?" cried Alec to Chip in disbelief, hitting the coffee table. But then he glanced at the kid. "You never entered probate with your dad's estate?"

"Why would I do that?"

"*Who is the fucking owner of my house!*" Alec shouted, jumping up.

That was followed by a loud crash upstairs. It sounded as if the dresser in the bedroom had toppled over. Then the ceiling and walls rumbled. The explosion made Chip and Robin look up, but Alec fell back on the couch and put his head in his hands again. He was getting so used to these noises that it hardly fazed him.

"Wow," Robin said, looking up. "The house really is haunted."

"Should we check upstairs?" suggested Chip.

Alec shook his head, running his fingers through his short hair again.

"Look, Dad disappeared after leaving the country years ago," Robin said. "I assumed everything in his estate went to me, including the house. Who else would get it?"

"You said your dad disappeared," Alec replied, glancing up at him. "Do you have paperwork showing transfer of title to you? Or his will? I just need the sale in writing so you can transfer this house over to me."

Then Robin made Alec feel worse by staring stupidly at him.

"Chip?" Alec asked, rolling his eyes. "I paid loads of money for the movers to haul all my stuff from California. I even had the car delivered. Now you want me to pay the rest of the money I owe for the house when you can't close escrow? When you can't get the deed for the house. Have you lost your fucking mind?"

"You've been in the house for weeks," Robin said. "Seems it's your house to enjoy."

Alec ignored his guest. Instead, he stared at his friend, dumbfounded. Chip avoided his gaze, staring out the window at the lovely view of the woods. *Again*, the spectacular yard he was now being told he couldn't have.

"Look, you don't have to leave," Robin said. "Just stay put and enjoy the place. You just need to transfer the rest of my money. Leave all your stuff here. I don't mind. I just need final payment."

"You don't own the fucking place, you idiot!"

"Hey!" Robin cried, jumping up. "Really? You have no right talking to me like that."

"Oh, I'm sorry, am I getting you upset?"

"Look," Robin said. He looked over at Chip, but Chip was staring down at the carpet again. "Look, Dad went missing... I've sold lots of his stuff without any trouble."

"Get the paperwork," Alec said. "Or hire an attorney and prove ownership, otherwise I won't pay you a dime. And you'll owe me my deposit back."

"I think you're making a big deal over nothing," Robin said. "This is all just a formality."

"Alec's profession was based on formalities," said Chip with a shrug.

"Seriously?" Alec snapped. "You don't agree with me, Chip? You said everything was ready to go. I figured you'd hand over the deed to the house this morning. Now you return here telling me the owner might not be the owner."

"I flew back here from L.A. to tell you, Alec," he said, raising his brow. "Jesus, look, I'm not pleased about all this either."

"Why hasn't the state taken the house if the owner left the country?" Alec asked Chip. "Maybe it's because there's an owner who still owns it who's not this kid? Maybe we just need to find the owner?"

"Dad hasn't spoken to me—"

"I wouldn't either."

"Hey, fuck off, man!" Robin cried. "I don't need your shit. Yeah, I'll get a lawyer, all right, if you don't pay up. You moved in. You signed escrow. The deal was made when you gave me your deposit. Everything is ready to go."

"Get out!" Alec shouted. "Neither of us owns this place."

And that's just what Robin did. He rushed out of the living room, threw open the front door, and slammed it behind him.

"God, Chip," Alec said running his fingers through his hair, "man, did you even meet this guy in person before signing?"

But Chip sank down in the chair. Then he put his head in his hands just like Alec had.

"Everything was done by email," Chip said. "I told you, he forged some of the documents. I didn't know it till it didn't go through at the bank. I would never have gotten you into this, had I known. Robin wants to make the deal. I mean, he traveled all the way over here, in the middle of nowhere, to do that. He might still be able to get legal ownership, as he's the closest kin I've been able to find."

"*Fuck!*" Alec leaned back in the sofa. "Chip…just go figure things out! No wonder the kid was selling at such a low price. It's not only haunted, it's not his house to sell."

"Yeah," Chip said, getting up. He patted Alec on the back. "Sure. Look, I'm sorry, man."

"Just…Just find the owner."

There was another rumble upstairs.

"Is that the noises you were talking about? That's the stuff keeping you up at night?" asked Chip, looking up. "How do you sleep at all? Jesus, it doesn't even seem to faze you."

"I…I've gotten used to it. Look, I still love this place. Find the owner so we can sign off and be done with this. I still want the house."

"I already found the owner," Chip said. "But telling you about it is not going to make you feel any better."

"Who is it?"

"The house was built and owned by a pop star. Her name was Fifi. Fifi Graynger. Ever heard of her? You might have heard some of her music. But we were never into pop, we were more into alternative music back in college. Fifi was in Hollywood too. Remember, Alec, the B-movies she did? *Lowry and the Cat.* That was a musical comedy about a stowaway talking cat. That was her biggest hit. That film *Idling off Soho* was good too. She was a really funny girl. Not only with an amazing voice, but cute as hell. Of course her music career is where she really got her fame. Well, she disappeared twenty years ago. Locals claim she committed suicide in your house, but there's no death certificate. Believe me, I've looked. Legally, she's missing. Sort of. Well, if she's missing, someone's been forging her signatures and paying her taxes. That's how I got so far into the deal without becoming suspicious. The banks just assumed the mortgage was legit. No one's been checking out the late Fifi, probably because all the bills are getting paid off so—I mean look at this so-called town—who the hell's going to investigate? I have loads of paperwork in her name, but the mystery is only going to send us sliding into a bigger rabbit hole. There's no explanation for how Fifi has continued to keep up the place, how's she's paying, or where she's disappeared to—if she's alive. It's a really weird mystery. And it hardly helps our situation, buddy. We need to have the owner to buy the house. As you said, it doesn't matter who the hell that owner is as long as they can sell it to you."

"It's like the dust," Alec said pensively, walking slowly over to the window. He stared out at the woods again. "Someone's been taking care of this place."

"I suppose. It's strange Robin didn't know all about it. The kid genuinely thought he was the de facto owner, and that he could work stuff out with the bank, as he's the son of Fifi's lover."

"Look for her. Or whoever's claiming to be her. We can work out all the legal shit when we find out who's maintaining the place. Maybe if we find that, we can have the house sold to us. Or, if this music star's missing, perhaps you can find—"

"You want me to find a pop star who disappeared over twenty years ago? She had a lot of fans, Alec. Don't you think her fans looked for her? Yes, there's paperwork with her recent signatures, but there's also stories about the house. According to the locals and rumors, Fifi committed suicide here. She's the ghost I warned you about when you opened escrow."

"That doesn't explain the upkeep. Maybe she's one of those famous stars that wanted to feign her death to be free of the spotlight? Maybe she faked her death for privacy? Dig deeper, Chip."

"I will," Chip said, heaving a sigh. "Sure. I will."

"I'm sorry I yelled at you," Alec muttered. "I didn't mean to be a jerk, but I've really been growing fond of this place."

"Don't worry about me, my friend, worry about Robin. You really pissed him off good. If there's anything still tying him to ownership and our sale, I don't think he's coming back."

"Do you blame me?"

"Nope. No, I don't." Chip took a deep breath, jumped up, and walked to the window. He shook his head, staring at the yard. "I'll make things right, man. You'll still get this house. Don't worry."

"Yeah, well… I'm sorry about yelling at the kid too." He jumped up and walked to the window to stare at the gorgeous view. "I was just so upset. I want this house. But I really didn't mean to shout at him. That was wrong."

"It's your anger problem."

"Sure," he said solemnly, nodding and still staring at the view.

"Don't be so worried, man. We'll figure all this out, still get you the house and close escrow."

"You asked me not to worry last time."

"Well, this time I mean it. We have leads, I just need to dig deeper. And, anyway, without anyone claiming the place, you don't have to move."

6

THE LADY BY THE LAKE

ALEC SAT ON LARGE ROCKS HANGING OVER THE SHORE OF THE LAKE with his computer on his lap. It was a lovely rocky outlook reaching about ten yards over the water, like a little natural pier. He had tried to write yesterday on a plastic chair on his balcony, with the same amazing view, but failed miserably. He thought perhaps sitting right at the lake would awaken his muse. Nope. Too beautiful. Birds chirped, leaves rustled, and it was quiet enough to hear the gentle lapping of the water. It smelled woodsy with an almost vanilla scent. He remembered that wonderful fresh air smell from when he used to visit the woods in the mountains in California. Rachel had reminded him about that in their conversation the other day, when he was trying to describe the forest smell to her. He already loved Plymouth Crest so much. But that only made him angrier when he thought about how he might have to leave.

A small bird hopped over some rocks and splashed near the water. Then he felt a cool, gentle breeze brush over his hair and beard on the right side of his face. He turned. For some reason, he felt like he was being watched. All he saw were the branches of nearby trees gently swaying.

As far as writing, things weren't going so well. He'd thought he was going to get so much writing done away from the noise in the city. He stared at the blank screen on his laptop.

249

"Beautiful, isn't it?"

Alec jumped. Then he nearly fell into the water. Looking to his right again, only ten feet away, stood a lady in a long thin white dress flowing down to her bare feet. She was hardly paying any attention to him. She was just squinting and staring at the glistening lake. The yellow light reflected, almost glowed, over her smiling face. It was her! It was the intruder who had broken into his house.

"Are you following me?" Alec snapped.

"I live here," she said, cocking her head back. Then she wrapped her arms around herself, closed her eyes, and smiled wider. "Smells so nice. It's so beautiful in the morning, isn't it? Near midday now, I suppose. I love mornings here by the lake. And summer is so nice and bright around Plymouth Crest, isn't it?" She looked back at him and nodded. "I would have explained myself further, had you not thrown the door in my face. That was very rude."

Alec said nothing. He just stared.

"I love this lake so much," she added. "Don't you?"

"Yes."

She giggled and nodded again, turning back to the view. Then she just stared out over the lake, ignoring him again.

Had this been some other stranger, particularly after breaking into his home, he would have raged at her or shoved her into the water. Not her. With her thin white dress reflecting the yellow rays of the sun, she was radiant, glimmering like a shining white-robed goddess. Wind brushed gently over her long dark hair. Her sleeves flowed down her arms to lace cuffs, seeming light, bright, and almost translucent as if they barely covered her arms. She was not only pretty, she seemed dazzling, like the lake. No, more like she *was* the lake. Under the bright rays of the sun, he could now better discern her face. Her skin was tanned, contrasting with her white clothes. She had narrow features, with a thin nose and dark eyebrows over almond eyes. Her eyes seemed sharp, marked with intelligence. And now those blue eyes just stared over the water. He felt that if he got up and headed back to the house, she wouldn't move. She would still be standing there, like a tree or stone, as if she were a fixture over the water. Her lips were her most striking feature, bright red, but seemingly always curved in a whimsical grin, as if curling over some joke that seemed to always be on him. But, whatever was so funny, even if she was poking fun at him, he liked her whimsical mood. She seemed so full of energy.

He found himself as mesmerized by staring at her as by Plymouth Crest itself. And it didn't really matter that she had broken into his home the other night. He didn't want her to leave. He'd be happy if she just stood with him, gazing out from the shore, the rest of the day.

"What?" She cocked her head and threw her long dark hair back.

"Who are you?"

"It wasn't right for that house to be sold to you," she said, brushing hair from her eyes and looking stern. "Particularly by a clod. That boy had no right to sell it, to tell you the truth. It's not his. Not even his dad's. Nothing idiots with fancy suits and signatures are gonna fabricate will change that. It belongs to whom it's always belonged to."

"My name's Alec," he drawled. "Let me try again. Who...what is your name? And, where—"

"Joy," she said with a nod. Then she furrowed her brow. "What are you typing on that computer?"

"Are you following me?"

"No one owns anything here. The house is like the lake. None of it really belongs to anyone." And she nodded then hugged herself again, gazing over the water. "That's why it's so absolutely wonderful. The house *is*. The lake *is*. Everything just *is*. It always is and always shall be. There's something so wonderful about that, isn't there? Permanence. It has nothing to do with ownership or anything human really. It just is. And I love that. If people would stop what they're doing and enjoy the moment, stop trying to think or own things, what trouble would they ever have?"

"What are you talking about? What's your name?"

"I told you my name. I'm Joy."

"Joy, how did you know there was something up with my purchasing agreement for my house? And what business is it of yours?"

"I read it. It was—"Then she spoke in a British accent—"*bollocks*, as the Brits say. The house is not owned by that kid or his dad."

"You read my purchase agreement? How? By breaking into my house again?"

"Stop," she said, raising a hand. "You're really on edge a lot, aren't you? That's one thing I don't like about you, Alec. You have a bit of a temper and can turn mean."

"How did you read it?" he asked, feeling angrier. "Was this after you broke into my house? Or did you break into my house again?"

"You mean when *you* came to the house, stranger. No one lived there for years. I told you already, a million times, that no one alive owns that house. It's like this lake. It just is. And that's how it will stay. Isn't that beautiful?"

"Where do you live, miss? Who are you? Stop fooling around. I was told there aren't any homes for miles. Plymouth Hill has a couple homes, but that's two miles from here. How come you keep acting like you live at my house?"

"Maybe I should question you. Why did you travel all the way across the country to sit before a lake and write? Do you think that's all that life's about? Writing by yourself over a lake? Staring at your reflection in the water. Seems a bit selfish, don't you think? What about your daughter back home, with her baby coming? Why not go back home to California and be there for her? That reminds me of my family."

"How do you know about my daughter?"

"Oops." She put her hand over her mouth. Then she snickered. "Well…well, I mean, you were talking to her on the phone."

"When?"

She shrugged. "Well—I mean…"

"Did you break into my house again? Are you spying on me?"

"Won't you calm the hell down?"

"The house is mine, miss," he said. "You can't be trespassing—"

"Calm down," she said, raising a hand. "Geesh. Fine. Whatever. You win. I suppose you got a problem seeing a woman here by your lake too? Am I not allowed here either? Do you own the lake? As if the lake isn't big enough for the two of us. You know, I was beginning to like you, Alec, but you need to be friendlier in a small town like Plymouth Hill. Anyway—" She turned from him and frowned. "Seems we're getting off on the wrong foot. Welcome to Plymouth Hill."

He just stared at her. Then he slammed shut his laptop, tucked it under his arm, got up, and made his way back up the trail to his home.

"You're creepy."

"You go have a nice life too."

He made his way back to the trail that led to the main road and then up the hill to his house.

"You can be a real asshole, Alec."

That made him look back. She shook her head, appearing stern, and quipped, "Good luck with your book."

Then she turned around, faced the lake, and held herself in her arms again. He gazed back at her when he was higher up the hillside, and she looked like she had when he first saw the house. She seemed to just be happy enjoying the view alone, as if she had never spoken to him.

7

DATE'S OUT COLD

"So you're a writer?" Sheriff Glen Denson asked Alec. He really didn't seem to care. It seemed the question was simply to strike up conversation.

Sheriff Denson had a look of suspicion on his face—that same look of distrust Alec had seen in the rest of the bunch tonight. Denson was an older gray-haired man wearing suspenders. For Plymouth Hill, he *was* the police. Yep, the sheriff of Badger was here, along with nearly all the others from the town, at their local Fourth of July party. Many sat on logs, others were cross-legged on the grass, but everyone circled around three large bonfires.

They were on an overlook far up in the mountains, at a much higher elevation than his house. It was a small glade, the ground mostly dirt and leaves. They had all hiked ten minutes up a trail after trudging through the deep forest. A young guy named Jed had told everyone he was a hunter. They had all followed him. Jason, his brother, even wore a hunter's hat.

Silvia and Garth seemed to be the nicest couple of the group, striking up conversation with everybody. They were a young dark-skinned couple with Latino accents. They had moved from Tampa to Badger just five years ago. They were vaping weed by the bonfire with Sheriff Denson.

Frazier was the most boisterous of the pack, engaging everybody with music, cards, footballs, frisbees, or whatever he could think of to maintain fun. He was a tall, very dark-skinned man in a brown wool sweater. And he was the organizer of the whole debacle. The city doctor was there too. Doctor Norman. Everyone called him Normie. And another couple, sitting near Alec and the sheriff, facing the valley, was Ted and Francis. That couple sat beside another couple, Donna and Terry. Both couples were hay farmers living in Badger. There were many, many others. He couldn't recall all their names. But everyone knew each other as if they were family.

Far down the hillside were rooftops camouflaged by the green forest canopy and a few streetlights under the starry night. These structures made up the town of Badger.

Alec gazed up at the night sky and took a deep breath, taking in the fresh air. One of the greatest things about living in a rural area, ever since moving to Plymouth Crest, was the star-filled sky. He'd sometimes sit on his balcony, just gazing up at all those stars, late into the night.

Alec had mistakenly thought Daisie had invited him to an organized firework show. That presumption had ended after Frazier presented a duffel bag full of firecrackers.

"Yeah, I'm a writer," Alec finally answered the sheriff. He hadn't replied for so long that it seemed to take the sheriff a second to remember what he had asked. "It's so nice out here at night."

"What do you write?"

"I started with mystery short stories for magazines. And an article here and there in some writing journals. Then I tried science fiction novels for a while with some A.I. stuff. Now I delve more into romance."

"He's very good," Daisie said with a slightly slurred voice, sitting beside him. She ran her fingers over his shoulder.

"How would you know?" Alec asked Daisie, amused.

"Just do," she answered with a wink. "Just do." Daisie swayed, seeming to have difficulty staying seated. "I just know." Then she patted his back.

Daisie had a flamboyant dress, this one rainbow colored, and was wearing a little too much dark makeup—and, of course, she had that distinctive moon drawn on her forehead.

"When are you going to invite us to your place?" asked Jed. "I haven't been in your house up there on Plymouth Crest for a long time."

"Seems everyone's been inside my house," Alec said with a laugh. "Daisie told me people have been breaking and entering for decades. You guys can come up whenever you want."

"That's why I'm sure glad you're finally living there," said Sheriff Denson, raising his beer can as if in a toast. "Now that someone's living at the place, I don't have to keep coming every time some idiot thinks they saw a ghost. You don't know how often people are making trouble reporting sightings. Many go there just to try to see the spirits."

"There are ghosts there," said Dr. Norman. "I saw a shadow through the windows when traveling around the summit of Plymouth Crest a couple years ago. I swear, it was just standing and glowing behind the window staring up at me. The place is damned creepy, if you ask me. Damned creepy." He smirked at Alec. "Good luck to you, sir."

"Remember when we broke into the house for our New Year's party a few years back, Sheriff?" Jason asked.

"That was fun," Denson replied with a nod.

Now Alec understood why the whole town disparaged Sheriff Denson. He seemed to talk about nothing but breaking the law.

"Alec?" Daisie whispered in his ear. "Alec? Alec, I really need to go to the lady's room. Can you come with me?"

He turned to her and furrowed his brow. Daisie looked pale.

"I need to go, like, *now*," she said quietly. "I don't feel good."

Alec nodded, got up, and took her by the hand.

"We'll be right back," Alec said to the group.

"Not till you tell us when we're invited up to your house," said Jed with a laugh. But Jed raised his beer can as if in a toast.

"You're welcome anytime," Alec said with a laugh, walking with Daisie deeper into the woods.

That was followed by another explosion. Someone shouted and everyone scattered looking up in terror. A rocket was flying straight up over the group. Thankfully, the firecracker fell off the cliffside. Everyone laughed. Then they started yelling at Frazier.

Daisie held Alec close in her arms as they wandered among the trees and through the thicket. She kept stumbling, tripping over branches and bushes.

"*Tha-nks Alec,*" she drawled, squinting up at his face. Then she reached up and touched his cheek, stroking his beard. "You're so nice. I think I drank just a little bit too much tonight."

When they were deep enough into the woods that it was difficult to make out the group, she surprised him by pushing him up against a tree trunk. There, she started clambering all over his body, kissing his neck and lips like crazy.

"Stop it, Daisie!" he snapped, pushing her off him. "Stop!"

"Sorry," she said with a burp. "Sorry… Alec." Then she put her hand on her forehead. "Sorry, I just, you know, can't help myself around a handsome man like you. We're still friends, though, right?"

"Are you okay?"

"No," she said with a chuckle. "No, I'm really not, Alec."

Then she opened her eyes wide, pushed herself away from his chest, and rushed to a bush under a thick tree trunk. She threw up.

Alec stood over her. To his right, he could still hear the laughter and barely make out the campfire about thirty yards through dense foliage.

"Sorry," Daisie said, leaning over, retching some more. "You're so damn nice. I'm really sorry I…kissed you. I just. I just drank…so frickin' fuckin' much, I think. But you are cute, you see. But we're just friends. I know."

"We are friends, Daisie. And I think I need to take you home."

"You can't do that," she said, holding his hand. "You've been…hey, you've been drinking too. I'll just suffer a little bit more. You go back with the others, and I'll just sit here by my lonesome. Nothing's happening here."

"I'm not leaving you. Maybe we can get Frazier to drive you now rather than later?"

"Are you kiddin' me? He's here to entertain. Ain't he funny?"

"What about the doctor?"

"*Normie? Normie!*" she cried, laughing like crazy. "He's fuckin' drinking too, Alec! Do you like 'em all? Huh? Do you like my friends? Everyone's nice but they…get tiresome. You know, they're totally like family. Shit, I've been here the longest in this dull, rotten town…I think. Just this fuckin' town wears you down after a while. I always tell you that, but you stick around for some reason. Let me tell you a secret." And she cupped her hands around her lips. Then she didn't say anything at all. She just furrowed her brow. She looked around, covered her mouth, and burped. Finally she said, "I love… I love, love, love, love, I just love it that you love being here. Nothing's really new, 'xcept you. And…but you'll learn every holiday's the same. Over and over. Guess what we all do for Thanksgiving? Guess. Go ahead, Alec. Take a guess. It'll be familiar. What do you think we do at every holiday?"

He shrugged.

"*That's it! That's what we do!*" she said, laughing and slapping her knee. "Nothing. Absolutely nothing. We drink around a table, shooting the breeze, talking 'bout absolute nothing. It's funny cause many people leave their old families to come here and live alone, only to find that the town itself becomes their family. You'll find that out soon enough. You just have to be careful you don't piss anyone off." She laughed. Then she covered her mouth and burped. "You just—"

"Francis and Ted are nice."

"Ted? Ted? He fucking cheats on his wife, Alec. Come on. You know better. He's a sneaky little fucker. Whenever a new girl arrives in town, he's all over her." She looked dreamily up into his eyes. Then she wiped her mouth. "Sorry. You don't seem to like it when I cuss. You're such a sweet man. Anyway…things aren't always what they seem. You're just too damn nice to notice." She tried to get up, but she swooned. "Damn, I drank *waaaay* too much tonight."

"Everyone's nice."

"Thanks for staying with me. I feel safe around you. The forest has dangers for a gal, ya know. You can go back to the others. I'll just rest here…for a little…while."

And then she just lay on her side under a tree. She closed her eyes. In another moment, she started snoring.

There was another explosion. That was followed by another burst of laughter from the group by the cliffside.

"She's got a point," said another stranger's voice. "These woods aren't as safe as they sometimes seem."

There in the shadows, by two trees, was a lady. His lady by the lake! Joy! She stood only about ten feet away, leaning against a tree trunk with hands in her pockets, wearing a black blouse and jeans. But even in darkness, her eyes, contrasting with her long dark hair, seemed to glow aqua blue—those inquisitive, sharp bright eyes.

Although he had shouted at her by the shore, he wasn't upset to see her. The feeling in his chest was like what he had felt when Chip first showed him his house. It wasn't anger at all. He felt happy.

"Afraid your date's out cold," she said, pointing an index finger at Daisie with a chuckle. "And you've been drinking a bit too much yourself, Alec. Shame on you. Is your car around here? I can drive you both home."

"What…" Alec looked all around him. "How…where did you come from, Joy?"

"This town doesn't care for me much," she said bitterly. "Not like her. She's native. She's as much a fixture as Plymouth Crest is to folks around here. Daisie could never be an outsider, like you and me, Alec. That's the thing about Badger. You'll always be an outsider if you weren't born or raised here. You and I will always be crazy Californians to all of them."

"You're from California?"

"Sure," she said, coming closer and waving her hair from her eyes. "Sometimes," she said in a near-whisper, "I'll tell you a little secret. Sometimes, I come by just to watch everyone make fools of themselves, especially during the holidays when they get drunk." She laughed, looking down at Daisie. "They're funny, like her. There's a few others, like Knoll at the gas station, who don't socialize, more like me. Even his dullness and dreariness can be refreshing. Sometimes. But that's about it. Not much else about us, really. Just trees. And our lake. Now you know everybody and everything there is to know about our small town."

And Joy laughed again. Her laughter made him laugh too.

Then he felt himself tremble as she walked very close to him. She seemed to glow, drawing down the moonlight as she searched his eyes.

"Do you…still…hate me?"

"What?"

"*Do you…hate me?*" she drawled with a big grin.

"Why would I hate you?"

"Because I broke into your home? I tried to apologize again by the lake, but I just managed to upset you more. I'm sorry. All that stuff about the contracts, I just learned when you were on the phone earlier in the day, with your daughter, when I did my morning walk. You talk to her a lot. I walk by the house every morning, hearing you calling her. That's all. But I haven't broken in since. I promise. You know, I just like to wander around the grounds of your place."

Daisie groaned. They both looked down as Daisie closed her eyes tighter, stirring on the leaves. That made Joy chuckle again.

"Wow," Joy said, shaking her head. "She is so fucked up. Good for her. Like I've said ever since I was little, you should enjoy yourself in life."

Joy gazed back up into his eyes again. And they just stared into each other's eyes for a moment. The only thing to move was Joy's lips. Her lips seemed to curl even more into a grin.

"Why don't you let me drive you home?" she asked.

"What?"

"*Why don't you let me drive you home?*" she drawled again, lifting her brow. "I owe you for all the trouble I caused you."

They heard yet another firecracker, and the group through the trees roared with another burst of laughter.

Alec looked down at Daisie. She was still sound asleep.

"All right, Joy."

8

HUMMING

Joy didn't say a word. The whole way down the curvy road, hugging the woodland mountain, back through Badger, and then up his hill to Plymouth Crest, she didn't say one word. She just hummed.

Her voice was amazing. Alec sat in the back seat behind Daisie, watching as Joy held the wheel with both hands, carefully watching the road and humming. He didn't recognize the tune, but her voice was enchanting. It was tranquil and so soothing. Or…maybe he was deceived after drinking so much? His eyes kept fighting to stay open…

No. Whatever she was humming, it was so melodic and so beautiful. It put him at ease. He forced himself awake just to listen.

"What is that you're singing?" Alec asked in a hushed voice.

"Hmm?" Joy asked, cocking her head back.

"What is it that you're humming?"

"Oh, it's just some tune I made up in my brain. I make up lots of music in my mind. Sometimes whole songs. Sometimes even whole albums come into my head in the shower. I'm kinda weird that way. Do you like it, Alec?"

She cocked her head back again and smiled. Then she winked.

"Yeah, I do."

"I'll try not to forget how it goes then," she said with a nod. Then she raised a finger and mimed making a checkmark in the air, as if marking a list.

Alec laughed a bit too loud and covered his mouth. Daisie stirred in the passenger seat.

"What?" asked Daisie. "What's going on? Are we back—"

"We're driving you home," Alec said, leaning forward. "Don't worry."

Daisie just nodded and fell backward in the passenger seat.

Then Joy went back to quietly humming. It was that same wonderful tune that the young lady claimed she had made up. And Alec just sat back and loved watching and listening to her.

9

TROUBLED STEPS

Alec practically dragged Daisie up the front yard along the concrete walkway to his house. Daisie was attempting to use her feet, sort of tripping along, but Alec kept shushing her, worried that she wouldn't watch where she was going if she didn't focus on the ground. Alec wasn't really all that steady either. All the while, Joy trailed behind, following him up the path to the front door. As the automatic lights lit up Alec's front porch, Alec fumbled with his keys by the front door.

"Hey," Daisie slurred, "hey, just you wait one second, misser. This isn't…this isn't my fuggin' house. Are you tryin' to take advantage of me, Alec?" She grimaced, looking up at him. "Ain't this your haunted house?"

Joy laughed behind them.

"We got a ride back and I figured I'd watch you for a little while," Alec said. "When you're better, I'll drive you home back down the hill."

"Aw, you're so nice."

He opened the door and Joy switched on the light behind them. From the entryway, the living room lit up brightly, too bright, in contrast to the darkness outside, and Alec squinted. He helped Daisie to the foot of the stairs, but by the base of the stairway, he nearly dropped her when she closed her eyes and fell completely limp.

"Where are you taking her?" Joy asked.

"To the bedroom."

"Why? Just take her to the couch in the living room. She's already out cold in your arms. Don't take her upstairs."

"I know, but the only bed in my house is in the bedroom."

"So? Look, my inebriated friend, you're going to drop her if you lift her up all these steps. You don't want my help, fine, but why the hell does she get to sleep in your bed?"

"Does it matter?"

Then he froze looking at her. Because she met his gaze with those eyes. It was so mesmerizing.

"Hey, wait a second," he said, "didn't you leave your car back in Badger? How are you going to get your car back?"

"It's a small town. I can hitch a ride. Or walk. It's a half day's journey by foot. I've done it many times at this time of the year. Don't worry about me, worry about you. Like, how the hell are we going to get this sloshed, unconscious guest up into your bedroom? Wouldn't it be a whole lot easier if you dragged her to the sofa? Can't we do that instead, Alec?"

That's when he looked down and noticed Joy's bare feet. They went in and out of focus as he stared at them on the white carpet. Did she ever wear shoes? And, if not, and she had been walking in the forest, why did her feet seem so perfectly clean? It was really weird.

She lifted her brow, still waiting for an answer.

"*Hey!*" Daisie suddenly jarred awake, opening her eyes wide in Alec's arms. "Hey, wait one second! Wait just one second. Ain't there a fu-gg-in' ghost in this house!" And that sent her barreling into more laughter than ever. "You, you, you tryin' to scare the shit out of me on the Fourth of July, Alec? It's the Fourth of July, not Halloween. I said take me home, mister. Home. My home. You take me home this instant. It's not—"She looked up into his eyes and suddenly feigned being coy —"well, it's not proper, you know, for a girl to be sent here when she's not herself. Take me back home or I'll climb down the hillside, trees and bushes or not, and go home myself."

"Daisie, I'm trying to help you. Why not just rest until tomorrow?"

"I say let her crawl down the hill," Joy quipped. "You wouldn't want to take advantage of her."

"What?" Alec snapped, looking back. Joy just shrugged with a smirk. "Look, can you help me get her upstairs?"

Joy frowned.

"Who are you talking to, Alec?" asked Daisie. "Is there somebody else in the house? I like you and all, I really do, I mean, you're so cute with that tight black shirt over your chest and arms." She laughed. "But, but, but, but inside I think you can be a bit looney. Sometimes. And…you know…you know what, I tell you what. I told you, I love that. I really do. I told you… I really love that a lot. You know what I'm gonna do because of that? I tell you what I am going to do. I'm gonna give you a free reading. You know, I'm really good with tarot. Would you like your future read from my tarot cards? A free reading? I think —"She suddenly opened her eyes wide and turned from him— "uh, oh."

"Joy, please!" said Alec. "Please help me get her up to the bathroom upstairs!"

"What's so goddamn joyful about this?" Daisie snapped, groaning.

"Take her back to the powder room near the kitchen, dummy!" Joy cried.

"How do you know there's a powder room by the kitchen?" he asked. "There you go again. Why am I thinking you've been in this house a lot more than just that one time?"

"What?" asked Daisie, barely opening her eyes. "What the hell are you talking about. I don't see how many…uh, oh. Here I go again."

Daisie opened her eyes wide. And then, it was too late. She threw up all over the carpet steps.

"Goddamn it, Alec," Joy snapped. "You're too drunk to think straight."

And Daisie didn't stop throwing up. She crouched over the carpet on the two bottom steps, vomiting everywhere while Alec held her.

Then, finally, she wiped her mouth.

"There," Daisie said. "Done."

That made Joy burst into laughter.

"It's not funny," Alec said.

"*Fu-nn-y?*" Daisie drawled, wiping her mouth. "This is hardly funny, Alec." But then she chuckled.

"I think she's very funny," Joy said, still laughing. "Don't worry about the carpet. I'll clean it up. It was worth it to watch that."

"You know, I feel a little better now," Daisie said, clutching Alec's arm. "But, God, it's like the walls are still spinning around and around. Why did I drink so much? I mean, why? Maybe I should go see a doctor."

"Normie?" Joy asked, still laughing. "Man, you are drunk, Daisie."

"Stop it, Joy." Alec cried in a forced whisper. "Please. Stop laughing."

"Joy?" Daisie said. "There's nothing… Wait, God, I'm sorry for yelling at you. I just feel…don't feel good, Alec."

"Just rest," said Alec. "Forget it. You'll be all right."

"You're so sweet," Daisie said dreamily, looking into his eyes.

"Now *I'm* gonna throw up," Joy quipped.

"We need to take you to bed," Alec said.

"But I'll need help changing, Alec," Daisie said. "I threw up all over my dress. I can't get in your bed like this. I'll have to change into different clothes before I get in your bed."

Then she looked up at him with a large smile.

"Course not." Joy rolled her eyes. "Wouldn't want her dirty tits and ass smearing up your bedsheets."

"Joy!"

"Why do you keep saying joy?" asked Daisie.

"I'll help her get undressed and into bed," Joy said, rolling her eyes.

"Thanks so much, Joy. You're being so nice to us."

Daisie looked up at him squinting her eyes. She shook her head. Then she held back a burp and guffawed in his face.

1 0

ORANGE JUICE

ONE OF ALEC'S GREATEST SURPRISES IN HIS HOUSE WAS THE FACT THAT the lake's horizon was to the east. Facing east meant that when dawn broke, beautiful yellow and orange rays of sunlight would reflect off the large body of water and slowly make their way over the trees on the horizon. And his long balcony afforded the brilliant view. It's one of the features that motivated him to get up early. That's what he was doing now. He got up before sunrise and walked down his long terrace to sit on a white plastic chair and watch the perfect view, waiting for sunrise. And while waiting in darkness, on his computer screen, he typed:

Nothing…

Absolutely nothing. He just stared at a blank screen.

He had only written twenty pages in the past month. The reality versus the dream of living in nowhere was settling in. He found that Plymouth Crest was too beautiful. Or was it his anxiety over the fact that he might not be here much longer? His realtor friend had still not gotten any leads. That was good and bad news. At the moment, that dunce Robin couldn't evict him, but it made his future very uncertain.

The horizon brightened and glowed orange. Then over the trees across the lake rose a single yellow dot. The sun. And the sun got bigger and brighter rising over the water. Wisps of clouds glowed the same red orange as the reflections of sunrays upon the lake. As the sun finally rose, the whole landscape turned a bright yellow.

Alec put on his shades and just leaned back in his chair watching. *Sighing…* Yeah, this was why he couldn't write.

He heard a bird flutter in the trees. It seemed to be at the crest of an elm. Otherwise, it was quiet enough to hear leaves flutter in the wind.

That's when he spotted someone standing below the terrace near his cement patio. She was so quiet that, for all he knew, she could have been standing under him since he got up this morning. As before, she wore her black shawl over her shoulders, a dark blouse and jeans, with her arms wrapped around herself. And she just stared out at the lake wearing sunglasses too.

"Joy," he hollered. "Joy. Hey, Joy!"

She cocked her head up and waved dismissively. Then she turned back, wrapped her arms around herself again, swayed a bit, and continued to watch the sun rise.

"Joy," said Alec, standing up and waving at her. "Joy. What are you doing down there?"

"Same thing you're doing, ding-a-ling," she answered with a smile. "Enjoying the sunrise. Do you know what's cool about sunrises over the lake, Alec? You get two for one up here off Plymouth Crest. Two. One reflected on the lake and another in the sky."

And they laughed.

"Come inside," he said. "I want to thank you for all your help the other night."

She walked right below the terrace. Then she looked up and smiled.

"Great weather we're having?"

"Is that small talk I hear?" Joy asked, tipping down her shades. "Small talk doesn't suit you. You are the least inauthentic man I've ever met."

"Oh, I just wanted to say something. Thanks so much for everything you did for us on the Fourth. What you did for Daisie was amazing. I'm so grateful. Did you get your car back?"

"Sure, it was nothing," she said with a nod. But then she cocked her head back at the sunrise. "The lake is so pretty, isn't it?"

Yes, Joy, sure is.

"Do you want to come up to my balcony?" Alec asked. "It's an even better view up here."

"Are you actually inviting me inside your home?" Joy asked with a smirk, bringing her shades down her nose a bit. "My, how things change."

"Yes. I… I can make you a cup of coffee?"

"I don't drink coffee."

"How about tea?"

"I learned long ago to avoid stimulants."

"How about orange juice?"

She turned back to the view, of course. Then she just gazed out quietly. Looking down at her, Alec wasn't sure which vision was more beautiful.

"Well?" he asked. "How about it? Orange juice?"

"Whatcha writing?" she asked, turning to him again.

"It's dead."

"You're writing about someone dead?"

"Uh…no. It's just an idea."

"What?"

"Nothing."

"Tell me. I want to know."

"It's just a story."

"About…" She gesticulated with one hand.

"Well, it's a book about a couple in St. Louis. The young couple meet each other on a train. He works in sales for a pharmaceutical company. She's a doctor. They talk about this new medicine being developed by a big Pharma company. Then they do the usual: fight bad guys. Well, the twist…you don't really want to know all this, do you?"

"Why wouldn't I?"

"It's just a story. You want to come up to my balcony and watch the sunrise with me?"

"No. I hate balconies. I tell you what, I'll take you up on orange juice—only if you tell me more about your story in St. Louis. I love stories, particularly love stories. Okay Alec, I'm coming through the kitchen door to get orange juice, but you best not throw the kitchen door in my face again."

"I won't," he said with a chuckle.

Alec laid his computer down on the cement under the chair. Then he bounded across his bedroom and down the stairs.

Along the inside balcony, he could see the bright sun was just starting to shine through the living room, and with all the windows, it was brightening the whole house. He made it to the kitchen before her, snatched two glasses, and poured some juice. And then he just sat down at his small circular dining table and stared at the door, waiting and catching his breath.

Joy arrived, still wearing shades, knocking on the glass of the kitchen door. When Alec opened the door, she reached out for a friendly hug. They embraced. She had this wonderful scent. He couldn't place the perfume, but he recalled smelling it in his car. It was a natural rose scent.

Then Alec squinted at her bare feet.

"Shoes are confining," she said with a chuckle and shrug. She walked to the kitchen table and plopped down on a chair. "This juice better be good, Alec." She removed her sunglasses. "I'm missing an amazing sunrise by our lake. My favorite thing is to watch the sunrise every morning here on Plymouth Crest, Alec. I absolutely love it. It's so pretty, isn't it?"

"You're funny, Joy."

"Am I? Friends always say I'm funny. Cause…you know, I'm full of *joy*. Get it. *Joy?* That's my name." And she grinned, picked up the orange juice, and toasted him. "Um, yummy."

But then they sat across from each other, gazing at one another, and falling into an uncomfortable silence.

"Where do you live?" he finally blurted.

She shook her head before sipping more juice.

"Me first," she said. "Tell me about this story about a couple in St. Louis. Why'd you call the story *"dead"*? *Dead* is so fascinating in such a grim, dark, and dreary sort of way."

"No, I meant I have writer's block. I can't figure out what to write. The idea was to talk about doctors and the pandemic, maybe bring out a connection with a patient the two lovers knew who died. I wanted to address all the post-pandemic angst. Maybe talk about how they find something that's tainted that the industry's selling. You know how there are so many conspiracies these days."

"You don't know what's going to happen next? No wonder you've got writer's block. You sort of should know what you're writing about before you write stuff."

"I have ideas."

"Ideas aren't enough. I knew this writer who used to outline from start to finish. She'd go through, like, four sheets of paper crossing stuff out with a red pen and planning everything. She was so organized. She always had the ending on the last page. She knew exactly where her story was going. So—"

"I never outline. But, no offense, what do you know about writing?"

"I know movies," she said with a shrug. "And I read lots of stuff."

She looked up for a second and smiled. He adored her smile. Then she put a finger to her chin, still looking up pensively. Those brilliant blue eyes were so pretty and alluring. It was electrifying when she gazed back at him.

"A couple meets on a train?" she asked. "Hmm… I'm guessing they're, like, sitting in separate rows and one is passing the complimentary lunch of the day to the other across the aisle or something. Maybe a plastic fork or knife falls on a lap?"

"You've never been on a train, have you?"

"Hey, what's that supposed to mean?"

But she sipped more orange juice.

"There are dining cars in trains," he said. "You get up and go to the dining car to order food for yourself. That's been my experience when I used to ride trains in the Midwest. Unless it's super expensive. Then, I think, you could pass a plate, I suppose, but I wouldn't know. I've never been on an expensive train before."

"Right, well, I've never traveled on a train, smarty. But I know dining cars. Seen them in the movies. All right. So…"

She put a finger to her chin and looked up again. She brushed her long dark hair back. Alec was taken by that. Just watching her run her fingers through her hair.

Looking back, her lips curled into a wry smile. "What?"

"Nothing," he said. "Why are you trying to help me, Joy?"

"I love, love stories. Okay, so, shh, stop interrupting me. Let me think." She looked up in thought again. "I'm here to help—since you don't have any idea what you're writing about."

She chuckled.

But then she sipped more juice. She wiped her lips with the back of her hand.

"You want some tea?" Alec asked.

"No, already. Shush. Don't interrupt. Let me think…okay, so they're both on a train riding through St. Louis, past that arch and stuff. Seen the arch a lot too. Well, maybe they meet in line at the dining car. So in the dining car he orders Cheetos—oh my God, Alec, I frickin' love Cheetos, especially red hot Cheetos, they're so good—but she orders Doritos." She laughed and it made him laugh too. "No accounting for taste. I mean, Doritos are amazing too, particularly Ranch Doritos. Anyway, she opens the chip bag because she's starving to death. Because she's a doctor and doctors are always working and don't have enough time to eat. She didn't have time to get breakfast. Right? But that makes some of the chips fly out of her bag and hit him in the face. How's that? Then they'll be like:

"Excuse me," Joy said in a different accent. *"How embarrassing."*

"No problem," Joy said in a lower voice.

Then he'll pick up one of the Cheetos that fell on her shirt collar and throw it in his mouth.

"I like Cheetos too," he'll say.

"See, then that strikes up a conversation about health food and how unhealthy their breakfast chips are, though they both love their bag of chips. And it leads to talking about vitamins and other boring doctor things—you'd have to look those things up, Alec. That author I was telling you about, she wouldn't even have started page one without already having looked stuff up. Anyway, this leads to talking about medicine. That leads to Covid. And they talk about how they didn't do much during the pandemic except drive to and from work. And that opens up the woman to finally being asked her name.

"What are we naming the doctor?"

Joy stopped talking and took another quick sip of the orange juice. But, after a silence, she gestured with both hands for him to answer.

"Elvira."

"Elvira?" she asked, scrunching her nose. "Eww. That's an awful name." But then her lips curled into one of her wonderful smiles. "Oh, *Elvira*. You're thinking, like, Elvira, the lady of the night? She was so very witchy, Alec. I loved her so much. Like vampires and ghouls movie host Elvira. I frickin' loved Elvira when she used to host scary movies. She was so funny. Did you ever see her when 3D movies were the rage? Remember those red and blue glasses? Those were such fun flicks. Okay. Well, Elvira would ask the guy what he does next, right?"

"I wasn't thinking of that Elvira. I just thought the woman would be named Elvira."

"Whatever. So they meander back to their seats, eating chips for breakfast, talking about the pandemic and their jobs as a doctor and a medical equipment salesman. Chip—we can call him Chip, cause of all this chip stuff I've been thinking about."

Alec frowned. And he felt all his excitement leave him.

"What the hell's the matter?" she asked. "Did I say something wrong?"

"Chip is the name of my best friend—my best friend who just ripped me off for this house. If he can't fix things, I'll be forced to leave."

"Wow, what the hell happened?"

"You don't want to help with my story anymore?"

"Not if something's really bothering you. If something's bothering you, Alec, I'd rather talk about that."

"Chip was my roommate in college. He sold me this place, but I recently found out that the place might not be mine. Turns out, the man who sold me the house didn't own it. It was some kid who believed he could sell the house without properly transferring the title. You were right. The purchase agreement was a sham—not sure how you knew…"

She shrugged.

"Well, apparently, the real owner is either some pop star who might have passed away here, or this guy, Fifi's agent, who skipped town and nobody knows where he is."

She sipped more orange juice and nodded. But then she quickly put the glass down because her hand had started to shake.

"You all right?"

"Diabetes, I think. Too much juice—"

"You've barely drank any." Her glass was still completely full. She was, oddly, sipping very little of it. It seemed she had hardly drunk any.

"Doesn't take much for me."

"Maybe I shouldn't have given you the juice?"

"I absolutely love drinking orange juice with you, Alec. This is totally worth it. Never mind. What are you going to do?"

"I don't know why I'm telling you about all this," he said, shaking his head. "You make me feel comfortable, I guess, Joy. You know something funny? For a while, I actually thought *you* might be Fifi Graynger's ghost."

"That's funny," she said with a laugh.

He leaned back in his chair with a nod. Then he glanced through the glass in the kitchen door. "You're right, I made you miss the sunrise. Sorry."

"I'd rather spend my morning drinking orange juice with you. You make me feel comfortable too, Alec. But, never mind… God, how can I help you keep your house? What the hell are you going to do? You love this place, don't you? How are you going to stay here?"

"Without escrow, I don't even know how or why I'm here. It cost me a fortune to move all my stuff in."

"Well, until you know, I think you should just carry on." She tapped her juice glass with red fingernails. "Don't worry about owning things. You know, everyone gets so hung up on owning stuff. Even if you received title and owned the house, Alec, you'd only have it for a few years. Maybe a decade? Most people move out of their house within five years or less. Nothing is permanent. Except the important stuff. Like our lake. Like the sunrise. If there's one thing I've learned from my life, it's that there's nothing permanent in this world. We all live and die. That was a mistake I once made. But the lake, like God, lives on. God's always with us, Alec. So, you know, why not just enjoy the sunrise? You know, enjoy your life. Forget the paperwork. Enjoy the lake. That's permanent. And the forest. That's why you left your job in California, right? To forget about all of this stuff. What did you say you retired from?"

"I never told you I retired," he answered, feeling suspicious of her again. "I was an accountant."

"What brought you here to Plymouth Crest?"

He raised his hand as she brought more juice up to her lips.

"If you have diabetes, stop drinking it, Joy."

"No. So, what brought you to Plymouth Crest? To nowhere land? You obviously love this lake and forest as much as me."

"I suppose I wanted to turn the page. My wife passed away a few years ago."

"God, I'm sorry."

"It wasn't unexpected. The worst was the years watching her suffer in pain. She died of breast cancer. She was young, only in her forties. But the treatment, I think, killed her. Yeah, it was so hard for my daughter Rachel and I. Very hard."

"I hear you talking to your daughter a lot. Or… I mean, at least, I heard the way you talked to her once and it was so nice. A true family is really special. My family was just me and my mom, but Mom was always working. Then she died when I was only a teenager."

"Well, you know—" And he looked into her eyes, loving them again.—"my wife's death taught me life is short. I learned I had to live life now. I suppose I did a little living with my own business as a CPA back in California, but my writer side wanted more. I wanted to live somewhere quiet to just do what I really love. Writing. That's all, I suppose. And now I'm here. The only thing I miss a lot is my daughter, Rachel."

"Well, you found quiet," she said with a nod. Then she lifted her orange juice glass, as if in a toast. "Hmm. I say…don't overthink things, Alec. Here's to Plymouth Crest. While you live in this house, I say live in the house. You needn't worry, like an accountant. This house has been abandoned for decades. So I say, enjoy it. It's yours."

"I wish things were that simple, Joy."

"They are. You believe something is yours, it's yours. I got stuck in a dream once. Got everything I ever wanted, but I was miserable. You know, with all my wealth, I never really was able to keep a thing. I moved here. Just like you. I thought it was temporary. Everything is temporary. But you know what I discovered? The sun always rises and sets. See, God is always here."

"What was your dream, Joy?"

She got up and walked over to the glass door pensively. Then she shook her head slowly, staring out at the trees.

"I spend most of my time outdoors now," she said. "I think, Alec, I don't really like the indoors anymore." She leaned her head on the glass. "But I love Plymouth Crest, and the forest and the lake are all I really need to feel happy. Things aren't so bad, I guess, if I'm here. It's so beautiful, and that's all that really mattered. Just enjoy what you have. The moment. Don't try to make it something it isn't. Don't overthink things. Just enjoy what you see and feel in your life."

"You're beautiful."

"What?" She spun around with a smile.

"Nothing," he said, getting up. "Sorry to bring up my troubles to you."

"Hmm, I'm almost sure I heard you say something else. I just want you to be happy. Happiness comes from not worrying. It's really about not worrying about anything at all. That's the Zen way, you know."

"Well, I have to thank you," Alec said, standing beside her. "You helped me and my friend so much. You even cleaned the stairs. I was too drunk to—"

"Don't worry about all that. That's what I'm trying to tell you. Stop thinking and…you know, enjoy the sunrise and orange juice in the morning."

He nodded. Then he rose and walked closer to her. Their heads were only a foot apart. Her rose perfume permeated the air. And he felt as if he were in a trance staring down into those bright blue eyes. She gave him that grin he loved. Then he reached out to touch her hand, but she quickly jerked it away.

"I… I'm sorry," he said. "I didn't mean—"

She shook her head, seemingly upset for a moment. But then she shocked him by throwing her arms around him. He gasped in surprise and just stood frozen and locked in her embrace. He was afraid to say a word or even move, because he hoped she wouldn't move either. Because, for some reason—he couldn't put his finger on it—but for some reason he feared that if either of them moved, or spoke, this wonderful feeling would end. Just as she had said, if he thought about it too much, she would be gone.

"I wish I had met you a long time ago," she whispered in his ear.

"You're wonderful. Thanks for the juice. You're such a good man. But now I've gotta go."

"What? Why so soon?" he asked, finally letting go. "Where? Aren't you going to tell me about yourself? Where do you live? I'll visit. Or… tell me why you love, love stories so much."

"How 'bout this one," she said, gently touching the doorknob. "I'm not a writer, but when I lived in L.A. I knew plenty of them. I'm also not originally from Plymouth Hill. We came from the same place. Los Angeles. And I came here for quiet too. You and I have a lot in common, I think. We seem to like the same things. Except accounting. Eww, I could never do math."

"When can we meet again?" he asked at the door. "Maybe we can go together to Badger."

"Badger?" She wrinkled her nose. "Eww, gross. You kidding me? Not much to do in Badger. It's really no different than here. If you stay around Plymouth Hill long enough, you'll learn there's nothing to do for hundreds of miles except enjoy the outdoors. That's why I'm here. I love it. How about we just take a walk together one morning?"

"All right. How about tomorrow morning?"

"Alec." She laughed. "Okay. I guess. I can knock on your door tomorrow morning. Sound good?"

"Just no breaking and entering."

"I'll knock. I promise."

Joy opened the kitchen door.

As she turned a corner around a wide tree, right before disappearing in the green overgrowth, Alec waved and said, "You can break in again anytime, Joy."

She waved back at him.

What are you doing, Alec? Are you falling for her?

Yes, he had that feeling in his chest again. That same feeling he had when he moved into the house. *Joy.*

Joy reappeared in an opening between more trees. She was walking so calmly and serenely. But as she passed another tree down the hill, she dipped her head, smiled, and waved.

"Can't wait, Alec," she said.

She was so lovely. So vibrant. So alluring.

But then he felt shock. Maybe she really was Fifi Graynger, the pop star? Had Fifi been hiding all this time in Plymouth Hill pretending to have died? She certainly was attractive enough and had that enchanting singing voice. Perhaps she had come here to escape the world, just like he had.

He took his cellphone from his pants pocket and searched the internet for Fifi Graynger. He had glanced at her image before but had never thought to compare her with Joy. No. In this image, Fifi held a microphone, singing to thousands of fans on an outdoor stage. The pop star's facial features were completely different from Joy's. Her skin wasn't as smooth as Joy's, and her hair was dirty blond and in braids, not black. Joy definitely didn't look like her. The only resemblance was the singer's age. And, if possible, Joy was actually even prettier.

He chuckled and shook his head.

11

BE WITH ME

ALEC WOKE UP STARING AT THE CEILING. HE WAS AMAZED HE HAD DOZED off at all after tossing and turning, his mind buzzing. He couldn't stop obsessing over the house he was now worried he'd lose. He wanted the place so badly. Maybe he had fallen asleep because of the lack of noise? The slamming of cabinets and doors and the footsteps had mysteriously disappeared last night. Now it seemed almost too quiet.

But his mind wandered again...

Was it over thoughts of the house or was it over Joy? Was he falling for her? He felt that same "crush" he'd felt so many times before, kind of like his crush on the greatest love of his life, his late wife. But was it love or curiosity? She seemed so odd. Maybe the unknown was what drew her to him?

No. Joy was truly the most beautiful woman he had ever seen, sure, but he was so much older than she was. And he still knew so little about her. She had intelligent eyes. She was smart, caring, and kind. And funny… She was very funny. Yes, she was perfect, as alluring as the house itself.

But she was so strange. Perhaps she lived in the forest? Then how did her clothes and her appearance always appear so well kept?

They hadn't kissed on the lips in the kitchen, but they had embraced for such a long time. Somehow, that had felt so much better.

No, it wasn't just suffering from insomnia over losing the house now, it was restless thoughts over Joy.

He turned to look at his clock beside his bed. It read two-thirty in the morning in digital red letters.

A gust of wind picked up outside. Trees swayed with the sound of rain pelting hard on the ground. Rain in July? Only in Plymouth Hill.

Then a flash of lightning lit up his entire bedroom.

He jumped. He wasn't alone in the room. Standing by the glass door before the terrace, in front of red velvet drapes shifting from a breeze that, queerly, was blowing inside the bedroom, stood a lady wearing a translucent white silk nightgown. By moonlight, he could make out the curves of her breasts and hips through the thin garment. But she was paying absolutely no attention to him. She was so quiet, it seemed she could have been standing there while he had slept for hours.

"Who's there?" Alec asked.

"Don't go."

The words didn't seem to come from the woman. They were whispered all around the room. And yet, it sounded like Joy's voice.

There was another flash of lightning. And she disappeared.

Thunder shook the whole room.

Alec jumped as someone, or some thing, appeared on his bed. She straddled him and he fell back in shock against his pillow. It was his lady by the lake. It was Joy! He couldn't fully discern her face in the darkness, but he smelled that familiar rose perfume. Her eyes, in the shadows, peered into his. She gently ran her hand through his thin beard and short hair while staring into his eyes.

"What's going on, Joy?"

"Shh, stop thinking, Alec," Joy whispered. She ran kisses along his neck, and then he finally felt what he had desired in the kitchen when they embraced—the gentle touch of her lips. "Please. Stop thinking or it will be over. Enjoy this night with me. You're sleeping."

He gazed at her breasts and along the curve of her stomach to her legs, through the translucent silk nightgown. She watched him undress her. Then she leaned down again and ran her lips along his beard. He heard their kisses as they made out. Then he felt fingers run along his hair again, massaging his head, hearing her breathing grow heavier. All the while, she kept shifting weight down, moving along his underwear and over the bulge from his cock, arousing him more.

"You're so attractive," she whispered by his ear. But that's what he had been thinking about her.

She squeezed him tight. Then she sat up tall, lifting her nightgown over her shoulders, revealing her soft breasts in the shadows of the moonlight.

"Joy!" he gasped.

"Shh," she whispered. "Be calm or this will be over. Do you want this to end, Alec? Just relax and don't worry. If you worry, you'll wake up from the dream and we can't do this."

"Am I sleeping?"

"Shhh. Yes. I told you you're asleep. This is the only way."

She gently ran her fingers through his beard. Then she shifted to his side and ran her hand along his legs.

"I wanted you in the kitchen so badly," she said quietly. "Shhh," she whispered in his ear. "Just rest. Now, I can feel you, only if you rest and allow me to. Do you want me, like I want you? I can leave you be to sleep if you want. I wish you would sleep better. You're always tossing and turning."

She leaned down and kissed his lips again. Then they were at it again, making out while he stroked her soft breasts, running his fingers over her nipples.

"Do you want to make love to me, Alec?" she whispered.

"Yes."

She gently took his fingers in hers and ran his hands along her soft breasts again. Their hands explored each other's bodies together, as she lay over him, gently rocking over his hard cock. She moaned. He felt so aroused. He pressed his fingers into her back, massaging her, then pressed along her shoulder blades. Gently, she guided his hands slowly down again, along her lower back, and then over the crack of her ass. All the while, she kept gently rocking over him.

"Joy…how did you appear and—"

"Shh, still your mind. Don't think, Alec, or it all could end."

As she sent more kisses along his neck, he answered by pulling down his underwear. And, before he knew it, he was inside her.

Another flash of lightning revealed her nakedness as she straddled him. She was sitting up, presenting her perfect body as she moved up and down over him. Thunder rumbled. And more flashes came, illuminating the room and their bodies, as bright as day. She grasped his hands in hers again, massaging them and bringing each finger up to her lips to kiss and suck. She seemed so focused on his hands. Every finger seemed to be more important than his body. Then she moaned as she grasped them tightly.

Darkness returned and, for a moment, it seemed as if her body had disappeared. Alec could only hear the sound of their lovemaking, still feeling her weight rock over him, which was just as alluring.

Lightning flashed. She appeared again in the shadows, staring into his eyes. That was wonderful—just gazing deeply into her eyes.

Then came another rumble of thunder.

"Is this really happening?"

"Yes," she whispered. "Don't think. Feel. If you think, it will all be over. We can only do this while you're sleeping. Oh, I've watched you and wanted to touch you like this for so long. Dance with me. Touch me. If you think, you might... Oh, that's it...you might...just ruin everything. Stay calm and serene and just be with me. If you only knew how alone I've felt for so long. Be with me, Alec. Be with me. You feel absolutely wonderful."

He threw her on her back making her gasp in surprise. But then she laughed. He adored her laughter so much. Her eyes widened as he lay on top of her. He couldn't make out the blue, but he could see them open and hungry. He brushed his hand along her soft cheek and then reached down kissing her lips again, running his tongue along hers. Then he pressed deeper into her body, and she moaned more loudly as she ran her fingers through his beard and over his arms and chest. All the while, in the shadows of moonlight, as he pushed, she gazed deeply into his eyes.

Another lightning strike lit up her eyes like sapphires.

"Yes. That's it. Please, touch me. Touch me and...fuck me."

All turned dark as the entire room shook. It was not just thunder—it was as if an earthquake had rumbled the bed and the entire foundation of the house. He ran his fingers over her butt, squeezing her ass and pressing down over her harder. All the while she kept stroking his back and arms.

"That's it. Yes, Alec. Oh, please stay with me. Please! Please be with me. Don't go. Oh, God, if you only knew how lonely I've been! I just want to touch and feel you forever!"

She took a deep breath and then fell limp under him. And he orgasmed with his weight over her. Then she caught him tightly in her arms and ran kisses along his neck and over his lips.

"Is this just a dream?" he asked, panting. "It seems so real."

"Can I stay in your arms while you sleep? I can help you…stay asleep, if you want. For a little while, if it's what you want, Alec. Then I can be in your arms longer. Do you want that? I'd love that so much."

"Yes."

"While you sleep, I can lie in your arms and finally touch you with my hands." He felt her running her hands along his back again, then over his hands, stroking his fingers again. "Lie with me, Alec. Lie with me."

They lay on their sides, staring into each other's eyes. He ran his hands along her back, pressing against her soft hips and breasts as she kissed him again gently on the cheek and lips.

"I want to touch you for as long as I can. I wish I could forever."

"It is a dream."

He awoke staring up at the ceiling again. Then he heaved a sigh. How could it not have been a dream? Joy wasn't in his room. How could she be?

But whatever it was, it was amazing.

"*Don't go.*"

12

SEARCHING FOR JOY

EVER SINCE MIDNIGHT, WHEN HE AWOKE FROM HIS VIVID AND unsettling wet dream, rain had continued to fall in a tempest of fierce winds, throwing branches and trees against the walls of his house, blowing away anything he had laid outside—chairs, vases, tables—right down the hillside and into the woods below. The wind was so powerful that it tossed his plastic chair right off the terrace. It had rained so hard that there was about a foot of water surrounding the foundation. *Well, there goes my walk this morning with Joy.*

Alec ventured downstairs, walking along the mezzanine, marveling at the inside of his home. Though it stormed outside, and he was surrounded by the sight of the outdoors, he was still warm and cozy. He loved his house so much. He headed to the kitchen to brew coffee.

That's when his cellphone rang from the bedroom.

So back he went, bounding upstairs and around the indoor balcony and running inside his bedroom to not miss the call.

"Yeah," he clambered, panting.

"Hey, man," Chip said.

"Do you have any idea what time it is, Chip? And…isn't it like three in the morning in Los Angeles?"

"Yep. Three in the morning. But six o'clock in Costa Rica. I told you I'd make things better. I found the owner. Or at least someone just as good, better than Robin."

"Really?" Alec asked, walking back down the stairs. "I don't know whether to kiss you or smack you in the face."

"Kiss me, buddy. Reggie's alive and well. He's not officially the owner, but he's got a better chance of taking possession of the place than his son. And here's the kicker. He doesn't give a shit about it, Alec. In fact, it's possible I can shave off more from the sale. He was in shock when I told him about it. He was led to believe the place burned down decades ago. All he wants is the money."

"His son didn't talk to him about it?"

"I don't think he's speaking to his son."

"What's the catch?"

"Why do you always think there's a catch, man? Well, time. I need to fax a ton of documents to the guy and wait for him to work things out. I might even have to take a vacation in Costa Rica. Could be worse, right? But at least this guy, unlike our music star, is alive and well. Really, the only catch is me. If I talk down the price, I get less of a cut for our sale."

"Fuck you, Chip."

"Yeah, I deserved that. Now"—He yawned—"I've really gotta get some rest. It's frickin' three o'clock in the morning here. I'll get everything arranged. I've arranged another phone meeting with Reggie later. He wanted to meet early. Now that there's a big deal for him, he wants to chat again. So I'll find out more soon enough and call you back. Don't worry. When everything's ready, I'll fax the papers back to you. Unless you want me to come by your house again? Please say you don't want me to travel back to Plymouth Hill, Alec."

"Email," Alec said with a chuckle. "But God knows where a fax machine is around here."

"Email can turn into faxing, genius. What century were you born in? Man, you really belong there in the middle of nowhere."

"Has he been the one forging Fifi's name?"

"No. I wondered about that. He said he wasn't sure, but he was certain it wasn't Fifi. He said he witnessed her death. I still haven't solved that riddle yet, but I will. Like I said, at least now I have a lead I can talk to, not some dead pop star."

"Fix it and get me the papers to sign the house over."

"Sure thing, buddy. Will do."

"Bye, Chip."

"Bye."

Alec hung up the cellphone. Then he just walked over to a lounge chair in the living room and gazed over his left shoulder at the outside. The rain was picking up again, and there was a wall of water outside the window now.

There goes my date.

He fell back in his chair. Did it matter? If he wasn't leaving Plymouth Crest, neither was Joy. There'd be plenty of chances to walk with her later.

Alec woke to knocking. Had he fallen back asleep?

Was it Joy!?

The thought was enough to stir him and make him rush to the front door. He still had his phone in his pajamas pocket. It read eight o'clock. It was still pouring rain outside.

He gazed through the peephole. Nope, it was Daisie. Daisie stood under the overhang by the front patio wearing a long red coat and matching beret. Her red hair made her clothes appear darker, like burgundy. Behind her fell a wall of water. And Daisie's coat was sopping wet.

"Hey, Alec!" Daisie said, walking inside. She took her coat and hat off and he grabbed them. Then she gave him a quick hug. She glanced around the house and scrunched her nose. "Hey ghosts, any of you creepin' round the house?"

Then she did what everyone did after walking into his home. She headed into his amazing central living room. Her eyes surveyed the upstairs balcony and all the windows.

"You know, last time I was here, a group of my friends smoked cloves by your fireplace in the middle of the night."

Alec looked outside the still-open door. Visibility in the downpour was terrible. He imagined Joy might be out there somewhere. But why would she walk in this storm? She'd definitely be indoors this morning. Where—that was the real mystery.

As Alec turned back to Daisie, she presented him a gold wrapped box with a red bow. She must have been carrying it under the coat. It was the only thing that was dry.

"What's this?"

"Special *Daisie* delivery. Amazon doesn't deliver in Plymouth Hill, you know, so we make do round here."

"Yeah, but what is it?"

"Open it, silly."

Alec opened the gold wrapper. Inside was a box with an image of a flashlight with a bright beam of light.

"That is the amazing one I was talking about. Remember I couldn't find it? Well, I had to order it. They say that thing can shine light for a mile. I wouldn't be surprised if you can spot deer all the way down the hill by the lake in nighttime."

"I just needed a light for the house," he said with a chuckle.

"Yeah, well, it'll sure do that too."

"Thank you, Daisie."

A strike of lightning lit up the living room, making it as bright as day. It made the recess light on the ceiling seem dim.

"Love what you've done with the place," she said, ignoring the weather. But she couldn't ignore the thunder. It seemed to shake the entire foundation. She shook her head. "What a terrible storm. Even for Plymouth Hill. Your furniture is really modern, Alec. So L.A.. Really, not all that different from what was withering here years ago. Your stuff fits the place and looks really nice. The house has always been totally L.A., I suppose. I mean, with that indoor balcony, California chic totally fits your weird mansion."

She went straight over to the floor-to-ceiling window and just stared outside at the backyard.

"How are you liking our rain?" she asked, cocking her head back. "Get used to it. This is a July storm. Wait till you meet December flurries. Then the road shuts down in January, and you'll be landlocked for the new year. Might finally turn you totally *Shining* nutso. You know, you best be walking on the main road then anyway because black ice is treacherous for your fancy car. But…hmm, there's not much stuff outside on your patio."

"It was all blown away."

"See. That's what I'm talking about. Rain in Plymouth Hill."

Lightning flashed again. It made Daisie glow yellow near the window and the whole living room flash brightly for a moment. The light was on, but it seemed dimmer when the flash of light left. Then thunder shook the room and all the windows again. For a moment, the weather reminded him of his strange, vivid dream last night.

Daisie plopped herself on his black leather couch—across from the chair he had been sleeping in—put her large leather purse on her lap, and just smirked at him. She wore a quarter moon on her forehead this time, but otherwise she seemed normal enough. And she wore a black sweater and dark slacks. She smelled nice, it was a strange mix of jasmine and mint.

She dug in her purse and took out a deck of cards. Then she laid the stack of cards on the coffee table before the couch.

"I owe you a reading. You were so nice to me on the fourth. You want to do your reading now? It'd be a lot of fun in this heavy storm."

He shrugged, sitting beside her.

"But you said you get up early, right?" Daisie asked, touching his leg. "Am I imposing?"

Only if Joy comes by.

Daisie shuffled the cards as if they were about to play poker.

"You want coffee?" Alec asked.

She shook her head. Then she started looking at a few of the cards.

"Isn't that cheating?"

"We're not gambling. These are tarot cards."

"How about orange juice?"

"No thanks. I hate orange juice."

"Okay, here," she said, moving the coffee table closer to them. Then she shuffled the cards, not looking this time. She took one card and pressed it against her forehead. "See this. Describe to me what the card looks like."

"The one covering your moon?"

"Uh, yeah," she chuckled. "Yeah. Describe it. Come on. It's your card, Alec. What does it look like?"

"It looks like a king carrying a grail."

"Oh, that's the king of cups. Yep. Wow. That sure fits you. It means you're sympathetic and kind. Artistic. A good listener. That's definitely you, Alec. Totally you. Now do you believe in the cards?"

Alec shook his head.

"Nonbeliever. Let's get to the good part. Let's see what your future holds."

Then she shuffled the cards again. She reached out to hold one of his hands. With the other hand, she kept moving the cards.

There was another strike of lightning. They squinted as the brightness rushed back into the living room. Then thunder quaked the glass windows.

"Jeesh, what an awful storm," she said. "But that could be good for my magical energy." She took one card, facing it down on the table. "Okay. Draw this one and show it to me."

There was another strike of lightning, and thunder that rocked the windows. But Daisie stared at Alec, waiting.

Alec flipped the card over. The card presented on the table was a guy on a throne. The bottom of the cartoon read "justice."

"An arcana card, Alec. Wow, an arcana. That's a goodie. Very good. Pull one more for your first reading. You need three for a reading. Three gives me the most information about your future."

"What does that card mean?"

"It means your life will be full of justice," she said with a nod.

He looked at her suspiciously.

"Do you know what you're doing?" he asked.

"What do you mean?" she asked, looking offended.

"Didn't you just read *justice* on the card?"

"I interpreted your king of cups, didn't I? Come on." She waved a hand at him dismissively and said, "Next card."

Alec chose a card with a cartoon of a naked couple under a woman with wings. At the bottom of the card it said "lovers."

"Ah, another arcana card!" she said with a large grin. "How about that! Another arcana. I can't believe it. I love arcana cards. And this one's the best one." She winked. "Wow, Alec, how unusual. You picked the 'lovers' card. See. That's a special one. And that card means—"

Another flash of lightning lit up the living room. For a flash, again, it was as bright as day. But then a gale rushed *inside* the house, shaking the windows and blowing through the room, throwing Daisie's stack of tarot cards off the table.

But although it stormed outside, none of his windows were open.

Then the whole room shook with thunder, this time more violently than ever. It was almost as if there was an explosion. And a cold gale still blew against his face. Alec turned to the windows, thinking maybe one was open. Instead, a large vase barreled into the bushes amidst the whirlwind. And all the trees were swaying like crazy.

"Do you have a window open?" asked Daisie, staring at the windows too. "They all seem closed to me." She got on her knees and started picking up all the cards. "Or maybe the door's open? That's so weird."

Flash came another lightning strike. This one was so bright that it seemed to have hit the house. Thunder exploded again. That's when a woman appeared right outside the windows, drenched, holding herself in her arms. A yellow glow surrounded her, as if she weren't real but a part of the thunderbolt. The flash lasted just long enough for him to recognize her face. *Joy!* God, was Joy outside in the pouring rain? She stood out there glaring at them. She looked pissed. Alec jumped. But the minute he approached the window, Joy was gone.

"You best stand away from the windows," warned Daisie. But she was on her knees, still gathering up all her cards from the carpet. "It sounds like the storm is right above your roof. You don't want to be struck by lightning." She looked up for a moment. "What the fuck happened? How the hell did the cards fly into the air *inside* your house, Alec? That is so weird."

Through the window Alec searched the woods for Joy. His small concrete patio was covered in a foot of water. But she wasn't there. Then he gazed farther up the hillside. No sign of Joy there either.

"Get that woman out of here," said a voice outside in a forced whisper. "Make her go. I mean it, Alec. Make her leave now!"

"Joy?"

"We're sure not having any joy if this storm keeps up, I'm afraid," quipped Daisie with a laugh. "Man, this is so bad. Good thing I drove. I was thinking of heading up the hill this morning. Walking would have been so stupid."

"You should probably stay until the storm lifts," commented Alec absentmindedly. He still searched the trees for Joy.

"*No!*" Joy cried.

Daisie threw a bunch of her cards on the table and then leapt up from her knees, rushing to the window. She searched the yard with him.

"You heard that?" he asked.

"Yeah." Daisie nodded, searching outside. "It sounded like a woman's voice outside shouting 'no.' Gosh, I hope there's no one out there right now in this terrible rain."

"I know a lady who keeps wandering outside. One of those drifters you were talking about."

"Well, she's stupid if she's outside of shelter in this storm. But I told you about them. I wasn't kidding. There are so many hikers and bohemians creeping about around this hill."

There was a bang. It wasn't thunder this time—it sounded more like a knock. It was coming from the kitchen. Then another gust of wind picked up *inside* the living room, and all of Daisie's collected tarot cards were tossed right off the table once more.

"What the hell is going on?" drawled Daisie with wide eyes. "Why is there wind *inside* your house, Alec. Alec... I... I think your house really is haunted."

"Wait a minute," he said, "I want to check around the house and make sure everything's okay. I'll be right back."

"Sure," Daisie said, with her eyes wide. "Sure, you do that. I'm not going anywhere." Because she was back to picking up her cards. "I don't believe this. This is wonderful, Alec. Your house is really frickin' haunted!"

"I'll be right back."

Alec rushed into the kitchen, where he had heard the knock. It was dark. The light switch didn't work. And there wasn't anyone there. Until another flash of lightning hit. Then, in the blinding white light, Joy stood shaking outside the glass kitchen door with her arms folded in pouring rain. When the lightning left, it turned very dark, but he could still see her standing outside. She wore a drenched dark blouse and jeans. Her dark hair was dripping wet too. And her eyeliner was runny. Drops of water fell from her face. But not only was she shivering, she was scowling.

He quickly opened the kitchen door.

"Let me—"

"Shh," Joy said in a whisper, shaking. "Shh, Alec. Shut up for a second. Be quiet." And she put a finger up to her lips. Then she looked toward the living room. The door was cracked open. She walked over and gently closed it. "Just be quiet for a sec," Joy said in a forced whisper. "Why is that woman here? Daisie's weird. And she's full of it. She knows as much magic as I do. She's just trying to seduce you."

"Go say hi to her, Joy," said Alec with a smile. "Come on. She'd love to meet you. You helped her on the Fourth, remember?"

"No," she said with a forced whisper. "Be quiet, I say. I don't want her knowing I'm here."

"Why? You helped her. Go say hi. You'd like Daisie."

"I don't want to right now. Not now. But you"—Her teeth chattered —"Hey, you promised to walk with me this morning."

"Seriously?" he asked incredulously, backing up. "You want to walk outside now?"

The funny thing was, though she was shivering and sopping wet, the idea of walking out in the pouring rain with Joy was the best proposition he had been given in years. She was all he had thought about since his dream.

Joy chuckled—but tried not to, covering her mouth, her body jerking. Then she laid a shaky finger over her lips.

"You're so cold," Alec said, searching all over the kitchen in the dark for a towel. "I'll find something to dry you."

A flash of lightning brightened the kitchen again. And then the house shook with another rumble of thunder.

"Alec," she whispered, "you invited me—remember?—to walk with you alone this morning. Not her. I knocked. Now get her the hell out of the house already."

"I'm ready," Daisie hollered from the other room. "I picked up all the cards. Unless that pesky ghost is going to mess them all up again." Daisie laughed. Joy narrowed her eyes. "You finished checking things over in your château, Alec?"

"Why the fuck do you think she came here this morning?" Joy snapped in a forced whisper. "Are you dense? She knows as much about tarot cards and witchcraft as you do. You can be so dense sometimes, Alec. Please make her go."

"But why?"

Joy threw her arms around him. He backed up, not because he objected to her embrace, but out of surprise. Her body was so wet and cold from the rain. But that made him squeeze her tighter in order to warm her. He felt the drops drip down all over him. A few drops even ran under his pajama shirt—he hadn't even had a chance to get dressed in regular clothes yet.

Then he felt her lips. Joy first kissed him gently. Then she pressed hard. And soon her lips were all over his beard and neck. He realized, though she had made love to him in his dream, this was their first real kiss. He had dreamt of being in her arms again, and now, even better, she was making out with him.

"This is why, mister," she whispered in his ear. "Okay? If you care about me like I do you, you'll honor this simple request for me this morning. Make her scram. No more questions. Just get that conniving witch to drive herself home. She'll be fine. She can drive straight down the hill to her store, but I don't want to see her right now."

"But…"

"But what?" She put a finger over her lips again. "No buts. Shh." Then she just looked deeply into his eyes. "Please, Alec. No questions. Stop thinking and do as I say."

Stop thinking…that's what she kept saying over and over in my dream.

She came closer to his ear and whispered, "This was supposed to be our morning. Remember? You invited me to come walk with you. Please don't be so nice to her that you hurt me."

"But we can't walk outside right now."

"We certainly cannot," said Daisie from the other room, laughing. "You can't expect to be walking outside in this rain, Alec. You're so crazy sometimes. Actually, I love that you're that crazy."

Thunder flashed again, lighting up the dark kitchen. Joy's eyes opened wide.

"Get her the fuck out now," Joy drawled in a whisper. Then she gnashed her teeth and raised her eyebrows. "She's not invited to join us. 'kay?"

Alec got out of her arms and rustled through drawers. All he had was a drawerful of small kitchen towels. He took the small towel out and presented it to her.

Joy rolled her eyes and snatched it. "Thanks."

"I'll stay," Joy whispered. "If she goes. But don't tell her I'm here. Please, Alec, please promise you won't tell her I'm here. Promise? Just figure out another excuse to have her go away."

"Let me at least get you a proper towel."

"Oh shit," Joy said, looking over Alec's shoulder. "Shit, shit she's coming! I'll just dry up in your powder room. Don't worry about me, worry about that witch. Get that witch the hell out of our house. You invited *me* this morning, remember? Not her. This…" She grimaced more deeply than ever and said quietly, with a country accent, "This town ain't big enough for the two of us, partner."

Then Joy ran to the nearby powder room and shut the door.

"Alec, you're so wet," said Daisie, opening the door from the living room. "Did you actually go outside in the storm? Are you crazy?"

"There's a lot of damage on the porch," Alec lied. Then he looked down at his bare feet standing in a pool of water. "I had to see if I could salvage some of my plants."

"Oh," Daisie said. But then she looked all around the dark kitchen. She switched on the light. The light switch worked this time. "I can't believe those cards were thrown off the table. We need to get a medium to check out this house—Luminous, or one of his friends. I'm only so good, you know. Most of my witchcraft comes from all the books I read and tidbits here and there from wizards I've met. In the city, there's some real good ghost hunters that would frickin' love this place. Have you ever seen anything else move inside your house? That was unbelievable. It could be the lightning's stirring up just the right amount of paranormal energy for awesome stuff like that to happen. Have you been having any strange dreams in your house?"

Uh, yeah…

The lightning struck again. Then it shook the kitchen.

He heard a grunt come from the powder room.

He thought of her plea. Perhaps he should ignore it, stop the nonsense, and just have Joy come out and talk to Daisie? He didn't get it. She wasn't shy. Besides, didn't they know each other? They had to in such a small town. But disobeying her wishes seemed disrespectful.

And also…deep inside, Alec wanted to be alone with Joy too. And he felt like if he obeyed her, for whatever strange oddball reason—maybe she had social anxiety?—if he obeyed her request, they would still have their date.

But…*walk outside in pouring rain?* Daisie was right. That was crazy.

"Daisie, I'm expecting someone to be coming by the house any minute to do some really important business," Alec lied. "I so like your gift, but I was wondering if we could meet again later? Maybe I can come by later this afternoon or evening."

"Oh," Daisie said, furrowing her brow. "Sure. All right. You don't have to be so formal about it. I told you I didn't want to impose. This was sudden. Just got excited when I got the flashlight delivered last night."

"You haven't imposed. I really appreciate you stopping by."

"Sure. But…before I go, maybe we could try just one more reading? I'll shuffle the cards and—"

"You sure you'll be all right driving down the hill in the rain?"

"Sure," Daisie said. "Sure. No problem. Alec, you haven't been around here long enough. It's a bad storm but it's nothing compared with snow. I'm sorry if I imposed."

"You didn't. You're a great friend."

"You are too, Alec." She touched his shoulder and then looked around the kitchen. "Wow, you live in a real haunted house. This place is so awesome."

Alec reached to hug Daisie. There was another flash of lightning and the roar of thunder. The two embraced quickly in the kitchen, but Daisie kept her distance. Because Alec was soaking wet.

13

____

ETHEREAL

Alec leaned forward, head in hands, on the black leather lounge chair in his living room, waiting for Joy to take a shower upstairs. His dream last night had been so vivid. And now she had come back to him to take a morning walk together. During a thunderstorm. Things were getting weird…

He jumped up and walked up to the window, stroking his beard and staring outside. Of course, Joy was right. The trees weren't swaying anymore, the rain was drizzling, and the clouds were dispersing, revealing the bright golden sun. Yes, they could walk this morning, but they'd have to keep to muddy paths. If he was honest with himself, he was excited at the prospect of walking with her.

That dream had been so real—too real to be a dream. The only answer he could think of was simple: he was slipping into psychosis. That's what Daisie had warned him about. He was simply getting "cabin fever." But how long did it take to develop cabin fever? He had only been in Plymouth Crest for a few months. It hadn't even snowed yet.

"Ready?"

Joy stood at the base of the stairs looking very excited. He loved her energy. But, typical of her weirdness, she wore the same wet clothes she had worn in his kitchen. Still, despite a damp shirt and pants, her hair had been straightened and she looked, if possible, lovelier than before.

"Sorry," he stammered, "I should have offered to dry your clothes."

"Forget it. I'm warm enough, Alec."

She sauntered over and put her arms around him again. That spread dampness, but she wasn't cold this time. They gazed into each other's eyes again. Then he looked at her shoes—or lack thereof. Her feet were spotless. They were always so clean. Come to think of it, even when she had walked into the kitchen from the woods, they weren't dirty.

"Oh," she said, looking down. "Kinda weird about my feet. Do you want me to explain?"

"There's so much about you that's a mystery."

"Well, if you love something, can't it be ethereal?"

"Huh?"

"Well," she said with a shrug, "I mean, that is to say, if you like someone or something, someone, you know, that gives you joy, do you have to worry? Isn't everything in this world fleeting? That's what the Buddhists say. Everything changes. It's like the house. You were talking about losing it, but eventually we lose everything, don't we? Eventually, when you die, you have to give everything away. So, why can't we just enjoy the moment? What we touch, what we see, what we hear—does it always have to be attached to some desire? Can't we just enjoy the world God gave us?"

"Sure, I guess. That all sounds pretty deep to me."

"I think we can," she said, nodding pensively. Then she shrugged and chuckled. "Well, you're the writer, Alec."

She took two slow steps away from him but hesitated. Then, with her back still turned, she reached out for his arm. "Shall we?" She hooked her arm around his, laughing happily again, and they passed over the threshold of his front door.

He had thought they'd head down the hill to the road by the lake, but she apparently intended the opposite. She headed uphill along a dirt path, now muddy, under a dripping wet canopy of branches and leaves that surrounded his backyard. He knew his grounds well enough to know where this trail headed: to an even higher lookout. Perhaps this peak was where she lived? Impossible. The pinnacle of the hill was just a small wild grassy knoll, hardly large enough for a home.

"I've been thinking more about your story," she said as they walked. "And I've got some ideas, if you'd like to hear them. Have you written anything else?"

"No."

"*Alec!*" she chided.

They turned up a steeper incline, up toward the summit of Plymouth Crest. And she held him closer.

"Well, why not have the couple meet on an airplane? Trains are so unfashionable these days. I was thinking you could turn the story into a destination novel. Wouldn't that be more exciting? They could meet on the way to Hawaii. Everyone loves Hawaii, right? The doctor could be sitting near the medical supply salesman on a plane. Or was he a pharmacist?"

"Medical supply. But the whole concept is a train, Joy."

"Well, hear me out. Maybe she's a new doctor and just hasn't had time to travel, but this is an exciting change. And he's getting out of some relationship and just wanted to let off some steam. He's single, so he figured he'd take a trip to the islands. Some people do that when they're lonely and single. Trust me, I should know. I did a couple jaunts myself back in the day. And, you know, if they're both going to a conference, Hawaii would be just the absolute perfect place. Wouldn't it?"

He shook his head.

"Why not?"

But he didn't answer. They just fell silent as they climbed.

Still, while his mouth didn't move, his thoughts were screaming. He couldn't stop wondering about her. Something seemed off. She had pristine bare feet, never with a blemish? He thought that maybe if he could solve that riddle, everything would become clear.

Is she the ghost of the house? Fifi's ghost?

She sure seemed like one last night.

But that was just a dream…wasn't it?

She seems as real as Daisie.

Was it possible a lady walked about everywhere barefoot? Didn't that cut up one's soles? Or did people get used to it? Cavemen didn't have shoes…did they?

"Hmm, Alec? How come you've gone quiet? What about Hawaii for your story instead of St. Louis?"

But what about her home? Where did she live? And if she was homeless, how come she always looked so clean and beautiful?

Because she's Fifi's ghost.

Impossible. Ghosts weren't real.

Her rose perfume permeated the air. That smelled wonderful. And he could feel the warmth of her embrace. And her heart—my God, her beating heart—he could feel it beat when she leaned against his chest. No, she was alive, more alive than anyone he had ever known.

When they reached the true "crest" of Plymouth Crest, Alec saw the view of the lake far below the trees, but from an even higher, more majestic overlook. It was stunning. And directly below, about three hundred feet down, sat his home. From this vantage point, he saw the back of his house and all those windows on the first and second floors of his main living room. Beyond this, he could just make out his dirt driveway meandering, under a canopy of trees, onto a single road that winded down the hill. The clouds, now clearing, reflected yellow over the lake. Joy was gazing down at the water too, running her fingers through her long dark hair, just staring. And the sun shone through the clouds, glistening over her pretty face, too.

"Isn't it lovely?"

"Joy, there's something about the way you look."

She turned with a smug smile. "What's the matter with the way I look?"

"I can't put my finger on it," Alec said, "all I know is, I don't think you're being honest with me. Some very weird things are going on, and you're not explaining them."

"Like what? So, what do you think about my idea of the destination being Hawaii instead of St. Louis? Everyone loves a holiday tale in Hawaii more than trains. I once saw a movie about trains. I tell you, it gets pretty damn dreary."

"Why are you so into helping me with my story?"

"I love love songs," she said gazing into his eyes. "I mean…you know, I… I love love stories, and stories are like songs. I'm from L.A.,

Alec, like you. Just a bohemian who loves the trees as much as you do, and a lover of art, like you. I used to write music. I love love lyrics."

"Like Fifi?"

"What?" she asked. It seemed to snap her out of it. "What do you mean, Fifi? You mean, like, Fifi Graynger, the musician who died in your house?" And she laughed.

"You're beautiful."

"You're not so bad yourself. I thought I heard you say that the other day."

"No, no, you're *too* beautiful, Joy," he said, shaking his head. "I want you to be honest with me. I think you're Fifi. Fifi Graynger. I don't know how, or why, but you never died, did you? You're Fifi Graynger. That's why you're living near my house, or on the grounds of her house? Or wherever you live. Where do you live, by the way?"

"Are you crazy, Alec? Do I look like that music star? Have you ever seen her?"

No, she didn't look like her. Maybe she'd had plastic surgery? Was that explanation any weirder than the alternative?

Before he could answer, his cellphone rang in his pants pocket. The contact read "Chip."

He raised a finger and walked a couple steps toward the edge of the grassy and muddy cliffside.

"What's up, Chip?"

"Bad news."

"So what's new?"

"Man, it's not that bad. I had my second talk with Reggie, a lot longer this time. He said our famous pop star moved to Plymouth Hill to get away from the Hollywood scene. She wanted to get away from the hustle and bustle, just like someone else I know. She was most definitely the owner. She built the place. She's the one who built your mansion."

"You already said she was the owner."

Alec looked at Joy. Joy just kept smiling, gazing down at the lake.

"Yeah, but here's the bad news. I also researched the tabloids. Alec, Reggie and Joy were *estranged* lovers. They didn't like each other when she passed away."

Alec froze.

"See, they had a huge falling out before Joy died, so I have my doubts, whatever Reggie's saying, that he has legal ownership of the place—unless he's lucky and she set up her will before their falling out. But from what I've researched in magazines and papers, Reggie and Joy were on awful terms when she finally moved into your house."

Alec glared at Joy. Joy didn't turn, but her smile narrowed.

"Are you still there…"

"Why do you keep saying Joy?"

"What?"

"Why are you calling Fifi, Joy?"

"Oh, Fifi was her stage name. Sounds like a stage name, right? But the name she was born with was Josephine. Fifi is a nickname for Josephine. Well, Reggie never referred to her as Fifi when he knew her. On our call, he kept calling her Joy. Apparently, Joy was her private nickname for only her closest friends. See, Joy's a popular nickname for Josephine too."

Alec felt his hand tighten into a fist. His whole body stiffened. Joy still stared at the view, but now she had what looked like a pained expression.

"Here's the good news," Chip continued. "Reggie's planning to visit you and work out all the legal avenues. If he can get legal claim to the deed, we can still do business with him. And why wouldn't he? Apparently, Reggie said that when Joy died, she left no next of kin or close friends. Reggie said he doesn't think there's a will. So who else can lay claim?"

"*Joy?*"

Joy finally turned.

"Joy, Fifi, Josephine, whatever," Chip said. "Does it matter? That lady had a lot of names when she was alive."

"But Reggie said the deceased woman's nickname was Joy? Are you absolutely positive, Chip?"

Joy grunted.

"Sure," Chip said. "So?"

Alec's heart grew heavy. He swooned, feeling dizzy, and the high elevation, which had been a pleasure, sickened him. The facts finally matched his suspicions, but he couldn't believe it. Even now, it looked like he was in the company of his neighbor, someone who had come to his house for a simple morning walk with him. Looking at her, he just couldn't believe the lady beside him was a ghost.

"How…did she…die, Chip?" Alec muttered. Joy grunted again, but he didn't dare look at her this time. "Did Reggie tell you how she passed away?"

"Oh, well, I don't want to tell you that."

"Please, man, tell me."

"If we finally get the deal on your house, you're not going to want to know this."

"How, Chip? I have to know."

"He said she fell from the bedroom balcony to her death. It was suicide. But he fled the country after witnessing it for fear of being accused of murder. There was never anything to implicate him. Ultimately, Reggie claims it was her fans that chased him out of the country. The whole ordeal apparently destroyed his reputation and career. Her fans suspected he killed her, because of their falling out, but it was never proven. I didn't want to tell you about the balcony because that spot is your favorite part of the house."

"He's sure she died?"

With little surprise, Joy looked deadpan now. Guarded. Almost angry. But a single tear fell down her cheek.

"What do you mean?" Chip asked.

"He's positive she died?"

And then, of all people, Joy nodded solemnly. That made Alec feel sicker.

"Alec," Chip replied, "your terrace is like three to four stories high when you account for the grade down the hillside. Anyone falling from your balcony wouldn't do well from that height. He witnessed her fall off the ledge and then he freaked out. He claims it was suicide, but he was so worried he'd be blamed, he ran. Well, he came back. Two days later, Joy's dead body was still lying in the front yard. He called the coroner, but it took the coroner another day to come by—you know how far away you are from everything. But then the body disappeared. So there never was a death certificate. You—damn, this is morbid, Alec—you know, you're in the middle of nowhere. God knows if some animal took her body. Her body was never found so, technically, Josephine Graynger is still missing."

"But Reggie saw her body. You're absolutely positive?"

"Yeah. He's sure. Why?"

"Two days later, he confirmed it? And... Joy is another one of Josephine Graynger's nicknames?"

"Yes. And yes."

Joy grunted yet again, folding her arms.

"Yes," Chip drawled on the phone. "Our pop star died falling from your balcony two decades ago. Why are you acting so surprised? Does it matter? I told you Fifi was the ghost of the house when you purchased it. Look, Alec, don't worry, I can fix all this. Reggie had totally forgotten about your place. He assumed it was taken by the state years ago. If he's telling me the truth, who else can lay claim? He wants to fly over from Costa Rica and see the place. He's saying he'll sell it to us if he can get the deed—unlike his son, who didn't know what the hell he was doing."

Joy shook her head vehemently.

"What?" Alec snapped, glaring at Joy. "What's the matter?"

"What do you mean, what?" asked Chip.

"No, Alec," Joy said in a forced whisper. "No. You can't let Reggie come here."

"Chip, just—"

"No," Joy said again quietly. "Don't let that man come anywhere near my house. Make sure that asshole stays far away from us. He's a very dangerous man."

"Why?" Alec asked.

"Who are you talking to?" Chip asked.

"I'll talk to you later, Chip."

"Sure. Sure. I'll send you all the details. But here's the best part. Because Reggie had thought the property had been destroyed, he said he's willing to take an even smaller cut than his son for the sale! Isn't that great! I tell you, if bad things keep happening, pretty soon you might have the place for free!"

"Bye, Chip."

"Bye. It's good news, right?"

No. It was some of the worst news Alec had heard in his life.

He shoved the phone back in his pocket. Then the trees and grass surrounding him swayed, and he fought an urge to vomit. He put his head in his hand and closed his eyes tightly.

"Whatever you do, Alec," Joy said, "you have to keep that asshole away from my house. You don't want him anywhere near us. He's a very dangerous man. If you—"

"*Shut up!*" Alec shouted. Joy lurched back. "*Shut up and just be quiet! You're…you're not even real!* Is he right? Are you Fifi's ghost? Of course you are. Where else can you live? You're a ghost. But you seem so real. How? How are you so real? Are you real? Is there anything about you…"

He ran his hand through his short hair. Then he just turned from her and stared at the view. The view, now with clearer skies after the storm, was gorgeous. Gorgeous like Joy. Joy…*his ghost?* For the first time since moving here, he loathed the view. Then he crouched down on his knees, sick.

"Alec, I'm sorry… I really am. I've been watching you for months. I really like you. I wanted to talk to you so many times, and then, when I felt like you liked me, I wanted to touch you. That's why I came to you last night. I watched you for so long, wanting to be with you, because… because…I'm falling in love with you."

"*How can you say that now!*" Then he shouted something completely incomprehensible. "You've been messing with me since we met! Why didn't you tell me from the start what you were?" He gazed down at her bare feet, her perfect feet, without a scrape or a bit of dirt. "No shoes? You never wear shoes, right? But you have flawless feet. That's a weird goddamn ghost thing, isn't it? That's why your feet are perfect, despite rain, thorns, or mud. You're not just Fifi, you're that pop star's ghost."

She nodded.

"Why don't you look like her?"

"I touched stuff up here and there on my face," she said with a shrug. "I thought you'd like me better this way. I suppose it's really no different from putting makeup on. I used to wear a lot of makeup back in the day. I was good at it. I'm good at all sorts of things I put my mind to, Alec. Just like—" She went on and on, but he stopped listening.

"*Why'd you lie to me!*"

"I didn't," she said, shaking her head vehemently. "I didn't lie. I never lied. I was going to tell you everything. I was going to tell everything right now on our walk. I think you were figuring it out. Honestly, it was nice to be around someone who didn't know."

"Did we?" Alec asked, disgusted. "Did last night in my bedroom really happen? Was last night real? I thought that was a dream? Did you seduce me and enter my mind in my dreams? In *your* bedroom, or my bedroom? Or… *Fuck!* Did we…did we make love or not, Joy?" He shook his head and shut his eyes tight. His embarrassment over it made him feel angrier. "How was last night not a lie? You were messing with my mind, hypnotizing me."

"You wanted it too," she said, shaking her head. "All I do is stay around that house all day, watching you. The idea of finally touching you, feeling anyone for that matter, was so… I just wanted to touch you, that's all. Was that so bad?"

"You've been spying on me too?"

"Look. Sorry, I didn't mean to hurt you. That's the last thing I wanted. I think you're a wonderful man. But now I don't care much for your tone."

"Oh, am I losing my temper with *a ghost?*"

"Yes, you are," she said, with eyes wide, nodding. "You sure are. I've learned in my life to avoid people with anger issues. You're sounding like a total dick right now, Alec, just like you did when you shouted at me at the lake when we first met. And the same way you did when you shouted at Reggie's son."

"Oh my God, was that your son!?"

"No!" she shouted, grinding her teeth. *"No! No! Fuck, Alec! No!"*

She turned from him and wrapped her arms around herself, shaking her head. Then her whole body started shaking.

Was she crying? *Was a ghost crying!?*

"Reggie had loads of women, okay, Alec?" she snapped. "I left him! Okay? That's why I came here. You're turning really mean. Reggie was a monster but, really, my relationship with him is none of your fucking business."

Alec just glared.

"You remember being with me last night, don't you?" she snapped, with her back still turned. "What happened between us in your sleep, happened. But it wasn't lust, it was love. I'm frickin' falling in love with you, 'kay? Keeping you asleep was…the only way I could feel you.

Touch you. You wanted to touch me back, didn't you? I didn't make love to you because I wanted a fling, damn it, Alec, I made love with you because I'm in love with you! Stop saying, damn it, just stop saying I'm not real! I am real. You see me, don't you? You felt me last night, didn't you?"

"You seduced me. I didn't know you were a ghost. *Fuck…what am I even saying! You're not real now!*"

She turned back. He stepped back in surprise at the sight of the tears now covering her cheeks.

"You have an anger problem! You're shouting at me like a complete dick! It's just like when you threw the kitchen door in my face. For the record, I asked you for consent a million times. I made love to you because I'm falling in love with you. That's all. I don't think I ever really loved a man when I was alive. Being a ghost allows me to…to watch you and I've watched you for months. You're in my house. What else am I supposed to do? I'm not *spying* on you, you're in my house… Look…you're a good man. It wasn't till after I died that I finally found one. God can be cruel. I just wanted to touch you, Alec. Was that so wrong? Sue me!"

She walked around him, hitting his shoulder, and then headed back down their muddy trail.

"Wait! Where are you going?"

Alec ran to her and snatched her hand to turn her toward him, but her fingers felt like fire.

"*Fuck, don't ever touch my hands!*" she screamed. "*I'm dead! All right! Why did it take you so fucking long to figure that out!*"

"You're a ghost."

"*Re-al-ly?*" she drawled, her eyes wide. "And you're *de-ns-e*." She nodded and laughed derisively. "I can't believe it took you this long. Footsteps? Moving furniture? Hovering cups in the cupboards? Well, the house is obviously haunted. Maybe that would have been enough for most people, but not you. How 'bout visions of my naked body popping up from nowhere in your bedroom? Maybe you didn't mind that so much because you desired me too? You needed your incompetent realtor to tell you I was a ghost? Or that slimeball Reggie? Well, I wouldn't be inviting Reggie to my house. Do you wonder why he left the country? It wasn't over me. I warn you. You want to join me where I am, go invite Reggie here."

"Wait!" Alec snapped, holding his head and shaking it. "Wait a second. Just…quiet for a second! Shit. I can't take all this. Just let me think."

"*Stop thinking!* I told you to stop doing that! That's your problem! It's why you're so miserable!"

"I can't believe this," he finally said. "Just give me time to think."

"You want something to think about? How 'bout you think of this!"

She grabbed his head with both her hands. The force was one surprise—her fingers burning his face was another. Then she lifted his head and kissed him hard on the lips.

It was a strange feeling of pain and desire. The burn was not just physical. His heart had burned to feel her again all morning, still desiring her, more than anything in the world. He had wanted to kiss her. Now it burned.

"I've fallen in love with you, okay, you jerk!" she exclaimed in tears. "But I'll go. Sure. I'll leave. You can only blame yourself. Cause you don't know how to live life, Alec, do you? You worry. That's you. That's why you needed to live in fucking nowhereville. I left because too many people wanted me, you left because you've got too much shit on your mind!"

"Leave me alone for a second so I can think!" Alec cried. "I came here for peace and quiet. There's nothing about you that's quiet!"

"Well, maybe it would be better if I left?" she asked with a devilish grin. "Would you like me to do that? Do you want me to disappear?"

"*Yes!*"

She nodded slowly, glaring at him with tears still falling from her eyes. But she wasn't sad anymore—she seemed pissed.

"That's not what I felt this morning," Joy said. "Or last night. Who's lying to whom? You don't want to admit your feelings for me, Alec? Fine, no more Joy. Say bye bye. Just don't you be calling me after I leave. Say *bye to Joy, forever!*"

And she disappeared.

And it turned quiet. Very quiet.

Alec heard birds and squirrels rustling the leaves in the nearby trees and felt a light breeze on his face as he was left alone by the overlook. It was as if she had never been there with him. Because…she hadn't. She was a ghost.

The silence almost made him feel worse than her shouting. If there had been any doubt remaining over Joy's identity, it had vanished with the disappearance of her body…unless his sanity had returned and she had always been just a hallucination?

"Fuck you, Alec!" Joy's voice shouted. *"Fuck you! All right? My house is not Reggie's or his son's or even yours! It's mine! Fifi Graynger's! That name once meant something in this awful world! Go away!"*

14

ALONE ON THE SHORE

The next day, after the storm, the appearance of the hillside of Plymouth Crest had not changed. That same green thrush surrounded all the large tree trunks and brush, but as Alec trudged down the hill, he was forced to keep to the main path to avoid sink holes and puddles under the foliage. Though the sky was clear, he could still smell fresh rain. Only a few wisps of white clouds floated over the lake now. He crossed the main road to the lake. Then he approached his favorite outlook along a natural pier of rocks. He plopped down on a particularly large rock, dropped his bag, and took out his laptop.

He was finishing his book. This was always the frustrating part—being close to being done but not finishing the story.

He typed.

Then he was distracted by the slapping sound of a few geese skidding across water. The wind picked up a bit, and leaves skidded past him. He shivered for a moment as the air blew past his cheeks. He recalled a similar light chill when he first moved here.

Did that herald his ghost?

"Joy?" he asked quietly. "Oh, Joy, I'm sorry. I couldn't believe you were a ghost. You seemed so real."

The wind stilled. Brushing over the water, yellow sunlight flickered.

All the while, waves kept quietly lapping over the rocks under him. And he heard an occasional stir of leaves by birds or squirrels in the trees up the road. Otherwise, it was silent. Perfectly still. Lovely…and lonely.

He couldn't type another word.

15

NOT THAT LOOK OF LOVE

As open as Alec's new home felt, his dining room was queerly small. When Chip introduced the room to him during his last walk-through of the house, it had been almost as an afterthought. A few weeks later, Alec made the room even smaller by adding his large walnut dining table, spanning the entire space. The room was awkwardly and inconveniently located on the opposite side of the house from the kitchen. And it was always dark. The window faced a bunch of trees in his woodsy side yard and, even when it was a bright, sunny day, the room felt shaded.

But tonight, the dining room was special.

Alec lit candles on the white silk tablecloth and poured red wine into two elegant crystal glasses. He straightened his best porcelain plates and silverware. Then he moved a basket full of rolls closer to a yellow and white flower centerpiece. Of course, in Plymouth Hill, there were no fancy restaurants in town. Actually, there wasn't a restaurant in Badger either. But there was Daisie.

After everything was neatly arranged on the table, he sat down on a wooden chair, staring out through the windows, and waited. Leaves rustled due to birds in the trees and a gentle outdoor breeze. The leaves outside were changing from green to yellow and red. It was the sign of fall that everyone raved about in all those pamphlets and state tourist guides.

He gazed down at his left hand, at the golden ring on his wedding finger, over the white linen tablecloth. *Sandra...* It had been over three years since his wife had passed. Her death still weighed so heavily. He remembered her in a formal black dress sitting at the head of the table —her long hair, darker complexion, and wry smile. They watched their little girl. Their daughter Rachel, barely eight years old, sat across from him with hands folded, looking down with eyes closed, saying grace. The little girl was in a white dress and old-fashioned cloche hat. She looked so cute. All the while Sandra sat beside Alec smiling.

That was when Alec remembered catching a stray glance from his wife. That's what he remembered most about that night. Her look: the look of love. That same feeling that he had felt only recently when gazing into...

The doorbell rang.

Daisie had on a long red coat over a lovely flowing charcoal dress and, when he opened the door, whiffs of her perfume smelled like cinnamon. Her long red hair was perfectly straightened, and she wore mascara. But none of that caught his attention as much as the absence of a design on her head.

Alec grabbed the large paper bag from her hands as Daisie hung her red coat on a hanger on a hook on the wall. Then they headed down a hall to their right to the small dining room.

"Hating our cold yet?" she asked.

"No," he said with a chuckle. "I'm loving the fall leaves. The leaves are turning yellow and brown, Daisie. It's wonderful."

"Yeah, suppose we got that. You don't have that much in California, huh?"

"Not like this."

Alec put down the large paper bag on the dining room table and then took out silver trays. Daisie surprised him by throwing her arms around him. It made him uncomfortable.

"This is going to be so much fun!" she cried with a laugh.

"Thanks for coming."

"No, thank *you*, Alec," she said, running her hand through his hair. "This was such a great idea of mine, wasn't it?"

She laughed and removed more white candles and plates from her large paper bag. Opening the trays revealed a large platter of vegetables, mashed potatoes, and a large pre-sliced chicken. Then Daisie sat down at the head of the table. Alec sat beside her, facing the window again. And then…they ate. Quietly. Alec didn't mind the silence. He just watched through the window across from him as the fall leaves stirred in the breeze.

Soon it grew dark. The darkness made their candles feel quaint.

"You still getting haunted by your ghost?" asked Daisie with her mouth full. She swallowed some chicken and then forked a few green beans. Then she touched his hand. "I never got my friend Luminous to come over and exorcise them."

"No," Alec said dismissively. He cut more meat. "This chicken is delicious. Who taught you to cook so well?"

"Mom was a good cook. Did lots of watching."

"The noises stopped about a month ago. I think the ghost got mad or something. She got really pissed at your cards, I think." He chuckled again. "It was right after that when she disappeared."

Daisie laughed and shrugged. But he wasn't entirely joking.

"Well, Halloween's coming. That would be the perfect time for Luminous to come here and run a séance. We can stake out the place and get rid of any ghosts. I'm sure if there's ghosts, he could exorcise them."

"What's Luminous?"

"Luminous is his name, silly. Oh, you should meet him—" She touched Alec's hand and opened her eyes wide. "He's a wizard. Like a *real* wizard, Alec. He's so good at the craft—and powerful. He likes chaos magic and is really amazing at it. He's even better with magic and the occult than I am." She forked some green beans. "How about the house? Did you finally sort out all the problems with the title?"

"Escrow's stuck in limbo," Alec said with a shrug. "The guy who, apparently, might be able to transfer title has to clear a legal mess. Suits me fine. The longer he takes, the longer I can stay for free. No one's living here, and neither the owner nor his son cares about me sticking around until all the legal paperwork is worked out. They just want the money. Problem is that the true owner was a pop star, his estranged lover, Fifi. Fifi Graynger. Also known as Joy."

Alec's red wine glass shook in his hand after saying her name. He had to concentrate to steady it. That was the first time he had mentioned Joy's name out loud to anyone since his mental breakdown…or his haunting… Really, neither madness nor a haunting was comforting.

"*That was that star's name!*" Daisie said, hitting the table. "That was it, Alec! I knew I'd remember it sooner or later. *Fifi. Fifi Graynger.* Yeah, her music was really cool. I copied a couple CDs to cassettes from years back. I should get a CD or stream it, or do whatever people do these days, to listen to her again."

"I'm finally finishing my book," Alec quickly said, cutting and forking some chicken. "Finally broke out of writer's block, thank God. I don't know what it was about this place, but I couldn't focus. I think it was just too beautiful."

"What are you writing about? A romance, right?"

Alec forked a green bean and then mixed it with some mashed potatoes. When he looked up, Daisie smiled demurely.

"A doctor and a medical sales guy meet in St. Louis on a train."

"Sounds like a joke."

He chuckled and shook his head. "They run from an evil pharmaceutical drug lord who's not only selling tainted pills, but smuggling drugs. Fentanyl and meth."

"And romance, right?" she asked with a wink and a nod. "I love romance. I really do." And she scooted closer.

"Sure."

"I'm happy for you, Alec. I really am. I know it's your dream to write. For some strange reason. I can't stand writing, personally. It's all work to me. I'm perfectly happy running my shop, jibber-jabbering with customers. But you know—" She scooted her chair even closer. Then her smile grew larger. "Well, you know, it gets lonely around Plymouth Hill. With all the snow and all, you can get snowed in. You'll see soon enough. Then not only can you get cabin fever and feel nutty, but you can get lonely." She gazed at the top of his head. She touched his bangs again. "You should…you know, you should let your hair grow out a little more. It'd be nice and wavy that way."

"I don't like my hair," he said as he brushed her fingers away. "I wish it was straighter."

She shrugged. Then she put his wine glass beside hers and reached for his hand.

"Gimme."

He pulled away.

"Come on, Alec. Gimme. Give me your palm. I want to do a reading. I'm not only good at cards, you know. How about a palm reading in your haunted house? I can tell your future. I'm good at divination. Let's try it. It's evening. Nighttime and all these candles bring out lots of magic too."

"I don't believe in all your witchcraft stuff."

"I know you're a nonbeliever. Ever since I met you, I've seen the way you look at the moon on my head."

"Why aren't you wearing it tonight?"

She shrugged. Then she gestured for his hand again. "Gimme. Come on, give me your palm."

He sighed, rolled his eyes, and handed his right hand over.

"Now let's see. Let me see. See this, this is your lifeline, Alec." And she slowly and gently traced his palm with her index finger. "And here is your heartline." And she moved her finger gently on that one too. "And here is your marriage. Hmm."

"What does it say?" Alec asked with a sigh.

"Come on, Alec! You have to believe. Magical intent happens only with belief. If you don't believe, no magic's gonna come of this. So believe and then we can proceed. See…see here, looks like you'll have a long life but lots of bad stuff near the end of it. See how the line gets all broken up. That's common, but yours has many more waves and broken lines than usual. You'll probably develop lots of health problems."

"Oh, great."

"Believe, Alec," she said, rubbing his hand. "Believe."

"I believe already."

She rubbed his palm all over with a chuckle. He doubted stroking his hand was helping with her reading.

"You have very cute hands," she said with a giggle. Then she lifted his palm and kissed it. "Okay, handsome. Let's not get silly or it will ruin my reading. So, your money line—"

"There's a money line?"

"There sure is."

"You're kidding me. How about a pickup line?"

"Hey!" she said, slapping his shoulder. "What's that supposed to mean? Do you want a reading or not?"

"Not really. I think you just want to hold my hand."

Daisie scowled, feigning anger. But then she leaned forward again with a grimace, rubbing his shoulder and chuckling.

Alec turned to the window and sipped more red wine.

"So you like the food, huh?" Daisie asked.

"Love it."

"Well, I have a confession. I got all of it in Badger. I'm not the greatest cook, Alec."

"Oh, I thought you made it and packaged it."

When he turned back, she was right beside his face. She crept closer, slowly touching her lips to his. And then he felt her hands stroke his hair and rub his back.

"Is this part of the reading?" he asked.

"Sure," she breathed, closing her eyes. "Sure it is, Alec. Aha. Hey"—She playfully hit his shoulder—"stop fooling around."

She grabbed his hand again, laughing.

"Okay, Alec, so you have quite a robust money line, unlike your health line, but, I mean, you were an accountant and you'd have to have money to snatch this place up."

"Just lucked out with a good deal."

"Yeah well, see this line? You can see that there will not be too many challenges with money. Unlike your health."

"Why do you keep talking about my health?"

She shook her head and ran her finger over and over the lines on his palm, stroking his hand more deeply, over and over.

"This, my dear friend, is your heartline. See it? It's got trouble about midway in your life. And here is your marriage line. Hmm…hmm, this is so very interesting. You have two marriage lines, Alec. Two. Not just one. Were you married before you were with your wife that passed away?"

He shook his head.

Then she just sort of stared deeply into his eyes. She reached over and…she was at it again, making out with him over the dining room table. This time, it was not only their lips, but her hands. One of her hands still held his palm, but the other wandered down his leg. She breathed more heavily. And her lips pressed his harder, as he felt her running her hand through his hair again.

Alec jumped as he heard an explosion. It sounded like glass shattering.

"What the hell?" Daisie asked, jumping. "I thought you said the ghost haunting stopped?"

"It did. I thought it had. Haven't heard anything for weeks. Let me" —He stood up—"let me go check. Just stay put, Daisie."

"No, Alec," she groped for his arm. "No. Forget it. You're in Plymouth Hill. There's nobody in your house. Let's get back to our reading."

But he left the dining room and headed across the hallway. He entered the dark living room.

The vision standing by his fireplace didn't surprise him. Half of him was surprised, he supposed, after not seeing her for so long, but the other half had known Joy was "real" all along. Still, had he seen a ghost like this, partly transparent, scowling at him, looking this pissed, when he first moved into this place, he probably would have turned around and run from his haunted house. But there Joy was. Or Fifi's ghost, standing in her usual casual dark blouse and jeans, with arms folded, leaning against the wall by the fireplace, in the darkness, looking furious.

"I don't believe it," he said.

"*This is your heartline,*" Joy mocked scornfully. "*And this is your lifeline. And this is your money line. And this is your 'I'm going to fuck you right now in Fifi's house, Alec,' line.*"

"Joy," he snapped in a forced whisper. "Joy… If…" He rubbed his eyes. "If you're really back, just leave us alone tonight. I'm having dinner with my friend."

"The hell you are. That friend is groping you in my goddamn dining room."

"I don't believe this. You're real."

"Yeah. Real. Stop saying I'm not real, Alec! That's pissing me off. I'm a real live ghost that's dead, right here, not in the flesh. Your haunting Joy."

"I kept calling for you," he said in a forced whisper. "I looked every day, all over the house, then down by the lake, calling out your name all over Plymouth Crest and feeling stupid. I kept asking for you everywhere. Why didn't you appear?"

"I needed a break from you. You really got me upset. Anyway, you told me you wanted me to disappear."

"I was in shock."

She turned her back on him and headed into the kitchen as if she were just one of his guests. But then she slammed the door behind her.

"Alec, is everything okay over there?" hollered Daisie.

"Just give me a second."

Alec opened the door to the kitchen.

Joy was leaning against the island with her hands in her pockets. She wasn't transparent anymore. She seemed as real as Daisie. And, unlike her look of rage in the living room, her lips were curled in her smile. Alec tried the kitchen light switch. It didn't work. Joy scrunched her nose and gazed out the kitchen window.

"You want me to disappear?" Joy asked with a shrug. "Fine. But I'm not gonna sit at home like some voyeur watching or listening to you make love to someone else. Watching or listening to people making love is just plain sick."

"Alec?" shouted Daisie. "What's going on over there? You all right?"

"I really can't stand her," Joy said, rolling her eyes.

"Stay there, Daisie," Alec hollered. "I found a rat in the kitchen."

"Oh, cute," Joy said, rolling her eyes. "I'm a rat now."

"Eww, gross," Daisie said. "I hate mice!"

"A rat?" Joy asked, squinting at him. "A rat, Alec?" That made him laugh. Then she laughed too. He hadn't realized how much he had missed that laughter.

"I never said I didn't want to see you," he said in a forced whisper. "I was in total shock, that's all. I kept asking for you. I've missed you, Joy."

"Actually, *disappear* is precisely what you wanted me to do, Alec. You specifically wanted me to *disappear*."

"You asked me if I wanted you to."

"Yeah. And you said *yes!*"

"Fine," Alec said, looking over his shoulder. "Just shush."

She shook her head and heaved a sigh. Then she walked over to the fridge. Raising a middle finger with her back still turned to him, she then, in fact, disappeared again.

"Joy?" he whispered in the darkness. "Joy! Stop it. Come back. Joy?"

"Now you want to see me, weirdo?" asked her voice in the darkness. "After you shouted at me. I like you Alec, and all, but sometimes you can be really weird."

The refrigerator door opened, lighting the room. Then a carton of orange juice floated out and across the floor and hovered over the island. The refrigerator door closed. Then a wooden cabinet door above the kitchen counter opened. A glass floated over to the island. The carton rose by itself and poured juice into the glass.

"Where are you?" he said in a hushed whisper.

"Everywhere. I'm Fifi's ghost. Duh."

"Yeah, but…why are you invisible?"

"You're being dense again, Alec."

"I thought you said you had diabetes."

She just snickered.

The glass was tilted back in thin air, but none of the contents were drunk. "Ah," she said. And then she snickered again.

"I had a lot of fun drinking orange juice with you," he said.

She reappeared and her countenance turned serious. "I enjoyed drinking orange juice with you too, Alec." She nodded. "Yeah, that was fun."

"Alec?" asked Daisie.

"Ohhhh! Get that witch out of my house!"

She slammed the orange juice glass on the island. Then she disappeared once more as Daisie opened the door from the living room.

"Alec?" Daisie asked, opening the door. "What was that? Trying to kill that rat?"

Daisie turned on the light. The light switch worked. Then she walked over to Alec and threw her arms around him, running her hand through his beard.

But she stammered, "Oh my God, babe, you look pale. Why do you look sick?"

"Now she's calling you *babe!*" Joy said. "She's frickin' calling you baby, Alec? Do you know what's next! Ohhh, can she please shut it!"

"*Quiet!*" Alec shouted.

"What?" asked Daisie with a chuckle. "Why?"

"She can't hear me, ditz," Joy said. "I'm only heard when I want to be heard. There's some perks to being dead."

"Just be quiet, all right?" asked Alec.

Daisie laughed again. "Okay." She ran her hand over his chest. "Okay, sure," she said with a shrug and kissed his cheek. "I'll be quiet, if you want me to be. But I can still touch you. Come on back to the dining room." And she grabbed his elbow. "Come. Let's go back to the dining room, and I'll work more of my magic."

"Course she wants you back there," Joy said, "I warn you, Alec, if you have sex with her, there's gonna be two ghosts in this house."

"You couldn't murder anybody."

"What?" asked Daisie with a laugh. "What's gotten into you, Alec? Why would I want to murder anyone?"

They returned to the dining room. Daisie scooted her chair back to the head of the table and sat down. Then she sipped from her glass of red wine. Alec sat back down and stared out the window at the trees again.

"There really was a rat in the kitchen?" she asked. "Ew, so gross. I guess I shouldn't be so surprised. Your place is really old. You probably should lay traps around the yard. I've got some back at my store I can give you. I set a couple around myself, during autumn, along the foundation of my place. We live in the woods, you know, and it's getting cold enough for them to come inside. Anyway…where were we, handsome?"

"Palm reading."

"Who were you talking to?"

"No one."

"Are you talking to yourself, Alec? That's okay if you are. I do that sometimes. There ain't many people around Plymouth Hill, are there? As long as you're not cracking up from that cabin fever I keep telling you about."

"Maybe I am," Alec said with a chuckle. "I don't know anymore." He lifted his glass and sipped more red wine. "Sorry. Maybe it is the beginning of cabin fever. Snow or not, yeah, it gets lonely here."

"It sure does."

"*Oh, shut up, Daisie!*" cried Joy. But it sounded like her voice was hollering from the living room. Daisie nodded slowly. Alec laughed, not at Daisie, but at Joy's rage.

"Now gimme." And she reached out for his palm again. "Gimme your palm. Let's read another line."

"*Another line?*" whispered Joy. "*How about more wine, bitch!*"

Alec lost control of the hand holding his wine glass and splashed its contents in her face.

"*Oh, my god!*" Daisie snapped, jumping up. "*Alec! Alec! What are you doing?*"

"*Daisie!*"

She grabbed her white silk napkin and quickly wiped the wine from her face. Then she blotted her face and clothes.

"*Joy!*" Alec cried, looking up at the ceiling. "*Joy!*"

"Joy?" Daisie asked. "Joy? What the hell is the matter with you! This is hardly joyful. Why do you keep saying 'joy'?"

But then Daisie stopped cleaning her dress and opened her eyes wide. Her lips curled in a large grin.

"*Joy,*" Daisie whispered with a nod. "*Joy.* Wait just one minute. Is that star's ghost here right now, Alec? You called her Joy? You told me that ghost Fifi was also named Joy."

"I did?"

"Joy." Daisie got so excited that she seemed to forget the wine dripping from her hair. "Yes, you did. Joy. That's your ghost's name, isn't it? The ghost's name is Joy."

"Hey, Joy!" Daisie cried, looking up. "Yoo-hoo. Joy! You around here, ghost? Why don't you come and show yourself to me." Then she looked down at Alec. "I'm a witch, remember? These sorts of manifestations come to me. I remember you calling out her name on July Fourth when I was sloshed. I was sober enough to notice, but I thought you were just jibber-jabbering drunk too. I thought it was weird you were talking to yourself, but…you weren't, were you? You were saying *joy*. And Fifi was also called Joy, you said. You're really seeing Fifi's ghost! I can't believe this. You're in contact with the supernatural. This is a haunting and you can actually communicate with her! This is, like, a total class five poltergeist!"

He shook his head. Then he went back to work helping wipe wine off her neck with another white silk napkin.

"I'm sorry, Daisie."

"Forget it. You'd never do this to me on purpose. You're too sweet. That's why I know it wasn't you. Where is she? Where is your ghost, Joy, hiding now? She obviously doesn't care much for me."

"She sure got that right."

Alec stood up. Then his hand was forced again to move without his control. This time, he picked up her red wine glass with a shaky hand and lifted it over her head.

"Alec, what are you doing!" Daisie asked, staring up at the glass.

Too late. The second glass of wine was spilled over her head. Laughter echoed all over the room, and it seemed like this time Daisie heard it too. The laughter circled around the room until finally stopping at the opposite side of the dining room table.

Joy appeared. But this wasn't the ghost Alec had been seeing. It was Joy's face, sort of, but her skin was as pale as the tablecloth. Her eyes were pearly white too, her dress was in tatters, and bloody gashes and cuts covered her arms and chest. Her tattered dress was crimson. One large gash was gaping open under her neck, revealing muscle and sinew. And though her face resembled Joy's, her hair was thin and patchy. But the worst was the bugs. Worms crawled all over her skin, with even a few maggots falling from the thin strands of her hair onto the white tablecloth. Yet all the while, over cracked gray lips, it was Joy's infamous grin.

Daisie screamed.

"Get out of my house!" Joy shouted, jumping up and slamming the table with her palms.

Joy disappeared.

Alec had to grab Daisie before she hit the floor. Then Daisie fought Alec, clamoring out of his embrace.

"I...I have to go," Daisie stammered. "You...you have to go. Oh, my God, Alec, what the hell is in this place? A demon? Get out. Leave this place. Oh my God, I saw her. I actually saw Fifi's ghost! I can't believe it. Alec, I think your house is really haunted. And you...you're talking to...that, that, that thing? Why? And how? You must get out too."

Daisie pulled away from him and clamored to the front door. She grabbed her red coat and hat, threw the door open, and darted outside.

"Daisie!" shouted Alec. "Daisie. Wait!"

In another minute, Alec heard the ignition of Daisie's brown pickup. Then he saw her skid along the dirt road and drive off.

There was laughter behind him. This time it was coming from the living room. He spun around and saw Joy crouched over in the living room, with her head in her hands, bursting into laughter. She was hardly a creature of the night now. As she lifted her head, she had the stunning face she'd always had, wearing her usual informal blouse and pants.

"Bitch. Showed her. Imagine if I looked like that when you first met me. Can you imagine, Alec? You'd already have called a shrink back in July."

"That wasn't funny! How could you do that to her? She probably won't sleep tonight. I should go see her."

"I wouldn't go to her now," Joy said, walking over. She waved her hand, and the front door slammed behind Alec. "Alec, come on. If you show up at her place, she'll freak out thinking I'm with you again. Let things simmer down. Look at how many months it took for you to accept me. Give her time. But"—She put her finger to her chin and looked up in thought—"she'll be back. She's a fake witch and all. She loves ghosts and magic and all this supernatural stuff. Eventually, she'll ask to see me again. Then I think you should just let the cat out of the bag. Let her know about everything, including our time spent together."

"You'll appear for her?" But then he rubbed his eyes. "Wait, I can't believe I'm even talking to you. You're not real."

"Righto. Well, there you go being rude again. You don't believe your eyes? Fine. Sounds like it's time to disappear again. And no, I ain't appearing for Daisie at your whim. I only appear before people I like— or want to scare the shit out of." She chuckled again. "Look, you can date that weirdo, but not in my house. Not in my goddamn dining room, Alec. Geesh. Anyway, I'll go. You want me to disappear, right? Bye."

And she disappeared.

"Wait, Joy! Wait! No, come back."

"You asked for me to disappear," she said in thin air.

"No, I want to see you."

"Nope, I'm still mad. I don't believe you really want to see me."

"I do, Joy."

"Alec, why don't you get out of my house too. Go spend some time with some *real* people. Just keep your lady friends out of my home when you return."

16

ALONE?

OF COURSE, ALEC COULDN'T SLEEP. HE JUST GAZED UP AT THE CEILING in darkness, like he had done so many other nights in this house. It was strange. He loved the house but it seemed to give him constant agitation. Lying on his side, closing his eyes tight, he heard his heart beating fast with his ear lying on top of the pillow. He felt a queer feeling of anguish mixed with excitement. It was a strange mix of feelings.

He sat up. Then he gazed at his bedroom windows. He had drawn the red velvet curtains closed. It was midnight, but moonlight was bright through the crack between the seams of the drapes. He looked outside and trees gently swayed from the breeze under a full moon.

He fell on his back and closed his eyes tight again.

If he was honest with himself, he had liked seeing Joy again…no, he had longed for her. And now, his mind raced with anticipation that, at any moment, she might appear again.

He listened for her. It was so quiet in his bedroom that he felt as if, by straining hard enough, he could hear the sound of his refrigerator downstairs.

The floor creaked. It sounded like footsteps! Someone was in the room.

Before the glass door materialized a woman in a nearly translucent white nightgown. It was the same clothes she had worn on the night of his dream—the night when they had made love. She stared through a gap in the curtains, paying no attention to him, probably gazing down the hill at the lake under the moon. Her profile, the most beautiful he had ever seen, shone in the moonlight. She ran her hand over her long dark hair. He could see her naked body under the thin white nightgown, as perfect and beautiful as her profile.

"Joy?"

She nodded slowly.

"I tried to leave you in peace," she said earnestly, "but I couldn't let you be with her. I just couldn't. Why'd you let that woman come into my home?"

"Did you know Daisie when you were alive?"

She smiled and nodded but still kept her back turned.

"I first saw her when she was a girl. A spunky kid back then too. She visited my home often. I see why you like her, Alec. I've always liked her… I just didn't like seeing her with you. So, you finally accept what I am?"

"Part of me does. The other part thinks I'm crazy."

"You've been tossing in bed all night. Why can't you sleep?"

"If you've been here this past month, why didn't you answer me? I called out so many times."

"I want you to be healthy and happy. Alive. I want the best for you. You should hang out with *real* people, not some *unreal* ghost, as you called me."

"Stop saying you're not real."

"You called me unreal."

Every part of her—her breasts, hips, arms, and legs—and her bare feet (of course)—appeared very real. Only the gown was translucent. And yet, under moonlight, her nakedness felt more natural and innocent than indecent. Though she didn't turn toward him, her grin seemed to reveal that she knew she was being watched.

"Why won't you turn around, Joy?"

"I'm dead, Alec."

"Like my book?"

"Is your book dead, Alec?" she asked with a chuckle, finally cocking her head back. He laughed too. Then their eyes met and, though she was in shadows, he felt as entranced by her eyes as she seemed to be by the view of their lake below.

"Thank you," he said.

"Thanks for what?"

"For letting me stay in your house, Josephine."

"You're the first one I ever let do it," she said with a chuckle. "I scared all the others away."

"Why?"

She shrugged again. "I think you know." Then she went back to staring outside.

He answered by doing something strange. It was the only "normal" strange thing he could think of doing in his haunted house. He turned on his side and closed his eyes.

"Goodnight, Joy. Don't leave me again. I don't want you disappearing."

But as he lay on his side, his heart pounded harder than ever, knowing she was still there.

Then he felt her. Her fingers ran gently through his hair, massaging his head.

"These past few weeks, keeping quiet around you, Alec," she whispered, "have been very hard. I've wanted to talk, to feel you again, for so long."

"I thought your hands were too cold to touch me?"

"Shh... You're finally sleeping. Rest, Alec. Just go to sleep, babe."

17

EVICTION

ALEC FELT THE SAME LIGHT STEP IN HIS STRIDE THAT HE HAD
experienced when he first visited Plymouth Crest. He bounded downstairs early in the morning. Then he opened his refrigerator door and laughed as he reached in for his carton of orange juice. He couldn't get his mind off her. When he first got up, just opening the drapes and gazing at the terrace reminded him of when he first saw her down the hill by the lake. Then, walking along his inner balcony, looking down at the living room, reminded him of the time Joy helped Daisie and him up the stairs. It seemed her image shone everywhere in his mind. She haunted him in more ways than with her appearances.

He sat down at his small kitchen table and poured himself a glass of juice, hoping his ghost would join him.

"Joy?"

When she didn't answer, he opened the laptop on the kitchen table.

No wonder she liked stories. She was Fifi the music star. She had been in movies and the entertainment industry. But where had she gone now? Where did she ever go when he didn't see her? If she was a ghost, wasn't she always in the house?

Thankfully, the keys on his computer moved under his fingertips. He wrote a full chapter in an hour. It was action-packed, with the police chasing his main character, the doctor. The doctor had acquired

328

evidence that the medicine was tainted and was planning on releasing it to the authorities—only the police were in on it too. Some of the cops had turned bad and were part of the conspiracy. So now the doctor was searching for her lover downtown, to warn him.

After editing for several hours, and realizing he'd have to add yet another chapter or two to finish his novel, he heard the front doorbell ring.

He gazed through the glass kitchen door—it was very foggy outside. The doorbell rang again.

Could it be Joy? But why would she ring the doorbell?

He ran excitedly to the front door. Looking through the peephole, he saw that Joy wasn't there. Three gruff men stood on his front porch. Two had the countenance of security guards. One reminded him more of a pimp—a tall, pale-skinned man with a mustache, wearing a violet suit and green driver cap. The other two burly men, one bald and the other with a buzz cut, wore sunglasses, black T-shirts, and pants.

Alec looked down at his robe and pajamas, shaking his head. "Who is it?"

"Name's Reginald Tealman," said the tall one in violet. "These are my friends, Oscar and Terry. Mind opening up so we can talk about the house?"

"My realtor didn't tell me you were coming today. Did you finally sort out the title?"

"Yes. And we came all the way here to go over it with you. How about you open up and we can talk. It was a very long trip, amigo."

Alec unlocked the chain and opened the door.

The three of them took off their coats and hung them on hooks by the door. Then the two giant men walked around him and did what everyone always did first upon seeing the house. They headed into the living room and stared up at the mezzanine. Reginald just looked around the foyer admiring the view.

"Reggie," he said, giving Alec his hand to shake. "I haven't been here in such a long time. Such a long time. I had been told the house burned down. Hearing it wasn't gone… I still figured it'd be all boarded up and in disrepair. No, no, this is incredible. It looks exactly the same as when Joy lived here twenty years ago. Except her furniture's gone."

"Your son sold or gave most of it away. Didn't he tell you?"

"No."

"I should get dressed," he said with a nod. "Why don't you guys stay downstairs, and I'll be back in just a minute. I can brew you three some coffee?"

"No need. This will only take a moment."

"Wow!" exclaimed one of the burly men—the bald one. "Wow, boss! This house is so good!"

"Told you," Reggie said with a laugh.

"But in the middle of the woods," said the guy with the crew cut, laughing and looking up too.

"Joy sure knew how to live," Reggie said, walking into the living room and staring at the upstairs balcony with them. "She made herself a castle in the forest. Only she would do that." Reggie shook his head and then addressed Alec. "You'll need to do more than get dressed, sir. You'll be needing to grab *all* your clothes. This mansion was never sold to you because it never belonged to my son. It belongs to me. Joy and me." Then he turned and smirked. "I'd like you to leave."

"Excuse me?"

"No one should ever have pretended to sell this place to you. After I receive title, trust me, you won't be able to afford it. I think I might stay for the winter." He walked to the living room window, gazing upstairs and shaking his head. "Wow, it's not only in good condition, it's in wonderful condition. You sure kept up the place."

"Do you have the deed to prove ownership?"

"Get out," Reggie said, losing his smile. He cocked his head back and glanced at Alec. "Why don't you get out now."

"Go," Joy said in a forced whisper. "Go!" It sounded like she was upstairs. "Get out, Alec! Reggie means it."

"What are you talking about!" Alec cried. "I already paid the deposit and moved all my stuff in."

"Stop it, Alec!" warned Joy in a forced whisper. *"He's dangerous!"*

Alec turned to his right toward the sound of her voice. Joy materialized in her blouse and jeans in the hallway, shaking her head vehemently. Her eyes were wide open with an expression he had never seen before. She looked afraid.

"Terry, go get my bags from the car, will you?" Reggie asked, feigning a grin. "We're moving in." Then he turned to Alec again with a fake smile. "You're moving out."

"The hell I am!"

"The offer given to you by my relation," Reggie said, "a boy who never owned this house, was not only inappropriate, it was ridiculous. Unless you intend to hand me ten times the said amount, title of this house will not be handed to you, sir. I might be willing to sell the place at a higher price... But…well, looking at it"—Reggie looked around him, shaking his head—"it seems my wife didn't just build herself a mansion, she built a little resort. A vacation home. People might come to the mountains for skiing, eh? Well, skiing was the lie that bitch told me to bring me here. With the place in such pristine condition, we could flatten more of the trees and make some slopes. Or, at the very least, make it into a place to stay for hunting. Joy ran a frivolous, wasted life, but she sure had an eye for fashion and architecture." He walked to the living room windows and stared outside again. Then he tapped the glass with his index finger. "I really had thought this place was gone," he said again, more to himself. "Oh, Joy."

He plopped down on Alec's black leather sofa. His goons were still staring at the mezzanine above them.

Reggie took out a cigarette and lighter from his pocket and lit it. Alec didn't have any ashtrays.

"The place will naturally fall to me, sir," he said, taking a deep drag and leaning back. "You certainly don't own my wife's house. You must get out now."

"Joy was never your wife!"

"*Shut up, Alec!*" Joy said between her teeth. "*Shut up and forget it! Stop being dumb and look. His guards are carrying guns.*"

Alec looked toward their large chests and protruding stomachs. Indeed, she was right, both guards were carrying sidearms.

"*Get out while you* can," Joy said. "*He means what he says. He will hurt you if you don't go. We can think of something later.*"

She appeared in the foyer. But she was translucent, and he could see right through her to the front door.

"Did he hurt you?" Alec asked.

Joy opened her eyes wide, vehemently shaking her head and putting a finger over her lips.

Then she completely disappeared.

"Is this guy loco, boss?" Terry asked with a laugh. "Maybe living out in the woods too long? Who in the hell is he talking to?"

"I get this is sudden," Reggie said with a smirk, standing up. Then he walked right up to Alec and got in his face. "But the house simply isn't yours. I can't have you stay. If you stay, you could be considered a squatter. Then you could go to the police and do what squatters do. Squat. I can't have you do that. In this state, you'd have rights to my house. Don't worry. I'll arrange for all your stuff to be sent back to you —all your chairs, tables, furniture, or whatever. I'll send you back your stuff. Just leave me an address. I just need your body to get the fuck off my premises now. Understand? And don't plan on coming back. My friends and I will be staying here for quite a while until all the paper-work clears with my attorneys."

"Then *you'll be* the squatter!"

"*Quiet, Alec!*" warned Joy again. "*Don't argue with him!*"

But somehow Joy's fear angered Alec even more. He glared at Reggie, ready to deck him. But, in his periphery, Alec watched Reggie's goons moving to stand behind him. Their hands lay over their gun holsters.

"I'm the owner, you motherfucker," Reggie said calmly, blowing smoke from his cigarette into his eyes. "Get dressed, grab your shit, and get the fuck out. *Now.* Or my two friends will help you out."

18

THE POLICE REPORT

Alec leaned forward, in a wooden chair at a desk, in a large room filling out forms. There were two large desks, though the one beside him was unoccupied. Three empty chairs were next to the main entrance near sliding glass doors. And to his left was a very small area sectioned off by blue-painted bars. Inside this cell were a sink and a cot. He had always thought jail cells at police stations were only in the movies. Sitting across from him at the desk in a tan police uniform, un-shelling peanuts and scratching his gray hair, was, of course, Sheriff Denson—probably the only police officer in the county. Peanut shells were all over his desk. Above him, "Badger Police Department" was painted in blue.

"I'm really sorry this happened, Alec," Denson said. "Daisie's told me how nice a person you are. I mean, really, we all appreciate you in our town. July Fourth was sure a lot of fun."

"All my stuff is in that house," Alec said, absent-mindedly penciling in more squares on the forms.

Denson offered him some peanuts from his bag. Alec shook his head.

"You know, I can't just throw him out," Denson said frowning. "The law protects people inside a property without a warrant."

"That's what he said. He forced me out so I wouldn't be the one claiming the property. He came in with guns to do precisely what he accused me of doing. He forcefully had me leave."

"But if I don't have the right documentation—"

"I know, Sheriff. I know. You told me all this already."

"Look, these crazy city-dwellers—unlike you, Alec—don't care much for our small town. Stay put until the snow comes. You'll see. The minute he's snowed in for a few weeks, he'll come running from your property. You'll see."

"The fool wants to rent the place out for skiers."

"*Skiers!*" Denson said, bursting into laughter. "Skiers? No one's gonna vacation at Plymouth Crest for skis and a creemee! Here? Never." Denson tried his best to stop laughing. "Ridiculous. We get hunters, but never skiers. That's why your house was abandoned for so long. The mansion's wonderful and all, but it ain't gonna draw tourists. There's not much here but a lot of snow and an iced-over lake with pretty fall trees. That's all and we love it. But just you wait for the mud season. If the ice doesn't get those strangers out, the mud will make 'em run away. You'll see. No, I figure only writers like yourself would be interested in living in that place."

"Then I should get it."

"I know, Alec. I know. Look, Daisie's sure fond of you. I knew her parents, you know. She told me how much she likes talking to you. I tell you, if there's anything I can do to get your house back, I will. I'll head on over the minute I have the necessary paperwork. But knowing the way bad people work—and I've been sheriff for thirty years, Alec, thirty years, mind you—bad people are impatient. Don't play their game. Don't you be impatient too. I advise you to just wait this out. Just talk to your lawyer folks back home, and we'll work everything out. Look, you've got the whole town on your side."

"Sure," Alec said with a sigh, turning the page over.

Denson threw more nuts in his mouth. Then he added, "I bet the minute he gets trapped in ice, he'll be itching to leave. Just give him a couple of weeks. Don't worry. I see them run all the time."

Alec nodded again, signing the bottom of the page.

"I sent one of them books of yours over to my niece, Emily. *Fear of the Spark.* An interesting book, Alec. I think she's liking it a whole bunch."

"Was it a paperback?" he asked, turning the next form over. There were more blank lines to fill out. He detested forms. He had spent years dealing with them and wanted nothing to do with it anymore. "Or hardback? Or an ebook?"

"Not sure. I can ask her."

"I can sign it if it's a book, Denson," he said with a nod. "Just let me know."

"That'd be really kind of you. You sure are a decent guy, Alec. I tell you, you have to be one of the nicest men I've ever known."

Alec looked up and forced a smile. He knew the old man was doing the best he could.

"Well, I got some police business to attend to." And he stood up. "When you complete all those forms, just leave it here on my desk and I'll sort it out. If you need anything else, anything at all, just come by the station and I'll see what I can do to help you."

When the sheriff left, Alec filled in his address. Again. The address of the house that was apparently no longer his. Then he reached into his pocket and took out his cellphone. His best friend had sent about a gazillion texts after Alec texted that he had ignored. He hadn't been ready to talk to his friend until now.

"Alec!" Chip hollered, answering the phone. "Alec, what the hell happened? That motherfucker threw you out of your own house!"

"Yeah. Looks like there'll be no commission for you."

"Shut up, man! I don't give a shit about my commission! You said he came in with guns. Was that a joke? Did he point a gun at you?"

"No, but his friends were armed and looked like bouncers from a club."

"I can't believe this."

"Forget it. If he's right and he's the closest kin to Joy, legally, he'll have the greatest chance of getting the house, whether he's an asshole or not."

"I'll talk to the kid again."

"I kinda doubt Reggie ever talks to his son. Anyway, he'll be able to claim the house before Robin can."

"Well, I can now tell you emphatically that Reggie never got married to Fifi. I haven't seen a marriage license or heard anything about that in all my research. Nor was it ever mentioned by her or fans in her magazine interviews, and I'm sure it would have been. I'm thinking we could have better luck if I can find Fifi's relations. Fifi's family might have better luck getting rights to the place." Chip heaved a sigh. "No direct relatives are known, but I don't know, maybe a cousin or uncle or...something. All this...sounds like now it's becoming dangerous. What a fucking mess. The greatest mystery is the signatures. I'm having a rough enough time just trying to figure out how the hell the property tax and insurance have been signed off in that pop star's name. Maybe if we can discover that mystery—"

"I think I know why."

"Why?"

"Forget it, Chip."

But his friend didn't stop yapping. Alec stopped listening. He jumped up, running his hand through his hair. He gazed through the sliding glass door at "downtown" Badger. From here, he could see the town square, old brick buildings surrounding their main street. About a block down was a gas station, hotel, and Walmart. That was the entire town. A few people in long coats walked along the sidewalk. It would be snowing soon. For Badger, this was the busiest thoroughfare in a hundred miles.

"Chip, it's not your fault this time," Alec finally said, heaving another sigh. "Just, don't worry."

"Actually the whole damn thing is my fault."

"I found the listing."

"I'm so sorry I called that jerk. That mistake is on me. I'll get it fixed."

"Forget it, I say."

That's when Alec spotted a woman in a black shawl passing the glass door. He'd recognize that face anywhere. *It was Joy!* He ran to the exit, but the glass doors couldn't open fast enough.

And the minute he stood outside, she vanished.

"Joy! Joy! Stop disappearing so I can talk to you!"

"Huh?" asked Chip on the phone. "What the hell are you talking about?"

"Forget it, Chip. Forget it. Yeah, everything's shit, but I don't blame you. It's all right. I'll figure something out."

"Hang in there," his friend said, sounding miserable.

Alec ran down the sidewalk, chasing his vanished specter in the direction from which she had disappeared. But by the time he reached the end of the square, he stopped running. Because she was gone.

19

GHOST MAKEUP

Alec ran his fingers through his hair, leaning over the white leather couch in Daisie's house. Across from him were two matching chairs and a small table. To his left, Daisie's kitchen was small enough to fit a mobile kitchen in a trailer. Daisie's home was just this room, the kitchen, and a bedroom and bathroom near the supply room in the back of her store. But everything was well maintained. The white couch didn't have a blemish on it. There were many plants and flowers, and a pleasant tea and ginger smell permeated her quarters. She had told him she was a green witch, whatever that meant.

"It's not Plymouth Crest," Daisie said, handing Alec a pillow, "but it's home. The couch folds out into a bed and, being that Plymouth Hill is in the middle of absolutely nowhere, you won't be waking up from too much noise." She chuckled. "Except coyotes. And there's an occasional idiot racing down the road honking his horn. You know, my place is by the main road."

It was approaching noon, but the only small window in her home, in the kitchen, admitted little light. The white mist was still thick.

Daisie wore no fancy makeup or moons on her forehead. Alec had surprised her so much that she was still wearing her morning robe.

"Anything," Alec said, shaking his head. "I mean, everything, every-

338

thing is great, Daisie. Just, thank you so much for having me here at your place. I'm sorry I barged in."

"Are you crazy?" she asked, sitting in a white chair across from him. "That fucking asshole had no right to throw you out of your house, Alec. I'd rather sock the creep in the nose."

"You heard what Sheriff Denson said."

"He's just scared of lawyers."

"I probably won't be here much longer to bother you."

"Where're you gonna go, kiddo?"

"Don't know," he said with a sigh. "I'll probably just need a place for the night. I can stay in the hotel in Badger tomorrow."

"Stay the whole week. I don't mind your company, Alec. You come by the shop every day to talk anyway."

"Thanks so much, Daisie. You're a really good friend."

She leaned over and gave him a squeeze.

"These last few months with you have been wonderful," she said. "I really love it when you come by. You've taken away some of Plymouth Hill's dreariness."

He nodded.

Then he stood up and approached the small window in the kitchen. It faced Daisie's "backyard" behind the store. There were maple trees and bushes out there, but this morning all he could see was a thick white wall of fog. Perfect for hiding things. Things like…

Ghosts? Joy must be out there, somewhere. Wherever did she go when she disappeared?

"You're a good friend," Alec muttered again. "I appreciate it but—"

"They really had guns?"

Alec nodded.

"And your ghost told you to run?"

"She was scared. That was so weird. I've never seen Joy scared of anything before."

"I find it hard to imagine that ghoul being afraid of anything."

"That's not the way Joy looks," he said with a chuckle. "She was just trying to scare you. Or at least it's not how she looks to me."

"How does she look to you?"

Alec shook his head and finally tore himself from her window.

"Daisie, I'm gonna wander a bit outside—step out for some fresh air. I'll be back in half an hour."

"Kinda dreary out there. This wet weather, you know, is a bit of a prelude before our real fun in Plymouth Hill: rain, sleet and snow."

"I'll be right back," he said with a chuckle.

He rubbed her shoulder on his way out and opened her door to the store. The Corner Store was the only way to leave her place.

But when he reached the exit, Daisie hollered, "Going to see her?"

Alec turned. Daisie was standing with her arms folded, leaning against the doorway to her home.

"Going to see your ghost?" she repeated sternly. "You can't walk far in that thick fog, Alec. I'm guessing you're going to try to find your new love interest."

"What do you mean?"

"I heard the way you speak to her. I saw it the night of our dinner when she was a ghoul—or before she appeared as a ghoul—and I remembered it on the Fourth. I've had my share of men, Alec. I'm no spring chicken, you know—just never really wanted to be tied down. That's my problem, I suppose. I never settle with anyone, except Plymouth Hill. But I know when a man cares about a lady. You are way beyond palsy-walsy when you talk to her."

"She's just a ghost."

"I know that. But do you?"

"What do you mean?"

"Look, I'm your good friend," she said raising her hand. "I don't want you to get hurt. Just because you don't believe in ghosts, doesn't mean they don't exist. Fifi's ghost has been haunting you. That's a fact. But, unlike our friendship, and after everything you've told me, this ghost seems to really like you. She seems far beyond the friend zone." She raised her hand again. "That's okay, Alec. Truly, I only mention this because I care about you. You're my good friend and that's all that counts. But I'm worried about you. You can't be in love with a ghost, Alec. You can't fall in love with someone who's passed away."

"Daisie," he snapped, "with all that's happening right now, are we going to talk about this now?"

She looked down. Then she shook her head. "Sorry… I just don't know when else will be a good time. Forget I said anything."

"I'd love it if you met her. Not the monster she showed you. Joy. Joy's wonderful. She's so happy and full of energy. She's kind and so caring. Just…thanks for letting me stay the night at your place. Thanks so much. I'll be in the hotel in Badger by tomorrow."

"The hell you will," she hollered as he opened the door outside. "You're staying until you get your house back, Alec."

"Okay. I'll be right back, Daisie."

Walking outside, he could not believe how thick the white fog had become. He couldn't walk much farther than five feet without nearly bumping his head into a tree. He couldn't remember Plymouth Hill ever being this foggy. But the weather fit his mood.

Of course, Daisie was right. He was looking for Joy. And, if he was being honest with himself, it wasn't just to talk to her about their problems. They had finally made up last night. He was so looking forward to spending time with her again. But now this had happened.

Not only did he want the house back—he wanted Joy. And he thought maybe if he was alone again she'd come to him.

Pretty soon, every tree trunk started looking the same in the white fog. He actually worried he might get lost. He tried to keep in a straight line from Daisie's house, and as he gazed back, he could barely make out the dim yellow light from her home.

"Joy?" he said among the white wisps of smoke. "I saw you in Badger. And then I saw you around Reggie. I know you're here. Somewhere. Just show yourself. Please. Come on. Where are you? Joy? Joy?"

"Seems there's not much joy around here now, Alec," Joy said, sounding morose as hell. He barely recognized her voice, as she had never sounded so down.

"Where are you?"

"Here."

She materialized before him in the thick white mist, wearing her usual blouse and jeans, only a couple paces from him. She was leaning on a tree trunk. She put out her arms and they embraced. Then she shook in his arms. Was she crying? He gently tilted up her chin. Sunlight shone through the fog, illuminating her eyes and cheeks. Her face seemed to glow in the mist as tears streamed from her eyes, despite her attempts at a smile.

"First he ruins me, now you." Though tears fell, her voice was crisp, almost angry. "I wanted you to have my house. I really did. Even if we never spoke again after our first fight, I always wanted my place to be yours. I think you're wonderful."

"Did he hurt you?"

"What?" she asked, wiping her eyes. "Why ask about me? I thought you were looking for my help?"

"Why do you seem afraid of him? Was he your murderer?"

"Yes."

She moved a few paces into the fog, almost disappearing. Alec reached for her hand, but she quickly snatched her fingers away.

"Damn it, Alec, don't touch my hand! Why don't you get that I died?"

Somehow shouting at him seemed to make her more upset than ever. She fell on her knees, covered her head, and wept.

"Oh, Joy," he said, rubbing her back. "Joy… I'm so sorry."

She lifted her hand, batting him away. He just stood over her.

"It's okay," he said, "if you…cry."

"It isn't." She shook her head. "What good does crying ever do? Anyway, you came for my help."

"I'm sorry, Joy."

"My name's not Joy."

She slowly forced herself up. Then she straightened and turned very serious.

"I'm Josephine. I loved the stage name Jewel, but it was already taken. Reggie loved Fifi. I think he picked Fifi because it sounded immature and easy to push around. Like, your fluffy feathery Fifi. Well, she became quite well-known, didn't she? The world knew me as the funny-go-lucky Fifi. I hated it. You called me unreal? Back in L.A., Alec, I was more unreal alive than dead. Even Fifi's appearance was made up. Well, not for you, Alec. I don't want to deceive you of all people. You don't deserve deception. Let me show her to you."

Her face blurred amidst the thick white smoke. At first, he felt as if the mist were simply thicker, but then he realized it was Joy's magic.

Joy transformed. She had the same face, but different. Her nose was hooked. Her eyes narrower. Her skin less vibrant and smooth. There were blemishes on her forehead. And her hair was dusty blond, not black. She was imperfect. Her makeup was thicker, she had hair in a ponytail, and she wore a T-shirt with baggy pants. This was like the picture of that rock star he had googled.

"This is Josephine when she was a star. This is how the world remembered Josephine Graynger: as Fifi. And this is what that asshole Reggie, my agent, created when he launched her career. I made up my appearance as Joy for you, just as Reggie made up Fifi.

"When I lived, Alec, I wasn't a singer, I was a goddess. But I was *Reggie's* goddess. Because"—Her voice finally broke again—"Shit..." She turned from him. "Joy might have been a fuckin' great singer, yeah, but inside Joy was never *joyful*. That was Reggie's worst joke."

Alec gently turned her toward him. She smiled woefully.

"No joy, Alec," she said, shaking her head. "No joy. Reggie came up with Joy as a pet name. But the thief could never give joy to anyone but himself. He might have given me stardom, but, yeah, he hurt me. He hurt me a lot. He even beat me. But his abuse was nothing compared with his blackmail. After creating Fifi the rock star, he pushed me around with money and drugs, told me who to hang around with and what to do with my time. I think it was when he finally proposed changing my stage name to our private name, Joy, that I mustered the courage to give him the middle finger.

"That's when I built our mansion on Plymouth Crest. Because Fifi wasn't as dumb as the world thought. I read every contract. I knew how to make my money. So many in the music world don't get that. And I think Reggie despised that I did.

"With my money I built our castle in the clouds. I worked with a contractor and built my princess palace with all the money I had made —not only to get away from Reggie, but to leave California, my fans, and the whole goddamn fake world. And I did. I ran and found peace here—until that motherfucker managed to come and rip that away too."

She shook her head vehemently, and her eyes opened wide.

"He took everything from me, Alec! Everything! He might have taken your house, but he tore up my dream! When I finally found real happiness, he killed me! I had only lived in the house for two weeks. Two goddamn weeks, Alec! That was it! Just two weeks before I died!"

Alec touched her back, but she shook him off. She raised her hand and turned from him.

"But you know," she muttered quietly, looking down. Then she even smiled. "When that dick finally managed to kill me, it wasn't so bad. Death freed me too. You know how much I love it here. Maybe that's why God made me haunt Plymouth Crest. Only when I died was I really able to enjoy it. Oh, I love it here so much." She smiled woefully at him. "And then I was lucky enough to meet you."

She reached for him and they embraced again. Then she reached up and kissed his cheek and lips. Their eyes locked in the white fog and, though it was Fifi's face, it was Joy's eyes.

"Then you came," she said with a nod. "After years of searching. So…what do you think of my depressing life story?"

"I only wish I could fix it for you."

"I know." She laughed, leaning her head against his chest. "You're such an amazing man. I had to die to finally meet one."

"Fifi's face is beautiful."

"Really?" She laughed. "You think so? I thought Joy would be so much prettier for you."

Alec shrugged.

That's when her face altered back to Joy. In a flash, her skin turned silky smooth, her nose straightened, but those eyes remained the same.

"But I love the way you look at me when I'm Joy. I've loved it ever since I broke into my kitchen. But, Alec, I heard what Daisie said to you. She's right. I *am* a ghost. Josephine died. You should be with someone real, like her, not someone who passed away."

She leaned her head gently against his chest, and they stood there, in an embrace, for a long while as the mist slowly cleared. And it was wonderful.

Quickly, perhaps magically, the mist cleared, and they were surrounded by the familiar trees and thrush with only wisps of leftover white fog. Sunrays shimmered between the yellow and red leaves as wisps of white smoke brushed over his ghost.

"Why were you looking for me?" she asked, letting go of him. "How can I help you? After seeing that creep, I guess I needed to dish out all my shit on someone. Thanks for that. But how can I help *you*, Alec?"

"I want your house back."

"You can't fight him," she said, shaking her head. "If Reggie came for the house, he already figured out a way to take it. He's a horrible man. Why do you think he left the country? It wasn't just me. It was probably over a bunch of his other crimes. His pen and paper are his worst weapon. He's an attorney. Those goons with him didn't come to shoot you, they came to drag you out the door with their meathead arms. The guns were just theater."

"What if you were to haunt him?"

"I don't think he'd scare."

"You might be able to frighten him. Or, at the very least, maybe grab their weapons and—"

"Alec, I said he brought those guns to intimidate you, but that doesn't mean he won't use them if he has to."

"I need to get your house back."

"Why is my house so important to you?"

"Not for me. For you. Don't you see, Joy? If I lose the house, I leave, but if you lose it, you're stuck here. If he keeps the house, he'll trap you all over again, this time not in L.A., but in Plymouth Crest as a ghost. I know you're the one who's maintained the upkeep of the place. Not just cleaning throw-up on the stairs, or dusting a stair rail, you've taken care of everything, Joy, for years. You love that house. So, why would you want to give it to a guy who murdered you?"

"I don't, Alec!"

"We both want him gone," Alec said with a nod. "Let's make him go."

"It's always been this way with him," she said with a nod. "He's stolen everything from me. He even stole credit for most of my songs. But he'll take more than your house from you if you confront him. He'll take your life. Just…just go on with your life without me. It's not safe. You need to leave."

"If you want me to go, I'll go," he said. "After we get your house back. It's not just for me, I want to help you now. You said he took everything. Don't let him take your house."

"Hmm," she said, cocking her head back, "I thought you were searching for my help?"

"Haunt him, Joy."

"I can…try. For you, Alec. I will."

"No. For us."

~

They returned together to Daisie's Corner Store. By the screen door, he caught Daisie doing her usual—leaning on the counter in front of her and thumbing through her cellphone. But just as Alec opened the door and the bells jangled, Joy vanished.

"Alec?" asked Daisie. "Did you find her? The fog's finally lifting."

"Joy, please show yourself," he said, searching behind him. "Joy, please?"

She appeared on the threshold beside him. She wasn't a creepy ghoul from a cemetery or a pop star. It was his ghost, Joy. And, as usual, she looked vivid, as if Alec had found a woman straying in the forest.

Daisie lurched back in surprise with her eyes widening.

"Hi," Joy said with a wave.

"I'm…Daisie," Daisie said, forcing a smile.

"I'm Josephine's ghost. I've known you all your life, Daisie."

2 0

GOOD OLE HAUNTING

"So what's the plan?" asked Daisie.

Alec and Daisie were lying on their stomachs on the cliffside, in thick snow coats, staring down at the house that had been stolen from him. Joy was on her stomach too, leaning her chin on her hands, wearing her blouse and jeans, barefoot. Alec and Daisie gazed through binoculars. The eye pieces were like her flashlight. They were military grade equipment and Alec could see, literally, a dime on his coffee table in the living room. It was bright down there. The lights in the house lit up the whole valley.

None of Reggie's goons were asleep yet. One of them was throwing sheets on the couch. The other was tossing a pillow on the floor. He couldn't spot Reggie. No…he could just make out the dick in a robe walking along the inner balcony, smoking another cigarette without an ash tray.

"What are you wearing?" Daisie cried.

Alec laughed. Joy had changed her clothes. She was wearing green army fatigues.

"It's a military strike, right?" Joy asked with a wink. "Figured I'd dress the part. I can change into blue SWAT gear if you prefer?"

"I can't believe I'm in the company of a ghost," Daisie said, rolling her eyes.

"Can't believe I'm hanging with a witch," Joy rebuked.

"Well, if you didn't know, witches don't like ghosts," Daisie said.

"That's not true. What about Wendy and Casper?"

"Was Wendy a witch?" Daisie asked, furrowing her brow. "I thought she was just a cute little girl in a red hoodie?"

"Can you wear your normal clothes, Joy?" Alec asked.

In a flash, Joy was back to wearing her blouse and jeans without shoes.

"Just trying to get us in the mood. But I don't think you want me to wear *normal* clothes, Alec. That'd probably be a white sheet. You know, like a funeral shroud."

"What's the plan, Alec?" Daisie repeated. "Why are we waiting till they fall asleep?"

"Joy's the plan," Alec said with a chuckle. "That asshole doesn't know we have his girlfriend's ghost. Joy's going to do some good ole haunting."

"Will you appear as a dead ghoul again?" Daisie asked. "That was really good. It totally freaked me out."

"The direct approach doesn't work as well as you might think," Joy said, shaking her head. "I find going all out gets the creepy supernatural lovers, like you, only more excited. You'd be surprised what actually scares people out of a house. It's small things: opening a door, turning off lights, running the faucet, footsteps. I've been haunting for years. Trust me, I know."

"I remember you doing that when we first met," Alec said.

"Kept you up at night, didn't I?" Joy said with a wink. "I'm good at what I do. I've always been good at everything I do, including haunting unwanted guests. Course, you were never unwanted, Alec."

"Do your best against him," Alec replied with a nod.

Then he looked down at his house through the binoculars again.

"What are you and I going to do, Alec?" Daisie asked.

"After you scare them, Joy, disarm them. Take their guns. Then, if they all go running from the house, Daisie, you and I will go inside and call for the sheriff."

"Sheriff Denson won't do shit," Daisie remarked.

"For sure," Joy said.

"But that's all he has to do," Alec said. "Nothing. If we disarm them and they vacate, we can take back the house. Then Reggie will have to throw me out again to reclaim it. We'll at least have the law on our side, for now."

"Reggie's too smart," Joy said, squinting and shaking her head. "A few doors opening is not going to scare that jerk. We have to do something big. He already heard the place is haunted. My usual tricks aren't going to work. And even if we manage to make them all run, what's gonna stop him from coming back?"

"You have to try, Joy," Alec said.

"Let's get your house back, Alec," Daisie said. Then she glanced at Joy. "Your house, Fifi."

Joy nodded.

Then Daisie took a compact from her pocket. She used the flashlight in her cellphone to check herself in the mirror. She took out a pencil and started darkening the edges of the quarter moon on her forehead.

"What are you doing?" Joy asked, amused.

"Re-drawing my moon. It brings down kundalini from Hecate above in the sky down to my center. It will help us fight."

"Well, I suppose, if you get to wear your moon on your head, I should get to wear my army fatigues. Right, Alec? You know my cousin Judy was a sergeant in the army for real. And I played a sea captain in high school. Or was it a pirate? Hmm, can't recall. But seems to me if we're gonna be creeping inside a house, I should look the part and be totally ready for a fight too."

And when Alec looked at her again, she had already changed back to her green army uniform. Alec laughed again.

"What planet is she from?" asked Daisie.

"Los Angeles," Joy said. "Same place as Alec."

"Okay, Joy!" Alec gestured to the house after the lights shut off. "Go! It's time. Do your worst... or, your best. Just scare the shit out of him."

For a while, it was just dark and quiet. Literally, all Alec heard were the shuffling of his and Daisie's bodies in the leaves and the crickets.

But then he saw lights flash in the living room. The brightness was jarring. It startled the men lying on the floor too. One of them jumped up and ran to the light switch, but the lights shut off before he could reach the wall. The other guard's sheets rose over his head and hit him in the face.

The two of them searched all over the room. Then they tried the light switch on the wall again. Those yellow lights, every time they switched on in the middle of the dark forest, were blinding in the valley. Alec could hear their shouting even from inside the house.

"She's doing her stuff," Daisie quipped. "Whatever she did, she spooked the hell out of... They're—" Daisie pointed at the inner balcony. "Look! Look over there, Alec! Look at them go!"

But Alec was watching someone run down the stairs. From the cliff-side, he could only make out a short section of the second floor and it was hard to discern, but it had to be Reggie.

"No, no, the driveway, Alec," Daisie said, pointing. "Look over at the driveway in the front!"

Alec heard the car ignition before he saw anything. And with it came more shouting. They were far enough away that the shouting was muffled. An old Dodge Challenger appeared, skidding along the drive-way. It nearly ran off the road into a ravine then sped down the windy road to the main highway.

"She did it, Alec!" Daisie exclaimed, putting her arm around him. "She did it! They're running!"

Daisie hit his shoulder again and pointed at Reggie, tripping along the driveway in the front yard, yanking up his pants, shouting like crazy. When his pants were up, he raised his fists. He was shouting for them to come back, but his friends were long gone.

But then...everything stilled. The sound of crickets seemed loud. And soon the lights in the living room shut off.

He heard the crunching of leaves. Then Joy's immaculate bare feet materialized on the trail up to the summit of their hill. That was followed by the rest of her materializing in her usual blouse and jeans. She approached and, standing over them, she frowned. She seemed so down.

She dropped two pistols on the ground.

"Here," she said solemnly. "At least there's that. I tried, I really did. But I told you Reggie isn't going anywhere."

"What are you talking about?" asked Daisie. "We saw them running."

"You saw his guards running," Joy said. "We need Reggie to run, not just hired help. I told you I couldn't frighten him. He's not going to run from an investment just because its haunted."

"Did you show Reggie Fifi's face?" asked Alec.

"No."

"Why not?"

"Reggie was smoking on the balcony when I messed with his friends."

"Why didn't you scare him when he was out on the balcony?"

"*Cause I died on the balcony, dummy!* Can you explain this to your dense friend, Daisie! Jeesh. You can be so fucking out of it sometimes, Alec. Maybe…shit, maybe…we'll try again tomorrow."

But then Joy turned back to the trail and headed down the hillside, looking depressed as hell. She just shook her head and disappeared.

"I'm sorry, Joy," Alec said. "Sorry."

"Whatever," Joy hollered back in the wind. "You can be so insensitive sometimes."

"We need to go home too, Alec," Daisie said. "It's getting cold."

"Wait, Joy. Don't go."

She didn't answer.

"We could still get rid of him if she'd just try again now," Alec said to Daisie. "All she has to do is just show him Fifi's face."

"Alec, forget it. She can't now. We'll try again tomorrow."

2 1

THE BROKEN RECORD

THE NEXT EVENING THE PLAN WAS SIMPLE AND STRAIGHTFORWARD enough: Joy would haunt Reggie again. Alec and Daisie went outside with her, under the cover of darkness, amidst thick undergrowth. Standing close to the kitchen glass door, they were cold. Alec had thought it would be a little warmer close to the house than on the peak of Plymouth Crest. At least they had come better prepared, wearing heavier coats. But it was still frigid.

The cold was the only thing reminding Alec that Joy was a ghost. It had never seemed to bother her until now. She started trembling. Or maybe that was fear. She also looked scared.

"Do your thing, Joy," Alec whispered. "We'll be standing down here waiting for you."

Joy nodded hesitantly.

"What's the matter?" asked Daisie. "You seem worried."

"It's like the time I opened for Madison Square Garden, right guys? I used to be so nervous performing in big venues. I loved it when I was finally up on stage, but that sea of seats made me totally freak out. Maybe it's like that? Right? But...what if he's on the balcony again, Alec? I don't know if I can go up there."

"You have to scare him tonight," Alec said. "Otherwise, he'll bring reinforcements. Besides, we already looked. He's not up on the terrace."

"All you can do is try," Daisie said, rubbing Joy's back.

"I know. I know. Thanks."

"If anything happens, I'll run inside," Alec said. "Come on. Face him. This is the house *you* built, not his." And he put an arm around her again and squeezed her.

"Why don't you turn into your monster *this* time?" whispered Daisie with a smirk. "It sure worked on me."

"Reggie would laugh," Joy said with a chuckle. "But I think I've got a better idea. I just have to get the nerve to do it." She nodded and met Alec's gaze again. "Okay, Alec. I'm ready. I'll get my house back for you."

"Not for me. For you, Joy."

"For you, Alec," she said with a smile, shaking her head. "For you."

And then Joy dematerialized.

Then it fell quiet. And Alec and Daisie were left shivering beside thick tree trunks, keeping vigil beside the kitchen door.

"It's really just as cold here as at the top of the cliff," Daisie whispered with teeth chattering. "Brrr. We should head home. There's nothing we're going to be able to do to help her."

"I thought it'd be warmer closer to the house."

"Not tonight. It's freezing tonight. I know you want to be here for her, but there's nothing we can do. She's a ghost. But, still… I like her a lot. And she said that asshole abused and killed her. I hope whatever she does, she gets even with that jerk."

Alec nodded.

Then they jumped. A scream was coming from right above them, on the balcony. They ran out in the open, risking being seen, and gazed up at the terrace. The light turned on in the bedroom, seeming to illuminate the whole forest, but Alec couldn't find anyone up there.

"That didn't sound like Reggie," said Alec.

"It sounded like Joy!" Daisie said.

Alec ran to the kitchen door, rustling for the keys in his pocket.

"Stop, Alec! Stop. She's a ghost. What are you going to do for her?"

"*Joy!*" thundered Reggie.

It sounded like it was right above them. He realized it must be coming from upstairs. And that jerk sounded far more pissed than scared.

"*Fuck you, Reggie!*" shouted Joy, sounding as if she was crying. "*Fuck you! Leave me alone! I came here to get away from you! You ruined me!*"

"*I ruined you? Me?*"

"*She sounds like she's in trouble!*" Alec said.

"Alec, think!" Daisie insisted, pulling at his arm. "How can a ghost be in trouble?"

"I don't know," he said. "I don't know. But I'm not going to stay outside and listen. I have to try to help her."

He finally managed the lock on the kitchen door and then, forgetting all stealth, he threw it open. Then he ran across his dark living room and rushed to the stairway.

"*I ruined you?*" Reggie shouted. "*No, no, no, you ruined me! You ruined all of us hiding in this shithole. Why? Why here, Joy? Hey, you, come back now. You come back! No! Come back to me! You—*"

"*I'm happy for once! Okay, Reggie? I like it here. Now, stay the fuck away from me!*"

Alec climbed two or three steps at a time and ran around the balcony toward the bedroom.

"You want to stay?" asked Reggie. "Fine. Not sure how it'll help your career. I can move in with you."

"You'll never move here, Reggie." Joy laughed derisively. "Why do you think I chose this place? There's no way in hell you, Travis, Jenny, or any of the others will come here. That's why it's so wonderful."

"You bitch! I made you what you are."

There were slapping sounds. It sounded like he was hitting her!

"*Go away!*"

"*Joy!*" Alec cried, finally rushing into the bedroom.

But then he stumbled back to the threshold. The light was bright, unnaturally bright, turning the whole room yellow. Then Alec nearly fell, witnessing the impossible. There were two Reggies in the room. Reggie "one" was far younger than the Reggie Alec remembered, wearing a black T-shirt, sports jacket, and slacks and without a mustache. He was attacking Joy in the center of the room. The other Reggie, the Reggie who threw Alec out of his house the other day, was wearing only pajama bottoms. He crouched by the bed, with eyes wide open, staring at the spectacle. He was in so much shock that he hadn't even seemed to notice Alec barging into the room.

"Get the hell away from me!" Joy shouted again. *"Don't touch me!"*

But Joy wasn't Joy either. She had Fifi's face, wearing a white beret and sweater, shouting, as the other Reggie—Reggie number one—rushed her toward the glass door that opened onto the outside terrace.

"Go away!" Joy screamed.

"Are you drunk again? Is that it!"

"I don't need alcohol," she said, wiping her eyes, laughing derisively again. "Not where I'm happy. Just stay—" She batted his hands away. "No! No! Don't you touch me! Just stay away from me. I told you not to touch—"

"Joy, I came here to marry you!"

They were on the terrace now. He reached for Joy's hand again, but she slapped it off her.

"I'd rather die than marry you!"

"Bitch, calm down!"

"Calm yourself! And…and…just go away!"

Joy, or Fifi, lost her balance, falling backward, and her whole torso tipped over the concrete ledge. For a moment, only her legs were keeping her from falling. Reggie tried to grab her arm, but she slipped through his fingers and tumbled backward over the ledge.

Reggie stared over the concrete ledge.

"Oh my God," Reggie said in a broken voice. But it wasn't the Reggie gazing over the wall. The Reggie on the balcony was simply staring down. The comment came from the one in pajamas by the bed.

"You bitch! I made you what you are."

Joy materialized in the center of the bedroom with tears streaming from her eyes. But her face, again, was not Joy's, it was Fifi's. Reggie had chased her in from the hallway—the younger clean-shaven Reggie, again, in his black T-shirt and sports jacket. He struck her a few times viciously across the face, making her stumble to the floor. Then he slugged and kicked her a few times and pulled her hair. She forced herself up, backing away from him.

"Go away!" she cried. *"Get the hell away from me!"* Joy, or Fifi in her white beret and sweater, shouted again. *"Don't touch me! Go away!"*

"Are you drunk again? Is that it!"

"I don't need alcohol," she said, wiping her eyes, laughing. "Not where I'm happy. Just stay—" She batted his hands away on the balcony. "No! No! Don't you touch me! Just stay away from me. I told you not to touch—"

"Joy, I came here to marry you."

He reached for her hand again and she batted it away.

"I'd rather die than marry you!"

"Bitch, you calm down!"

"Calm yourself! And…and…just *go away!*"

Joy, or Fifi, lost her balance, falling backward, and her whole torso tipped over the concrete ledge. For a moment, only her legs were keeping her from falling. Reggie tried to grab her arm, but she slipped through his fingers and tumbled backward over the ledge. All over again.

Reggie stared over the concrete wall.

"My God," Reggie said quietly, shaking his head. "My God, please stop this. Please. Stop this. Please."

"You bitch! I made you what you are."

And Joy was back in the center of the bedroom with Fifi's face. Once again, Reggie stormed in from the hall—Reggie, the younger clean-shaven Reggie, again, in his black T-shirt and sports jacket. He struck Joy over and over, until she stumbled to the floor.

"*Go away!*" Joy, or Fifi, shouted again leaping back up. "*Get the hell away from me! Go away!*"

"It keeps happening over and over," Reggie said by the bed, shaking his head. "Why?" He stumbled on the bed. "Why?" He put his head in his hands. "Why doesn't it stop?" And tears fell from Reggie's eyes too. "Please make it stop."

"Alec?" cried Daisie, rushing into the bedroom.

"I'm happy here," she said, wiping her eyes, laughing derisively again. "Just stay—" She batted his hands away. "No! No! Don't you touch me! Just stay away from me. I told you not to touch—"

And now Daisie, standing in the doorway, was watching the fight too. Over and over it kept playing like a broken record. Joy would appear in the middle of the room. But it wasn't Joy, it was Fifi. Then Reggie would attack her. Joy would get up, and then he'd chase her to the open door onto the terrace. Rushing her, he'd try to stop her, but she'd trip and fall over the ledge to her death. And once she fell, it would start up all over again. Over and over and over again.

"I don't understand what's going on," said Alec.

"She's haunting him," said Daisie. "She's showing him what he did to her. Good for her. If that asshole ever lets it sink in."

Reggie leaned over the mattress. It seemed he wanted to look away, but he couldn't. *"Go away,"* he said, shaking his head with a nervous laugh. He looked at Alec but seemed to look through him. *"Go away."*

"Cabin fever, Alec," Daisie said with a big smile. "I told you this house does that to people sometimes. Or shock. Whatever the case, we can get him the hell out of your house now."

"Throw him out of my house now, guys!" shouted Joy in a disembodied voice.

Meanwhile, Fifi was being pushed to her death. Again. Over and over and over again…haunting Reginald again and again.

22

PASS THE MASHED POTATOES

Alec and Daisie sat across from one another on white leather seats at a tiny wooden kitchen table near Daisie's kitchen. Alec wore a pressed brown suit. Daisie was formal in a very pretty draping dark green floral dress. But they weren't on a date this time. They were meeting as "family."

After Alec uncovered the meat, stuffing, potatoes, and vegetable trays, he poured gravy over his and Daisie's sliced turkey. Then he sat down.

"This is so wonderful, Alec," Daisie said. She reached over the table to touch his hands. "Thanks so much for picking it up, especially with the weather turning so icy. I'd kind of rather you didn't, honestly, but you know I can't cook. Going to Badger in the snow must have been so difficult."

"I saw two cars off the side of the road just on the way over," he said, nodding and chewing on a roll. "Another had turned three-sixty on the road on the way back. Thank God it didn't look like anyone was hurt. A police officer had his patrol car with its red and blue lights flashing in the middle of the highway, slowing down traffic. Traffic is one thing I never thought I'd see here around Plymouth Hill. But"—He forked some turkey into his mouth—"the cop was familiar enough. Sheriff Denson. When he saw me while directing traffic, he hollered

'*Happy Thanksgiving*.'" You know, as much as we poke fun at him, he told me he works every holiday season."

"Who else is gonna take his shifts?"

"That's my point." Alec shrugged, chewing on stuffing. "He's not so bad, is he? Last week, I passed by the police station, and he told me that if Reggie ever returns, he'll chase him away for me. Of course, all it would take is documents showing Reggie's ownership and suddenly Denson would be saying he can't do anything again."

He sipped some white wine.

"You still haven't seen her?" asked Daisie.

"Hmm? Who?"

He cut some turkey with his fork and knife.

"You know who," she said. "You still haven't seen her since she haunted Reggie?"

"No."

And that made that familiar sense of unease return. He felt deflated. Daisie frowned.

"Oh, I'm so sorry, Alec," Daisie muttered.

"Yeah." He shrugged. "Well, I don't get why. I've called her name aloud a million times, but she won't show up. I've even walked around the lake and the hills in the snow shouting out her name. There's no sign of her. But she's disappeared before. She always comes back..." He shrugged. "God, I miss her, Daisie. God...if she's really gone, it's terrible. But if she is, I just wish...I could have said goodbye."

Daisie reached over and touched his hand again.

"If she can see me, I know she'll show up again," Alec said. He forced himself to spoon some mashed potatoes into his mouth. "I know she will. She'd at least say goodbye."

"How about the legal stuff?" she asked. "Do you at least finally have possession of the house?"

Alec looked up at her and was amused by the moon sketched on her forehead. She always changed the drawing to match the current phase of the moon. Tonight the moon was apparently full, but with all the clouds outside, he could only tell by looking at her head.

"I'm firing Chip," he said with a chuckle, cutting more meat. "He's a good friend, but makes a lousy realtor."

"That's not what I asked," she said with a chuckle. "You should have done that a long time ago. Who owns the house now, Alec?"

"Joy. She's always owned her house."

And that's when she appeared. She materialized in her usual dark blouse and jeans, standing over them by the small table.

"Joy!"

Alec leapt up and took her in his arms—but she stepped back. From the corner of his eye, Alec saw a wooden cabinet open and a crystal wine glass and plate float to the table and land beside Alec's plate. Then their bottle of white wine lifted itself and filled Joy's empty glass, while a matching white leather chair from a corner of the house by the bathroom slid over.

Joy sat down beside Alec.

"Can you pass the mashed potatoes?" Joy asked, heaving a sigh.

"It's so good to see you, Joy," Daisie said.

"It's great seeing you!" Alec echoed, sitting back down.

"Hi, Alec," Joy said with a chuckle. "Daisie. It's so great seeing you guys again." But she seemed depressed. She raised her wine glass, forced a smile, and toasted them. Then Joy sipped it (but she didn't drink any, she just pretended). "To friends. Happy Thanksgiving. It's nice to spend this special time together."

"Where have you been?" Alec asked.

"Wait," Joy said, raising her palm. "So, um—" She sipped more wine. "How will you keep the house, Alec? If you know Reggie like I do, he'll be back."

"After what you did to him?" asked Daisie.

"You don't know Reggie. He doesn't like heights, but he'd climb Mount Everest if it meant making money. Even if he has to come back in a straightjacket, he'll be back." She laughed. "Yeah, I scared him good though, didn't I? But for only so long. Trust me. The mighty dollar always brings that jerk back. Still—" She tapped her red fingernails on her wine glass. She wagged a finger. "I think I've got a plan."

"You always had the plans," Daisie said, sipping some wine. "You were the one who threw him out."

"Yeah," Joy said with a thin smile. "Sure did. But I couldn't have done that without you and Alec. You guys gave me the courage to do it."

She turned to Alec with a rueful grin. There was something about that smile that really hurt—a smile he had longed for so much these past few days, but now it seemed so sad.

"You two gave me the strength," Joy said. "That's what this day is all about, you know. Giving thanks to the people you love."

"Where've you been, Joy?" Alec asked again. "I've been calling out your name everywhere. I wandered around the house, went up to the top of the hill, even hiked all around the lake calling out your name a thousand times. I've missed you so much and—"

"Wait," Joy said again, raising a hand. She shook her head and stared up at the ceiling for a moment. "Wait…just wait one second… I know you did." She looked back at him and flashed a grin. "I have an idea to finally straighten things out. See, I've been signing checks with the bank for years. I've sent checks for taxes and the mortgage on the place, just like I did when I was alive. To the world, maybe not my fans, but to the banks, Josephine Graynger is alive. I was never pronounced dead. So, I figure, why not use my signature one final time and transfer the deed of the house to you? That way Reggie won't vie for control of our place anymore. He won't be able to, legally. And then if the brute comes back, our sheriff can actually be of help for once."

"But you'd need a notary to make it legal," Daisie said.

"Doesn't Plymouth Hill's Corner Store have a notary?" Joy asked.

"Hey, how did you know I was a notary, Joy?" Daisie said, slapping the table.

"Been snooping around for a while," Joy said with a shrug and smirk.

"But why didn't you give it to Alec in the first place?" Daisie asked.

"Well—" She turned back to Alec and frowned. "I really don't think I wanted to give my place up. Even to you, Alec. You don't know how mad I was when Reggie's ditzy son had movers take my stuff away. Nobody really knows how hard it is to give things you love away until you pass away."

"Sure, you can hand it all over to me," Alec said with a big smile. "Sure, Joy. That'd work for both of us now."

"No, Alec, it won't work for *us*," she snapped, shaking her head. "That's what I'm trying to tell you."

"What do you mean?" asked Alec, furrowing his brow. He reached over to squeeze her hand, but her hand singed him like an open flame.

"*Fuck! Damn it, Alec!*" She slammed her fist on the table. "*Stop touching my hand! Why do you keep doing that! How many times do I have to—*"

"Sorry."

"*He's so dense, Daisie!*" Joy exclaimed. "So dense! What the hell's wrong with him?" But then she looked down, shaking her head, and chuckled. "Like, he doesn't get I'm a ghost. I guess it's kinda cute." She heaved a sigh. "Alec, you'll take my home. It's yours. That will take care of all your problems in Plymouth Hill."

"But you can still stay in the house with me."

"Not after I give the house away."

"Why?"

She gazed into his eyes for a moment. Then a tear fell from her eye. That tear stung his heart more than the burning her hand ever did.

She quickly turned back to the table and served herself some turkey with a fork from the open silver box. She cut and sliced a piece. Then she pretended to sip more white wine.

"Who chose the wine?" Joy asked, swallowing.

"Me," Daisie said.

"I bet you have really good taste, Daisie. I wish I could taste it."

"Why do you look like someone—"

"Like someone died, Alec?" Joy snapped, pretending to sip more wine. "Like someone died? Hmm? Why do I look like someone who died? Cause I did. And I think it's about time you realize that." She looked angry, but her comment brought even more tears streaming from her eyes. Then, with a measured voice, she said, "Shit. All right… well, you see, Alec, I now know the reason I was haunting my house. It had always been about Reggie. All ghosts haunt things when trying to fix past traumas. I read it"—She cupped her hand, winking at him and gesturing to Daisie—"I snuck into the witch aisle of her store and read some witchcraft books on the end of life."

"Joy!" Daisie snapped.

"Sorry," Joy said with a shrug.

"Anyway, a haunting, I learned," Joy continued, "means repeating over and over again, and it's done by spirits that feel like their lives need something that's been left unfulfilled. My situation was obvious. I had lost my dream, ripped from me by my manager and agent. Worse, I thought I had escaped him and finally found happiness on Plymouth Crest. He stole that happiness from me when I died, just like he had when I was living in L.A. Well, with your help, I fixed it. You guys gave me the nerve to finally do what I had to do to Reggie."

She looked pensively toward the small window for a moment. Then she looked pained.

"Can you explain the rest, Daisie?" Joy said finally, with her voice breaking. "Alec is sweet, but he can be so dense…you know, and I don't think I can keep going on. Fuck… fuck… I hate byes so much, just like I hate cries." She glanced at Alec and wiped tears with the back of her hand. "Just, you go tell him the rest, Daisie."

"You're leaving me," Alec said somberly.

"Yes, Alec," Joy said. "Yes. I have to. You love my house? Well, now you can have it. You can live happily ever after here." Then she looked down at her plate and sort of swirled her mashed potatoes. "I fucking love mashed potatoes, guys. Just as I loved drinking orange juice with you that morning, Alec. God, I'm going to miss you so much. Just like I'm going to miss this special night with my friends in Plymouth Hill. Thanksgiving with family is something I didn't have when I was alive. It's so special."

Joy raised her wine glass to toast, but her hand shook. Daisie raised her glass too.

Alec didn't. He felt horrible.

"Did you finish your book?" Joy asked Alec, throwing her long hair back and bringing more wine to her lips. Then she brought the plate closer and cut some turkey with a fork and knife.

"I don't care about my book."

"She has to go, Alec," Daisie said.

"How the hell would you know, Daisie," Alec snapped. "Some witch you are, you probably didn't even read the book she's talking about."

"Now you're being mean," warned Joy.

"More like woman's intuition," Daisie muttered. Daisie's voice cracked. She was on the verge of crying too.

"It's taking all my effort to spend this little time left with you," Joy said quietly, trying hard to force a smile. "I only came back to make the transfer of my deed official. You notarize my signature, Daisie. Then I can go. God, sorry…it all sounds awful. I'm sorry, I really am. Oh, Alec, if this was only about you, it'd be different."

"What is it about?"

"It's hard to explain."

"Try me."

"I want to go," Joy said. "If you saw what I saw, you'd want to leave too. So…" Joy cut some meat. She chewed. (But she was pretending. The meat remained on the fork.) "I came by to say goodbye to my friends. I love you guys so much. I'll sign the deed to Alec, Daisie will notarize it, and we'll be done with this whole debacle. Reggie will have to stay far away, where he belongs. And we all will live, or die, happily ever after."

Then they returned to quietly eating. Only the sounds of dishes clinking and forks and knives moving were heard. And Joy seemed content just pretending to eat and drink with them.

"I don't get it," Alec finally said, running his hand through his hair. "You can give me the house legally and still stay there. No one will know. Why don't you stay in the house with me? You like me. You told me you *loved* me. Why would you want to leave me?"

"She said she wants to go, Alec," Daisie said, wiping tears. "She said her haunting's over."

"*She's not done haunting me!*" Alec snapped, slapping the table hard.

That quieted everyone all over again. Daisie and Joy just froze, staring down at the table.

"I never liked your temper," Joy muttered quietly. "You're not making things any better, Alec."

"I'm…sorry," Alec said solemnly. "Sorry, Joy. Sorry, Daisie."

"It's okay, Alec," Daisie said.

"Let's try to enjoy these last moments together," Joy said.

But that was an awful thing to say. Joy raised the wine glass once more, and they all toasted each other and forced a smile.

2 3

SNOW, SNOW, AND MORE SNOW

Chip stood at the living room window, staring outside as icy flurries fell on trees and shrubs, covering everything in Alec's backyard with a white blanket. Sipping from a small cocktail glass, he peered upstairs through the second-floor window. He kept shaking his head. Alec wasn't sure if it was out of rage or if he was in awe of his view. Maybe both? All the while, Alec sat on his black leather sofa, typing the last chapter of his novel on his laptop. Normally, he wouldn't type with company, but this was Chip's fourth day staying at his house.

"Well, Merry Christmas," Chip said, heaving a sigh. "Suppose vengeance is yours. Inviting me to your house only to get me trapped here."

"I didn't know," Alec said, shaking his head. "Really, I didn't. Sorry. But thanks for coming."

"Fuck you," Chip said, shaking his head. "Really. Fuck off, man. Cheryl is expecting me back home for the holidays, you jerk. If this snow keeps up, I won't make it back in time."

"Your family will understand."

"They won't." Chip turned around.

He walked away and angrily plopped back down in a chair. But then he grinned and pointed at Alec with the hand holding his cocktail glass. "I don't really get you, Alec. How and why did you decide that you want to live here? It's so boring. Oh, it's that writing thing, right?"

"It's amazing here," Alec said, shrugging and typing more.

"Let's talk about our deal," Chip said, leaning forward in the chair. "You're really going to pay me 10 percent off the original asking price? Why? Is this my Christmas present?"

"Merry Christmas," Alec said, looking up with a smirk.

"Mind telling me the secret of how you got this incredible deal? Did you send some commandos in to get rid of Reginald and commandeer the mansion? More importantly, how did you have Fifi Graynger sign the house over to you? A *dead* Fifi Graynger."

"If I told you, you wouldn't believe me."

"She's not dead? That's it, isn't it?"

A shadow crossed the kitchen door. Alec stopped typing and stared. He thought, or hoped, that it wasn't just outside the window. He so hoped it was Joy. He had hoped his ghost would appear every day since she left two weeks ago. But the shadow came and went as fast as it had appeared. It was probably just a bird in the branches.

Chip was still staring at him.

"You found Fifi?" Chip said. "That's it, right? Fifi Graynger is alive, like some of her fans guessed, and she sold her house to you, but you swore to never tell anybody. That's why you won't tell me—even though I'm your best friend."

"Not exactly," Alec said with a chuckle. "Or, I suppose…well—"

Chip gesticulated for more information.

"Does it matter?" Alec asked.

"No." Chip sipped more whiskey and shook his head. "Not if you're giving me 10 percent." He sank deeper in the lounge chair. "Hey, are there any restaurants around here? Or do I have to keep eating your frozen food?"

"Frozen. Nearest restaurant is—"

"Three hundred miles by the nearest airport."

"I'm really sorry, Chip," Alec said with a laugh. "Really I am. I didn't know the roads would close. Daisie told me this snowstorm hit a bit early this year. She said the road will probably still reopen by Christmas."

"Probably?" Chip said, jumping up. "*Fuck, you did this on purpose!*"

"I didn't," Alec said with a laugh.

"Alec, I'm telling you, I mean, I guarantee, I promise you, I will slush my rental Toyota through ice, sleet, and then down the frickin' hill itself, if I have to, to get back to the airport and fly home."

Chip frowned. But after he sipped more whiskey, he smirked at him.

The doorbell rang. Chip jumped up, probably excited to see *anyone*. Alec followed, knowing who it was before Chip opened the door.

"Hey, Alec," Daisie said, in her red coat and hat, reaching for a hug. She handed him a large bag of groceries. "I waited till the snow quieted to get you all this stuff. These flurries are so early this year."

"Are the roads open?" Chip asked.

"Not yet." Daisie laughed. "It took me an hour just to get up Alec's hill." Then she handed Alec her coat and hat and walked inside. She shook Chip's hand. "I'm Daisie. You're one of his foreigner friends from the other side of the country?"

"Chip," he said with a nod.

"Oh, you're *Chip*," Daisie said disdainfully. "You're the realtor."

"Hey!" Chip snapped, turning to Alec. "What the hell did you tell her about me? What does she mean by looking all disgusted when saying *the realtor*?"

"I told her you're my realtor. Did I need to say anything else?"

They all laughed.

"You can't get on the roads yet, Chip," Daisie said. "You'll have to wait just a couple more days. I drove slow, real slow, with chains up the hill, but I've been stranded a couple times. At least Alec's hillside is not too curvy or steep, so if I slip down the hill, I don't crash to my death, I just land in a ditch. But I wouldn't be driving anywhere farther than Plymouth Hill."

"Great," Chip said.

"You came just in time, Daisie," Alec said. "You can talk to him. I've just been writing, and he's bored as hell by me."

"He gets really boring when he writes," Daisie said with a chuckle. "Well…" She hooked Chip by the arm and walked with him into the living room. "I work the Corner Store at the bottom of the hill, so, if you're looking for supplies this week, Chip, look no further. I don't have much business this time of the year, so you can have my personal "Daisie" delivery service. I've got plenty of windshield ice scrapers and spare shovels." She laughed again. "So, tell me, how long have you and Alec been friends? I feel bad Alec drew you all the way here for the winter."

"This house was quite a good deal for me," Chip said, shaking his head.

"I thought you fired him?" Daisie asked with a smirk, looking back at Alec.

Alec shrugged.

Alec walked to the entryway to close the door, but before he shut it, he thought he saw something heading up the snow-covered hiking trail. At first, he thought it was a deer. But then he noted only two legs. And the lady wore a blue coat with a fur collar. That was the jacket Joy wore when she first met him in the kitchen.

"Joy!" Alec said, running outside. "Joy? Joy!"

Alec rushed onto his snowy driveway. It was so frigid and he was just in a T-shirt and sweats with slippers. He didn't care, as long as Joy was back. He'd fight a blizzard all the way up to the top of the hill for a chance to see her again. But as he gazed at the trail, going farther up the hill, now covered in a foot of snow, she faded away.

"Alec," Daisie said behind him. "Alec, come back inside! Are you crazy? It's so cold outside."

"I saw her! I saw Joy, Daisie! I'm sure of it. She came back!"

"She told you," Daisie said, shaking her head. "She left for good. Now come back inside before you freeze to death."

2 4

THE NEW YEAR

Alec sat on his white plastic chair in a coat. Although snow still covered the leaves and branches below, it was warm enough to sit on the terrace that he loved so much. The sky was hazy and there was a pleasant smell of snow, but the clouds weren't as dark and foreboding as yesterday. At the bottom of the hill, about a foot of snow had accumulated over his patio. The roof provided some cover over his terrace, but he'd still had to clear ice from all the windows before he'd started writing this morning. There was a constant dripping sound of water running down the slope of his roof. In the distance was the iced-over lake. It was a bit dark without the sun's glow, but the vista over the woods was breathtaking, as always.

This week marked the new year, and it meant good tidings. Alec had managed to stay in Plymouth Crest until winter. Daisie had wagered he'd be gone by now. And Chip had left Plymouth Crest and made it back home for Christmas.

But there was a negative side to the new year. January first had heralded his deadline to finish his novel. He was supposed to have had the manuscript in his editor's hands last month. So he finally did what he really didn't want to do. He called his agent.

"Happy new year, Phoebe."

"Hey, Alec. Happy new year! Your house buried in snow yet?"

"Snow's thick and it's very cold, but the view is still stunning. The house is gorgeous. How's the rest of your gang back home?"

"Great. Great. Family's great. Look, I'm going to send you the cover for your new book. The artist we got is amazing. The image is bright, like you requested, with a yellow tint to mark the sun's rays. For the back, the publisher was thinking it'd be good to get some pictures of our bestselling author. You keep telling me how amazing your town is, so why not let your readers see who their writer is with that lake and forest of yours as a backdrop? Can you send me some photos of you beside your amazing home?"

"Sure I can."

"Did you make a decision about coming back to L.A. to do a book tour?"

"I'm going to try to make it back there to see my grandson born. But I told my daughter that I won't be able to go if I'm snowed in. She's not due for another month. But with the weather, I really don't think we should plan a tour, Phoebe."

"If you change your mind, I need to schedule the dates with stores as soon as possible. You know, people prefer seeing you in person."

"I wouldn't schedule anything now."

"Hmm, you never liked public appearances."

"Yeah. Listen, I've got some bad news."

That led to silence. After a month's delay, Alec didn't think he needed to say much else.

"What is it with you lately, Alec? You never had writer's block before? Maybe this middle of nowhere stuff isn't helping your writing career like you thought it would?"

"I just need another month for the final chapter. Promise."

"The editors have a schedule too."

"Just one more month. I promise. I just need to finish this last chapter."

"Alec, you can write a chapter in an hour."

"Just one more month."

Phoebe went silent again.

Alec jumped up and stood closer to the concrete ledge, just staring out at the lake below. He wandered a bit too close to the ledge with a sudden terror of falling. That was the first time he realized why the ledge was so shallow. Joy had built it low so as not to obstruct the view. She had loved this view so much that she had died for it.

Phoebe heaved a sigh.

"Please, just one month," he repeated.

"We might have to delay the launch. But you only need one chapter? I don't get it. Just write the goddamn chapter, Alec."

"I think I can make the story so much better. At least two more weeks. Please."

"Fine," she said with a sigh. "Happy new year, Alec. We'll make do, as we always do. I can't wait to read your novel."

And she hung up her phone.

Then Alec sat back down in his chair and stared out at the view again. Yes, maybe it was too beautiful for writing. But now he had bought himself a little more time to enjoy it.

He forced himself to do some typing—just when the cellphone buzzed again in his pocket. He expected Chip, or his agent again, but it was his daughter.

"Daddy?"

"Hey, Rachel. Happy new year!"

"Thanks, Dad. Happy new year. I tried to reach you yesterday but your phone was down."

"It was probably snowing too hard. You know how the reception is when it gets stormy here."

"Well, Dad, my water broke so I'm in the hospital now. The baby might come at any moment, and you insisted I call you and let you know when that happened."

"I'll be right over!"

"What?" she asked. "Wait...what? Wait, you're really gonna fly all the way over now? But I know how far away you live. And you said it's been storming. Isn't it snowing there? I'm just calling because I promised to let you know."

"Never mind, I'll be right there, Rachel. You're at the hospital already? Wow. This is so early. So sorry about yesterday, babe, it's just that when the clouds are thick, the phones—"

"Just be careful, Dad. I'd love it if you came, sure, but don't do it if the roads are too dangerous. Please, just be careful."

"I'm so happy for you, babe."

"Me too. I'm really excited. It's going to be wonderful. I'm getting contractions a lot. The doctor says the baby could come anywhere from a few hours till tomorrow morning. They already checked with an ultrasound, and everything seems to be going fine. I'm just a little nervous. It's really exciting."

"You'll be fine. I'll—"

It was then, further down the hillside, surrounded by snow-covered trees, that a woman appeared. The lady was staring out at the lake, wearing a dark shawl and pants. The same clothes she had worn on that first day he had visited the house.

It was Joy!

"Babies come when babies come, I suppose," Rachel said.

"I'll… I'll be right there, Rachel," Alec stammered, jumping up. "But I have to go now, babe. I'm so happy for you. I'll see you soon."

"I love you, Daddy." She hung up the phone.

"Joy!" Alec hollered and waved. "Joy! Are you back?"

She shook her head slowly, wrapping her arms around herself, as if feeling cold. But he caught a smile from her profile—Joy's smile, the smile he had fallen in love with and missed so much.

But she wouldn't turn.

"Joy!"

She just stood there with her arms wrapped around herself in her dark shawl and jeans, barefoot, staring out at the icy lake. The sun peeked through a cloud, and rays of sunlight reflected off the lake. That gold light shimmered over Joy's face.

"Joy, answer me. Come on. Joy!"

Alec rushed back inside, ran around the inner balcony, and dashed down the stairs. But when he threw the front door open, she was gone.

2 5

RACHEL

Alec walked through the double glass doors of the hospital, past a reception desk, and then into an elevator. He checked his cellphone. Somehow, he had made it back to California in less than a day. Somehow. He'd had to. But he was exhausted. He had driven through treacherous, slippery, and icy roads with his Lexus, sliding some of the way, for the three-hundred miles to the airport, and all the way, other cars had been stranded off the road in the thick snowfall. Then came the lines in the airport and the flight itself. There were threats of delays. But he would get there to see his daughter, somehow. Somehow, he'd make it for the delivery of his grandson. With his heart beating hard in his chest, excited, now walking fast down a hallway, he was finally on his way to the hospital room number she had texted him.

He didn't make it. That is, he didn't make it in time for her delivery.

Rachel lay in bed, in a blue hospital gown, exhausted, with a baby lying on her chest. His daughter looked weak and pale, but she smiled when he entered the room.

"Where's Matt?" Alec asked, looking around.

"He stepped out for breakfast, Dad." Then she smiled and nodded at the baby on her chest. "Daniel. Your grandson. Isn't he wonderful, Daddy?"

"He sure is."

373

"Do you want to hold him?"

Alec carefully lifted up his grandson, wrapped in a baby blue blanket. His eyes were closed. He was quietly sleeping. Alec gently kissed those chubby cheeks and rocked him a little. Then he gently laid him back down carefully in his mother's arms.

"I'm so proud of you, Rachel." He kissed his daughter's cheek. "Wow. He's so cute."

"I…" She tried to sit up on the hospital bed, but Alec gestured for her to stay put. Instead, he sat beside her on the bed, holding her hand. "I felt bad calling you. Matt said asking you to be here was a dumb idea. But I told him you insisted I call when the baby was coming. But he's right. You just live too far away. And it's snowing, right? I wasn't thinking straight, but I just—"

"I don't care. I'm so glad I came."

"Well, we still need to come and see your place. We so want to visit."

"When you're well. I'd love you to see the house. I'd love for Danny to see it too."

"Hey, Rache, brought you a bagel," a man said, barging into the room. "If you're hungry. The cafeteria was busy. I heard—"

"Oh," Matt said. He walked over and gave Alec a hug. "This is a surprise. Wow. Hi, Dad."

"Hi Matt. Congratulations."

"Thanks," Matt said putting an arm around Alec. "Congratulations to you, grandpa." He laughed. "It was so sudden, right? She kept talking about how she kinda wanted to run postterm just so you'd be able to come for sure after winter. Came preterm instead. Man, you came all the way here from your place? You live so far. You staying in a hotel?"

"He's staying with us, dummy," Rachel replied.

"Oh, of course," Matt said with a chuckle.

"I hope I can return the favor soon," Alec said, "and you two can come visit when the winter's over. We were just talking about that. You two bring the baby. You'd all love it there."

"I saw how beautiful your house is," Rachel said with a nod.

"We kept checking out the pictures together," Matt said with a nod. "It's incredible, Dad. What a gem. I can't wait to visit."

Then Matt sat by Rachel's side in the same place Alec had a moment earlier. He took her hand. But the baby opened his eyes and started fussing, so Rachel started opening her gown to breastfeed.

That's when a nurse walked into the room. She looked at the plastic wires and machines by the bedside. Then she looked down on Rachel and the baby smiling. She reached for Daniel and transferred him to a wheeled bassinet.

"Kiddo will be right back," the nurse said.

"You made it just in time to see him, Dad," Rachel said. "They're gonna take Daniel away just for a little bit."

"He'll be right back," the nurse repeated.

"He looks so cute, Rachel," Alec said. "I'm so proud of you. So happy for both of you."

"I think Mom would have really loved him," she said with a nod.

2 6

JOY

Traveling back home was not nearly as easy as flying to California. When he landed, the snowstorms had only gotten worse. There was zero visibility, and Daisie had suggested on the phone that Alec stay away for a month. Daisie offered to watch over his place, but Alec wanted to be home nearly as much as he had wanted to be there for his daughter (and, secretly, he didn't tell Daisie, but he also had hopes of seeing Joy). As usual, Daisie, the Plymouth Hill native, was right. First Alec had to spend the night at the airport. Then it took him an entire day, late into evening hours, to get home. The slick windy drive of three hundred miles took over sixteen hours, and nighttime felt even more treacherous. Once again, he saw cars turned off the road and stranded along the shoulders of the white-blanketed highway every few miles. His biggest fear was that they'd close the highway down. Daisie had warned him about that possibility too.

When he finally made it back to Plymouth Crest, he dropped his bags by the front door, hauled his body upstairs, and just plopped onto his bed.

～

Morning came, shining sunlight through the open red velvet drapes of his bedroom. Ironically, after terrible travels, the sun shone brightly with clear skies, heralding the end of the storm. But it was still very cold outside. He had to wear a heavy coat as he sat on the terrace, just so he could be outside and enjoy his view. With his laptop on his lap, he stared at his unfinished book—the book he was supposed to have finished.

The air smelled of snow and maple trees. And the lake, far below, reflected golden, shining more sunrays than ever from an icy lake-mirror. Daisie told him the lake iced up every year. Only once or twice in her life had she not seen it freeze. Right now, it nearly blinded him with its reflected yellow light. It was as enchanting as the vista in the summer or the autumn leaves in fall.

He typed, not out of inspiration, but because he had to. All the while, birds rustled in the leaves fighting for his attention.

But it wasn't the sound of leaves rustling in the wind or squirrels climbing trees that finally stopped his fingers from moving. It was a far lovelier sound. Something that brought that feeling deep inside his chest again—that same feeling he'd first felt when he came to Plymouth Crest.

Joy.

Joy was humming. She was humming betwixt singing. It was her lovely singing voice, that same voice he had heard humming on the Fourth of July when he and Daisie were in need of a designated driver. She hummed and added words to that same tune, a song she had supposedly made up, but one she undoubtedly figured Alec would remember.

He stood up and, following her voice under the terrace, he saw his ghost. Joy stood barefoot in her coat staring at the lake with her hands in her pockets, squinting at the bright light, humming and singing. All the exhaustion from his trip left him.

"Joy!" he cried. "Joy!"

He leaned over the concrete ledge and cried out her name over and over. All she did was nod slowly while still gazing out at the lake.

"Wait, Joy. Wait. Please don't go this time! I'm coming down."

She didn't turn. But she nodded again.

He ran downstairs, nearly tripping over two steps at a time, and right out the front door. Then he rushed to the side of the house where he had seen her. He followed her voice. Finally turning the corner, he saw that same lovely profile, a face that had seemed to be imprinted in his mind during his whole journey to California: splashed on his passenger window, appearing in the window beside his seat in the airplane, on the windshield of his rental car in California. It was not Fifi's face, it was Joy's—those almond eyes with dark eyelashes, large red lips, and long flowing dark hair, staring at the icy lake, just as beautiful as Plymouth Crest itself. She had told him she created this vision for him. Her profile haunted him, just as that vision of his wife at the dining room table still haunted his memories. These pictures in his mind were more valuable than any photograph. And something about the fact that her face was Joy's, Josephine's creation created specifically *for him*, told him that she knew he was waiting for her.

"I love you."

That made her turn. But she looked confused.

"How did your trip go, Alec?"

"I still haven't finished my book. Maybe you could help me write the last chapter?"

"I'm not talking about your silly, dumb book," she said, shaking her head. "I'm asking about your daughter. How's her baby? Your grandson?" She forced a smile and squinted up at the sun. "That was so wonderful. I can't believe you went there through the terrible storm. There are two things I have always misunderstood about you. Your relationship with your family and your temper. I thought, being so like me, you didn't get along with your family. Seeing you battle the snow and sleet just to see your daughter's newborn baby was…amazing. I wanted to tell you that before I go. But as far as your anger problem…"

"Nobody's perfect."

"Yeah." She shrugged and smirked at him. "That's exactly what I was going to say. Nobody's perfect." She pointed her index finger at the sky, as if ticking an imaginary box. "There's something else about the two of us. I guess you can read my mind too."

"Please look at me, Joy."

"I really shouldn't," she shook her head. "Why haven't you gotten closer to your neighbor, Daisie? She's such a nice woman. I like her a lot. She would make a wonderful companion in your life."

"She's a witch."

"Nobody's perfect," Joy repeated with a laugh.

"I don't love her, Joy. I love you."

"How can you love someone who's dead? I'm like your book. I'm not real. Daisie's *real*. And she likes you. Or are you too dense to notice?"

"I noticed."

Alec touched her back, but her body recoiled from his touch.

"I… I can't, Alec. I can't… I told you. I have to go."

"Okay. Just know I love you so much. God, I'm going to miss you so much. I love your smile. Your energy. There's so much, you know, I love about you."

And she laughed.

"And I love your laughter."

She gestured back at the lake.

"When I first came here," she said, "I was looking for a place to start a new chapter in my life, just like you. Some stars get an island, or build themselves a castle, but I chose to live in the woods out in the middle of nowhere. Beside our awesome lake. Nobody understands how wonderful all this is to me, I think, except you. You and I."

"I love the view, just like I love you."

"Yeah? Well, stop saying that you love me already and go have a nice life."

He laughed. That made her laugh too.

"You really can't stay?"

"Are you crazy, Alec! You want someone who's not real to hang with you? I'm not real. Okay? You were right. I'm not real. Fifi died. I changed my look for you. This is all a fantasy, Alec. I'm not real. It's like…ghost makeup."

"I have no objections to you looking like Fifi, if you prefer. You can even look like that ghoul you once showed Daisie."

"I don't think you'd want me to look like that," Joy said with a chuckle.

Then they were caught staring into each other's eyes. It was that look of love.

Alec came closer. He noticed her breathing more softly. Then he ran his hand gently through her hair and she seemed lost in his eyes.

"If you must go," he said, "then…but if it's up to you, and you can stay, please don't go. You obviously haven't left yet."

"You have no idea what I'm missing," Joy said, breaking his gaze. She walked over to a tree, leaned against the trunk, folded her arms, and looked up at the clear sky. "When you die, Alec, there's this brilliant yellow light, and this amazing feeling of warmth and goodness that is so magnetic, and really the only thing, I think, that can keep you in this dreary, dark world is someone or something that haunts you. In my case, it was my hatred for Reggie. You know, I was never happy as a star, and when I finally found happiness, he ripped it from me. Now he could come back and hurt you."

"So you're here to protect me?"

"Of course. I would never want anything bad to happen to you. But I mean…no. I told you, when you die the only thing that can keep you from moving into that light is something that haunts you. Reggie haunted me first. I took care of him. Then there was…"

"Me."

"Yeah, you. But you have to think of your future, Alec. Think about Daisie, your good friend, or maybe someone else alive that is *real*. You know, someone who—"

"Joy," he said, coming closer again. He ran his hand through her long dark hair and over her soft cheek. He felt tears fall from his eyes. "You told me that we should be happy without thinking. You're thinking. You said we shouldn't worry, and, like the lake and the woods, enjoy the moment. You said this so many times. Why can't we enjoy our moments together? Even if it's only for a little while longer?"

Joy slowly shook her head.

"For a little longer?"

"I'm still here, Alec, aren't I?"

He embraced her so tightly over that. Then she touched her lips gently to his. And he kissed her soft lips harder. His hand ran through her long hair and he felt her arms around him, squeezing him.

"If you have to go, then go, Joy," Alec whispered. "But if you're thinking of my welfare, don't go for that. Because I don't want you to leave."

But then she started shaking in his arms.

"Why are you crying?" he whispered.

"You make me so happy, Alec. Yes, I love you. Yes. I didn't think I'd ever meet a man in my life like you. I suppose I never did."

"So you'll stay?"

"Yes," she said, squeezing him tighter. "For you, Alec. Yes, I'll stay for you. I will."

"I will," Alec echoed, kissing her lips.

2 7

THE LAKE

ALEC SAT ON A PLASTIC CHAIR ON THE ROCKY AREA OVERLOOKING HIS lake. He had been coming down to the shore like this for so many years that he and Joy had finally just left chairs. It seemed it had become a tradition, when weather permitted, for him to walk down the hill every morning and write beside her. This morning, like so many times before, bright yellow light reflected off the water under a clear cerulean sky. And his ghost, as usual, sat by his side, wearing shades and sitting quietly, loving the view.

It was a warm autumn day with leaves turning that wonderful orange and brown. A perfect day, if it had not been for his hand shaking. That wasn't from the cold. His nerves were getting worse—that, along with a growing unsteadiness whenever he walked. When he had first arrived at Plymouth Crest, he could get to Daisie's place in less than an hour. Now, if he didn't drive, it could take two or three hours to make his way down the hill—despite Joy's help, supporting him along the way.

He glanced at Joy. The water reflected the sun's rays over her profile. For years now, she had worn her long hair white with blemishes on her perfect face and wrinkles on her skin. He never recalled asking her to do it, she just did it. But she never lost that whimsical, joyful countenance that he had fallen in love with. And she wore the same clothes—a dark shawl with jeans, without shoes, that she had worn when he saw her the first day he arrived at her house.

She seemed to notice she was being watched.

"You always have trouble finishing your books," she said.

"And you always help me finish them."

"But you really need to lay off the writing now, Alec. Or…stay inside the house. Your body's telling you to stop. You need rest."

"Never."

She reached over and put an arm around him, kissing his cheek. Then she just leaned her head on his shoulder.

"You know Danny is almost due for the birth of his granddaughter," Alec said. "He was hoping so much that I could come by and visit them in a few months, in Denver, around springtime. I thought—"

"No, Alec," she said, letting go of him. She shook her head. "I'd love for you to go, but you can't. You need to stay put in Plymouth Crest. This is what I'm talking about. You have to think of your health now."

"And I can't bring you along."

"Well, that too." She shrugged. "But you know I'll always be here when you get back."

And she always was. Joy always remained at Plymouth Crest, waiting for his return, every time he left: when Danny's daughter was born, when Danny had a son, and when Alec spent a month by his daughter's side before she passed away in California. Back home in Plymouth Crest, Joy stayed by his side at every birthday, at every meal, and during leisure time. She had been his constant companion for decades.

There was a white plastic chair, thrown on its side, now brown and dirtied from the passing of time, stuck in the rocks and sand behind Joy. That chair had once belonged to their friend Daisie, who had loved to spend time with them here by the lake years ago. All three of them had so many fun times together over the years. Daisie had passed away not long after his daughter, Rachel. But unlike at his daughter's death, Alec remembered fighting with Joy in a fit of mourning, demanding that she somehow magically bring Daisie back to stay with them as a ghost. He thought, if Joy could be back, why not his best friend? He couldn't imagine Plymouth Crest without Daisie. Daisie never returned.

But Joy never left his side.

"Why'd you stay with me all these years?" he asked. "How could you do that? Why didn't you leave, like Daisie did? You told me how much you wanted to go."

It was hardly the first time he had asked. She turned, removed her shades, and smiled.

"I love you."

"No, tell me," Alec said, shaking his head. "Don't just say you love me. You always say that."

"But I do love you, Alec," she said with a laugh. "That's why. I love you so very much."

"But you wanted to go. You said how beautiful it was on the other side. Why didn't you go?"

Joy looked down pensively. Then she laid a hand on his.

"Do you remember when we first met? You traveled to see your daughter in California when she gave birth to Danny. I'll never forget that. That was so amazing. I was going to leave, and I planned to go after Thanksgiving, but...I heard you talk to her on the phone. And then I saw you run to help her with her birth. For her. It made me think that you and I were missing something. Maybe life isn't just about the lake, or the trees, sun, clouds, Alec, or all the wonderful things we love so much in Plymouth Hill. Maybe it's about people. And I do love you. I love you so much. That's the reason, honest. I never loved any man more than you. You see, all this time you've thought your ghost, Josephine, had haunted you. That was one winter. You've haunted me ever since for the rest of your life."

He nodded pensively. But then, he shook his head.

"But you would never have heard me talk to Rachel if you had left after that Thanksgiving with Daisie. It wasn't just Rachel. It couldn't have been."

"No," she said with a nod. "It wasn't just that." She leaned over and kissed his white beard. "I already told you why. I kept being drawn to the light but... I love you, Alec. That's all. I don't know how else to put it. I wanted to spend more time with you. That's all."

He nodded.

"Thanks for letting me stay with you in your house all these years," Joy said.

And they laughed together. Alec remembered saying those exact words to her when he finally acknowledged she was a ghost.

But then Alec's hand tremored again. Then it burned. He grasped his fingers tightly, trying to stop the tremoring. He rubbed his shoulder, which had started to ache. He couldn't type. He couldn't hit any of the keys this morning.

All the while, Joy hummed. It was a different tune this time, one he had never heard. She did that, occasionally coming up with music in her head. Now she hummed and occasionally, quietly, sang words with the tune. It was a beautiful tune, as lovely as the view. And even though he wasn't feeling well, her voice soothed him. Did she know her singing soothed him? Her company soothed him so much too.

The pain came on sharper than ever. He struggled with a deep breath.

"Are you okay, babe?"

"No, I'm…having trouble breathing," he said, shaking his head. "I'm feeling that pain in my chest again."

His hand tremored more, not from nerves, but this time out of fear. And his fear seemed to only make his heart thump more crazily in his chest.

"It's okay," she whispered in his ear. "It'll be all right."

"I'm afraid, Joy. Do you think it's time?"

"Don't be afraid. Aren't you anxious when you travel, Alec? Is that nervousness or is it excitement? I'm excited. You're right, I've waited long enough."

"You're not afraid?"

"I am," she said, squeezing his hand. "I never saw what lies on the other side. I'm scared, for sure, but… I remember it being so tranquil, and I felt more at peace than I had ever felt in my life."

She took his shaky hand and brought it up to her lips, kissing it. Then she brought it down on his lap and played with his fingers. He stared at their hands together, something that had never before been possible.

"It is time," he repeated to himself with a nod.

Joy nodded back with her rueful smile. "I think so, Alec."

She helped him stand. Then she held him as they stood by the edge of the shore.

It seemed that the light shone brighter, not from the sun, not only over the trees and the water, but from everywhere—from the air itself. And in a flash, Joy's features altered into Joy's younger face, which he remembered from when he first met her. Her long hair turned from white to black again. And her perfect face with almond eyes and perfect eyebrows, like her feet, had no blemishes. Both of them just stood before the brightest lake as yellow sunlight reflected off everything. It was not just the water that reflected the sun now. There was a yellow light glowing from the fall leaves, the autumn tree trunks and branches, even along the rocks on the wet sand at their feet.

They stood and waited. Then finally, hand in hand, they walked past the ledge and onto the water. But they didn't go in. They seemed to hover over it.

"I love this lake," Joy said.

"I love you, Joy."

"And I love you, Alec. Before I came back to stay with you, I caught a glimpse of this. Oh, I've been wanting to show you this for so long. I think waiting has been the hardest. You're right. But I wanted to wait just to show you and be with you. That's why I never left you. See, as much as this light attracts me, you attracted me more. Do you…feel it? Do you feel the light as it moves us towards it? Just wait. Oh, I think it's going to be wonderful."

"With you, Joy…it will be."

And he squeezed her hand tight. She squeezed his hand back, but as he turned to her, he couldn't see her anymore. The light blinded him too brightly. Yet all the while, he heard her humming her beautiful tune.

Then, as Alec felt the radiance surround him, he walked forward, while Joy held his hand.

THE END

PHANTOM MASQUERADE

Mina Daaé dreams of performing like her ancestor, Christine Daaé. Her close friend Toni Vollini surprises her by offering her a role in his play mixing Mozart with clowns on Broadway. Toni and a ghost vie for Mina's love, but she thinks the ghost is just an illusion. Or is he a phantom of the opera?

1

THE HARLEQUIN

AND HERE IS WHERE I FALL.

A fire truck of laughing clowns with squeaky horns, dangling over a red-and-white striped engine, rushed from the left side of the auditorium toward center stage. Behind came the lion trainer, slashing the air with his whip near an empty diamond-studded cage. And acrobats in striped tights jumped and tumbled beside the fire truck, up and down, doing somersaults and flips, with jugglers not far behind. Then music: a disturbing mix of puissant class with the frenzied Big Top. An orchestra triumphant thundering *Don Giovanni* in D minor. Then light shone down on raspberry lips and the white-and-black painted face of the Don Juan himself.

Mina leaned forward, captivated. She recognized this clown. This was Monsieur Antonio Vollini, her teacher and close friend back in the university in Paris. An older man with a dark beard and thick black eyebrows. A vibrant man, now thrusting his hands high, wearing a bright-red flannel suit with a tail and a sad painted smile. His face was powdered paler than the fools around him, yet he walked across the stage, emitting grandeur. The sight of him bordered between ridiculous and brilliant—exactly like his play. Exactly like him. Antonio Vollini. The harlequin.

He stiffened his body and held his head high, demanding attention.

And she was close enough to the stage to see a smile behind the painted frown. Then he waved his hand in broad strokes before the audience and bowed, seemingly adoring the adulation as the crowd applauded. But when she turned and looked behind her, there was no one there. The seats of the auditorium were empty.

The harlequin removed his red coat and spun the cloth around like a magician, and pigeons flew out from within the satin folds. Then the clown gave another majestic bow, throwing his coat to the crowd amidst thunderous applause—from no one.

"This is my favorite part," whispered a male voice.

Mina was surprised to see a man sitting beside her, wearing a shiny black mask covering one eye and much of his face. This stranger touched her fingers with soft white gloves, which contrasted with his pitch-black mask. As she gazed at him, trying to recollect who he was, he leaned forward in his seat, just as enthralled as she was. The open part of his mask revealed a goatee and stubble extending up his hard cheekbone. It made for a handsome portrait. Then she felt tingles as he pressed her fingers again with those soft cotton gloves. She followed his muscular arm and chest in a sleeveless tuxedo up to his broad shoulders. He turned and flashed a smile, looking at her with bright jade eyes, rubbing her fingers some more.

"Enjoying the play?" he asked.

She recognized a French accent.

"Yes." *Who are you?*

The crash of drums jerked her eyes back to the performers. Two women wearing tall, frilly hats and white tights rode on tall bicycles—penny-farthings—to center stage. They circled the Harlequin and jumped off, swaying and contorting around him. Their white spandex pants and thin shirts twisted over their shapely hips and chests. Then a third ballet dancer interrupted the dance, rushing to the clown. She kissed his white-painted cheek, running her fingers along his beard and gliding them over his chest and stomach. She touched his shoulder then grabbed him, swaying and dancing to Mozart. And the Harlequin, in his ridiculous flabby white pants, twirled in a senseless bourrée.

The sound of a trumpet, an odd, shrill instrument in the midst of such lovely strings and choral music, broke the spell. Lights dimmed. The music stopped. There was a roar of applause—from no one.

When a yellow floodlight lit the stage once more, two tall steel towers rose until they nearly touched the ceiling; a tightrope stretched between them. To Mina's right, the Harlequin sat very high atop one of the towers on a narrow pedestal. It grew dark, with only an array of rainbow light shining over him. He shifted his balance and, for a moment, it looked like he was going to fall. There were gasps. He threw up a white-gloved index finger. His hand seemed to be in step with the orchestra. One solitary finger. He dropped it and raised it again, miming a conductor's movement, as if he were conducting a great symphony with the colored lights. A few onlookers in empty seats laughed.

Then the strangest of strange things happened. Although the Harlequin was painted in clown face, wearing baggy pants and ridiculous circus shoes, and at times swayed stupidly as if about to fall from the rafter, he sang a baritone accompaniment to Mozart. He sang and the circus transformed into an opera. Although his huge red clown shoes were barely balancing atop the narrow platform, he was absorbed by the music, looking into the bright light as his voice bellowed.

Mina recognized the song as the second and final act of *Don Giovanni*, playing again. There Toni stood, high above Mina, with his lovely baritone voice, singing his best Italian. She mouthed the words as if accompanying him. Back at the Conservatoire de Paris, they had sung this opera together. The orchestra thundered and, as he sang, she no longer thought of music. She thought of him. Toni. Her harlequin. Her clown. Her dear friend. But he seemed sad, with his painted frown, singing to her. He looked right down at her, only her, for there was no one else in the auditorium … except the stranger.

"Enjoying it?" the stranger asked again.

She nodded and pulled her fingers away from the stranger's soft glove to wipe a tear running down her cheek. The orchestra finally rang in a crescendo.

And here is where I fell.

Toni cried out a shrill scream of terror, so unsettling and discordant from such a jovial man. The shriek shook her. She felt dizzy. Everything spun and grew dark.

When she opened her eyes, a flood of bright red and purple and green began shining up from below. Now she was atop the high precipice, naked, looking down over her chest and shaky legs. She adjusted her bare feet, trying to balance on the cold, narrow steel ledge, in the same place Toni had been standing, singing his opera. She had replaced him. The light brightened, nearly blinding her. She could barely balance.

And here is where I fall.

2

MACARONI AND
CHEESE ON BROADWAY

Mina sat in a large booth by her lonesome, waiting for Toni, in a swanky downtown Manhattan restaurant. It was an elegant establishment, lined with windows, with white-columned walls and waiters wearing formal suits. Really swank. A single candle flickered on the center of her table. And quaint. Her booth was surrounded by a three-walled window overlooking the bright lights of the New York City skyline. The city was absolutely breathtaking. But she was high—too high—over fifty floors up. The street was so far below her.

She spotted Toni. He approached the maître d' and bound inside. He wore an elegant black suit. His short black hair and thick beard were perfectly manicured, and his skin was a bit tanned. The only major imperfection was his nose. It was a little round and ruddy, perfect for reminding her of the clown in her dream. She was surprised at how little he had changed.

She stood up and embraced him as he kissed her cheek.

"Oh, Mina, cara mia … cara Mina, you're so lovely." He had a thick Italian accent. "Absolutely lovely. I'm so happy to see you."

"Me too, Toni. Hi."

"Sorry I'm late but, believe it or not, it had to do with our play."

"*Our* play?" she asked with a chuckle.

"Si. You look breathtaking. Stunning."

"Thanks. It's great to see you too. You look pretty good yourself."

"Time moves fast, eh?" He removed his suit jacket, draping it over a seat across from her at the table. Then he sat down with her and looked outside the window, taking a deep breath as if enjoying the fragrance of the view.

"Quite a nice table you arranged," she said with some smugness.

"Meeting with you, my dear…" He gestured with a swoop of his hand. "I planned the best. The very best." He smiled again.

She loved his smile, but his broad hand gesture disturbed her a little, reminding her of her dream.

He shrugged and stared into her eyes for a moment—just stared. Then he looked some more.

"What?" she asked with a nervous laugh. "What is it?"

"Bellissima." He shook his head. "Simply bellissima. Did you order anything yet?"

"No. It's so great seeing you. And thanks for the invitation. This place is amazing."

It really was. She looked up from the menu, under the candle-light, and admired the view again. Then she laughed as he tapped his fingers on the table, thumbing through the menu as if it was a bother.

After brushing through a couple of pages, he put it down. "How are you, Mina? Tell me. I mean, how are you *really*?"

"What do you mean?"

"Not just hello. How are you? Are you still living at the university? That's what you said on the phone. Painting? You have so many talents. I introduced you to Blateman when you first arrived in New York. Did he help display your artwork?"

"No. He … well, it just didn't work out."

"Dancing then?" He leaned back in the chair, stroking his beard.

A waiter in a double-breasted navy-blue suit came back with two glasses and a bottle of wine before she could respond.

"What's this?" Mina asked.

"Celebration," Toni said with a smile and a wink. "For you."

"Celebrating what?"

"*You.*"

The waiter uncorked the bottle and presented the cork to Toni to sniff, then offered it to Mina. She waited until both glasses were poured by the waiter and he left.

"I'm doing fine," Mina said. "Thank you, Toni."

"That makes me so happy." He raised his glass. "To you and I, my dear. And the past. I've missed you so. Your voice is exquisite, but it is not as welcoming as the vision of your soul."

"Oh Toni, you still talk silly."

"Arabesque?" he asked, laughing with her. "True, true." He stared at his wine glass. "I like to have fun."

"You *are* fun."

He raised his glass to that. Then he cocked his head and looked at her curiously. "You remember before, no? Remember what I said right before you left Paris with that gentleman you were with? I can't remember his name."

"It didn't work out between us."

"You told me. But do you remember what I offered you?"

Yes. She remembered. Toni had offered her a job. She hoped that's what he was proposing tonight, and that's why she had spent so long fixing her hair, applying the perfect makeup, and putting on an attractive, but professional, navy-blue dress in her apartment. She had chosen her finest clothes. Even around her neck, she'd added her favorite diamond stud silver necklace. The diamond was tiny, but the chain was her best silver.

"I sent you my screenplay," he added. "Did you read it?"

"For sure." After all, it had imprinted itself in her dream.

"What did you think?"

A black shadow brushed by the window and drew shade over their table. At first, she mistook it for a bird, but then she realized that was impossible in the middle of the night. Toni still stared at her, waiting for her to respond.

She looked outside and jumped. A black figure in a cape stood like a perched raven with hands tucked in coat pockets and head tilted downward. Although the man gazed down, he wore a mask—the same half-mask that the figure in her dream had worn. He seemed very real, only he stood midair and she could see two buildings through him.

The waiter returned.

Mina forced a fake smile at the waiter. Toni glanced at the window a couple of times and then just furrowed his brow. The waiter had placed a salad plate before each of them and a basket of bread. Mina quickly grabbed her fork and stuck it into a carrot. Her hand shook as she brought it to her mouth.

"Are you all right?" Toni asked.

"Um-hmm." *Get it together, Mina. Not now.*

"So ... what did you think?" he asked again.

She took a deep breath, squeezed her hand under the table tight, and closed her eyes for a second.

"Hmm? What'd I think about what?"

"My musical, Mina? Did you like it?"

"Uh-huh."

She dipped another carrot in the dressing and tasted it. It was sweet and tart—absolutely delicious. She savored every bite.

"Umm," she said. "This food is really good."

Toni raised his eyebrow, staring impatiently, waiting for her response.

"Oh, Toni, well ... it was different. But yes, it was good. All your stuff is really good." She swallowed some kale and finally summoned enough courage to glance back at the window. The apparition was gone.

"It will be the number-one show on Broadway. *If* you help me. Remember what I offered you before you left? That offer is still good, now on Broadway. What do you say?"

"Well, well, well. But I haven't danced in a long time. Not since we lived in Paris."

He just smiled.

"A show on Broadway?" she asked.

"Si." He folded his arms.

Mina swirled more leaves into her salad dressing, enjoying whatever heavenly stuff it was. The food was so good. It was a pleasant distraction from the window.

Toni looked at her with a warm smile.

She stabbed some more leaves and crunched on them, patting her chin with her cloth napkin surreptitiously to make sure the dressing remained inside her mouth and not on her lips. She laughed inwardly as he just attacked his plate, seeming not to care about his appearance or the food. It was cute.

"Why Mozart?" she asked.

"Che?" he replied with his mouth full.

"Why Mozart, Toni? I don't get it. I never did."

"I love Mozart."

"I do too. But why did you stick him in a play about clowns?"

"The play is an adaptation of *Don Juan*."

"I know."

"Don Juan was in Mozart's opera *Don Giovanni*," he said matter-of-factly, shrugging. Then he chuckled. "So why not have Mozart in my clown musical about Don Juan?"

"It's theft, for one thing."

"It's not theft." Toni threw his fork down, laughing. He pointed at her. "Only you'd say that. Mozart didn't end his opera with a clown atop a pedestal."

He has a point there. "But you used his work to conclude yours. His conclusion. His music. His art."

"All art is theft, Mina. The best is what you steal from life." He picked up the fork and pointed it at her. "Anyway, it was the perfect finale."

"A clown falling to his death, singing *Don Giovanni*?"

"No, a harlequin taking off a clown *mask*, singing a eulogy before death. Remember the end of Act II of *Don Giovanni*? Don Giovanni faces a statue for the sins of his past. Yeah? The play, which is largely a comedy, becomes a masterful statement of life and death. Don Giovanni refuses to repent for all the sexual conquests of his life. He is threatened by the statue and told he will go to hell if he does not repent, but he ignores the warning. That would be against his nature. He is a libertine, no? More so, he is human. And so he falls. In so doing, Mozart takes light opera and turns it into a piece of pure genius. That is art that touches God."

"And what does that have to do with *your* play?"

"It, it, it …" He stared pensively outside at the view for a moment and then took a deep breath, turning and looking into her eyes.

She had always loved his eyes. They were hazel and almond shaped, under bushy but well-groomed brows.

He smiled. "It's a show of sensuality. A dance with a clown and ballerinas on stage. It's, of course, absurd, as the clowns are dressed in white baggy pants and in clown face. Ridicolo. But that draws you to watch. Why do lovely clowns dance around the Harlequin? And, of course, all dance is sex."

She raised her brow at that.

"By the end of my play, the clown sits atop a pedestal and tempts a fall. That temptation excites everyone. That is life. Death at any moment. It draws them to look and listen to me."

"Which you love," she interjected with a chuckle.

"Which allows the Harlequin to sing. But, it … it, it is not only the end of *Don Giovanni*; it is a harlequin singing *Don Giovanni*. A clown close to you and me. Not just a libertine, a clown. A mask. Us."

"Do you two know what you'd like this evening?"

Toni jerked in his chair and turned to the waiter standing beside the table. He had been so engrossed in explaining his play that the man had surprised him.

"We have a special dish tonight. Crab-stuffed shrimp with a pepper sauce. Absolutely delicious."

"La bistecca alla fiorentina, please," Toni said in his exquisite Italian accent. "I'd like that. How about you, Mina?" he asked with a wink. "Do you remember our evening in Naples?"

"Oh, Toni," she said, laughing. Then she leaned forward. "How do you remember that?" She turned to the waiter. "I'll have your Florentine steak too. And …" She searched the menu some more and pointed at a side dish. "With this side. The mac and cheese."

"Excellent choice," the waiter said.

For a flash, she caught him wrinkling his nose. It didn't seem like the macaroni and cheese was an excellent choice to him at all.

"The food here is fabulous," Mina said, enjoying her salad.

"Si."

Mina smiled at Toni's dismissal.

He had another taste and put his fork down again. "A human falls, no? Literally, Mina, the clown dies. The symbolism becomes direct metaphor. We live, we love, we die."

"On Broadway?"

"Of course." He nodded. "On Broadway. The threat of the

Harlequin's fall clinches it. It's why people will come. They're going to wait for the platform to sway or for a foot to slip. The rest, the depth, nobody cares. I brought the fun of the Big Top under the sway of Mozart. And what better composer to showcase such a feat of brilliance. Those around him said Mozart laughed like a clown." And then, indeed, Toni laughed just like a clown. He struck his chest with his hand and acted with silly bravado, like the performer in her dream. "Ridicolo. Divertente! Mozart e Antonio Vollini!" Then he burst into laughter.

"You're so conceited." Mina laughed while dabbing her mouth with her napkin. "I can't believe you."

He just nodded.

"It's adorable." She touched his hand.

"Food is food. A face is a face. You can do what you will to hide it, Mina, but ultimately you are what you are underneath. God gave us purity. It is what we choose to cover it that leads to our fall."

He grabbed some bread, pushed it into his mouth, and said, "Mina, tell me, I thought you said on the phone that you were dancing at the university? What do you mean you haven't danced in a long time?"

Uh-oh. "I'm modeling. Not dancing."

"I see."

She touched his hand again. "I'd be honored to dance in your play. If you want me to. Crazy or not, it's your play. I warn you, I haven't danced in years. But I've always loved your work."

"With clowns?" he asked, looking down at her hand with a playful grin.

"Yes. Clowns, Toni."

She sighed and forced a look out the window again. It was just a gorgeous view of skyscrapers and twinkling lights. Her heart quickened, but not out of fear this time. She was going to get a job tonight. She knew it! That's why she had gotten all dressed up. She had been excited to see her friend, but the prospect of working on a play on Broadway excited her so much more.

She shook her head and turned back to him. He wasn't eating. He seemed to be watching her.

"A clown singing *Don Giovanni*," she said, shaking her head. "Why not? The Big Top and Mozart? On Broadway."

"We're ar-*tists*," he said. "You sing. You dance. You paint. Hell, you know more about classical music than I do. You know Bach provided foundation, Mozart colored it, and Beethoven hammered it in. Their best works touch God."

"And you think your art touches God, Toni?"

"I know it does. This will be like the mac 'n cheese you ordered with our Florentine steak. In this restaurant. Food is food, Mina. That is my play."

She paused in thought and then nodded. "So you're throwing mac 'n cheese all over Broadway?"

"Esattamente," he said with a chuckle, holding his arms wide open again. "You got it. I knew, of all people, you would."

"No, Toni, I don't." She furrowed her brow and shook her head. "I don't get it. I really don't understand it at all."

"I think you do." He turned stern, leaning back in his seat, and folded his arms again. "And it will be the number-one show on Broadway … *if* you help me."

"How can I help you?"

"I want you to be in my play. Can you? What modeling job are you doing? What agency are you using?"

"I'm a model for art students."

He nodded.

"A nude model, Toni."

He furrowed his brow, put his fork down on the plate, and turned to the window. He looked uncomfortably somber for a moment. She had never mentioned it to him on the phone.

"Why me?" she asked. "You need another ballet dancer in the ensemble?"

"Hmm? No. I don't want you in the ensemble. Mina, I told you many years ago, at the institute, what I thought of you. Your face. The way you smile. You have a glow. It's in your blood. You know your great-ancestor, Christine Daaé, was a famous performer in the Palais Garnier. You're a talented dancer … but dancing is not what I want from my Mina Daaé."

"What do you want then?"

"Your voice. You have the voice of an angel. A voice that touches God."

She nodded thoughtfully again. "I haven't sung in a long time, certainly not Mozart. I'm probably more rusty at singing than dancing, even."

"But you did in school. You know the opera. You were in *Don Giovanni*. I would like you to help with my show. So how 'bout it? Do you want to be in my mac and cheese play on Broadway?"

"I said I did. Of course. What will I be singing?"

"Don Giovanni, of course." He gestured with wide-open arms. "You're to have the starring role as the Harlequin." He smirked. Then after a moment, he laughed more heartily than ever.

She dropped her fork and it clanged on the fine china. A few people from other tables turned. Then she heard herself gasp and felt her face flush and her eyes bulge.

Of course, Toni didn't lose his smile. He laughed harder than ever.

"Is this a joke?"

"No, I'm quite serious. You're a star, Mina. I've always known it. Now that it's my play, I consider myself lucky to be the one debuting you." He reached for her hand, but she pushed it away.

"What's wrong?"

"I thought the Harlequin was a man's role?" she said, staring at the table. "I read it. He has women accusing him of being a libertine. A Don Juan."

"I've changed that. Now they're men accusing you. And women too."

"You're absolutely crazy, you know that?"

"Si." And he took a deep breath. "Mina, I know your voice and I've seen you dance. It's my play and my choice. But I also know you're the only one crazy enough to refuse. So—I ask you again and, truly, as your good friend, I urge that you say yes to me—this is the chance of a lifetime, and I can't offer it to you again. Will you perform as the Harlequin in my play? You will be my main character. The Harlequin. On Broadway. We open in three months. Do you accept?"

"For sure," she said, throwing her long hair back.

Then it became oddly quiet. Too quiet.

He lost his smile and became strangely contemplative, nodding and turning back to their view—much as he had after she'd told him she was a nude model. She just stared at the flickering candle on the table.

She had been nervous about what he'd intended for the meeting, but she never would have guessed this. The starring role? She really thought that because he was moving to the States he just wanted to see her again—perhaps become closer to her. And maybe he'd offer her a bit part that would make her some money. And she would have been happy with that. But this, this was different. The starring role?

She risked a gaze out the window again with him. It was still just the lovely Manhattan skyline. But when she saw how high up they were, she didn't want to look there either.

"Isn't it an insult for a woman to play a clown?"

"Che?" he asked, furrowing his brow. "No, no, no. Do not think that. I told you that the head clown can be either male or female. The clown covers who she truly is. Not a fool. A mask. With you, a woman. But you of all people—Mina, if you perform it, I will never disrespect you. Not you, my jewel. Of course, you are to be a female Don Juan. A female lost in lust. You are fallible and you shall fall, just as my man did in Paris. But as for you being a clown, I would never dare cover your face. I shall be discreet. For why would I foolishly cover such beauty?"

"Oh, stop." She laughed.

"Mina, you will be dressed like a Pierrot, but I will barely cover you. I will not disrespect you. Everyone in my play is a clown." He pointed to people at the other tables. "Because … after all, every single one of us is."

"But I don't care for heights."

"But you will soar, my dear."

After sipping some red wine, she said, "Mind telling me why *me?*"

"I already have. Your voice touches God. We shall receive ovations from heaven!" He drank some wine, laughing, but then became stern. He lifted a finger, just like he had atop the pedestal in her dream, reached back into his blazer on the seat, and took out a single red rose. He handed the flower to her. "Mina, my jewel, you shall steal the sound and sight of angels and bring them down to Broadway for every clown to see and hear."

3

MANNEQUIN

MINA DIDN'T LIKE HER JOB. SHE WASN'T ASHAMED OF NUDE MODELING per se; she was more ashamed that her ambitions in dance and theater ended in modeling. That's why she had felt ashamed when she told her former instructor, Toni, about it. It seemed like her life was a dead end — until last night at dinner with him.

Nude modeling was the most lucrative job she could find. It paid well, and soon the students, even the new ones, didn't seem to pay any more attention to her than they would a mannequin. Her boss—a very nice, short, Asian woman with small, thick glasses named Ms. Kuni— was one of the sweetest ladies she had ever known. Ms. Kuni was sensitive, unlike her instructor a year before. On her first job, the teacher embarrassed the hell out of her by walking up close, touching her boobs with a stick, and gliding it along her ribs down to her ass. Ms. Kuni never disrespected her.

The worst part of her job now was not embarrassment; it was physical demand. She had to remain in the same position, like a statue, for fifteen, even thirty minutes at a time.

Today, on a very hot summer morning as the students settled down with their paints, Mina stood beside her stool, holding her long black hair back behind her head and looking straight out in no particular direction. Ms. Kuni liked this position because it accentuated Mina's firm breasts. She could feel the students' eyes tracing her hips, the curvature of her breasts and tanned and flat nipples, and her arms. Since it was such a scorcher outside, her sweat likely helped accentuate the lines of her body. Then there was the pyramid formed between her two breasts at mid-chest. It was so quiet that she could hear the brushstrokes. She imagined them touching the shadows of her belly and her ribs. Then drawing the small hole of her belly button. Next they'd fill it in, softening the lines a bit to mimic her smooth skin.

She saw her reflection in a large mirror from the corner of her eye. Her forehead was a little larger than the norm. Her nose was a bit sharper. Her lower red lip was a little thicker than the upper one. The students would be painting her face, too.

It was not such a terrible job. She could focus inward on her problems or just think of nothing at all as she posed. Perhaps meditate, as she had learned to do, and focus on her breathing. And the benefit was she could do all this while getting paid.

Cocking her head back ever so slightly, to look away, she saw students touching up her body and shading it with brushes.

Ms. Kuni signaled for Mina to change positions.

Mina sat down on the stool and leaned forward while covering her breasts with her arms. She liked this position, because now she could look into their eyes. They were shy, too. All of them avoided her gaze while painting.

In the front row was a tanned boy dressed in a T-shirt and shorts. She imagined he was from California or Florida. A surfer. She studied his body, for—it was a secret—later at home, she used the students for her artwork just as they used her.

His nose was like hers, sharp but short, and she could see it wrinkle in the middle as he worked, brushing her on the canvas. He had a strong forehead, a faint dimple on his chin, thin, light-red lips, and chiseled cheekbones. He wore a white cotton tank top, but she could see the lines along his muscular chest and upper arms. She could imagine the skin along the ripples of his abdomen. She pictured what it would be like tracing and painting an image of his skin over the angles of his deltoids and biceps with her own brush. Then she looked down at his jeans. He sat uncomfortably on his own stool, frequently rising to dab paint in different directions, while gazing at her. Having him stand, she would run the lines down around his well-developed quads and the tight crack of his ass. The athletic hardness would be easy enough to recreate. The subtlety of the softness of his stomach and ass would be the real challenge.

"Fifteen more minutes," said Ms. Kuni. Then she crouched down and looked at Mina with a sweet smile. "Are you doing okay, Mina? Can you do fifteen more?"

"Sure."

At the end of class, Mina threw on her white robe, which had been lying on a chair by the curtain, and ran to the door before her teacher left.

"Ms. Kuni," Mina said. "Ms. Kuni." Everyone else was gathering their things to leave too.

"Yes?"

"This is my last class."

"Oh. All right." She adjusted her glasses and looked up at Mina with a sweet smile. "Thank you for coming, dear." She didn't seem too surprised. Mina knew people had come in and out of this job many times before. "Did you tell Dr. Ruthers?"

Mina nodded.

"Did you find a modeling job elsewhere?"

"No. I'm spending my time in a play. You never know. It could be a big break. Or I could be back. We'll see how it goes."

"A play." Ms. Kuni smiled kindly. "Oh, yes, you said when you started that you liked theater."

"Really? I don't remember."

"I do. When I showed you our classroom. I hope your successor is as disciplined as you. You know, the girl before you was always late and she was always taking too many breaks." Her teacher shook her head, and Mina laughed. "You've been perfect."

"Thanks, Ms. Kuni."

"Hey, you're not going anywhere." Her friend Gail sprinted into the room, pushing her way past two students making for the door. She was a pretty girl with long blonde hair and a pale complexion. "You best not be." Gail was fun, and Mina liked her. Always smiley, like her friend Toni, Gail was the type of person to never be angry over anything. Except now.

"Hi, Gail. I didn't see you."

"Oh, I was…" She opened her large eyes wide and looked nervously at Ms. Kuni, who readjusted her spectacles and cocked her head back in irritation. "In the back. You didn't see me? I was tracing you, Mina." When Ms. Kuni turned back to Mina, Gail waved her hands back and forth to get Mina's attention. "Where are you going, anyway?" she asked.

"She said a play, Gail." Ms. Kuni looked at Gail over her glasses. "And where were you this morning?"

"In the back row," Gail lied, nodding.

"Show me your work tomorrow. I think you just came in. I don't think you were here during class at all."

"She was," Mina lied. "I saw her when I was standing."

"You were standing at the beginning of class," Ms. Kuni replied, raising her eyebrows. "She was definitely not here when we started."

Gail put her hands on her hips and opened her eyes wide, behind her teacher, pissed at Mina.

Mina chuckled. She couldn't help it.

"Your finished work tomorrow, Gail," said the teacher. "And I already collected the work from yesterday, so if you come up short, I'll know." Then she put a hand on Mina's arm and said with a sweet grin, "Bye, Mina. Thanks so much for helping me teach our painters."

When the door shut and the teacher left, Gail and Mina were alone.

Gail whirled around. "Fuck, can't you lie a little bit better?"

"Sorry."

"Well, I've been sketching your figure for weeks. I'm sure I'll remember your tits and ass. I can probably sketch you in my sleep tonight."

"All right, Gail," Mina replied with a chuckle.

Gail smiled. "Where are you going? What's this about leaving? What sort of play?"

"It's *The Harlequin*. It opens on Broadway in a few months."

Gail's mouth opened and her large eyes grew wider. She froze. She was speechless. And that wasn't like her at all.

Mina felt like closing Gail's eyes and mouth. "You okay, Gail?"

"Bullshit."

"It's true."

"Bullshit."

"I'm not joking."

"I thought you said you weren't dancing anymore?"

"A good friend came to town from Paris. He's the producer. He offered me a role. The starring role."

"Shut the fuck up."

"Gail, stop swearing." Mina walked behind the curtain. "I'm gonna get dressed."

"Let's go to lunch so you can tell me all about it."

"All right."

There was silence and, as Mina got dressed, she reflected that this could very well be the last time she dressed in the art room. She hoped it would be. She was sweating terribly from the heat, and she didn't like putting her clothes on over her wet body. She buttoned her blouse, thinking her young friend could have left—Gail had become so quiet— but then she heard a voice say, "It's hot as hell, isn't it, Mina?"

"Yes."

"Do you remember that boy who liked you? Rhett. The tall guy with the tattoos of lizards all over his neck. You know, the one we saw at the bar last week. Remember? He's the one who had the ponytail. He liked you. He kept talking to you as you sucked on your beer. Do you remember him, Mina?"

"Yeah. What about him?"

"He's going to a party tomorrow and he invited me. And you know what he said?"

"No. What?"

She laughed. "He said to ask my radiant friend to come. *Radiant.* Funny, huh? Can you believe that?"

"What's so funny about that?"

"He wasn't the kinda guy to say that kind of word. I was surprised he even knew what the fuck *radiant* meant. He was a bit of a moron. Cute, though. But he couldn't recall your name. I thought it was fun because he asked for you to come with me. My *radiant* friend."

"Oh. Okay. Maybe."

"What do you mean, maybe?" She actually sounded hurt.

"I'm sorry, Gail, but Toni hasn't told me yet when rehearsals begin. If I'm needed Friday, I can't come."

There was a mirror beside the curtain, and she took out a comb from her handbag and ran it through her hair while gazing at her reflection. Then she cleaned some smudges of runny mascara and sweat from under her eyes.

"Toni, huh? And … what's this Toni like? Is he cute?"

"Gail, why do you think all men are just here for a date?"

"Because I'm not old like you."

"Well," she said with a laugh. "I suppose he's cute. But he's fifty."

"Oh."

"Uh-huh." Mina walked around the curtain and smiled at her friend.

"You're not really leaving, are you?" Gail asked.

Mina lost her smile looking at Gail's expression. "Stop. Broadway's in Manhattan, not LA. We can still hang out."

"For sure," Gail said with a nod and a tight grin. Gail looked depressed as hell.

So Mina extended her arms out wide and gave her friend a big hug.

$$4$$

THE PEDESTAL

"WHAT WOULD YOU LIKE ME TO SING?"

Mina heard her voice echo through the empty hall. A few curious people backstage turned at her question. As the lights shone on her, she squinted. She couldn't see Toni or the rest of them, but she knew they were in the center of the third row, staring at her just as they had stared at the redheaded singer who had auditioned that morning.

"*Zaide*." Toni's Italian accent was amplified by his microphone. "Sing *Zaide*. You know, our favorite: 'Tender Is My Smile.' You know the one. We performed that one countless times."

"I know the song, Toni," she replied with a nod. It was "Ruhe Sanft," which meant "rest in peace." A lovely song from Mozart's unfinished opera *Zaide*. But she didn't want to sing it after hearing the exquisite voice of the redhead singing it earlier.

How can I sing better than that?

"The orchestra will play. You sing. You remember the German, no?"

"Yes."

And she waited for the orchestra to begin.

The amphitheater looked like it was capable of seating over a thousand. Old-fashioned and opulent, with a giant polished wood stage and old seats covered in velvet, matching the red satin curtains on the stage, it held a power all its own. It was as if the architect had made a building so grand it moved the crowds even without a performance. The balconies and great crystal chandeliers above her appeared to have been there for a hundred years. She loved the yellow webbed design on the red carpet, the decorative wooden columns, and even the modern neon-purple lighting along the ceiling rafters. But the strangest thing, the thing that really disturbed Mina, was that she recognized it all. Certainly, the theater was old. Perhaps she had seen pictures on the internet? But it was more than that. This fit her dream... No, it perfectly mirrored it.

Beside the stage, a few stagehands ran about while three girls in bright-red pancake tutus marked their dance steps. One dancer dipped down, touching her toes, another was putting on pointe shoes, and the third was moving her hands and feet in ballet positions.

The flute and violins began playing a lovely composition from *Zaide*.

Mina looked down and tightly clutched the microphone. She hadn't sung in so long, but as she heard her cue from the music, she performed and that finally relaxed her.

Her voice rang out, surprisingly strong. It bounced off the walls—the acoustics in the building were perfect. Throughout the hall, all she could hear was her voice, and it was lovely in the magnificent theater. She sang to them as if she had planned the performance for months but, of course, she'd had no preparation at all. She probably hadn't sung on stage since she was in Paris. Certainly, her performance was not as good as, if not far inferior to, the woman she had seen when she first arrived. But they didn't tell her to stop.

Mina looked around the auditorium as she sang; dancers were warming up backstage. They were no longer stretching. They were gazing at her, frozen, as if in surprise. Had she done something stupid?

As the song ended, she looked down at the producers, shielding her eyes from the glare of the lights. There was no clapping. No applause.

Then she heard the sound of a microphone being tapped. "Bring the platforms." It was Toni's Italian accent. There was some objection from below, and he snapped something inaudible in Italian. "Bring the pedestals. Mina, I want you to lead the song in our last act, the final act in *Don Giovanni*, up on the platform. Can you do that? I want to show them this. You see, they're still a bit twitchy about my show."

"But a male voice leads the song."

"No matter. I'd like you to sing it. We spoke of this."

"But … it's a baritone accompaniment, Toni. It's famous as—"

"Yeah, yeah. I can't wait to hear *you* do it."

Mina waited for them to arrange the stage. She must have sung well, otherwise they probably would have hauled her off. Or perhaps she'd sounded so awful that Toni was trying desperately to save her by having her sing another song? She didn't know. But the dancers and stagehands stopped what they were doing and sat in chairs, curled up on the floor, or leaned against the wall to watch her. Everyone did. They all waited as a giant tower was rolled onto the center of the stage. And a group of people in black clothes were tying a net to the two platforms. Then another tower was rolled onto the other side of the stage. The towers were tightrope platforms, though no tightrope was being hung.

"Mina, I told you this was a rehearsal, no?" Toni asked. His amplified voice echoed through the hall.

"Yes."

"Well, I need you to sing the last act for my friends. Some of them will not be here tomorrow. Can you do that for them?" He sounded so serious.

"Did … did you like the way I sang *Zaide*?"

Toni chuckled. "This is not an audition, Mina. Please climb the steps above us and sing. If you look down, you'll see the entire orchestra accompanying you."

"I just sing—"

"Yeah, yeah."

"All right."

Mina climbed the ladder and looked up. The platform seemed to touch the dark-purple lit ceiling. But Mina had read the screenplay. She knew the Harlequin had to deal with heights. She wondered if this was another reason she was so shaky this morning.

As she climbed the last few steps on the ladder, her feet trembled. Then she was stupid enough to look down. She was no longer blinded by the light, but Toni and the other producers seemed so far below. She could see the orchestra pit too. It was full. So many people had gathered to perform this morning. For her?

She got to the top and it was worse. It was a narrow platform with a microphone tied to a metal pole. Mina found it hard to swallow. Her heart raced. Somehow, she managed to climb the last step and kneel on the ledge. She didn't dare look down at the stage below.

"Are you at the top?" Toni asked.

"Yes." She was surprised to hear her voice shake.

"Turn the spotlight on her," Toni directed.

It was bright again and Mina shifted in surprise, feeling a rise by her butt and her familiar terror of falling. Her legs shook violently. She crouched down and carefully moved her legs, one at a time, over the ledge. She wondered if her heart would explode from all the stress. What an odd combination of excitement and fear. But ... if she could just finish this ... this "rehearsal"—which she now knew full well was a complete farce—if she could do that, she might win a lead position on Broadway. On Broadway, her life dream.

The orchestra rang out with the familiar drums and violins. The rumble made Mina more nervous, as the vibration shook the steel platform. Then she prepared to sing "Don Giovanni."

She knew the song. Just like *Zaide*, she had sung it in the university in Paris. But that was school and so many years ago. And that was accompanying a male Don Juan, never leading the aria.

When it came time for her to sing, she fell mum. The orchestra stopped.

"What's the matter?" Toni asked through his microphone.

"Uh ... you want me to start the song with the music—"

"The lead role, Mina. I do."

"The baritone section? The part of the accuser?"

"Si."

"In ... low notes?"

"No, no," Toni said with a laugh. "In your same lovely tenor."

Mina swallowed. "But ... it doesn't feel right. It's not supposed to be like that."

"Portami pazienza. What do you mean, it doesn't feel right?"

She didn't know Italian, but she guessed what he meant.

"Mina," Toni said, clearing his throat, "this is not the best time to discuss this."

That was an understatement.

"Well, I mean, it's not just the change in voice. You're asking me to sing the accusation. But I thought the Harlequin was acting as Don Juan. Why am I the accuser?"

"Try it. *You* lead the song. *You* accuse. There are other singers you can't see who will provide additional vocals to defend. Everything is reversed again. It will work. Most in the audience will not know what you know. This is for effect. Trust me."

"But, shouldn't—"

"Mina, the musicians are waiting. They've all come to hear your wonderful voice this morning. Can you do this?"

That question was terrible, because if she said no, she would probably lose the part.

"Play the music," Mina said.

"You make me so very happy," Toni said.

It didn't sound like she did. And that was the first time ever that Mina wasn't fond of his expression.

The music in D minor thundered. Once again, it was so powerful that it shook the foundation of her narrow platform. Her legs shook over the hundred-foot precipice, and her body trembled.

When it was time, Mina sang. She sang "Don Giovanni." And, once more, she liked the sound of her voice with the orchestration, even though the piece sounded very different with her high notes. Then she was shocked to hear a male voice accompanying her. As she sang, she looked down. Toni's seat was empty. He was walking to center stage, holding a microphone and singing. In Mozart's play, his voice would have represented Don Giovanni and his companion defending himself from her, the accuser. But in this rendition, as he stood on stage pointing up at her, Toni's hand gestures were at times contrary to his actual words. He was pointing at her as if she were Don Juan while defending himself, as if he were Don Juan, with his vocals. The whole thing was backward and confused. The actions were reversed. On purpose? But would anyone watching the play who didn't know the words in Italian even notice? Or indeed, as Toni had said, even care?

Mina let go of all concerns and allowed herself to get lost in song. Even the accusations became robotic. It was as if she had left her body. And she loved it. She enjoyed accusing him. It felt powerful. She wondered if this was why Toni had set it up this way. It was so powerful that she almost stood up with excitement, forgetting her fear of heights. It was as if her voice and Toni's fought one another, but really they complemented each other. Neither missed a note. Neither missed a tone. It was exquisite. She wasn't sure how she sounded to her critics, but she enjoyed the thunder of the orchestra and the sound of Toni's voice. She didn't even mind the vibrations in the steel platform anymore.

As it was coming to a close, a spotlight fell on the other pedestal, across the stage. A singer in Pierrot clown face, but wearing a black cape and a black mask, appeared on the other side. He reminded her of Toni in clown face in her dream. And now this clown pantomimed silently to the sound of both of their voices, swaying his arms in time with the music. The clown reached out a hand to her. Was this another one of Toni's surprises? Toni just kept singing.

Then Mina recognized this clown. She recognized the shiny black ceramic mask covering half of his face. It was the mask of the handsome man in her dream. And then she remembered his soft gloves. But, instead of facing the empty auditorium, he looked at her, miming her words in silence. He gestured with wide arms for her to rise. And she obeyed, while singing to him and Toni. All three clowns sang now. Then, as the final notes of the piece played, she stood up straight, no longer fearing the height. She reached out to touch his hand.

And here is where I fall.

5

REST IN PEACE

BRIGHT LIGHTS DANCED, SOME RED, BLUE, AND PURPLE, SWIRLING around her and waking her from tranquil peace. There were flashes of yellow light as she focused on faces hovering over her. She blinked her eyes. She touched her aching forehead. Then she looked behind the faces and saw the steel platform, now towering over her. She was on her back. All the lights were on. And a bunch of performers whose acquaintance she had just made, and many she had seen backstage, were huddled over her.

"My God, Mina, are you okay?" Toni knelt over her, holding her hand.

"What happened?" she asked. Someone helped her sit up. Another ran over with a cup of water. She took it, but her hand shook terribly. She handed it back to Toni without drinking it. "What happened?"

"You fell. Into the net, thank God. Why did you do that? Are you all right?"

"I'm fine." Mina lay back down. "I ... don't like heights. I just fell. That's all. I'm okay."

She thought about the man on the other side of the theater. She turned and searched for him. Where was he? He had fallen, too. The man in her dreams. The man with the mask.

"Should we call 911?" a dancer asked.

Someone helped her sit up and leaned her against a large pillow. Then Toni pushed the cup of water back into her hand. She sipped it.

"I'm okay," Mina said to everyone hovering over her. "Really, I am. But … how did I do, Toni? Did you like the way I sang?"

"Young lady…" A gray-haired woman with a crew cut crouched beside her with a smile. Mina had been introduced to her earlier; Daniella was their lead choreographer. "If you sing like that live, during the show, our production will be a smash," the choreographer said.

"Yeah, Dani." Toni nodded. "Yeah. Incredible, Mina. I told you."

"Well, I'm more interested in balletomanes," Daniella added. "I can work her feet. But that was stupid. Real dumb, Toni. You shouldn't have had her up there so soon."

Toni nodded.

"Your voice is amazing, Mina," said a white-haired, dark-skinned man above her. He had been introduced earlier as Vince, the main coproducer. "I really hope you'll join our production."

Mina sipped more water. All the anxiety of the morning left her and she felt fine. No, she felt better than fine. She felt happy. They liked her singing. They were asking her to join them based on her "rehearsal." She felt wonderful.

"But Toni, is the other performer all right?"

Toni furrowed his brow.

6

MORTE

Mina was outside her own body, watching, as a dim gray light cast a shadow over pale skin. Her black lips cracked open ever so slightly. They opened and closed rhythmically—as undulating breaths emerged in a mist—as if in song, as she lay on top of wrinkled white sheets. But she couldn't move. Behind her bed, through her wall, were shadows of trees and a dirt trail that meandered among thick brush and bushes beside a small stream. She could hear the trickling water. And a full moon lit the shadowed forest behind the wall.

There was music. Wolfgang Amadeus Mozart: the start of Mozart's "Requiem."

Fingers slowly crept along her belly, tracing her belly button, gliding along her naked skin, and making its way under the curves of her breasts, pressing deeper, and then touching her leaden-colored nipples. Her nipples were hard and she felt aroused, but she couldn't see the fingers touching her. It was too dark. She could barely see herself.

"You were the singer on the pedestal?" she asked. "The man I saw fall with me?"

"Oui."

She heard that recognizable French accent again.

Then he appeared, clearly visible, standing over the bed—the man with the mask. But that was all he wore. He was nude, and behind him and what once was the wall in her bedroom was the woods, still shrouded in darkness. The mask covered half of his face, revealing part of a thin goatee. His face, what she could see, was handsome. His fingers slid delicately, like flowing water in a forest stream, down her side, over her soft skin.

The view changed. Still outside her body, with everything gray and black, she watched herself under him on the bed. His broad, muscular shoulders and his powerful arms and legs flexed over her. His ass rose and fell as he thrust into her, straddling her body. As he moved, one powerful hand grasped the bedsheets as the other pulled her closer to him. She felt the pleasure between her legs, though she still watched from the ceiling. She felt every hard thrust from his tight, muscular physique and the wetness and tingles of pleasure inside.

The view changed again. His lips pressed against her passionately now, and she felt the stubbles of his beard as he ran it along her lips while gliding his hand down her naked hip. She moaned from another hard thrust. He fucked her, over and over, while firmly sucking her bottom lip. His other hand wandered under her side and along the crack of her ass.

"What's your name?" she asked breathlessly between kisses. "Tell me. Please, tell me your name."

"Je suis la mort transcendante."

"Tell me. Please tell me … Please."

"Erik."

She was under him now, his eyes so close to hers. She remembered those emeralds sparkling in the light, and even illuminated by rays of moonlight, they glowed jade. She ran her hand along the open side of his mask and then up along the thin hair of his head. She pressed up into him, and he gave a satisfied groan. He was handsome, so handsome, but he wore that black mask. Why? Why should he cover such a gorgeous face? She wanted it off. She wanted him completely, his face and body, with nothing covering him.

She grabbed him and turned him on his side. As he pressed deep inside her, she grabbed his mask, trying to take it off. He turned his face away but brought her close to him again. She tried to pull off the mask once more.

"No," he snapped, snatching her wrist. "No, Christine."

"But why?"

"Je suis Don Juan."

He thrust inside her hard, as if punishing her, then squeezed her wrist and twisted it.

"Oww. Erik, stop it. You're hurting me."

"Ne retirez pas le masque tant que vous n'êtes pas prêt."

"I am ready. Please, Erik. I want to see you."

Darkness.

A light shone on five dancers in clown face, moving slowly, with hands held over their heads. The dreary gray faded and light became vibrant. Colorful. Bright. A rainbow shone over the five dancers as they danced. Mina recognized this as the stage of the Harlequin. Three women wearing long, fluffy blue and saffron dresses, with tall, white headdresses, danced with two men in gray coats, breeches, and white wigs. They swayed back and forth, smiling behind painted frowns, on the wooden stage as an orchestra played. The music was still the "Requiem" by Mozart.

Her head turned from the stage and she saw Erik. Just like in her dream, he was watching the play with her, but this time, they lay on their sides together, naked. She admired his rippled abs and muscular arms, and his bright-green eyes gazed into hers while he ran his fingers over her breasts and fucked her. He cradled her tightly, as if not wanting her to get away. The seats in the auditorium were gone. Only a single bed lay in front of the stage. And as he pressed into her, still fucking her, they watched the play.

Mina felt embarrassed. But she didn't get up. They were in public, but in an empty auditorium. Something about the weirdness of that made her not disengage. Or was it the pleasure?

As they fucked, the dancers paid no attention, continuing their trot back and forth, back and forth, with hands held high, strutting to orchestral music.

"Stop. Stop it now, Erik. I'm scared. It's … it's indecent."

She looked away from the stage and stared at those bright-green eyes. Then he breathed heavily beside her ear but didn't say anything.

His tongue ran along her neck and he grasped her more tightly. She tried to look away, but she couldn't turn from him. She couldn't look anywhere. So she buried her head in a soft pillow. Part of her wanted to get away, but the other part didn't.

She was afraid. She was scared that she wouldn't be good enough. That she couldn't sing. That she couldn't dance. Surely, she couldn't perform as well as these dancers on stage. She wasn't good enough for Broadway. She knew that. And she was afraid that they would find out and see that she was a failure.

"Stop," she said. "Stop, Erik. Stop it now. That's enough."

"No."

She looked up as the actors, in clown face and colonial dress, continued to trot forward and back, forward and back, amidst the music of Mozart.

"Who are you?" she demanded, turning from him and closing her eyes. "You must tell me. Tell me now, Erik. Stop and tell me." And when he didn't, she felt trapped and cried out, "Stop! *Stop it!*"

He finally let go and she pushed herself off.

"Why the mask?" She touched the half-mask. It felt metallic and cold. "Why?" It was pitch black, so dark that it felt like emptiness itself. She felt like if she reached in, her hand would fall inside. "Please. You're frightening me. Tell me."

She tugged at the mask but he snatched her wrist again and twisted it hard.

"Je suis le Don Juan triomphant! Je suis mort! Morte, Christine Daaé!"

Mina jerked. Her eyes opened in pitch darkness. Her hands clutched wrinkled sheets. Only a dim light appeared, from a crack in the window by the wall. The darkness made her more uneasy. And it was quiet, with only the humming of her refrigerator. She breathed heavily and felt wet from perspiration.

She looked around until her eyes fell upon a painting of a screaming face on an easel beside her mattress. And next to that was an image of a naked man with arms being stretched, gashes with dripping blood, and a face with gnashing teeth and eyes squeezed tight while being tortured on a rack. She took a deep breath. These were her works of art, but her subject matter wasn't making her feel any better.

When she sat up, she was surprised to see that she was naked. That was weird. Usually she wore a camisole and panties to bed. Or when cold, a nightgown. Never naked. She took another deep breath; then she forced herself up and turned on the light.

All the easels and canvases leaning on the walls disturbed her. Seeing her art—demons, vampires, mutilation, and torture—beside her bed after her dream was the last thing she needed. Then she furrowed her brow. On a pillow was a single red rose. She picked it up and clutched it to her chest. It was so important to her. It was as if it was some magical charm against all the darkness. But how did it get there?

She remembered. It was the rose Toni had gifted her at the restaurant in honor of her accepting the role in his musical.

7

THE ACCIDENT

THE FIRST DAY MINA DID NOT SHOW UP FOR REHEARSAL, SHE TOLD herself she wasn't feeling well. She spent the whole day in her apartment, sitting on a couch, eating chips, drinking Coke, and staring at her TV. Sometimes the screen was on, sometimes it wasn't. It didn't matter. She didn't want to do anything. She told herself she needed a respite after falling a hundred feet. And why wouldn't she? The very last thing she wanted to do was climb that ladder again.

The second day she used the same excuse.

But on the third day, she started looking at her rather paltry pantry. And she thought of Ms. Kuni.

It was on the third day, in the afternoon—while binging on reruns of her favorite classic TV shows, *Gilligan's Island* and *Bewitched*—that she heard a knock on her door. She jumped from her couch and looked down at her red silk robe. It would have to do. She touched her hair. Of course, her long, dark hair looked like a bird's nest and she had no makeup on. She hoped it was her friend Gail. It probably was.

She looked through the peephole in her entryway and saw that it was her second guess. A man with a beard in a brown beanie, white button-down, and dark slacks was standing outside her door.

"Hi, Toni."

"Mina." He flashed a fake smile. Then he peered behind her and removed his hat, scratching his head. "Mind if I come in?"

"How'd you find me?"

"Mina, I've been sending you Christmas and birthday cards for years." Then, for a flash, he looked like the old Toni, with a jovial grin, as he put his beanie back over his head and walked through the door. She shyly ran her hand over the knots in her hair. He didn't seem to notice. He seemed too busy looking over her apartment disapprovingly.

Actually, she was quite proud of her place. It was a nice pad for Manhattan. The kitchen and living room formed a single-studio unit, and there was a small room, if you'd call it one, off to the side—her bedroom and art studio. It was close to the university, and it was cheap and rather spacious for New York.

Toni sat down on her ratty beige couch. Then he smiled at the TV. Jeannie was on the screen, in her silly pink genie getup, in the classic sitcom *I Dream of Jeannie.*

"I see you still have the same taste in shows."

"Only the best. You want some coffee?"

"No, I'm okay."

No time for coffee? Hmm. Boy, he must really be mad.

She felt him watch her as she walked over to the other side of the couch, yawning and stretching, and sat down. She leaned forward, folding her arms over her lap, and faced him.

He put a finger to his chin and said in his thick Italian accent, "You don't look good."

Mina laughed. It was the first time he had ever insulted her appearance. "Sorry, Toni."

"No, I'm sorry. I'm very sorry. I understand. What happened was absolutely terrible. You have every reason to be avoiding us and to be angry with me."

"It wasn't your fault." She shrugged. "I knew the dangers."

He took a deep breath. Then he said very carefully, "If you come back—and I think you know that's why I'm here—I want you to know that you'll be safe. The height is meant to alarm the audience, not you. Once, I'll admit, it wasn't safe, but that was a long time ago in Paris."

He's lying, Christine.

Mina searched the room for a voice that seemed as clear as Toni's.

It was a voice with a French accent. The voice of the man who had come to her bed last night.

"Something the matter?" Toni asked.

"No, nothing. Perhaps some music?" Mina asked with a forced smile, grabbing the TV remote off the coffee table.

Toni shrugged. "Whatever you like."

Mina turned the TV channel to a classical radio station. Ironically, it was—

"Herr Mozart," Toni said with a nod. "Coincidence, eh? I wonder?"

"He's a popular composer, Toni."

"Si, but I don't believe in coincidences. No, not like this one." Toni chuckled and nodded, and his laugh made Mina chuckle too. But then Mina wrinkled her nose, recognizing the musical piece. "'Sonata Semplice.' I loathe 'Sonata Semplice.' It has to be the most popular piece of shit Mozart ever wrote."

"Popular like *I Dream of Jeannie?*"

"You have a point there."

"Yes, but only you, my dear, would know the name of Mozart's piece." He took a deep breath, scooted forward on the couch, and looked very stern. "Mina, I'm sorry. So sorry. But I need you to return and attend my rehearsals. You see, I wrote the play for you."

"What do you mean?"

"I wrote *The Harlequin* for you." He took her hand and she felt herself blush. Then he moved closer and pressed her hand between his fingers. She wondered how he could even touch her with her hair looking so ugly. "I mean, not the original performance but the Broadway play. This rendition of *The Harlequin* was made for my star, Mina Daaé. In Paris. I invited you then, but you were set on leaving. But when you told me that you had moved to Manhattan, I suspected your dreams. Was I wrong? Was it not your dream to be in a show on Broadway?"

Mina nodded.

"I made the play for you, Mina. That's the truth. Your grand entrance. My star. I wrote it all for you."

"Because I'm a clown?" She forced a laugh.

"No, because you're a star. You are the so-simple, rare, beautiful bird, so majestic and soaring. Human, yes. A clown. Sure. Like all of us. You will fall. *Figuratively*, my dear. But you are my star. Your voice touches God, Mina. You're an angel."

"Come on, Toni. You've said all this already," Mina said, laughing, and pulled her hand back. "Many times."

"I know, but…" He gently touched her hand again. "I'm serious. Very serious. Vince said he had never heard anything like you before. After hearing you sing, he said that he knows the show will be a hit—if you're in it. Daniella said that, movement or not, your voice is enough for—"

"I'm not sure I like her."

"She's rough around the edges. True. She's gay, you know."

"So?"

"She's a lesbian, Mina. She said that not only is your voice exquisite, so is your body and face. She's attracted to you. I tell you this because … well, we all are. Even if she weren't gay, I think she would find you beautiful. As lovely as your voice. That is why you are my harlequin. That is why I am not. You are a star, Mina. She thought so. She said that she can frame your movements so that we accentuate the motion of your figure in dance. She thinks it can work. But it will take time. And practice. Rehearsal. And—"

"I haven't been dancing. I don't know."

She was surprised at how red his face had become after calling her beautiful. That was so cute. She met his gaze and smiled.

He smiled back, a genuine Toni smile.

"Will you come? Please, Mina. Please. Mina, I can't picture anyone else taking this role. I heard that you saw one of your standbys when you came early. I have a list of singers who can try out for your role. But I say *try*. I don't want them. I want you. Vince and Dani want you, too. It was a rehearsal. I told you this. For you."

"You sang with me. Are you also planning on being in the play?"

"You shall see if you return," he said with a sly grin. "But really, Mina, I'm getting old."

"Not so old." She grasped his hand in both hers and massaged it. Then she leaned against him.

And for a moment they fell silent, staring at the TV screen, sitting quietly beside each other. There was nothing on the TV, just a blue background with music playing. But they sat close, shoulder to shoulder, and just stared at the TV while listening to Mozart. She really liked that.

"Will you come?" he finally repeated, looking again into her eyes. "Please?"

"You're begging," she said with a laugh. "Just stop."

"Si."

"I can try. But, Toni, I'm … scared. I'm afraid of falling. I hate heights. You know that."

What if there's no net? What if it's like it was for me, Christine?

She looked around the room again. She knew the voice was in her head, but it seemed as clear as Toni's.

Toni jumped up and that broke her thoughts. He headed for the door. "Tomorrow morning by seven, okay?" he said. "I'll come by and drive you. You'll meet in the dance room with Daniella while others will practice the first act. She really wants to work on your steps for Act II. Okay?"

"What about the pedestal?"

"With a net, my dear."

He placed a hand on the doorknob. Then he turned and looked at her pensively for a moment.

Mina jumped up and came over. She took his hand and ran the fingers of her other hand along his cheek and over the hairs of his beard. She smiled, looking deeply into his eyes, and gave him a peck on the cheek with her lips. "I'll come. Thank you, Toni. Thanks so much. I mean it."

He nodded sweetly. But then he looked sad.

"What's the matter?" she asked, searching his eyes. "I said I'll go with you, okay? I'll come."

"That's not it."

"What's wrong then?"

He rubbed her fingers and shrugged. "I was afraid you wouldn't open the door."

His hand trembled in hers with those words. He seemed almost coy, which was ridiculous for such a boisterous, extroverted man. Their eyes met, and she felt mesmerized. Like she had with Erik in her dream, but

Toni was not a phantom. This was Toni. He was here and now, in the flesh.

"Oh, Toni. Thank you. Thank you for everything." Mina leaned her head against his shoulder. She embraced him and kissed the back of his hand. "You're so sweet."

He remained frozen by the door. She kissed his hand again, and then a couple of fingers. She chuckled and looked up. He was peering at her nervously. She reached up and pecked him on the lips. It was meant as just another goodbye kiss but, somehow, their lips found each other's again. It became more. They stood kissing for a long time by the door. Then she said, almost in a whisper, "Thank you for believing in me."

"You are a star."

She embraced him again and pressed her lips harder against his, her tongue entering his mouth. She desired this. She had never thought of desire with Toni. She knew he had always been attracted to her, but he was her friend. Yet now, she wanted him. Why? Was it because of his play? Or was it those last words: *I was afraid you wouldn't open the door.*

He was unhappy. Why? This was Antonio Vollini, ringmaster of the circus, the most happy-go-lucky guy in the world. Now he was sad. Why? Because he had been afraid she wouldn't open the door? Afraid she wouldn't be in his play? Or … was it because he was afraid he would never see her again?

"Tomorrow, okay, Mina?" he said, tearing himself from her embrace.

He turned back and touched the doorknob again, but Mina snatched his arm and turned him toward her. Then she pushed him against the wall. He gasped in surprise. She pressed her lips against his, very hard this time. He jerked back, she figured more from shock than displeasure. She made out with him again.

"Mina," he said between kisses.

"Yes?" She kissed him some more.

"We shouldn't. We're friends."

"I know."

"I don't want anything to happen to that."

"It was cute seeing you blush for me. I saw you blush when you said

I was pretty. I'm pretty, huh? And saying the play was made for me. An angel. Oh, Toni. You're so sweet."

"You are a star. And pretty, si. Bellissima. I swear it."

"*Your* star?"

"No, everyone's star. If you will be."

"Oh, Toni."

She pulled his shirt from his pants and ran her fingers across his stomach. Toni was overweight, but it made no difference. She liked the smell of his cologne and, more so, his touch. No, most so, *him*.

Her fingers glided along his stomach and up over his chest. Then they moved down, touching his belt. She opened the belt buckle, unfastened the button, and unzipped his pants. She felt him pull away, but she pressed her lips on his, tasting him again. Her palm ran along his cotton underwear, over his bulge. He moaned. That made her press more firmly, up and down, while making out with him. Then she yanked down his pants, reaching inside his underwear and touching his hard cock. She rubbed the skin while they continued to kiss each other's lips.

"Mina, oh Mina. But I ... I don't think—"

"You don't want me to?"

"I ... yeah, of course I do. But ..."

Mina pulled his underwear down and held his cock in her hand.

She was surprising herself. Everything was happening so fast but, somehow, it had to. She knew Toni. If she didn't act quickly, she might never touch him again. He treated her like a little girl, despite always throwing stray glances of desire her way. She knew he had always liked her. And now ... she liked him. He had made a play for her. *For her.*

She rubbed his shaft as he held her closer. He moaned again. His pants were on the floor now, while she tasted him, caressing his tongue and sucking his lips. She finally yanked his underwear all the way down his legs, while his hands ran over her body to the crack of her ass, pulling her closer to him as she continued to run her palm up and down his cock.

"God," he said between kisses. "Oh God, Mina. Mina."

He still sounded a little afraid, but his reticence drove her harder. She could hear him breathing heavily. She wanted him to breathe more heavily.

She wanted to take it in her mouth. Not his tongue—his cock. Inside. She felt the pleasure wetting her panties as she touched it.

She let him go for a moment and removed her robe. She wasn't wearing a bra, and his eyes widened at the sight of her boobs in the broad daylight of her apartment, but he couldn't enjoy the view for long as she pressed her chest against him, pushing him against the wall once more. Now, with just red silk panties and her naked bosom pressing against his chest, she kissed him over and over while still stroking him with her palm.

For a moment, she let go and pulled down her panties, letting them drop to her ankles. He looked down her body with wide eyes. She giggled and embraced him once more, pressing her naked skin against him. Then she grabbed his cock once more.

"Mina, wait. Maybe—"

"What?" she whispered, breathless. "What is it? You want me to stop?" she asked, stroking him.

"No, no, I don't … but—"

She felt something warm spill over her hand. The liquid trickled down her hand and dripped over her bare leg. It surprised her so much that she nervously laughed. As Mina backed away, he had a look of shame.

He leaned his forehead on hers. "I should go."

"It's okay, Toni. Forget it. I wanted this. Really—"

"No, no. I … I should go. I should go."

He quickly pulled up his pants, opened the door, and left.

8

PAINTING

Mina would paint. She always painted when she was upset. It made her happy. That's what she needed now. She wanted to be happy.

She wasn't happy.

What the hell was she doing? She had heard about producers black-mailing actresses for sex. She had been warned in school in Paris about that. But she had never heard of an actress offering sex *after* she was given the starring role. Why? Was she crazy?

Or did she actually like him?

She mixed a little water with the paint. Then she applied initial strokes. When she was in the mood, she could paint very fast. Today she was in the mood, so much so that she had barely prepared her work-space. It was like her bizarre sexual advance on her friend. She hadn't even bothered to properly place the mats on her floor. She'd just grabbed the paint and dove into the act.

Toni had given so much to her. And he was so sweet. And she adored his spirit. And he seemed to care so much for her. No one else cared for her. He had given her the starring role in his play.

Mina was a lonely girl. Her only real friends were Gail and Toni, come to think of it.

She painted. It took her mind off things—and the voice in her head. That odd French voice kept muttering, now coming so frequently that she did everything she could to ignore his words. She figured if she painted, she could ignore that too.

She first painted a frail man in a park. The day after her fall, she had walked the lovely Central Park Mall alone. The old man was an ice cream vendor selling cones by the side of the path, beside the benches, near a picturesque arch bridge. She enjoyed listening to him, he was so nice, as he scooped her some strawberry ice cream. She thought of trying to recreate all the wrinkles she had seen along his face and forehead, his large nose, and his bushy white eyebrows, thin gray hair, and sparse beard. He had light-cerulean eyes. Really lovely blue eyes. She remembered that—cerulean, like the sky. The eyes were a bit sunken in. He was a thin man. Yes, she could paint him. She knew she could.

No. Her mood was somber.

You shall fall again.

"Shut up!" she snapped, looking all around her. "I don't want to hear you anymore. Stop talking. I can't take it anymore!"

She could paint clouds. The clouds had been thick. The gray above the New York skyline that afternoon had been beautiful in its own way.

No, she didn't want to paint scenery.

She started mixing paints and faced her blank slate.

I made love to you.

She shut her eyes, taking a deep breath. Erik, her phantom, sounded pained, or … jealous?

She started painting a child. She had watched a boy throwing a Frisbee to his dog while his mother read a book on a grassy hill.

No, that would turn into another poodle sketch. She had so many poodle paintings lying against the wall.

The canvas was taken off the easel and changed again. More words were heard and ignored. She thought he spoke in French.

She started sketching the people who she had watched sitting on blankets, picnicking, near the mother and boy beside the water. It had been nice and tranquil. But she didn't want to paint people either. She threw the brush down on the mat on the carpet in a huff and folded her arms.

How strange. She felt such an urge to paint, but she couldn't find a fucking thing to work on. Then she took a very deep breath and …

We made love last night.

"Fucking shut up! Damn you! Shut up! You're just a figment of my imagination … and I … I think I must be going crazy."

You're not crazy. I'm the phantom from the theater.

"Yeah? Why are you in my apartment, then?"

Why do you think you're crazy?

"You're speaking to me even though you don't exist. And … because I heard you talking when Toni was with me this morning, but he didn't hear you."

I don't want him to hear me. I only want to speak to you, Ms. Daaé.

"You were in my dreams. How is that?"

Then she felt a touch. It brushed against her neck and pulled down her suspenders. Then it ran across her breasts, along her hips, and down over her butt. Then it pressed where it was most pleasurable.

"Stop," she said, closing her eyes. "Stop it."

You don't want me to touch you again?

"No. I don't even know who you are."

I was an actor in your lover's play.

"My lover? He's not my lover. Toni's a friend."

That's not what I saw this morning.

"That's enough." She searched the room, wide-eyed in fear now. "Stop playing games with me."

She felt fingers gently touch her again. It tugged on her hair, which she'd tied back in a bun, then ran along her ear and neck before caressing her chin. But then the touching stopped. It became quiet, with the exception of some murmuring from neighbors through the walls.

When the voice quieted, she started another painting.

She painted a group of people dancing around a fire. It was ancient man, dancing in some sort of mystic ritual frenzy. These men, dancing around the pyre, were half-clad in animal fur. She made the background twilight. She used orange and red along the horizon. Then she painted figures moving up and down to a beat that only she would ever know.

But it didn't take long for her to abandon this too. By the time she had worked on their faces, she was bored. And she felt like the figures were disjointed and not moving in unison. It was another failed piece of artwork.

Some painter she made. Maybe Toni was right. Maybe she was a better singer.

You sing like an angel.

She quickly changed the canvas yet again and brought up another blank slate. She stared for the longest time, sucking the tip of her brush and biting her nails. Meanwhile, she heard incessant chattering from her French ghost. She tried to do everything to ignore it or, at the very least, ignore what he was saying.

She painted with more fervor.

She gazed at her left hand as she painted with her right. Her naked hand would be her model. And she brushed fast, surprised at her vigor. She probably needed more nude model training to get the borders and angles perfect. She had painted subjects before but had always felt her education rather inadequate in regard to human anatomy. Nevertheless, she did her best at her self-portrait. And she didn't do a half bad job.

Her goal for this new piece was to bring out the three dimensions of the hand. Like her all-time favorite, the *Virgin of the Rocks* by Leonardo Da Vinci, she wanted the hand to appear as if it were reaching out to the viewer. This proved ambitious. And it took many efforts. But her hand furiously attacked the canvas.

After she was satisfied enough with the painting, she created an effect with color, particularly red, of paint dripping from the hand as if it were a melting hand of wax. It looked pretty good. When she had finished with the colors, her only regret was that it looked darker than she had intended. She wanted the hand to be dripping into obscurity, not appearing monstrous. But there was something frightening about the hand. Like all her paintings. Dark. Foreboding. All her work was like this.

She stared, while sucking on the brush, at her likeness of her own hand. Then she jumped as it started to move. At first, it turned. It fell perfectly still. Then it reached out to grab her.

Let me touch you!

"Stop it!" she screamed. *"Get out! Please leave me alone! Get out of here!"*

9

***

JUST A FRIEND

THERE WAS A KNOCK ON THE DOOR. SHE CLEANED HER HANDS ON A towel and walked over. True to form, Gail was pressing her eye against the peephole while banging obnoxiously and laughing, jumping up and down.

"Hey, bitch," Gail said with a wave as Mina opened the door. "About time." Gail barged in as if the apartment were hers. She always did that when she visited. She meandered straight over to the refrigerator.

"Mina, I don't believe it. You have food."

"Not funny."

"But … where's your fucking beer?"

"Keep looking."

Mina regretted saying that. Gail started pushing stuff all over the place. Then she took containers out and stacked them on a countertop. Finally, she found what she was looking for. She had a bottle opener attached to her keychain. She opened two beers and gave Mina one with a large grin, as if Mina were *her* guest. Then she looked at Mina's clothes with distaste. Mina likely looked like a complete mess, wearing a long white frock covered with paint. Her hair was still tied back in a bun, and there was paint on her fingers and arms. Gail, on the other hand, looked very pretty in her white sleeveless T-shirt and black pants.

434

Gail jumped on the couch. "Whatcha doing?"

"Painting."

Gail raised the beer in a toast then squinted at her friend. "Hey, you wanna go with me and my gang tonight? We're clubbing. It's gonna be so much fun, Mina."

"I …" Mina bit her lip.

"What?"

"I just have to be ready for rehearsal. I promised Toni. Gail, if I don't go, I might be back working for Ms. Kuni again."

"She's so pissed. You should see her." Gail opened her big eyes wider and nodded. "She's using her fucking cat. Can you believe that? Everyone's drawing a fucking pussy. A real purring pussy, Mina. Not yours."

"Stop talking like that." But Mina couldn't help but laugh. "I told you, I don't like your trash talk."

"Just kidding. Actually, she's got some surfer boy who was in the class. Can you believe that? Anyway, a male's form is cute and all, but it's not like yours."

Mina wondered if it was the cute painter she'd ogled on her last morning there. He had a nice face and a hard body. He'd make a good model.

"Ms. Kuni's really pissed, Mina. You were such a great model. Poor teacher's not the same." Gail drank some beer to that. Then she smiled a playful smile at Mina.

"What?"

Gail shrugged, jumped up, and sauntered into the adjoining bedroom. Mina followed. Her failed paintings were all over the floor. Gail maneuvered around them and walked right up to the easel. Still sitting on a tarp was Mina's *Hand*.

"This one's good," Gail said after staring for a long time. "Wow!" She touched the frame. "Really good."

"You think?"

"Yeah. This is the best shit you've ever done. What … what is it?"

"What do you mean?"

"Well, I see it's a hand. What's it supposed to mean?"

"It's art. I don't know. Does it have to mean anything? It was more of a feeling than a scene."

"I fucking love it."

"Really?"

"Yeah. It's intense. I love it. It's like the hand is weeping, you know." Gail turned and gave Mina a very bright smile. "It's like anger. Rage. It's fucking intense. Reaching out. It's great."

"I'm glad you like it."

Gail laughed. Then she brushed her hand along Mina's arm. "Sometimes you talk so formally. It's cute."

"You know," Mina said, folding her arms and looking at her work, "I think good art, I mean really good art, doesn't always have to have a point, right, Gail? Sometimes it just *is*."

"Yeah. That's what's great about art. It's whatever it wants to be. It's not a thing. It just *is*."

Mina loved that. She nodded at Gail and realized that's what she loved about her. Gail was one of the few people who understood art. Like ... Toni.

Gail turned and came right up to Mina's face. She seemed to search Mina's eyes.

It made her a little uncomfortable.

"This is anger, right?"

"Huh?"

"Anger? You're angry about something?"

"I guess."

"What? What are you angry about? The whole world's at your fingertips. I don't get it. Why are you mad?"

Mina nodded. She stepped back a little. "I don't know. I just don't know."

If Mina had the nerve, she'd have told her about the mishap with Toni. Of course, she'd never have told her about the voice. Or the moving hand. But she would have told her about her favorite clown. She really needed counsel, but she was shy.

Gail turned back to the painting. "It's fucking great, Mina. I mean it. It's you. It's fucking great. The best thing you've ever painted."

"Thanks."

"I guess ..." Gail said. They both kept staring at it. A hand reaching out but dripping into obscurity. It was reaching out to them but disappearing. "It's kinda, horrific. It's like it's going away, right? Like the hand is disappearing. And yet, it's desperately trying to touch someone. Almost violently."

"For sure."

Gail smiled at her then looked back at the canvas. "It's your best work." Then she ran her fingertips along Mina's arm again. "So, what do you think? Can you go or not?"

"I really have to get up early tomorrow for rehearsal. Tonight's not a good night." But Gail nodded so smugly, as if this was just an excuse. For all Mina knew, this might be her last day off. "All right. Fine. As long as we're not back too late."

"Really? For real? Awesome!"

"We'll be back early? Like midnight, okay? You have to promise. I can't miss tomorrow. My friend will kill me."

Gail nodded. But then she lost her smile.

She walked really close to Mina's face again, as if examining her once more. Then she touched her shoulder, gliding her fingertips along Mina's shirt and against her skin. She looked up and stared into Mina's eyes. Then she leaned close with a smile, parted her lips, and tried to kiss her.

Mina abruptly pushed her away.

"I'm just fucking with you," Gail said with a giggle. "Can't wait to see you tonight."

Mina took a pin from her hair and started to quickly pick up her paintbrushes.

"Is it finished?" Gail sat down on a small purple beanbag chair near Mina's bed. It was the only other furniture in the room. "Huh? Is it finished?"

"I don't know," Mina snapped. She ran the brushes along some paper and wrapped them in Saran wrap. Then she gathered up the mat under the easel. She liked the painting, so she wouldn't take it down yet, but she turned it away from the bed.

"What's the matter?" Gail asked. "Are you mad? I was just messing with you, Mina."

"Gail," Mina said, violently pushing paint into another bag. "I told you before. I'm your friend. And I like men."

"Geesh. I know." Gail leaned back and stretched out her arms on the beanbag chair with a bubbly smile. "Sorry … still, sometimes the wrong thing to do is … the funniest, right? Relax. You're so serious." Gail smiled widely, then she frowned at Mina's response. "Come on. You're acting like the world's about to end. I was just messing with you."

"Sure."

"I fucking love you, Mina. That's all. Just like your painting. I love that intense shit. It's just you. You're so quiet, but inside you're like ready to explode. I fucking love that. I'm with you. As long as I see you."

Mina leaned against the easel and faced her friend. Then she said sternly, "But are you?"

"Am I what?"

"Are you gay, Gail?"

Gail lifted an eyebrow and there was an uncomfortable silence.

With all of Mina's stress right now, that wasn't the response she was looking for.

Then Gail said, "I really need you tonight. That's why I came over. I need my *friend* at the bar. 'Kay? Get it? My *friend*. Can my *friend* join me?"

"All right. As long as you stop saying *fucking* and *bitch* and other trashy talk."

"Ooh, but I love it when *you* say it."

1 0

THE FALLEN ANGEL

A LITTLE AFTER TEN O'CLOCK, MINA SAT ALONE, GRIPPING A METAL POLE on the New York subway. She was on her way to the bar. She chuckled to herself about Gail's meeting time—so typical of her. A man across from her stood with his head dipped down, staring out a dark window. He looked homeless, with ragged clothes and disheveled hair, but he seemed oblivious to anyone, just staring. Closer to her, a young couple was pushing and pulling at one another, goofing off and laughing, with an occasional glance in her direction. But no one bothered her.

It was cold. Summer was over. She wore a white cotton sweater and clutched her arms close as she made her way up the tunnel escalator and across a seedy alley. Gail had told her that the Mole Hole was a new bar set in a basement. When Mina found a painted wooden sign with a mole hanging from a hole, holding a bottle, she knew she'd found the place.

The place was packed. There was a long line, but the bouncer let Mina pass the moment she arrived. She made her way down a very narrow and steep flight of stairs, shoulder to shoulder with strangers. It was crowded and dark, lit only by a handful of neon lights flashing red and green from the bottom of the stairs. And it was loud. Many shouted and hollered, but their voices were muffled behind the blaring thump of techno music.

Downstairs, the room extended almost like a warehouse with a bar, surrounded by bodies, at each end. Although it was cold outside, all the people dancing made it warm. She took her sweater off, wrapped it around her waist, and looked around. While gazing at a couple inappropriately grinding beside her, she was startled when someone yanked at her elbow.

"Haeey, hun!" said Gail. She staggered and smelled of alcohol as she kissed Mina's cheek.

Gail stumbled, and Mina had to catch her. Then they walked through swaying bodies to a raised table at the other side of the club.

"Cra-azy shit, eh, Mina!"

Sitting there on tall stools were Gail's friends. To her right were Lori and Raoul. She knew them from meeting with Gail in a restaurant a month ago. Lori was a dark-skinned girl with long hair. She wore a cute long-sleeved lime-green shirt and jeans. Raoul had on a preppy white button-down and brown slacks. They were Gail's best friend and Gail's brother. Raoul nodded, acting cool. Lori lifted her martini glass and smiled. Two girls Mina didn't know stood by the table, to her left, pointing and laughing at people while drinking from beer bottles. One of them nodded at Mina.

"Know my bro?" Gail asked, sliding Mina a beer bottle across the table.

"We met," Mina said, raising her beer bottle. "Hi again."

"Hi, Mina." Raoul nodded across the table. "Gail was talking about how you used to be together in class?"

Lori and Gail laughed. Raoul just furrowed his brow.

The two strangers beside the table laughed too, apparently in on Mina's former job. Lori leaned over and pointed at the two strangers. "That's Tiffany and Beatrice. Beatrice goes by Bee for short. This is Miss Mina Daaé, ladies."

The strangers nodded and went back to staring at dancers and gossiping. The two of them must have been close friends because they chose to wear nearly matching glittering rose skirts and kept talking between themselves.

Mina drank. She could barely hear a thing except the weird techno-heavy shit, thumping and pounding. It was pretty awful.

"How you doin'?" asked Lori, leaning over again and touching her arm.

"Great," Mina said with a smile. "Not as good as you guys, though. Seems I'm late to the party."

On cue, Gail closed her eyes tightly for a moment, dipped her head down, and quickly opened them. She looked up at Mina, smiled, and clumsily raised her beer. Lori laughed at her.

Mina turned to the couple grinding toward the center of the room. Everyone had made space around them and was clapping and cheering the couple on. It was a short bald guy, shirtless, with tattoos covering his arms and shoulders, abs cut as hell, a thin mustache, and blue jeans. He looked like a professional dancer and certainly moved like one.

"They're pretty good," Mina said, pointing. She turned back.

Gail wasn't looking at the dancers. She was smiling at Mina.

"How'd you find this place?" Mina asked Lori.

"I used to work here, when it was called the Rush. I bartend outside college."

"Really?" asked Mina. "I'd love it if you'd make me a drink one day."

"Oh, yeah? What's your taste, Mina?"

They had to talk loudly. Whether people were shouting, staring at the improvised entertainment, or jumping up and down senselessly to the thumping music, it was hard to hear.

"Beer," Mina said stupidly. "Oh … or margaritas. Martinis. I like sweet drinks."

Lori nodded with a kind smile.

"Sheez fuckin' good with mar—eenies," said Gail, nodding and cutting into the conversation. She spoke a little too loudly. "Try 'em. Made me a cosmo once, bitch."

"It wasn't that good, boo," said Lori, laughing.

"I'd love it if you made me one," Mina said. "What do you have there, Raoul?"

"Coke."

"L'il bro's underage," Gail said with a wink and a laugh. She put a finger to her lips and it sort of slid off her face. "We snuck him in."

"Where are you working now, Mina?" asked Lori.

"The theater."

"The *theater*," echoed Lori with her best British accent. "*The theater.* What are you doing at the *theater*, Miss Madam Mina?"

"I've got a part in a play," Mina answered with a laugh.

"*The Harryequin*," said Gail with a nod. "She's in *The Harryequin*."

"*The Harlequin*," Mina corrected.

"Wow," said one of the two strangers leaning on the table. "*The Harlequin*? I've seen the posters in the subway. It's a really big play."

"Actually, she *is* the harryequin," Gail added, raising a finger.

The two friends stared at Mina. Then Gail caught everyone's attention as she started to tip over on her seat.

"Come, come, come bitch," Gail said, opening her eyes wider than normal. "Come with me to the bar. Let's see some other shit I can get you and me. Come on!"

"Sure you can manage?" Mina asked.

"Let's go!" Gail grabbed her by the arm and led her to one of the counters. She seemed to be using Mina more as a crutch than a companion.

The crowds along the bar were terrible. She wondered how Gail would get anything. But Gail fumbled her way through, tapping a shoulder or shoving between couples with a big smile. People made way for them and, somehow, they made it to the counter. She didn't have as much success with the bartender, though.

"I'm so glad you came, babe," Gail said in her ear.

"Thanks for inviting me. I think I needed a break before rehearsal."

Gail leaned over the counter, searching the bar. Two bartenders were really busy. "Fuck, Mina. We'll be here all night."

"You two care for a drink?" asked a tall, curly-haired young man leaning over the counter beside them. He was dressed sharply in a navy-blue suit, carrying two drinks in his hand.

"We're waitin' for 'em." Gail nodded and pointed at the bartender.

"You'll be waiting a long time. Here." He handed the two drinks to them.

"What's this?" Mina asked.

"You want a drink?" the stranger said. "Well, here you are. Got these for you."

They were purple and over crushed ice, in margarita glasses. The violet color looked weird. Gail didn't hesitate. She took her glass and started drinking it down.

"Umm," said Gail. "Not bad shit, Mina."

Mina hesitantly sipped hers. It had juice and some spices, with something alcoholic.

"Whas in it?" Gail asked. She had to tap on the man's shoulder to get his attention.

He was swaying to the music, acting all cool. He shrugged. Then the young man looked at Mina, top to bottom. "Where are you two from?"

Mina wasn't sure she liked this boy. He was alone. He didn't seem to have any friends, and yet he had this arrogance about him.

"Here," said Gail. She giggled. "How 'bout ya?" And she ran a single finger down his chest.

"Just visiting. I go to school in Georgetown."

"New York town?" asked Gail.

"He means Georgetown in DC, Gail," explained Mina with a laugh.

"Right," he said, raising a drink with a smile. "You've been there?"

"Yeah, I visited a friend going to school in DC once." Mina sipped more of her mystery drink.

"At Georgetown?" he asked.

"Um-hmm … This is good. What is it? Where'd you get it?"

"I don't know. I think they're mojitos. I just asked for something different. Purple. Wild, huh?"

"Yummmm," said Gail, practically hunching over. "Hey man, whas your mayor?"

"Political science."

Gail's eyes opened wide. "Reeeally? Come fuck o'er with us. You need to see my bro."

"Why, does he go to Georgetown?"

"No, he's one of your mayors."

"How much did your friend have to drink?" he asked Mina with a laugh.

Mina just shrugged. "How did you come across these drinks?"

"You shouldn't question gifts, my lady," he said with a smile and a wag of a finger. "Anyway, I was expecting two friends and got it for them. Seems I was stood up."

He acted nice. A little *too* nice. Mina didn't like that. She started looking at her drink with distaste. And why was the drink violet?

Gail gestured for him to follow them, but he put his hand up.

"Gotta use the bathroom," he said. "I'll be right back."

"How will you find us?" Mina asked.

"I'll look around."

Gail stumbled back into Mina's arms, nearly spilling the rest of the purple stuff all over Mina's shirt and white sweater as they went back to their table.

Mina leaned over and whispered into her ear, "Gail, why did you tell me to arrive late? I told you I had to be home early tonight."

Mina had been trying to summon the nerve ever since she first saw Gail drunk. Gail looked down and then seemed a little guilty.

"Don't worry 'bout it."

"Tell me," Mina insisted.

"Mina, I love you," Gail said with a guilty smile, flapping a hand over her arm. "I mean, I reeeally love you. But don't get me wrong. I just had to get them ready."

"Ready? Ready for what?"

Gail laughed.

Two drunken bastards fell right behind Mina, hurting her heel, and draped themselves over some bodies, laughing. That got them into a row with a few other bystanders and, for a moment, there was lots of shouting and pushing near them. A huge, burly bouncer came in the nick of time.

Gail almost fell over again. Mina grabbed her in her arms.

"What do you mean, *ready*?" Mina let Gail lean against her on their way back to their table.

"Mina," Gail said, with a slur, in her ear, "Mina, you know, baby, you're shy."

Then Gail pressed her lips against Mina's cheek. It was just a peck. But it bothered her. No, what Gail had said bothered her more.

So she was invited to come late in order to not … what? Bore her friends? Embarrass her? Jesus, was she that bad?

Mina felt warmth rush to her face. Gail was telling her that she was so awkward that her friends had to be drunk in order to be in her company. That was seriously fucked up. And worse, Gail seemed very serious about it—even in her inebriated condition.

Mina tried not to spill Gail's drink. She had it in the same hand that held Gail as they made their way back to the table.

When she finally reached their stools, she felt angry. So mad that ... no ... she started ... to feel dizzy. Really dizzy. Or was she just that upset? She really didn't feel that angry. So why was she dizzy? Was it the drink? She had only drunk one beer and this purple drink. She was swooning a little and, for a flash, returning to her spot at the table, Gail lost her smile and looked sick too. Had they been poisoned?

"What you got there?" asked Lori.

"*Mo-hee-tos!*" cried Gail, falling into Lori's arms.

"And you didn't get us any?" Lori added.

"Sorry," said Mina. "It's not as good as you could have made them."

"Let me try," said Lori. She took a swig of Mina's drink and shrugged. "Tastes a little sour. There's some..." She swished a little in her mouth. "Vodka. Maybe lemon. But I don't know what the other shit is. It looks like a Purple Rain."

Gail shrugged and burped.

Mina felt nauseous. And she hadn't liked the way that boy looked. He seemed too preppy and fake. She pushed her cocktail glass onto the table and grabbed her unfinished beer.

"So ... what'd I miss?" asked Gail. Then she fell off the stool. Everybody burst into laughter. Gail raised a finger over the table.

"We were talking about football," said Raoul. "You like football, Mina?"

"No." Then Mina thought of what Gail had said about making sure she came late. "I mean ... it's okay. It's okay, you know. I guess."

"I fucking hate football, bro," Gail said while being helped up by Lori. "I haaate football. And leave Mina the fuck alone." And Gail pinched her brother's cheeks.

Raoul just sat there and looked annoyed. Everybody laughed.

"I wonder if we can do pool?" asked Gail. She started searching the room. "I wonder. Is there a pool table here? Want to do that, Mina? Mina, you want to play pool with me, Mina?"

"If they have one," replied Lori, "people are dancing on it. Anyway, you really should just chill out."

And that's when it happened. Mina looked out at the people dancing, and she could have sworn their bodies were swaying like waves on the ocean. She rubbed her eyes. Her vision blurred. Her heart raced. She felt sweaty and terribly dizzy. For a moment, she thought she was going to throw up. Gail wasn't looking good either. But then again, Gail had an excuse, having probably drunk six drinks by now.

Mina closed her eyes. When she opened them, the swaying bodies looked normal again.

"I don't feel well," Mina admitted.

That seemed to alarm Gail. For the first time since seeing her friend, Gail seemed to become sober. "Are you okay, Mina?"

"I don't know. I just don't feel well. Maybe it was the drink."

Mina closed her eyes again. She was swaying on the stool.

"I don't feel great either," said Gail. Then she vomited all over the table, sending everyone reeling. But Gail was so drunk that she laughed, burrowing her head in her arms.

Raoul rushed over to Gail. Lori grabbed her over her shoulder and held her.

Then Lori cocked her head back at Mina. Lori became a blur.

"You okay, Mina?" someone asked.

"I think it's the drink."

"The Purple Rain?"

At that precise moment, a man tapped on Mina's shoulder. She figured it was the Georgetown stranger who had brought the drinks, and she intended to spin around and give him a piece of her mind, but it wasn't. It was a man dressed in a dark mask and cape. Erik. Her phantom. He looked ridiculously elegant surrounded by T-shirts and jeans in the nightclub. But he looked good. He always looked good.

When Mina turned back to her friends, they were still busy helping Gail and cleaning her mess.

Erik gently tapped on her shoulder again. Then he leaned beside her ear.

"Come join me, Miss Daaé," he said softly.

"Leave me alone, Erik."

"Join me," he whispered. "I'd like to show you something."

She shook her head.

"It's about your friend. You need to see this."

Mina turned, and he had a kind smile under his mask. He sort of faded in and out of focus and, for a moment, he even disappeared entirely. But his eyes, those striking jewels, came back into focus. They seemed kind. He touched her fingers with his soft white gloves—those lovely soft gloves.

"Come. Come with me."

Mina got up and followed, more out of curiosity than desire. She didn't even know how he was there. Or how people weren't staring at him in his dark nineteenth-century cape. People swayed around her and Erik as they seemed to pass them in slow motion under the bright swirling lights.

Somehow they made it to the center of the dance floor beside a bunch of kids jumping up and down like fools. He stood close to her and gently kissed her cheek. Then all the surrounding bodies seemed to slow. He gently rubbed her fingers with those soft gloves again. He turned her gently so she faced the strobing lights. Then he ran his gloved fingers along her long hair and they embraced, slow dancing. Mina would have thought everyone would be staring at them, but they didn't. They all kept pogoing along.

"I'm sorry if I gave you a fright," he said quietly in her ear, "but I'm a ghost, my dear. I'm not always in control of how and when I appear."

And somehow that all made sense in his arms. And, as if proving it, his face blurred and for a moment she saw dancers jumping through him. But it didn't scare her. She felt at ease in his arms.

"Particularly with your psychic perception. Sometimes you pull me through at the wrong time. But I'm here now, Christine, so happy to be dancing with you. And not startling you."

She wasn't sure if he was referring to now or when the painting of her hand tried to grab her in her apartment. He gently brought her into a closer embrace.

"You did scare me, Erik," she admitted, nodding and leaning her head on his shoulder. "You did. Oh, Erik, I can't even be sure you're here now."

"But I am."

His cologne smelled nice. And she liked it when the bristles of his thin goatee ran against her cheek as he held her. Although everyone else jumped up and down with the hip-hop, she and Erik danced their slow dance. And it seemed lovely and felt right.

He kissed her on the lips.

"But why are you here, Erik? Why?"

She got lost for a moment in those lustrous eyes.

"Are you happy I'm here?" he asked in a whisper. His lips, half hidden under his mask, curled into a smile under the flashing light.

"Yes."

"Then that's all that matters. Follow me, Miss Daaé." He let go of her and took her hand again. "I want to show you so much more. Something about your friend."

They were off again, with him guiding her between bodies with his gloved hand, until they approached a wall beside a bar. Erik walked through the wall, reaching back for her. Only his gloved fingers were visible. That frightened her. Even though it was his soft white glove, having it emerge from the wall reminded her of her painting. It was so weird. Yet no one around them paid any notice.

"Come. Join me." And his white-gloved fingers reached for her again. "Come."

She gave him her hand and he helped her through the wall. She blinked and shaded her forehead with her free hand as a blinding yellow light shone over her eyes. It took a moment for her to adjust.

Her eyes focused on a grassy field and the sound of running water under the bright sun. There was bird song and a trickling brook near them. Her clothes had changed to a pitch-black dress. The sleeves were trimmed with frilly see-through lace ending near her fingers. Its long skirt extended down to a pair of glass slippers. She looked up at the clear blue sky, between branches, and realized that she was under a large leafless maple tree. Behind her was a forest of thorny maples, but in front of her was a steep, grassy hill. And at the top of the hill perched an elegant white medieval castle. The castle was perfect, without even the slightest blemish. It seemed to sparkle in the sunlight. Everything around her was bright and beautiful. And the air smelled fresh and clean. It was wonderful.

She walked by the side of the brook. Water trickled down a collection of jutting rocks and boulders, making a lovely waterfall. And thick, grassy moss clung to the rocks and boulders around the water. She stopped and looked down at her reflection in the water. She was surprised to see herself wearing a see-through veil, like a wedding veil, but black, pulled back behind her long, dark hair. She saw Erik's reflection beside her. His face in his shiny black half-mask, though handsome, looked a little disturbing standing over her. He leaned down and kissed her on the lips. They looked down at their reflections as they embraced. She closed her eyes and enjoyed the lovely sound of water as he entered her mouth again, dancing with her tongue. They embraced gently under the sound of bird song. Then he brushed her cheek with his white-gloved hand and gestured up to the castle.

"Come with me."

They walked hand in hand up the grassy knoll, Erik still in his black cape and mask and Mina in her matching ebony dress and veil.

There was a drawbridge over a shallow moat. They crossed creaky wooden planks over the bridge, and she heard music. It was a trance-like music, blaring from within the castle walls. It was as if they were approaching a house party, which was weird coming from such a lovely castle. Erik led her, holding her hand, until they reached giant wooden double doors.

"Welcome to his castle," Erik said with a smile and an exaggerated bow. It almost seemed like a joke.

"Erik, stop," she said, chuckling and pulling her hand from him. "What is this place? Where are you taking me?"

"The ruler's domain," he said, turning serious. "The king leads you to me. Our ruler. But the secret, Christine, is 'tis our kingdom. For he does not hold the courage that you and I hold. He is not willing to see what lies behind the mask. But if you join me, I will show you. Come and see."

She looked at him and those bright-green eyes behind the mask.

He smiled.

"I … I don't know where we are. Aren't we at the bar?"

He laughed. Then she laughed too, at the ridiculous sound of her question.

"This is the festival. Do you not care to meet the king?"

"Who?"

"Of course, you'll need a mask. Only certain guests are allowed.

Are you a werewolf, vampire, angel, demon, witch, warlock, ghost, griffin, fae, fairy, nymph, mermaid, merman, satyr, mummy—"

"Out of all that," she replied with a laugh, "I suppose the closest would be an angel. I'd like to think so, anyway."

"An angel?" He nodded. "All right, that will do."

And Erik reached into the pocket of his long, dark cape and pulled out a black velvet mask. He handed it to her to wear over her eyes. "Here is your mask. Behind your back, your wings are folded."

"But what of you?"

"I am a phantom. Ghosts are always welcome at the gates."

"What is the place? Please tell me. Is this another dream?"

He furrowed his brow, and those green eyes stared for a moment. Then he pinched her arm.

"Oww!"

"Did you wake up?"

"No."

"Then it is not a dream. But are you sure you're an angel?"

She looked at him funny. "Yes. Yes, I'm very sure. I am an angel."

"Welcome in then, angel. Welcome, Christine the angel."

He opened one large wooden door and gestured for her to enter with a sweep of his hand. But as she entered, he remained standing by the threshold.

"Aren't you coming with me?"

He shook his head. "It's for you to know what's inside. Look at my mask. I already know."

Somehow, that made sense.

Mina walked through.

She found herself at the summit of a rocky ledge. She had to shield her eyes as the sandy valley below was so bright. Above the valley was a giant dome, blocking parts of the sky. The sides of the dome were made of turquoise stone. The center was a dusty glass dome. This dome was huge, towering very far above her. Directly below, along sand dunes, black stones moved like ants. She squinted and peered more closely, realizing that these black "rocks" were people. Thousands of dancers in dark leotards, covered in black paint, were moving on top of each other over a field of sand dunes. The black paint, like tar, dripped down their faces and hair, and they smeared it about their bodies and the bodies of their partners. The chaos was such a huge contrast to the quiet forest and grassy fields outside the palace walls. And the music blared in step with the chaos.

Mina looked back at the doors but Erik was gone.

A small man crouched beside her, hunched into a ball, with onyx paint upon his face. He had a violet lyre on his lap, but he didn't play. The hypnotic music blared. Then a violet light was cast over the small man's face, almost like a purple floodlight. She jumped back, seeing him open more than two eyes. He had rows of eyes along his face. Then he pointed down the ledge with a very sharp stump of an arm.

"Enter, Mina the angel."

The man stood on eight legs and scurried quickly, like a giant spider, down a dirt trail by the right side of the sandy ledge.

Among the dancers covered in black paint, down the valley, was a motley crew of circus freaks: jugglers, pipers, green-skinned witches, knights, kings and queens, acrobats, puppeteers, tightrope walkers, children in brown tatters, and mimes. Some of them were trapped in a rocky wall, with half their bodies emerging from the walls. Their chins rested on the backs of their hands. They appeared to be deep in thought, reminding her of that famous statue, *The Thinker*.

And then came the Harlequin. A man dressed in thick, white frills making his way, weaving this way and that, in the pandemonium. Bucking and jumping, he danced toward a central wooden stage on the opposite side of the valley. On stage, naked men and women contorted and twirled like ballerinas, spinning about and carrying streamers of all the colors of the rainbow. So many naked bodies, some white as sand or black as obsidian, dancing or fucking on the large stage above the tar dancers in the valley below. As the fluffy white clown made his way through the tar-dripping dancers, they ran their fingers and palms over his face, along the sides of his body, and over and under him.

"May I introduce an angel," someone announced.

Three more black spiders with large torsos and eight pointy spidery stumps crept beside her. Multiple eyes alternated from open to shut. She didn't flinch. Standing wide-eyed and frozen, she was too shocked at the nonsensicalness of it all to move. There was a sandy path, to her right, that led down the incline and to the central stage. Something drove her to go there—to visit her clown? She wasn't sure. But as she heard the tapping of eight more legs and a shadow passed over her, she decided that she'd fare better among the dunes of tar-drenched bodies than up on the cliffside with arachnids.

As she made her way down the dirt trail, mimes with part of their bodies trapped in the dirt walls gestured for her attention, life-size marionettes dropped down from wires hanging from high atop the glassdome ceiling, and merchants, artists, and shopkeepers by tents along the walls just stared at her.

There was art on the walls. Beautiful paintings and sculptures fixed to the dirt walls mixed with vibrant green vines and carmine and lavender rose petals. It was elegant and regal, and ... colorful. She loved to look upon the earthen walls as she ventured down among the dancers.

Soon she was in the middle of the hornet's nest. Close to the dancing figures, she found that there was more space to navigate around them than it had seemed from the summit. She walked down dirt steps, dodging a group of contorting bodies. Some smiled, but most ignored her. Then a couple of them stopped spinning and grabbed her hands, helping her make her way faster to the stage across the valley. She didn't like the feel of their wet, blackened hands, and some of their tar adhered to her fingers.

By the time she was helped up steps to the stage, the Harlequin was sitting on an elevated throne, looking past the squirming nude bodies to look at her. She recognized this harlequin. He was fatter than Toni, but he had the same short black hair, ruddy nose, and hazel-brown eyes. Yes, behind the clown face, the man behind the mask was not just a harlequin. It was Antonio Vollini. But a big Antonio, so large that he could barely move from his throne.

"May I present Mina Daaé the angel," someone announced.

Toni looked down, seeming to recognize her. He lifted a glass of wine and toasted to her. "Si, si. But this is a fallen angel, no?"

Then, as quickly as it had begun, the sound of the dancers stopped. The naked bodies fornicating at her feet faded. The arena emptied. It was just her and Toni.

Mina looked at Toni's face and recoiled in fear. He was contorted in pain. He leaned against the side of the throne as bright red oozed from the folds of his white puffy clothes. His face winced behind the painted frown. There was a gurgling sound. And then he cried out, like that terrible cry he had uttered during the fall in her dream. He suffered as his white chest and legs were coated in crimson.

Mina turned to run, but she couldn't. Something pulled at her to stay.

When she looked at him again, it only became worse. What was once a frilly white clown was now a red-dripping wad of flesh. He attempted to stand, but he was too big. Then she watched as pails of red liquid were thrown over him from behind. This liquid was the same blood color as his now-drenched suit. It hit his face, turning his makeup from white to crimson. And as the blood splashed across his face, he seemed to suffer more, unable to avert the deluge. Mina ran as hard as she could back up the dirt trail.

Red rained down from the rafters of the glass-dome ceiling. It began as a drizzle of blood spotting the sand. Then it became a down-pour. She was desperate to not be covered by it. It was as if it were poison.

She had to get away, but she couldn't. Her lacy black dress was soaked now, just like the Harlequin's white suit. Then she looked up, and what seemed like bucketfuls of blood fell over her face, her hands, and her head. She threw the wet veil over her head, but this only splashed more blood on her hair and face.

"GET IT OFF ME!" she screamed. *"GET IT OFF! OFF!"*

She turned back. Her "king" was no longer recognizable. Toni had become a mass of bloody gelatinous pulp, bubbling on center stage.

"Get it off me!"

Then she saw a spider with tar dripping from his face. He crept toward Mina on eight long, spider-like legs, removed a mirror from behind his body, and gestured for her to look at the mirror. Mina's face was covered in blood. It was so red that she could barely recognize herself.

"GET IT OFF! OFF ME!"

11

OFF

"GET OFF ME!"

"Mina, I'm trying to help you!"

"*Get off!*"

"Are you okay?"

"Get off me!"

"Wake up, Mina. Come on! Wake up."

"Huh?" She sleepily cracked open an eye. Gail was leaning over her. Mina shook and looked around. She found herself lying on a couch. She saw a dimly lit room and the night-light from a kitchen—her kitchen. Then she looked at the beige cloth of her couch. She was home.

"Morning, crazy," Gail said, her voice bubbly. "Hi."

Mina felt dizzy. Gail fell out of focus and the couch seemed to move. Even the ceiling swayed. She turned to the floor and threw up beside the couch. Gail had been ready and pushed her head close to a bucket. It helped. She felt a little better. But she still felt terribly sleepy.

"That was a good idea."

"It wasn't the first time. You've been throwing up for hours. Made me sick just watching you. And you've been talking all kinds of weird shit, in different languages. It's been really scaring me. You're totally fucked up like me, bitch, which … I really don't get. You had like two drinks. Did you drink before you came?"

"No. I think I was drugged."

"We had the same drinks," Gail said, shaking her head. "I had a lot of them."

"Maybe roofied. Or like PCP or something? That guy looked really suspicious, Gail."

"You're crazy." Gail shook her head with a laugh. "You just drank too much. Maybe you're not used to it. I don't know. Or maybe he spiked yours with too much vodka."

"That guy from Georgetown looked suspicious."

"Yeah? Well, he was worried about you when you drifted off. He was helping Raoul and Lori get you into the car—along with me."

Had she passed out and had it all been a nightmare? It must have been a long time. Gail was barely slurring her words now.

Mina tried to sit up but felt too weak. Then she gazed at her clothes. Her dress and veil had disappeared. For a moment, she had been terrified that she would be dressed in a black gown, lying beside a dead tree or something. The dream had been so real. But she was wearing her red silk robe instead.

"You changed me?"

"Yeah. You vomited all over your clothes."

"Shit."

"It can be washed," Gail said, with a chuckle and a yawn, touching her arm. "Relax."

Relaxation was one thing Mina could do. In some ways, that was the thing that made her so nervous. Not only did she feel numb, but she felt so tired that she could barely move her arms or legs. She felt like she was above her body. Almost as if she were floating as Gail crouched over her.

"What's … wrong with me?"

"Rest." She shrugged. Then she ran a hand along Mina's bangs. "You're home. Maybe you should sleep."

"What time is it?"

"Around ten."

"Ten!" Mina jumped up. Gail quickly grabbed her wrist, but Mina wasn't up for long as the walls swayed. And now she noticed daylight from the kitchen window and through drapes in her bedroom.

"Ten?" she asked. "Why is it day outside and—"

"Ten in the morning."

"Huh?"

"Mina, relax," Gail said, chuckling, grabbing her. "Come on. Just stop. It's okay."

"But the play! Fuck. I promised Toni, Gail. Oh God, he's going to kill me."

"I spoke to him. Don't worry. When he saw you, he said he'd be back in the afternoon to pick you up. Just rest. It's okay. He said you could miss the morning rehearsal."

Mina squinted at Gail. She still wore a white cardigan, sports bra, and jeans. Her long golden hair was disheveled. She hadn't even changed her clothes since the bar.

Mina laughed.

"What's so funny?" asked Gail with a smile.

"You look like shit too."

"Hey, thanks." Gail fell back on the couch, bringing Mina into her arms. "I feel like shit. My head is splitting. But I'm all right. When I'm with you." Gail held her, stroking her hair.

Mina closed her eyes.

"Let's just go to sleep together again."

But a little later, Gail asked her quietly beside her ear, "Do you like me, Mina?"

"Huh? What do you mean?"

"I mean, I feel so incredible when I'm around you. I fucking love you. But I'm so fucking lonely. Last night was amazing. My bro and Lori are nice, but Lori's distant. And I don't see much of her anymore. Anyway, I don't feel the same way I do when I'm with you. I don't feel the same way with anybody."

"Then why'd you invite me so late to the bar?" Mina surprised herself at the edge in her voice.

"I had already promised to meet her stuck-up friends."

"They didn't seem so bad."

"They're Lori's peeps." She felt Gail shrug. "I don't mind getting plastered with them, but that's it. With enough liquor, Tiff and Bee lighten up. Without drinking, they're just bitches who set you up through a barrage of fucked-up questions. I didn't want them to do that to you. They were already saying stupid things about your model job."

Mina nodded and closed her eyes again. She felt so tired.

"Yeah, I like you, Gail."

Gail kissed her cheek and hugged her close again with a giggle. "Me too. Feeling better?"

Mina nodded. Soon her friend's rhythmic breathing helped soothe her.

Later, she didn't know when, Gail leaned over and pecked Mina on the cheek. Mina could smell the alcohol still on her breath. Then Gail touched her lips to hers. Mina opened her eyes. Gail smiled, looking right at her. Then she leaned back into the couch, closed her eyes, and clutched Mina close again. Mina thought nothing of it. She drifted off again.

Still later, she heard a giggle. She felt fingers glide along her chest under the soft robe, exploring her breast and nipple. And then another hand moved the robe back and ran along her leg. Mina gently pushed her hand away, but Gail seemed persistent, continuing to touch her breast with the other hand. Then Gail changed position, moving on top of her. She kissed her lips again. "Mmm." Gail sucked Mina's lip and entered with her tongue, kissing more passionately while gliding her fingers along Mina's belly button. "That's nice." Then a hand ran down to her legs again, sliding under her underwear.

Mina opened her eyes wide and then … threw Gail off the couch.

"I like men!"

It wasn't the first time a girl had touched her. She had met a girl in high school who liked her too. But this was different. Gail was her best friend.

"Sorry," Gail said, stretching an arm on the carpet, laughing nervously. "Geesh. Couldn't resist. Anyway, it's no different from how you touched me in your ramblings earlier."

I did?

Gail jumped up and laughed. "Phony," Gail accused, flashing her a big grin.

"I like men," Mina said again. But she felt so tired saying it. She leaned back in the couch.

"Well, I like you," Gail said with a shrug, cocking her head back. "Perhaps later."

Then, with her back to Mina, in the light of the morning sun streaming through the drapes, Gail removed her sweater and sports bra, pulled down her jeans and panties, and stood naked for a moment. Her blonde hair was disheveled. She stretched her arms high with a yawn, tightening the crack of her ass, and ran a hand down the side of her breast, silhouetted in the light from the kitchen window.

Her standing like that there nude, on display, was seductive. But before Mina could say anything, Gail cocked her head back with another yawn, giggled, and said, "Excuse me. Gotta shower. I can only hold you for so long, bitch. And these clothes smell."

Mina closed her eyes. She heard the shower turn on.

Her friend Gail was gay? This in and of itself was not a problem. But she had the hots for her? That could be a problem for their friendship.

Gail had said she had touched her. She didn't remember that. To be honest, Gail was attractive, but Mina had never instigated touching another girl, unless she touched Gail last night? It was another piece of this mysterious nightmare. The whole evening scared her. She felt so confused.

After a long time spent staring at the dim light of the kitchen, Mina heard the water turn off. Then she heard her friend's bare feet walking toward her. Mina looked up and Gail stood in front of her again, her naked body now dripping wet. She ran the towel over her chest, drying her breasts, and then along her sides. Then she just held the towel by her side and stood there for a moment, looking deeply into Mina's eyes.

"I have a confession to make," Gail said terribly earnestly. She dried her ears and ran the towel up over her hair. "Maybe it's the beer—well, at least being drunk has given me the nerve to finally tell you—but, Mina, I've had the hots for you. I've been attracted to you ever since you first posed for class. It's not just that you're a drop-dead gorgeous model, or how fucking amazingly nice a friend you are. I'm really into you. And God, your body is, like, so incredible. Like really hot."

Gail reached out her hand and Mina took it, gently lying Gail back onto the couch beside her.

"And you want to fuck me," Mina said softly with a chuckle, putting an arm around her.

"Yeah," Gail replied too seriously, cocking her head back. "Yes, I do. I want to fuck you, Mina. Really badly, actually."

12

THE HANGOVER

Mina woke to a pounding in her head—or was it a pounding on her front door?

She squinted and recognized her kitchen and living room. She was lying in her red robe on her couch again. Then she heard the door open and Gail's voice.

"Huh?" asked Gail with a yawn. "Yeah, what? What is it?"

"Is she better?"

Mina recognized an Italian accent. Toni. She turned and saw him standing by her front door in jeans, a striped button-down shirt, and loafers. True to form, he turned to her and nodded. Mina groaned, rubbing her head.

"Mina, it's time," Toni said with a smile. "We've gotta go." He walked over and crouched beside the couch, touching her arm. "I'm not letting you play hooky anymore. You promised, yeah?"

Mina nodded.

"She's still not feeling well," Gail said, brushing her long blonde hair back and hanging by the door.

"No matter," Toni said, raising a finger. Then he gave his infamous grin to Mina. "It's time. I have my driver waiting. You promised."

"Sure, Toni," Mina groaned. "Sure." Then she sat up. The whole room spun for a second. "Shit, Gail, I knew I shouldn't have gone."

"She's still sick?" Toni asked Gail.

"Too much fun last night," Gail said with a shrug and a giggle. Then she walked into the kitchen. Mina noticed Gail was wearing the matching red robe from her closet. "Before you guys go, I'll brew up a quick brew, babe. 'Kay? It's my special concoction made to end all hangovers. Trust me."

"What's in it?" Mina asked, sitting up and holding her head.

"Aspirin and chamomile with a dash of honey."

Mina laughed. Then she rubbed her forehead again.

"Mina, I left your clothes on the bed next to mine," Gail said from the kitchen. "I remembered your rehearsal. You better go now."

Mina shuffled off the couch and hunched over it for a moment. Finally, she forced herself up to make it to her bedroom.

The thin red curtain, only partly open, let in the bright light of the morning. The white sheets were wrinkled and all over the place, half hanging off the mattress.

Though her bedroom was small, a door demarcated it from the rest of the studio apartment. So she closed her door and got dressed.

She didn't hear a word from Gail or Toni. She pictured Toni pacing and looking at his cell phone and Gail ignoring him. His smiles didn't hide his true feelings. Mina knew full well he was pissed.

The room spun as she put her pants on and, although she prided herself on her balance as a dancer, she fell over onto the mattress when lifting her other leg.

Shit, I think I'm going to throw up again. How can I go to rehearsal?

You have to, Mina, for Toni.

When Mina opened the door, indeed, a very agitated Toni was sitting on the couch, staring at his phone. Gail ran over with a giggle and handed Mina a paper cup of her hangover tea. It smelled awful. She didn't want to eat or drink anything.

"I'll have it on my way."

Gail nodded, hugged Mina, and kissed her cheek. Then she hugged her again—a little too tightly—chuckled, ran a finger along Mina's bangs, and whispered in her ear, "It was fun last night. *A lot* of fun."

"Close up the apartment, will you?"

"For sure."

On the car ride, Toni stayed quiet—weirdly quiet. He just looked out the window as they drove through downtown, periodically checking his phone. But he forced a smile whenever Mina looked over.

Mina felt her bowels turning. Would she make it to the theater without having to use the bathroom? Just like at her audition, she began thinking about her abilities—how she was inferior to the professional dancers, how her voice was unpracticed, how she couldn't live up to Toni's expectations. And then she thought of the pedestal. Would she fall again?

You will fall.

"Shut up!" Mina snapped.

Toni jerked and turned. "Che?"

"Nothing." She looked down and rubbed her head. "Shit." Then she turned to Toni. "Not you, I was just thinking … out loud. Sorry."

"You've been doing that a lot lately." Toni nodded and patted her hand.

"I'm so sorry, Toni."

Toni shrugged. Then he turned back to the window.

A quiet Toni was worse than a loud one. He was too frenetic a man for silence to be normal. After Mina had waited long enough for a response and was about to turn back to her window, Toni laid a finger on his cheek and said, "This Gail … this Gail of yours, she's a good friend, no?"

"Yes. I met her at the university. She's a student."

"From your art class?"

"Yes."

He didn't like that. It seemed he had thrown the suggestion out, hoping she'd say no. "She seems to like you."

"She's a really nice girl. She's got so much energy. She's young."

"That's what I think of you," he said with a tight grin and a nod.

"I don't have a lot of energy," Mina said with a chuckle. "And I'm not all that much younger than you."

"Twenty years."

She shrugged.

Then they went back to looking out their respective windows. And Mina thought of Toni's patience. How could he wait the whole morning for her? The director must have been livid. Toni must really want her in the play to be this patient.

"I'm sorry," Mina repeated. "I really am."

Toni nodded. Then he turned to her with a fake grin and said, "Tell me … is this Gail gay?"

The car stopped at a red light just at that moment. The same moment Mina froze. She furrowed her brow. Then a car beside her window honked and made her jump. But it probably wasn't the car that had startled her.

They say that a woman possesses a special intuition. Well, right now it seemed Toni did. Had they been that obvious?

"I … I don't know," Mina replied.

"I'm very in tune with this sort of thing, you know. I'm also very observant. I like to think that's what makes me a good writer and producer." Then he nodded. "Don't worry. If she is gay, I don't mind. I have nothing against lesbians, of course. I suppose it's—"

"Then why are you asking?"

He nodded in thought and turned back to the window pensively. For some reason, his silence made her angrier. It would have been better if he had shouted at her. But she had never seen Toni get mad. She didn't even know if it was possible.

But Mina got mad—very easily.

"What happened between us happened," she snapped.

"Che?" He turned to her and almost tried to force a grin. "Between you … and I? Or Gail and …"

"Between you and me. What happened in my apartment, happened, Toni. And it's okay. I'm okay with it."

"I wasn't going to even mention that."

"Well, it happened. Okay?"

Toni nodded.

"And what else happens in my apartment, with other people, is my business. Not yours. You might be…" Mina looked at the driver. He was playing music softly—some sort of hip-hop—and he looked like he had no idea what they were talking about. But it didn't feel private. "You might be my producer, but what I do outside the play is really none of your business."

"I know." Then he turned and gave her his famous smile, but somehow it looked very fake this time. "Sorry if you thought otherwise."

She nodded. Then Toni turned morosely back to the window, and Mina felt awful.

"Oh, I'm sorry, Toni," Mina said, touching his hand. "Forget it. And … thanks for being so patient with me for your play. I don't know how you could wait so long for me."

"*You* are my play, Mina. I told you that. Are you feeling better?"

"Yes. I suppose."

"I am so glad."

"I won't do it again."

Won't do what again, Mina? Fuck Gail?

Really, if Mina was to be honest with herself, she had more problems with what had happened than Toni did.

Why did she touch Gail? What was she thinking? She had never slept with a woman before. Was it the alcohol? How? She'd had less than two drinks! And her nightmare. But she had been awake. Had she been awake?

You're losing it, Mina. You need to see a psychiatrist. And this isn't your phantom talking—it's YOU, your conscious mind. Your conscious mind mulling over the fact that yes, Mina, YOU DID, IN FACT, FUCK Gail last night. WHY!? Maybe you are gay?

She started crying. She couldn't believe it, but tears were running down her face and she shook a little. She did her best to turn and hide it from Toni, leaning toward the window. Then she gulped hard, straightening her body and using all the strength she had to stop. She didn't want to fall apart. Not in front of Toni. Not after everything this man had done for her. The last thing she wanted was for him to comfort her. And how could he?

But she knew she was crying for him because she felt like she had hurt him.

Or maybe I like Toni?

She glanced over, but he was still staring out the window. If he had noticed her crying, he wasn't admitting to it.

She forced down some of the tea in the cup she'd brought. Then she thought again how strange it was that she had a hangover at all. It must have been that suspicious man who gave her the purple drink. He must have poisoned her.

No one poisoned you last night, Christine.

13

THE REHEARSAL

For Mina, a girl who was pathologically shy, the crowd hanging around the stage to greet her that afternoon—literally a frenzied circus —was overwhelming. But she liked the attention. She had so many things on her mind and she needed distractions. It was the oddest motley crew she had ever seen. Only Toni could mix such extremes of art.

Two strongmen, as wide as Mina was high, stood by the end of the stage. Their long, thin, Salvador Dalí–like beards draped down over their lips. Jugglers dressed in clown face laughed and threw all sorts of trinkets into the air. One hurled a rainbow scarf at Mina's face. Acrobats ran and flipped over one another. There were singers practicing single notes over and over again. A man on stilts, in a suit—with a way-too-wide smile painted on his face—walked to and fro across the stage. And there were animals. A cage of birds and a young man, in jeans and a T-shirt, sitting beside a metal cage big enough for a lion. But there wasn't any lion—none that Mina could see or hear anyway. All the while, ballet dancers in tutus turned on their tippy-toes, practicing their routines in any space they could find. And gymnasts walked on their hands or landed in somersaults.

But the "normal" ones were just as fun. The "normal" ones hugged and kissed Mina, their star, on the cheek, shaking her hand or offering to meet for a drink at break time. They were all overly smiley, as if they had known her all her life. And all thrilled to see their main performer, Mina Daaé, sing again. Some might have been in suits, but they were ar-*tists*, just as looney as the bohemians. They reminded her of all her roommates and friends at art school in Paris. She loved them. They scooped her in their arms and acted as if she were their long-lost best friend. And as they embraced her, she caught Toni in the background, flashing a warm side glance. Finally, a genuine Toni smile. He knew theater was her home. And she supposed, from his grin, that he also knew that it was *his* show making her dreams come true.

It went on like this for half an hour, until Toni's claps echoed through the hall. He was clapping as loudly as he could at the center of the stage.

"Get to your places, everyone," he shouted. "You see her. Now the break's over. It's time to practice."

"Till later, Mina," said a dancer with a wink. Dressed in a light-blue pancake tutu, she looked like a dancer in *Swan Lake*. "Promise?"

"Don't forget to text me the link to your paintings," said a young man in glasses, a hoodie, and slacks.

Toni clapped some more.

When enough space had cleared, Mina spotted Daniella, dressed in a navy-blue suit and high heels. She and a gentleman were walking toward Mina and Toni, from stage left, and binders were tucked under her arm. The man walking beside her also had papers in his hands. This guy was a short, bald man in his thirties, who seemed to be taking in everything around him.

"Hi, Mina," said Daniella. "Let me introduce you to Henson Jenny. Our director."

"Mina," Henson said, sticking a hand out.

Mina shook his hand.

"Wait till you hear her voice," said Toni with a gaping smile.

"I'm more interested in seeing her dance," said Daniella. Then she examined Mina head to toe. "You'll need to practice. You're mine after rehearsal from five to seven every day. Got me?"

Mina nodded.

"She won't disappoint," Toni said.

The raucousness only increased. Toni looked around, annoyed. "I don't know what to do with these people."

Henson looked around too. Mina jumped when he shouted, *"Get the fuck out! Unless you're up! Get out!* Now that she's here, we're starting from the beginning. And if you're not in the first act, then … fuck! What are you doing here?"

And they obeyed. Toni looked at his director and shook his head.

Henson smiled smugly.

"You need to change, Mina," Henson said, his demeanor completely changed, almost sweet. "You don't come in until later. I'm sorry I missed hearing you sing at the audition. From what I hear, you were incredible. Let's do that again opening night, shall we?"

Mina nodded.

On a stool before a huge vanity mirror in her dressing room, Mina stared at herself. She took deep breaths. She was wearing a red silk bra and matching panties, sitting beside a glittering, puffy scarlet dress, trimmed in gold, hanging over a chair. She didn't have to apply makeup; it was a rehearsal. But she did want to brush her hair and look more presentable, rehearsal or not.

The dressing room was full of pomp. It was the most prized dressing room in the theater. And it was huge, with a lounge with a TV and sofa. Chairs surrounded the green leather couch, adorned with expensive mauve and cherry-red suede pillows. Elegant lamps surrounded the sofa. Thick gold coils framed a sign reading *The Harlequin.* Even the door was of a finer, darker wood than everybody else's. The room was gaudy and ridiculous. It was "Toni." And she figured that was why he had been so excited to show her this dressing room when she had first arrived.

The stark change from the production crew crowding around her to the peace and quiet in her dressing room was a little unsettling. Only a few dancers had nodded at her as she had walked down the dark hallway. Now it was completely silent, though she knew that, above her, the orchestra was playing and the dancers and jugglers were performing.

She sat like this for a while, just gathering her thoughts. Her dizziness had lifted. Now she was just plain nervous.

In the mirror, she noticed a shadow among the boxes and hangers and an old costume in the far side of her room. At first, she thought nothing of it, for it was still. But then something shifted in the darkness. She spotted the form of a body. Looking closer, she saw that the figure wore a black cape and a familiar black half-mask. It was Erik, sitting on a stool, hands folded, staring at her. Erik. Her phantom.

She whirled around and quickly drew her hands over her chest and waist. "I'm not dressed!"

"I've seen it before," the man quipped in his French accent. He chuckled. "Anyway, this is my dressing room, fallen angel."

He was so still and quiet that she could almost believe he hadn't said anything. He seemed to blend in with the shadows.

"I'm not dressed," she said again, jumping up and pointing to the door. "Get out of here."

He turned from her. "Go ahead, put on your costume. I'll turn. Wear it if he must humiliate you like he humiliated me. It only brings you closer to your fall."

Mina's heart was racing. She slowly leaned back in her chair, but she didn't dare take her eyes off him.

"I said leave. I'm—"

"Not dressed? Oui. I told you, I saw more than that in your forest."

"What forest? I don't know what you're talking about."

"Faker. I call you that." And he raised a finger. "You are a faker, an actor, and a good one but … not a liar. A faker. My mademoiselle, Christine Daaé, could never lie. You're too sweet an angel to lie. But fake you will. You will fake. And you will fake all the way until your end, won't you, Christine?"

Mina reached over to the other stool facing the mirrors and grabbed her huge frilly dress, because there was no way she was going to make a run for it half naked. The creep was right next to the door. She stood up and started pulling the dress on, but she didn't stop glancing at him.

He actually looked bored. He kept his hands folded and gave a few sighs.

"You can't be here," she said with a nervous laugh. "Not in my dressing room. You don't exist."

"The dressing room is mine, ma chérie."

"Why?" She straightened her red dress over her shoulders. It was so heavy she had to strain to lift it. Thankfully, it was to be worn only for a short while at the very end of the first act. It weighed down her shoulders. "This is my dressing room. I've been given the starring role."

"No, this is my dressing room. It says 'The Harlequin' outside the door, does it not? And I was given the starring role in Paris when you weren't even out of school yet. You know, you're a careful bird, but you're a little too trusting of Toni. Sure, your fuck-clown has a painted smile, but sometimes the nicest of clowns are the most vicious. Did you look up Monsieur Antonio Vollini's record in Europe? Did you check his show? Did you surf the web and look up what it was about before the circus came to town? Or did you just sign up like an imbecile? Stupide like me?"

Mina didn't answer. After all, he was just a figment of her imagination. She never saw him across the stage when she fell. Nor did he ever show her that nightmare castle. And if all of it had been a figment of her imagination then, certainly, he was a figment of her imagination now. He was a hallucination. He wasn't real and he wasn't here. So she ignored him.

No, I am here.

"*Goddammit!*" Mina put her hands to her ears.

She faced him again. He was motionless, which seemed creepier. And this time, he stared with glowing green eyes behind that shiny mask.

She turned back to the mirror and leaned her head in her hands. "Why do you keep haunting me?"

"Am I frightening you? Oh, but I must. I must. When it's showtime, do not play the role. No. Let Antonio play it. Let him kill himself, not his lovers. That was his intention. His plan was to be the Harlequin if you didn't reprise the role. That would have been better. I would much rather throw Toni to his death than you. You're too nice."

Mina picked up her scarlet hat. It was a ridiculous, huge, feather hat.

"You're not actually going to wear that?" he asked with a laugh.

"Really? A fucking burlesque hat? Why not go naked? Reprise your modeling role."

Mina refused to respond. She simply readjusted the tall, feathery hat.

"Quit, Christine. Don't go on. Let him wear that and make a fool of himself. Don't strut your tits and ass and dance for a fuck-clown. I showed you the valley. I showed you who he really is. Do you wish to be like him? Let him be his own peacock."

"Why do you care about me?" Mina asked, spinning around again. "You—"

He was gone.

"Oh, my God," she said to herself, raising her hand to her mouth.

She found it difficult to breathe. She felt trapped. She took a deep breath and looked at herself in the mirror—while doing everything she could to keep her eyes off the shadowy corner of the room. Her face was white as a ghost.

She jumped from a loud knock on the door.

"You're almost on, Mina." It was Vince. "We're all waiting for you. You doing okay with that heavy dress?"

"Yeah. I'll be right out, Vince."

14

THE SCARLET DRESS

Henson Jenny might not have made her apply makeup, but her dress was so thick, heavy, and ridiculous that she would have preferred to hide behind clown face. Everyone turned, and it wasn't just because she had the starring role this time. She wore the bright, puffy, gilded scarlet dress with a matching red train that ran fifty feet behind her. In fact, she had to wait about fifteen minutes just for the crew to hang more frilly cloth along the sides, properly attach the tail, and be ready to follow her out onto the stage. The train was carried by stagehands dressed in red and black camouflage meant to blend in with the shadows. And it seemed, as Mina made her entrance—now for the twentieth time—that Henson was more interested in the waves the stagehands made with the tail than in anything she was doing. The only thing she was asked to do was lift her head up high as she entered. It was physically exhausting, a bit like her nude modeling job, but she endured.

Meanwhile, two singers wearing eighteenth-century clothes were singing Mozart to the empty audience. The blue floodlights over them looked cold, and the director had already explained that there would be fake snow during the play. A woman wore a red and gold dress with a hoop, to widen the hips, and a tall, white wig. Beside her was a man in a gray coat and breeches. Of course, as they sang, the audience would not have their eyes on them. They'd be staring at the red dragon with the feathery burlesque hat.

"Keep your head high, Mina," said Henson. "That was fabulous. Absolutely fabulous. You're doing fantastic. Let's try it again, and when you come in from stage right, I want you to walk a little slower but your helpers—guys, for fuck's sake, move the dress up and down, carefully up and then down, with taller strokes, okay? Damn it. How many times do I have to tell you? The audience is watching Mina for the first time. Let her look like waves on the sea coming to the shore. 'Kay? Get those waves high, rolling, rolling up and down and washing onto the sand. We'll have to get this right or we'll spend the rest of the week doing it. Okay? Get it? 'Kay? And not to the side. No one walk to her side. Stay right behind her, single file, carefully and exactly the same distance apart. They don't want to see you. No one wants to see you. No one cares about you. They want to see Mina. All right? Damn it! You all fuck it up and we might as well call it a night. The whole musical will be shit. Right, Toni? Okay? Fuck! … Mina, we'll perform the singing later, 'kay. You'll be accompanying the others on stage, but we'll practice that later. All right, Mina? You're doing fabulous."

She just nodded. She didn't have a microphone, so she couldn't say anything anyway.

"Get back behind her and then we'll have another go. For the hundredth time. Ready?"

She looked out into the audience as she walked on yet again. It was hard to see as all the lights were shining on her. But she could see the shadow of the director. And Toni. She spotted his beanie and his signature theatrical gestures when talking to Henson.

After about the thirtieth take, Henson said, "Okay. Finally. Brilliant! Now bring in the clowns."

15

THE TAXI PIROUETTE

Mina learned to loathe Daniella. Of course, she was exuberant over opening night being only a month away, but rehearsal was grueling. Her body suffered under the weight of her ridiculous red dress—which was even more unbearable when she sang. Then her acrophobia was toyed with by her practiced performance on the dreaded pedestal. By the time she worked with Daniella in the evenings, the strain was complete. She was asked to perform contortions, spins, and jumps in ways she hadn't thought possible by Dani the choreographer bitch.

After the end of one particularly grueling evening, being made a complete fool of by Daniella's Russian girlfriend, Sonia—a far better dancer than Mina—she was absolutely exhausted. One consolation was that it was Friday, which meant she could sleep in a little tomorrow.

She lugged her large duffel bag through the glass doors of the theater, wearing a long coat over her leotard. It was so late that she turned around and locked the theater behind her. Then she made her way to the side of the street to call a cab.

She shivered, realizing it was not only really late but cold. Then she hailed a cab.

"Hey, Mina."

She recognized the voice immediately. Gail stood by the curb, wearing a fuchsia coat and blue jeans, smiling widely but seeming uncharacteristically reserved.

"Gail? What are you doing here?"

"You told me about this theater. I thought I'd accompany you home. If that's okay? It's Friday and I was … well, I was hoping to join you." Then she looked down the street for a moment. "I texted you but you never returned my messages."

"I've just been so busy."

A cab stopped by the curb. Mina walked toward it, but she wasn't going anywhere. Gail stubbornly stood, obviously vying for her attention. So the cab left.

"We have a new female model," she blurted out.

"Yeah? How is she?" *Oh, Gail, I need to go.*

"Not as cute as you."

"I like men."

"I know." She quickly nodded, putting her hand up. "I know. I hope that isn't … I mean, well, I hope that's not why we haven't talked. That night at your place—"

"I was very drunk."

"You barely drank anything."

Another cab drove down the street.

"Look, can we talk later?" Mina asked, gesturing to the cab. "I'll give you a call. I promise. I told you, I've just been so busy. And I'm so tired, Gail. I have to go."

"Ms. Kuni misses you too. The new girl, her name is Carla, is always late. And she's asking for breaks like ten times a session. Anyway, the class is ending soon, so it doesn't really matter. But when I look at Ms. Kuni, I can tell behind her spectacles that she doesn't like this model. But … I mean, it looks like you got your shit together here, didn't you? I mean, a big Broadway play. Wow. How incredible. I'm so proud of you, Mina. You used to talk about your dream. Now you're living it."

"Thanks, Gail." Another cab stopped by the curb.

"You know," continued Gail, ignoring the cab, "I've been working on painting scenery. You should see my work. You know how I like to ski and stuff back in Colorado. So I've been working on mountain ranges and snow on landscapes. Being that so much of our work in class lately had consisted of flowerpots, I thought I'd expand a little, you know. I've gotten really good—love to show you at my place sometime. I really would like to show you. Perhaps we can arrange a time when you can come over and look at my stuff. Are you still painting?"

Gail's gaze wandered anxiously around the street as she fidgeted with some gold bracelets on her wrist. Then she chewed at her lip.

Mina pulled out her cell phone from her purse to check the time. It was almost ten thirty.

Another cab left.

That's when Gail sort of fell apart. She put her head in her hand and started crying. "Oh, Mina. I miss you. When can we see each other again? I'm your friend. I don't want what happened to come between us. I hope that isn't why things haven't been the same. I just want things to go back to the way they were. I really miss you. I can't believe that—"

"It's not going to go back to the way it was. Not because of you. I only have a month left to get ready for this play. On Broadway. I don't know … honestly, I don't know what the fuck I'm doing." Mina shook her head as Gail wiped her teary eyes with her sleeve. Her sobbing didn't make Mina feel sorry for her; it made her angrier. "Look, it's not just that night. Things have changed. I just need time right now. Maybe we can meet, but just not right now. Okay, Gail?"

Gail nodded solemnly. But she became so serious and that bothered Mina more.

"I mean, we were drunk, I suppose," Gail said with a shrug. "You did what you wanted to do. You touched me first. I was thinking maybe … I don't know, I mean—"

"I don't want to talk about it," Mina snapped. She hailed another cab. "Anyway, you're not convincing me. Sounds like you're accusing me."

Another cab came by the curb.

"You could have said no, but you didn't. But I'm not accusing you."

"Sounds like you are."

"I'm not. I'm not, Mina. I just want to talk to you. I just want you to answer your phone."

"I don't want to talk about this anymore."

"Well, I want to." And she touched her arm, trying to turn her from the cab. "I mean, not about that. I don't care about that. I just want to talk to *you*. I don't get why ..."

Then silence. No one said a thing. The taxi driver did. He shouted something about having to leave through an open window.

"I have to go, okay, Gail?"

Gail nodded, somber as hell, opening the cab door for her. "Bye, Mina."

"Bye, Gail. I'll call you."

Mina cried the whole way home. She would never see Gail again. For every time she thought about Gail, she didn't think of sex or that Gail was gay. She didn't care about that. She thought about Ms. Kuni and her life before Broadway. Her job, which she had convinced herself, for two years, was a legitimate art job. Modeling wasn't what she had gone to the academy for. She didn't need that sort of work anymore. She was a fucking star. She didn't want to ever go back to that life again. She had been so miserable, barely making enough money to eat. Seeing Gail again would bring that life right back to her.

She whimpered, pressing herself closer to the window so the cab driver wouldn't hear.

Gail knew. Somehow, Gail knew they would never see each other again.

Mina cried for Gail. She felt so guilty because she didn't want to hurt her. But she would never see her again. Never.

And the tears kept flowing.

Or was she crying because she was just tired? Daniella was such a bitch. As much as Mina loved singing for Henson, she detested dancing for Dani. She didn't need to be reminded every day how bad a dancer she was. She knew it. She knew she was only in Toni's play because of her voice. Well, Daniella knew it too but, for some reason, she made it her business to remind her every night.

Gail was her friend.

Maybe she was crying because she was afraid of being alone. After all, who else did she have?

You have me, Christine.

16

———

FROM THE FIFTH BALCONY

A BODY HUNG OVER THE RAFTER OF THE TOP BALCONY IN THE THEATER. It hadn't been taken down yet when Mina arrived. Hanging there motionless under a bright-yellow floodlight, it seemed more like a sick prop or decoration than a person. Mina had been in her changing room when she had heard the screams. She had rushed to the back entrance, through the dark tunnel beneath the theater, hearing shrieks and the sound of her sandals clapping against the stone floor echoing through the tunnel. But she didn't know exactly what all the hubbub was about until she reached the auditorium. Then, as if that were not grisly enough, when she got to the side aisle, stage lights were shining up on the dead body. But the absolute worst was when she recognized the jacket on the body. It was purplish-red and flashy. Gail's jacket. Then she recognized Gail's face.

Mina didn't scream. There was enough of that surrounding her. Nor did she turn away. She just stared, not saying a word. She just stared.

"Oh my God!" Toni was beside her. "Poor girl. Poor, poor girl!" With wide eyes, he turned to Mina. Then it all seemed to register with him, and his surprise turned into a pained look of pity. "Oh Mina, I'm so sorry."

It wasn't until she saw Toni's dreadfully morose expression that it

477

finally sank in that something had happened to her best friend. Gail was dead.

Mina turned from him and closed her eyes. She felt him hold her. Her heart raced and her head spun. She forced herself to turn and look upon Gail's face again. That's when she noticed the oddest thing. Gail's eyes were closed but her youthful face looked serene, oddly tranquil.

"Let's just get out of here," said a girl wearing black tights and carrying a duffel bag.

"I don't think we're going to have rehearsal today," said another.

Henson ran down from the stage, shouting, as if hearing them, "No one leaves! The police are on their way. They'll be questioning us. Everyone stay put. But we're locking all the doors. No one else will be coming in." Then he turned toward the stage. "My God! Turn the fucking lights off! Jesus, as if it isn't horrible enough!"

And everyone obeyed their director, like they always had.

"Oh, Mina … I'm so sorry," Toni said again, gently holding her.

"I don't even understand how she's here," he remarked, more to himself than her.

Then there was weeping. It wasn't Mina. Instead of emitting shouts and cries of shock, people cried and many put their arms around each other. But they didn't know Gail. Only Toni and Mina did. And Toni didn't really know Gail either. If anyone should be crying, it should be Mina. But she didn't cry.

"Mr. Jenny?" a shy young girl in a black leotard asked. She walked up to Henson, who now had his hands on his hips, staring up at Mina's hanging friend. "We ran up to the balcony and found this. There was a note."

Henson looked at the girl strangely, squinting. Then he said quickly, "Hand it to me."

Henson read it and he only seemed angrier. He pushed it to Toni. Then Toni glanced over it, shook his head, and handed it to Mina.

My dear ARTISTS,

Surely this first feat of brilliance is a warning, no? You will henceforth halt all practice of your production. I am sorry it has come to this, truly I am, but it seems that the only way to end further harm to my dear harlequin is a petty show of force. I warn you that if you dare hurt her again, I will deal another. Then there shall be more interruptions. You want to see the horror that lies behind the mask? Look no further. Take a glimpse at the girl hanging from the top balcony who hurt my Christine. The next one will suffer far worse.

Fakers. This is act one of your opening night. Behold what happens when lovers defile an angel. I cannot wait for the final act when my angel falls. Do not touch her. Only on opening night shall we have our end. A fall to end all falls, no?

No loss for words,

Your phantom.

"*Artists*, Mina?" Toni asked, whirling back at her. He stared at her in shock. "*Feat of brilliance?* Those are my words."

"Are you kidding me!" Mina yanked him off her. "What are you saying, Toni? I had nothing to do with this." Then tears finally streamed down her cheeks. She turned from him. "My God, Toni, she was my best friend."

"Si ... si. My God, forget I said it." He laid a hand on her shoulder. "But, Mina ... the words in that note mock me. Those are the words I used to describe the play to you. Who else would use them like this, unless—"

"Unless what? They're your words." She pulled away from him again. "You tell me."

"No," Toni said, shaking his head. "No, they're ours. My God, Mina, I didn't write that. You didn't either. But ... if she was your good friend and I didn't, who did? She didn't know me."

Indeed, who?

Henson kept looking up, with his hands in his pockets, probably asking himself the same thing. So did everyone else in the auditorium.

But there was another possible culprit. Not *your* phantom, as he had written. *Her* phantom.

Mina fell into an auditorium seat. She just stared at the stage in shock. She didn't dare turn and look up at the balcony again. Henson leaned over to comfort her, touching her shoulder as Toni had.

"She knew this girl?" Henson asked Toni.

"Yeah. I met her a couple of weeks ago at her apartment."

"Then you two are going to have a lot of explaining to do to the police. But … don't knock yourselves out. Toni, you're the last one who would sabotage this play. And I don't think Mina could hurt a fly."

Mina just stared at the stage. A few others came over to her. She barely noticed them. She felt numb. But numbness was good. Better than crying. She didn't want to do that anymore. She didn't want to feel anything.

What about the voices in my head? My God, maybe it was me?

"Get Mina out of here," said Daniella. She sounded uncharacteristically gentle.

"I'll take her to her dressing room," said Toni.

"No!" Mina snapped. "Not there! Anywhere but there!"

17

———

ALONE

Mina didn't answer the cell phone vibrating in her coat pocket. She sat shivering instead. Water trickled down the outside of a metal pipe, forming a very unnatural, yet oddly tranquil, waterfall. It was beside a bench. Mina liked the sound of the water dripping. She turned and looked at the fluffy white frost that covered the pipe. This early in the morning, the water had iced. Strange. Winter had come so fast. She reclined a little more and turned toward the fields, folding her arms. The grass was sprinkled white from frost too. As the sun had just risen, the park was pretty vacant. She was alone. This she usually loved, but not this morning. She really hadn't liked anything all week.

The phantom had gotten his wish. The show had been placed on hold, pending investigation of Gail's suicide. So Mina did nothing, feeling stuck at home like a bird in a cage. But she probably wouldn't have done anything anyway.

For a moment, Mina felt tranquility, enjoying the stillness of the air. She heard a blue jay. A squirrel rummaged through some leaves close to her bench. And for a second, a brief flash, she forgot why she was upset.

Then, between shakes and twitches, she thought of what had happened. Her closest friend had hanged herself after their fight. Her guilt was nearly as strong as her sorrow. She hated herself. She kept thinking she could have stopped pushing Gail away, especially that night. Maybe Gail came to her because she needed her? Not for their friendship, but over something else? Mina had been so self-absorbed that she only thought of herself. But it was too late. She died.

Monday, rehearsal would start again. What an odd mix of triumph and failure in her life. And yet, Mina Daaé was a star. In less than a month now, she would have her opening show. The biggest show on Broadway.

Mina sighed, leaned on her knees, forced herself up, and walked. She dug in her purse and put on shades. As cold as it was, the sun was out. Then she headed to her favorite part of Central Park: the Mall.

She walked the broad street alone. A couple of stray bicyclists and pedestrians passed, wrapped up in coats, but the park was largely deserted. And so, as she sauntered, her imagination wandered. She wished it hadn't.

She pictured herself wearing that ridiculous red dress with the trailing tail for her first act. She had held her head high, with her tail carried by a hundred clowns somersaulting along the walkway behind her. Mina Daaé, the star of Broadway, the clown. And everyone she passed bowed before their clown. She walked as if it were a parade.

A parade for what? A clown?

Did she murder Gail? Or was it her ghost? Was there any difference?

Ghosts aren't real.

When she was questioned by the authorities, she recounted every step with them. She admitted having spoken to Gail on her way home, but she said she left her on the sidewalk and jumped into a cab. It must have been someone else. It must have been.

But she had locked the doors behind her. She had the keys after being there so late. How did Gail get in? Daniella? Daniella had extra keys. Could it have been Dani? No. Impossible. That woman was a bitch but hardly a murderer. Sonia? Maybe. But Dani's girlfriend didn't seem to have had much of a motive either.

She looked back at the fields of white and found the place where, not so long ago, she had been sitting. It still had the mark of her body where she had cleared the ice to make space. She shivered some more. It was so oddly frigid for the first weeks of fall.

She admitted she had been angry with Gail. That much was true. That's why she hadn't answered her calls. But Gail hadn't really done anything. When she had touched her that morning, Mina had let her. It wasn't just because of alcohol. Hell, she'd had only two drinks. It was consensual. Honestly, Mina found Gail attractive. But Mina wasn't gay. She felt manipulated. Obviously, Gail had been attracted to her when she started class. That's why she had lunch with her every day. She had probably planned that night months beforehand. That was probably the only reason for their friendship. Just to touch her and make love to her. Right? It was all about sex. Wasn't it? Did it matter? Gail was so nice. Was it that wrong that Gail was attracted to her? Gail was her best friend.

Gail died. She hanged herself by the fifth balcony.

Oh my God.

Mina didn't do it; her phantom did. Her imagined ghost killed Gail. *Imagined?* No, it must have been him. The note sounded like the phantom. The phantom that had infamously tormented her great-ancestor Christine somehow now haunted her.

The theater ensemble all thought it was suicide, but the police officer who had questioned Mina seemed to think differently. The officer acted like it was murder. And based on the notes and the fact that Toni had left the auditorium by three, the investigator seemed sure Mina had killed her. Who else could have done it?

There was no proof. They had let her go.

Her phone buzzed again. Mina sighed and walked off the path. Standing beside a statue, under a tree, she dug through her small purse for her phone. "Huh, what?"

"Hi," Toni said. "Are you feeling all right, Mina?"

"For sure."

"Hmm. You don't sound like it."

Silence.

"Are you coming to my place Friday?"

"Friday? Something happening at your place, Toni?"

"The get-together. Don't you remember?"

Yeah, she remembered. But she couldn't believe they were still having it after the hanging.

"I ... I don't think—"

"Mina, I think it would do you some good. You can accompany me. I so want you there. So does everybody."

"It's at your new place?"

"Of course it is. Everyone will be there. I'd love to show it to you. We all want you to come."

"I want to. I really do. It's just … I'm so upset, Toni."

"I am too."

More silence.

Mina walked back to the center of the Central Park Mall. She passed a man on a bike and a woman in sweats "wogging." And then another woman with long blonde hair talking on a mobile phone.

"You still there?" he asked.

"I can't stop thinking how sweet she was. I can't even believe it happened. Gail was such a good friend. And I think she looked up to me, you know. Like a big sister. I … I just feel like I let her down. She was reaching out to me, and I abandoned her. There was so much shit she was going through, and I wasn't there for her anymore. I've just been so busy. I feel so bad. God, if I had known she was thinking of this, I would have done something that night, anything—"

"We've been through this. You didn't do anything wrong. She did it to herself."

"Yeah. After *our fight*. I could have been there for her. And … what about the note? I told you I've been hearing things. I can't …" She took a deep breath and heard her voice cracking. "Jesus, Toni, I can't stop thinking it was me. God. You even said I've been acting weird. God, I—"

"Stop it, Mina. You must stop thinking like this."

"I guess. I can remember everything I did that night. I wasn't with her. I mean, I left her after I got in the cab to go home."

Mina watched a couple walking down the wide walkway, hand in hand. Both wore long coats. The view was romantic, with benches and huge towering trees behind them.

Mina sighed and plopped on the nearest bench beside the walkway.

"She was upset," Toni said. "It was suicide. It's not your fault."

"She never talked about taking her life. Yeah, she was mad at me, but there was never any sense that she was going to kill herself. If I had known that—"

There was silence again. It was almost as if Toni had interrupted her, but he hadn't. He didn't need to. There was nothing he could say to make the situation any better.

She made her way back to the walkway and went all the way to the fountain without hearing Toni, but she knew he was there on the line. She could hear his breathing. And she liked that. By the fountain, she sat down and just stared at the lake.

"Mina, it would mean a lot to me if you came tonight. We're gonna take it easy with rehearsals. I don't think it'll matter much if you have a little fun. And from the little I saw of your friend, and what you told me about her, she wasn't someone who'd mind if you had fun."

"No," Mina said with a chuckle. "Gail never minded fun."

"Mina, I know this is so hard for you. I'm sorry. Really. But, believe it or not, it's been very hard on me. I need to pick up the morale of the crew. And we need you. I need you. Everyone wants to see you. And I want to see my friend Mina again. Can she come?"

"What should I wear?"

"A semiformal dress. It's a little fancy. But I'm supplying masks by the door."

More silence. "All right."

He took a deep breath. "That is so good. I can't wait to see you." Toni sounded a little like his old bubbly self. "I love you."

"Bye."

18

THE MASQUERADE BALL

The cab took Mina close to Central Park in northern Midtown. She tapped her long red fingernails nervously on her leg, staring out the window. Her lovely gold-beaded yellow dress draped close to her figure, leaving her back bare. She was adorned with a matching fake gold necklace and saffron high heels—the closest color to her dress—and her hair was up in an elaborate chignon. She looked good, but worried that she had dressed too formally. She had opted for opulence, knowing her good friend Toni.

After going up the elevator to the eightieth floor and being ushered through the door of Toni's penthouse, she was satisfied with her decision. Men with their hair perfectly groomed were wearing double-breasted suits and women wore elegant, long, flowing dresses, some far more expensive than her own. Some, she suspected, wore very real gold and diamond necklaces, too.

Toni's penthouse was breathtaking. The entryway opened into a grand room spanning what must have been nearly half the skyscraper. Everything was modern, with beige painted walls, sharp angles, and walls of windows admiring the Manhattan view. She had to remind herself that the place was Toni's, her friend's. She remembered him being very poor in France. His benefactors for the upcoming Broadway performance must have paid him plenty for him to have afforded this prized place in Manhattan.

Yet she was reminded that it was Toni when, in the midst of all the formality, Lady Gaga's music blared, with colored lights shining over two small stages, featuring a pair, a man and a woman, in lavender and turquoise tights, dancing sensually. The dancers could have been from his play. She was unsure because, like everyone else in the penthouse, they wore masks.

And that's when a girl handed Mina a mask.

"Ms. Mina Daaé," the girl announced loudly by the entrance.

Nearly a hundred people, who had been socializing, eating hors d'oeuvres, and drinking wine or champagne, cocked their heads, raised their glasses, and hollered out her name. She felt her face redden.

"Hi, Mina," said the girl, with a smile under her purple lace mask. She handed Mina a black lace one. "Cindy," she said quietly with a chuckle.

Mina recognized her. This was Cynthia, one of the other ballet dancers.

"Hi, Cindy."

Cindy chuckled again and touched her arm. "No one knows who anyone is. Isn't that fun? Leave it to Toni. But everybody goes crazy when someone comes in and gets announced. Especially you. Fun, right?"

"For sure."

"It's really good to see you." Cindy leaned forward and kissed her cheek. Then she frowned. "We've all been sad, especially for you."

"Thank you."

"Well," Cindy said, smiling again, "just walk down the steps. You can hang out and dance down in the living room or just wander anywhere. Toni said he doesn't give a shit where we go. He said it's our house. And I know he's gonna be so happy to see you."

Mina made her way through the colorful flashing lights. She didn't recognize anybody, but they kept greeting her. She recognized some of their voices. The living room was full of their bodies swaying to the music.

She wandered into the kitchen. It was even busier there. No one was cooking, but a few people wearing black suits grabbed silver trays and pardoned themselves as they grabbed more food for the guests. So Mina sauntered back through the living room. Less people greeted her as she began blending in with everyone else. Then Cindy called out, "Vince Aster and family" from the front door, and she heard more shouting.

She headed into an adjoining den. Just as in the living room, there were glass tables, curved suede seats, and low couches. It was the same furniture, but the couches were all sorts of ridiculous colors—mauve, pink, violet. And the walls here weren't full of windows; they were covered with paintings.

She enjoyed perusing the artwork. Then her mouth fell open when she saw one of the oil paintings. A rush of fear rose to her chest. This painting was of a king wearing a white puffy outfit, like a clown, with a crown on his head, atop a throne over a desert valley. Blood was oozing along the folds and crevices of his obese body. And blood was being splashed on his face. This was her work. In normal circumstances, Mina would have been super honored that Toni had decided to display one of her works. But that's not what made her dizzy. She clenched her fists and shook her head, trying to calm herself. This was her hallucination. This was the vision she had seen when she had been "drunk" with Gail. Why hadn't she put the two images together? She had vaguely recalled painting it years ago, in Paris, but it had been so long ago and she had never associated it with her dream. Of course, in her dream, the clown had been Toni.

Gail had comforted her after that hallucination. Gail who then …

Get it together, Mina. It's just an old painting.

She shook her head, told herself to stop being stupid, and quickly turned and walked back to the living room.

After greeting Daniella and Sonia, who wore lovely long black dresses and were cordial enough—and were easy to identify because, apparently, they were the only ones refusing to wear masks—and being offered hors d'oeuvres and champagne twice, she headed back into the to-die-for main living room.

The view through the walls of windows was so amazing that it calmed her. She took a deep breath, touched the glass, and looked out at the twinkling lights. But she didn't like looking down.

She spotted her beloved park. The yellow-green lights crossing into the rectangle below her were gorgeous. She couldn't imagine affording a place like this. It must have been, like, a hundred million dollars or something.

"Do you like the view?" asked a man quietly behind her. She would have recognized that Italian accent anywhere.

Mina spun around and put her arms around Toni.

He wore a gray satin mask with a matching gray suit. But his beard hinted at his identity. "I'm so glad you came," he whispered in her ear and kissed her gently on the cheek. "I've missed you terribly."

"How did you know it was me?"

"How could I ever not recognize such beauty?"

Mina cocked her head and squinted. She didn't believe him.

"Cindy told me," he confessed.

"Uh-huh. Well, your place is absolutely breathtaking."

"'Tis." He let go of her and looked out the window beside her. "Well, of course, it's a fortune," he said with a smile. They laughed. Then he playfully wagged a finger at her. "You better not disappoint on opening night or I'll have to sell it."

"I'm already under enough pressure as is." She bit her lip.

"I only jest. But why … you're empty-handed." He raised his glass of champagne. "Would you like a drink?"

"Are we celebrating again?"

"Yes. To the future. No doubt the horrible event has rocked the show, but we will persevere. I must say, I wish I could leave and let someone else run everything now. The stress is—"

"Perhaps you should." Mina gestured to the room. "If you can afford all this, maybe you should go to Santorini and let Vince run things."

"I would never let anyone spoil my circus, Mina."

He tapped on the shoulder of a black-suited server. He grabbed a glass of champagne and handed it to Mina. She hadn't drunk anything since that weird night—that night she had seen him in the desert valley like the man in her painting. But, with his smile, she couldn't refuse.

"I saw my painting in the other room," Mina said, sipping her drink. "I noticed it was not far from a Picasso. Picasso, right? Don't tell me the Picasso is an original? Tell me it isn't. And near my work? Toni? Come on. That's quite a ridiculous compliment."

"Yes, it is a Picasso. And yes, it is his original, near Dalí. But no, it isn't ridiculous next to yours. All these paintings are original, so I hung them up. All three are ar-*tists*."

Mina laughed. "You're mad, Toni. Absolutely mad."

"Si." And he raised a glass with a wink.

Then both of them turned and enjoyed the view again. The music changed to "Mary Jane Holland."

"Lady Gaga, Toni?"

"Are you a fan? I figured the crew had enough of Mozart. I suppose I could have played *The Marriage of Figaro*. Or perhaps Copland's *Rodeo*? Whatever the case, we needed something uplifting. I thought this would be fun."

"Yeah, I'm a fan of Lady Gaga."

"Hmm," Toni said with a solemn nod, raising his champagne glass again. "Me too."

Mina chuckled again and said, "Why the masks?"

Toni cocked his head and folded his arms. "I didn't want to be accosted everywhere I went. I didn't want to run the party like I run my show. I wanted to relax. And, sorry, but I didn't particularly want to have to talk to anyone … except you. See…" He put his hand on her shoulder. "Most importantly, Mina, I wanted to spend time with *you*."

Mina blushed. Then he took her hand and played with her fingers. She turned and watched the dancers, on their mini-raised stages, dancing to Lady Gaga. She didn't pull away from his hand.

She laughed.

"What's so funny?" Toni asked. "With everything that's happened, you don't know what it means to me to hear you laugh."

"Toni, it's just … look around. You're absolutely crazy."

"Thank you," he said with a thin smile and a nod.

Then she felt him pressing along the bones of her fingers.

"No, thank *you*, Toni. You're so sweet."

He gently kissed her on the cheek. "Would my star care to dance with me?"

"To this?"

"No, no." Then he gave a playful smile, let go of her hand, and reached into his pants pocket, taking out a remote control.

"I'm beginning to think you had other intentions than just a party this evening, sir."

Toni shrugged and pressed a button. The song wasn't finished and everyone looked around in surprise. Even the dancers on the stages froze. Then Toni pressed a few more buttons and slow music erupted.

Mina recognized it, of course. Rachmaninoff—probably "Piano Concerto Number 2." Yes, that's what it was. A solitary piano played a lovely soft concerto.

"Would you care to dance with me, Ms. Mina Daaé?" Toni reached for her drink. He put both their drinks down on the floor and held her hand again. "There's enough open space in my living room."

Mina shook her head at Toni's bravado. Any other music would have felt contrived and cheesy. But not this one. Mina loved Rachmaninoff. And Toni knew it.

She nodded.

"You make me so very happy."

They walked hand in hand and many turned, noticing the couple. Toni might have been trying to be inconspicuous, but Mina was quite sure, with his beard and his mannerisms, they all knew their producer. He took her to the center of the room, with her hand raised, and many people moved aside, giving them space. Mina reflected that even now, at this very moment, her friend was producing a show. The change in music and the two of them making their way through surprised guests was drawing everyone's attention.

They took center "stage." A few people yelled out "Toni," but she didn't hear anyone mention her name. Perhaps they didn't recognize her.

They did a simple slow dance, on the wood floor, in the middle of his living room. In this area, all the furniture had been cleared for the party. Before, people had been just bobbing their heads or jumping up and down to hip-hop. Now, a few other couples joined them in the slow dance. The rest stood crowded around the room, watching.

"Perhaps you should have included this one in your play," Mina whispered into Toni's ear as they swayed.

"No, no. That would have been theft of a much higher realm, Mina."

"Why?" Mina asked with a chuckle.

"You see," he said, rubbing her back and bringing her closer, "that would have been like recording your voice. Your voice is angelic, touching God. I would have had no right to steal such a bright light."

"I do believe you're flirting with me, Toni."

"I've been very worried about you," he said, sounding serious. "And I've missed you. I've missed you so. Perhaps being away has shown me that."

All eyes in the penthouse were on them as they swayed. But soon, she lost sight of them. She felt only Toni's embrace. His hand on her waist, his body touching hers, and his beard lightly brushing along her cheek. His cologne. And his trained steps. Even this, the simplest slow dance, he danced professionally. And she let him lead her.

She thought of what he had once said to her over dinner. *Dance is like sex.* She felt close to him like that now, moving in step with him, enjoying the sound of his breath and the touch of his fingers on her back. His hands roamed close to her hips. She felt a desire to be closer, not unlike the frenzied desire she had felt in her apartment, but tempered now. Patient. Love? His embrace made her feel better than she had felt in a long time. But they were just friends. She didn't want to lose their friendship like she had with Gail. And then the thought of Gail made her a little nervous.

"Mina, I love you," he whispered in her ear.

And that was far worse. But no one else could have heard him.

"I'm sorry," he quickly said. "I … I love being with you. Close like this. I really do. I really do like you, Mina. I like you a lot."

"Oh, Toni. I know. I like you too." Mina swayed, patting his back. "I like you so much. I'm so grateful for what you've done for me."

She noticed many others dancing around them now. Married couples or dates, it didn't matter; so many couples were slow dancing close to one another. Some were close enough to caress each other, and others were looking deeply into each other's eyes. It was beautiful.

That's when Toni moved back. Someone was tapping on his shoulder.

"Sir, would you mind if I have a dance with this angel?"

It was said so formally, in an old-school manner. And how could a classy man like Toni refuse? But Mina recoiled when she recognized the stranger's French accent and black mask—a tall, strong man in a flashy red suit and a ridiculous red tail. At first glance, the long, shiny, black mask reminded her of her phantom. But that was silly. After all, the man in her head was a figment of her imagination.

Toni nodded and smiled at Mina. "Till the next time," Toni said.

Then the stranger embraced Mina. And he danced as elegantly as Toni, perhaps better, moving professionally with polished grace. He held her close, too. But when he spoke, she recognized his voice again. And that made her shake.

"Lovely Ms. Daaé, I've missed you. I thought the shock would necessitate a break from my appearances, but it's been hard. Dancing with Antonio—well, that was a bit too much."

She didn't stop. She kept in step with him. She just pulled her head back a little to look at him. She stared at his black mask. This one covered nearly his entire face, but it was similar to what he had worn before, though more elegant, decorated with wavy rows of small glistening diamonds. And he had the same glowing green eyes. This was the fiend. This was the monster who had killed Gail. It had to be, but Mina would have had to be insane to accuse him publicly. He was a hallucination, after all. A figment of her imagination who now danced in step with her.

Her thoughts of Gail, her anger, gave her courage to dance on. Without stopping, she said, "My phantom? How did you get in here, Erik?"

"A night with Princess Charming does me wonders, no? It is quite a psychic effort, I can tell you. But seeing you close to my fuck-clown in this gaudy new penthouse provided me just enough impetus to appear before you as Cinderello. For one night, to dance with my Don Juanita. It is a great pleasure to dance with you, Christine."

"Did you kill Gail?"

"So forward." And he actually laughed. "I thought you did? I like how direct you are. Actually, I pity you. I figured from the note that you must think it was you. That maybe you thought you were losing your mind, perhaps? But surely, now that the phantom who wrote it dances with you, you can be reassured that you are not mad. I am here, in the flesh, dancing with Ms. Christine Daaé."

"You do scare me, Erik."

"Don't be frightened," he said almost mockingly. He turned and swayed with her beside another dancer. It was Cindy, smiling at her while dancing with another man. "Gail wasn't killed by me either. Of course it was suicide. She was in love with you, and you rejected her. I watched the two of you fight, by the street, from a window upstairs in the theater that night. I watched her, in a fit of sorrow, head back into the auditorium, tie a belt around her neck on our prized balcony and hang herself. But don't be upset. I mean, you didn't love her. Did you? You're not gay … are you?"

"You do frighten me. What are your intentions? If you love me, why do you torment me?"

"I am a hideous monster behind my mask, just like you and your fuck-clown. Only your masks are more elaborate."

"Why do you call him that?"

"What?"

"A fuck-clown."

"Because he fucks clowns." And he shrugged as if it was a nonsensical question. Then he led her past two other dancers, closer to the window.

"Toni is the nicest man I've ever known."

"Yes. I suppose he's a good faker, like you."

"How do you know him?"

"I was you in Paris." He smiled and backed up enough to show her those beautiful green eyes, which seemed to hypnotize her. She nearly forgot her hatred for a moment. "I was the Harlequin. Ask him."

"I can't believe you are even here."

"I am, Christine. And … do … do you know why?"

Mina didn't answer.

He stopped dancing and stood still, looking deeply into her eyes. His gaze and countenance seemed so serious. "I want to fuck you, Mina. Really badly, actually."

Gail's words. Those were Gail's words. And it even sounded like her voice. That was finally enough for her to break from him.

Was he making fun of her? The cruelty tore her heart. And incensed her.

In a fit of rage, she slapped him as hard as she could across the face, knocking off his black mask. With horror, Mina finally looked upon Erik. She had expected a scar or disfigurement, but it was more than that. Without the mask, his entire face was full of gashes. Not just the single scar on his right side, which his mask covered, but now it seemed his entire face was disfigured and scarred. His lip was deformed, revealing mottled and broken teeth. His nose was missing and his face was swollen. It was so hideous that she turned away and her rage became disgust.

"*Do you see what your fuck-clown did to me, Christine!*"

19

THE BEDROOM

MINA WOKE IN A LARGE BED, FACING A WALL OF WINDOWS LOOKING OVER the twinkling lights of Manhattan. She was lying on top of the covers on the soft bed, still wearing her gold dress. It was oddly quiet. The bedroom was large, with a furry white carpet, modern mahogany furniture, a huge flat-screen TV, and a lovely vanity mirror. It looked like she was still in Toni's suite.

"She's awake," someone said quietly outside the door. "I heard her stir, sir."

When the door to her right creaked open, she feared it would be her ghost. But it wasn't. It was Toni. His mask was off and he was looking down at her with such concern. He had taken off his suit and was wearing just a simple T-shirt and sweats. He sat by the edge of the bed and ran his hand over her shoulder.

"Mina, I think you weren't ready for this."

"Did you see him? Did you see that man? The man who killed Gail?"

"Che?" Toni squinted and quickly shook his head.

"The man I danced with after you."

He shook his head again. "Vince wanted to introduce me to a new actress. There was no one else who danced with you after me. You were alone."

496

"No. It was Erik. I danced with him. The man I danced with was Erik."

His expression of confusion changed to fear. He quickly turned from her.

"What's the matter, Toni? You did see him?"

He shook his head. He laughed nervously. "You're giving me a fright, Mina, saying that name. I wish you wouldn't say that name."

"Erik?"

He nodded and turned back, forcing a smile. "Erik was someone I worked with many years ago."

"Yes!" Mina sat up in bed. "Yes. So you saw him?"

He shook his head. Then he quickly, but gently, took her hand and laid her back down on the bed. He smiled. "Calm down, dear. You have to just rest."

But her heart was racing and she was having trouble breathing. She shook her head. "He came to me tonight. Butted in on our dance. He denied having killed Gail. He said Gail committed suicide."

"Gail did kill herself."

She nodded. "He said he had nothing to do with it. But he started spewing all kinds of things about you. He said he hated you. He called you a fuck-clown. Erik said you—" She stopped.

Toni looked pale and his face looked pained.

"What? What's wrong? I keep seeing him, Toni. God, I'm afraid! I see him in my sleep. I see him, God, I see him everywhere. I hear him in the cab. I hear his voice in the morning. He laughs at me. Taunts me. I hear him in the dark. I see him reflected in the window when the cab takes me to the theater. I must be going crazy … I don't know. I think I … I think I did kill Gail. God! Not because I wanted to. I loved her. But I think I'm losing it. I saw a vision the night before you met Gail. I saw you covered in blood. It was just like your painting, but the clown was *you*. And Erik invited me in to see you bleed. He hates you."

Mina laughed and that seemed to upset Toni even more. "I see him everywhere. I saw him performing the morning I fell during my audition. He's been coming to me ever since you gave me the part. Do you know him? His name is Erik. Erik."

"Erik Belles?" Toni asked, with eyes a little too wide to be normal. "Si. I know Erik Belles. And I remember the words *fuck-clown* too."

"Yes. Yes. Thank God! Maybe I'm not crazy. That's what he said his name is. Erik."

"Erik used to work for me. Where did you hear that slur: *fuck-clown?*"

"He wrote the note, Toni."

Toni took a deep breath and slowly shook his head. "No, Mina. No. He didn't. That's impossible."

"Yes, he did. He said that he came tonight to make me feel better." Mina laughed. "Can you believe that? He's sadistic. He acted like, after he took my hand from you to dance, he acted like he was doing me a favor by seeing me. To prove that I'm not crazy. To prove that I didn't kill Gail. He said that Gail took her own life."

She turned on her pillow and stared at the yellow wall. The yellow in the shadows in the dim evening light matched her golden dress.

She heard Toni breathing but he had stopped talking. He just sat over her, rubbing her shoulders and back.

Most of the light in the dimly lit room was cast by the city lights outside. She looked back at the large window, facing the incredible view.

"Mina, you danced with yourself. You swayed alone. Vince came up to me to introduce me to one of his friends, and we stopped dancing. Then I looked over and caught you just swaying back and forth to the music. I thought you were just enjoying the music, but I saw you close your eyes and put your arms in the air as if around someone. Now I get it. No one thought anything of it, because we love you. But I thought it was odd. Now I understand you thought you were dancing with someone."

"I was!" Mina snapped, spinning around to look at him.

He had a smile now. He was back to being the kind Toni she loved. He gently shook his head.

"Then you went to the window in the living room," Toni continued. "I heard some gasps and rushed back to you. I picked you up from the ground where you had fallen. Then you fainted again in my arms."

"Is this your room?" she asked, looking around.

"Si."

"And the party?" She sat up, but Toni helped her down again. "Oh, I'll get right back to the party. You need to attend to your guests."

"The party ended three hours ago."

Three hours!

That did it. She felt an out-of-body sensation, as if she were finding out that her life was unreal. Like everything was a dream. Like she was falling forever. She needed Erik to pinch her skin again. But this was reality. *Her* reality. Not a dream, or maybe some kind of nightmare. Mina stared at Toni and shook her head.

Ended three hours ago!

She felt a tear on her cheek. Her hands shook. Her heart pounded.

"I'm scared, Toni. I … I don't know what's happening to me. I keep fainting like a stupid, weak girl. And ending up waking in places … and seeing things. What's wrong with me?"

Toni took her shaking hand and leaned down and hugged her gently. Then his eyes teared up too. "I don't know. But it will be all right. Rest. Forget everything. Don't worry. Forget about all of it. I only care about you. You have me so worried. Whatever's happening to you, I think it's the stress of the play. Yes, Gail killed herself. God, Mina, you're dealing with enough. Don't feel guilty, as if that were your fault. It wasn't. Don't ever think that again."

"Maybe it was Erik? I don't like him. I don't trust him."

"It couldn't have been Erik, Mina. Erik died years ago."

20

DINNER AT TONI'S

TONI CONSTANTLY WATCHED OVER MINA THE WHOLE WEEKEND, insisting that she spend the nights as a guest in his own bedroom. He wouldn't let her leave, checking up on her every few hours and having Jacque, his butler, serve her meals as if she were a queen. When Monday morning came, with the return of rehearsals, they were driven to the theater in his Bentley. Then he sat quietly in front-row center seats the whole day, staring up at the stage while she rehearsed the second act under the witch, Daniella. The attention made her feel silly, but she never spoke to him. Come to think of it, she had barely even spoken to him the whole weekend. But when the afternoon rehearsals came to an end, and Daniella wanted to torture her some more with extra evening dance lessons, Toni intervened and took Mina back to his penthouse.

Dinner was incredible. He might as well have met her in a fancy restaurant. They sat alone every night, like tonight, in a dining room with a wall of glass affording a gorgeous view of the twinkling lights of the New York skyline. Toni sat across from her at the middle of a long oak dining table that looked like an antique. Behind him was the breathtaking vista of Manhattan.

Jacque brought in an ornate dish of roasted duck decorated in garnish, surrounded by feathers, on a silver tray. Jacque was a short man with auburn hair and a mustache, wearing a black suit with a tail. He methodically cut two slices of meat and placed them on silver plates. Then, ridiculously, he cut them into small, edible pieces. He put a serving of fresh, steamy bite-sized potatoes, green beans, carrots, and kale on each plate. Then he drizzled a sauce over their steamy plates. No, the finest restaurant could not have served her better. Red wine was poured in two lovely crystal glasses.

Far in the background, Mina heard music—Mozart, of course. It was so elegant. But the funniest thing about the whole affair was that Toni was wearing a black T-shirt and gray sweats. And Mina had on a simple silk blouse and black slacks. She had even washed off most of her casual makeup after the rehearsal. But Toni had readied himself in his room before dinner, showering, combing his short hair perfectly, and even applying cologne. It might have been casual, but the restaurant ambiance made it feel a little like a date.

"I really should go after this," Mina said.

"No." Toni smiled, biting into the duck, and raised a finger. "No, no. Stay. Stay longer. Please. You've given me such a scare, Mina. Once I know you're better, you can go. Consider this insurance. I must help the star of my show."

"Well, you've helped, Toni." She chuckled. "Thank you. You've helped a lot. And you're right. After yesterday, it would have been hard for me to come in today."

"So," he said with a grin and a broad hand gesture. "What's the problem? Mi casa, su casa, as they say. I'll wait for whatever it takes for you to recover."

"Okay, Toni."

"You did very well today. I feel like the show is going so much better now. There's less of a shadow in the air from what happened. I know the dancers, at least, are back to laughing."

"And I'm singing."

"Si," he said with a warm smile. "I couldn't ask for more than that. Things are starting to settle back in again."

"For sure."

She dipped the duck in the sauce at the edge of her plate. It was exquisite. "I heard Vince is spreading gossip around that I have seizures to explain my falls?"

"Could be true," Toni said with a shrug. "Of course, I don't want anything to be wrong with you, but it would be nice if there was an explanation. Do you want me to go with you to your appointment with the doctor Thursday?"

"Oh stop, Toni. You've done enough already."

"You could have some sort of seizure condition, you know. I'm so worried about you."

She sipped some wine and nodded. The red wine was smooth and delightful. "Wouldn't it be nice if all I needed was medication? I don't know. I'm just worried that if I faint again, it could ruin the show."

"Stop worrying. Everything will be fine." He smiled but his grin was fake.

Toni was more worried about this show than anyone else.

It fell silent. Mina didn't mind. She just heard the sound of their silverware scraping the plates. And lovely Herr Mozart playing in the background.

She gazed in rapture at the view behind him while enjoying every morsel on her silver fork, all the while catching his stray glances at her. Indeed, she was grateful. He cared about her. But she felt uncomfortable when their eyes met in the candlelit room.

"How did you know Erik?" she asked.

That question seemed to be the last thing he'd expected. He lost his smile. Then he wiped his beard and quickly turned to the window. "We shouldn't talk about that. It, it, could bring back what happened."

"I know. But Toni, I feel like if you tell me, I'll be less worried. If he's real, maybe I'm not crazy, you know? Just like seizures. Maybe there's something going on that can help explain things? I mean, it's not just Gail now. I'm freaked out about sleeping for so long through the party. I still don't even know what happened."

He nodded slowly but hesitated. "You don't understand. I wasn't only talking about you. I don't want to bring back what happened between Erik and *me* either."

"Please, Toni. Tell me. How did you know him?"

"He was a good friend," he said with a sigh. "Like you. But it was years ago. You remember my calls? I told you about a man I had met who could both dance and sing. A man who was the shining light of my show."

"Yes. I think I remember. Tell me about him."

He nodded. Then he traced the stem of his wine glass with his finger, staring at it.

After he didn't say anything, Mina said quietly, "Please, Toni."

"In Paris…" He stuffed some meat into his mouth, looking like it was more of a chore than a pleasure. "We had the circus, if you remember. I worked on it while I taught. Loved it. But I didn't focus everything on it until after you left."

"So you said. You stopped teaching."

"Yeah," he said with a nod. "Well, after I met him, I decided to devote everything to the show. Erik was a unique soul. A boy bounding with energy."

Mina dipped more delicious meat into the sauce and tasted it.

He sighed. "We met in a café, of all places. Not the theater. Over cappuccinos, we hit it off. I tell you, he had so much energy, it was infectious.

"But I didn't know at the time he was destitute. No, not just destitute … desperate. He had run from affluence, preferring madness. You know, what we call *art*. He had no money. Everything was about art. But watching him, even that first time in the café, made me realize that, like you, he was a star."

"Really, Toni?" she said with a chuckle, feeling her cheeks blush. "Like me? How? How could you tell? Especially in a café?"

"I just knew."

"And like me?"

"Look at you. Your voice is not the only thing that touches God. Look at your face."

"Please, Toni," she said, turning from him.

"'Tis true. Anyway, I'm quite astute at finding talent. And beauty. Erik and you." He stopped and drank wine pensively. Then he took a deep breath and turned away from her, preferring the view again.

The butler returned, swinging open the door. It was so still that, even though he had just walked through the door, it felt like he was bounding in a rush. "Antonio, are you and Ms. Daaé going to want chocolate soufflé? I need time to prepare."

Toni turned back to Jacque with a faint smile and said, "No. Thank you." But then he squinted at Mina. "Oh, but how 'bout you?

Jacque makes an incredible chocolate soufflé. You really should taste it."

"No. I don't think I'll fit in my costume if I do that."

"Just coffee, Jacque," Toni said with a laugh. "With perhaps a pinch of chocolate."

Toni sat sideways, looking outside, sipping more red wine and staring pensively out the window again. It was as if he was done with his story.

"He had acted in various plays," he continued. "But his true talent was dance. He was so graceful, incredible movement, so flexible and fluid. I never would have thought someone could move like that. Especially a man. It was so odd that a dancer with so much talent met me in a simple café." He sighed, forked a couple of potatoes, and ate some. Then, with his mouth full: "I got to know him. We became the best of friends. You can figure out the rest. That's all."

It didn't sound like that was all. It sounded like there was hours more.

"He probably met you on purpose at the café," Mina said. "You were known for the theater even when I was your student."

"I thought that. I suppose, after seeing him perform so well at the audition, it sure seemed planned to me too at the time, though."

"Rehearsal or audition?"

"Audition." Toni laughed. "I hadn't seen him perform like I saw you perform in the university, darling. He was good. Incredible. I was shocked at his gracefulness. In tights, he danced elegantly, even better than you."

"Really?"

"Even besting my angel, Mina, si. Well, you can guess where this is going. I hired him for the show."

"I remember you telling me about a dancer after I came to New York. You fell in love with him, if I remember?"

He looked disturbed by that. He ran his hand over his head and shook it quickly, turning stern again. "Mina, I don't want to talk about this."

"No, please. Please go on. I feel like if I know, I'll better understand who this man is and why his ghost is haunting me."

"There's no ghost. Erik never went to the US. He was born in Strasbourg. He could barely speak English. Whatever vision you saw, it wasn't Erik. Could be a phantom, like the legendary phantom that haunted your great-ancestor Christine. But not my Erik. Unless you spoke with him in French."

"I speak to him in English most of the time. He has an accent. I speak to his ghost. And he wears a mask too."

"Oh Mina, come on."

"You saw the note. You know it wasn't you. So either I'm insane or there's a ghost haunting our play. Please go on. Tell me so you can prove I'm not crazy. Is he the man you fell in love with?"

"You're not crazy."

"Then tell me. Was this the man you spoke of that you fell in love with?"

He didn't respond. But that was the answer.

Mina dipped some potato into the sauce. The sauce was salty and sharp. Exquisite. She could have just dipped the fork in the sauce and enjoyed it alone. She ate more and, for the moment, didn't care if Toni stopped telling his story. It was all so delicious.

"He played the Harlequin," Toni finally admitted. "He had your role."

Mina had a little difficulty swallowing. The role that Erik had told her, time and time again, would make her fall.

"And … I suppose he knew me as well as you do. Si, if my Erik was conjured up from the grave, he could have written that note."

"Tell me about him."

"Mina."

"Please."

"I loved him." He flashed a fake smile. "I'm not really gay, but you should have met him. If you knew him, you'd understand. Any man would have been attracted to him."

"I don't have a problem with whether you're gay. I'm not anti-gay."

Of course she wasn't. She had sex with Gail before she died. And, for a second, Toni looked at Mina smugly, as if thinking—*obviously*.

"I'm not gay," he replied. "I don't have a problem with it either. But I'm not gay. I don't even think I'm bisexual. I experimented, I suppose. It's … it's difficult to explain. Erik was more than a man or a woman. He was…" Toni raised his hand, staring at his fingers, trying to gesture something to make Mina understand, but then his hand dropped. He smiled. "He was a god. An Adonis. Like the *David*. You should have seen him. Pretty and handsome. Exuberant. All of it. Our theater was a paltry dump of rats, dust, and filth at the time. And so, when Erik performed his ballet, the audience thought they were going to see a circus. No. No, not Erik. When the light shone over him, my Erik, just Erik in the center of the stage, he held everyone's attention with his perfection. Everything—the seats, the audience, everything in the auditorium—became unimportant. Only Erik's movements mattered. He was more like a light than a human form; he moved as if he wore skates: gliding, jumping, and twirling, as fast and smooth as an ice skater. It was something I had never seen—something I will never see again. They watched him spin and twirl. He was so good. All eyes turned to him, just as all ears turn to you.

"Many of the movements Daniella showed you were choreographed by him. He was our original choreographer. You once asked why I stole from Mozart. I didn't. No. No, I stole from my Erik."

He fell silent again, just nodding to himself.

Mina stared at him in the dim light of the room. She didn't care for the view or the food anymore. She was captivated by him and this story.

He was so serious, almost solemn. It was a side of Toni she didn't see often except, when she thought of it, when he was alone with her.

But most importantly, for the first time in months, someone was talking about her hallucinations. Perhaps she wasn't crazy? Whatever the case, it was quite clear that Toni had loved this man.

"Toni, did you have a falling out with him?" Mina finally asked. "Is that why you never mentioned him again?"

"Fall? No … I loved him."

"Then what happened?"

"A fall," Toni said, chuckling and nodding. "Hmm. Si, si, indeed, that's it, Mina. It was a fall, but not over love. I told you my circus in Paris was in the American style, where classical music did not fit jugglers and acrobats. The introduction with the ballet pieces was different. It was the opposite of our Broadway play. In Paris, it was a circus invaded by Mozart; in Broadway, it's Mozart invaded by the Big Top. Of course, Erik exhibited high class with his feet. But, well, one night he fell from the tightrope in the third act. Unlike you, he had no net."

"Oh no," Mina cried, putting her hand over her mouth.

"He was instantly paralyzed. He never danced again."

"Oh my God."

"Si. He never walked again." And that was too much. Toni put his head in his hand. Then, in a broken voice, he said, "And he blamed me, Mina."

"I'm so sorry, Toni."

"It's been so long, I thought I had gotten over this. When you fell, it brought the horror right back to me."

"Can you describe him?"

"Che?" he asked, looking up in surprise. "Why? … I did. He was the most beautiful man I had ever known. What more can I say?"

"No, I mean, can you actually describe his features."

Jeesh, can you be any colder, Mina. But I have to know!

"Toni, I saw him during the audition. Or I dreamt him up. Then I danced with him in your house. I even see him in my dreams. Can you tell me what he looked like?"

"Why?"

"Did he have bright-green eyes? And a goatee?"

Toni stared at her and grew pale again. He didn't say a word.

"And scars running from his forehead down his right cheek? A disfigurement along his nose?"

"Stop," Toni cried. He jumped up. "Stop it."

"Toni, I'm sorry, I—"

He stared up at the ceiling and cried, "Mio dio! Mi perseguiti anche adesso?" And he slammed his fists against the window overlooking the view.

"I don't speak Italian, Toni."

Mina jumped when the dining room door swung open. Jacque walked in, carrying another silver tray. This one had two white porcelain mugs and a silver coffee brewer. He poured fresh coffee into both cups.

"Give her a little chocolate," Toni said dismissively with his back still turned.

Jacque smiled at Mina and nodded.

Toni ran his hand along his beard, staring out the window. "Jacque knows just the right amount to make it exquisite."

"What is it, Toni?" she asked him, as the butler drizzled melted chocolate in her cup. "I … I don't know Italian."

Toni sat back down and ran his hands through his short, feathery hair. "Did you see footage from the old show? That must be it. I thought everything had been taken down from so long ago. I tried to get rid of everything."

"I didn't."

Jacque bowed and quickly left the room.

"Of course he had a scar on his face," he answered, as if she were dumb. "A head injury. Probably much more damage underneath. He was never the same after the fall. I told you, he never walked again. And a joyful man became depressed and bitter. As tragic as Gail, I guess. And green eyes. Yes, the brightest green I had ever seen."

"So, it is him. What happened? How did my phantom die?"

"No," Toni said, shaking his head. "Not your phantom. Stop this! I can't believe you saw him. It's just not true. You must have seen an old picture of the performance."

"Is that any better? Then we're back to me being crazy. That's why I have to know."

"Please, Mina, not tonight. Let's not talk any more of this."

He made his way around the table and crouched down on a knee, leaned over, and gently kissed her cheek. "Goodnight, cara Mina. You can use my bed again. I am so happy for you to stay with me one more night."

"Wait a minute." Mina snatched his arm. "What happened to him? You're not finished. You said he never danced again. You didn't say how he died. Oh Toni, tell me. How did he die? Please. You have to tell me!"

"Just know that he died. There's nothing else to tell."

And he was going to get up, but she grabbed him again. She shook her head. Then she ran her hand along his short, feathery hair. "I'm staying for you to help me, right?" she asked. "To feel better? So finish your story. I need to know what happened to him. If I can put reality into this, then I'll know that, perhaps, I'm not crazy."

"Mina, please. Forget it."

"You have to!" Mina snapped. She searched his eyes. He actually smiled at her outburst. Oh, she adored Toni. They never fought. Even when he had taught her onstage and she forgot lines, he was always patient, respectful, and kind. But she had to know.

How did Erik die? How was his ghost a threat to her?

He started getting up again. This time she brought him close and pressed her lips hard against his. He gasped in surprise, blowing against her lips. Then she pressed harder, licking and bringing her tongue along his while she pulled his body close. She ran her fingers along his short hair again as she kissed him.

"Tell me," she said between kisses. "Or else."

"Or else, what?" he asked, laughing. "What are you talking about?"

"Or else I'm fucking you in your dining room."

"Mina, you *are* crazy." And he laughed nervously, backing away. "I don't have to tell you anything anymore. You just proved you are crazy."

They laughed again. But she pressed her lips passionately on his again, as if ready to carry out her threat.

"There's not much else to tell," he said, gently pulling from her. He looked down for a moment and lost his smile. "It's terrible."

"Please, Toni."

"I ruined his life. He turned to drinking. He lived off the streets. He sold himself." He turned his head from her and tried to get up, but Mina kept a vise-like grip around his arm. He looked down at it and nodded slowly. "Soon he really didn't have to blame me—I blamed myself. Time passed and I missed him. I loved him. Si. I will always love him. Just as I will always love you. But more, I felt responsible. The stagehands were paid a paltry wage. The horrible mistake and neglect in safety wasn't all that surprising."

And he met her gaze. Tears were forming in his eyes, and it made her want to weep too.

"I just didn't have the money … One day, on a frigid, snowy day, I saw him near the theater. He was without shelter. I took him in. Cared for him. Let him stay with me, like I am letting you stay with me now. And finally, in the evening, I asked him what I could do to fix this. I told him I'd do anything for him." He laughed bitterly. "He suggested the one thing I didn't want to do. He wanted to perform in my play again. What's more, he wanted to go up to that pedestal. Of course I refused.

We fought, as we often did. He called me a *fuck-clown*. Eventually, after being called enough stupid names and being reminded far too many times that he had nothing left to live for because of what I had done to him, I capitulated.

"He thought of singing *Don Giovanni*. He couldn't dance, but he could sing. He may not have had the voice you have, but he had vision. So you see, it was not Herr Mozart that I had robbed; it was Erik. We had used Mozart, snippets from *The Marriage of Figaro*, with our choreography for years, but never *Don Juan*. But Erik *was* Don Juan, for women and men. Literally a living libertine, more so than anyone I had ever known. Even with his disfigurement, his body was attractive. And he had used sex to woo both men and women, even as a paraplegic. Now, asking to be back in my play, he wanted to fight his challenge and conquer it. So he devised a plan to sing up on that ledge. It was a way to thumb his nose at death."

He stopped and lowered his head onto her shoulder.

"Oh, Toni."

"At first, I didn't want to do it. I thought it was a terrible idea. He wanted to go right back up to the pedestal where he had fallen. We'd have to carry him up the ladder for the final act.

"It was this performance, Mina, that got us our fame. We made the fall as real as we could, just like in our Broadway play. The audience filled the stadium and watched the whole show just to see our finale. Whereas before they had watched his body, now they listened to his voice and his performance. Just as they do with you now. The strange accompaniment of Mozart and the Big Top. The singing was scant in the rest of the play, but we gathered up all the money we could for the finale, even adding an orchestra. I felt I owed him. Hell, I told you, I would have done anything to make him better. And it worked, for a little while. The audience loved him. It was such a bizarre twist in the act. I heard his voice and it touched God, like yours. He was so talented, Mina. He was, like you, a star."

He paused. But then ... he wept bitterly.

"Oh, Toni, what's the matter?" She embraced him while he was still on his knees, crying.

"That ... that is how he died," he said, with a shaking voice, between sobs. "I killed him. That's why I didn't want to say. It was because of me. It was my fault. You asked. That's how he died. He gave up, not only because he couldn't walk, but because he couldn't dance. His dream. The singing was a temporary thing. I destroyed him."

He stopped talking and wept more in Mina's arms. Then, when finally able to speak again, he said, "One night, we had a huge fight. You see, despite success, he told me many times that all he had ever wanted to do was dance. I had destroyed that. He drank too much, as he often did. But the intensity of the fight was different. We carried him to the top of the tightrope pedestal in the final scene, as we always had. Of course, now there was a net below. Only he made sure to cut it on that final night. I should have known. He said it would be the best show ever. He kissed me before we went on and whispered in my ear, 'in boca al lupo,' which in Italian is like saying 'break a leg.' The whole end performance was no longer a ruse. It was real."

Toni stopped talking. He even stopped crying. He just froze in her arms.

"God, Toni, I'm so sorry." She kissed his forehead. "Forgive me for asking. Forgive me."

"No. No. I understand."

She didn't let him go. She held him like a mother holds a baby, cuddling and swaying, back and forth, with him in her arms. She went right back to kissing him, now gently along his beard, neck, and forehead. She held him tight.

"You're too good to me," he said.

"Me? How could you say that, Toni? After everything you've done for me here, how can you say that?"

"I don't know how you saw him. I tried to get rid of all traces of him. Not because I didn't love him, but because of what I did to him. I couldn't face seeing him. I couldn't look at him … It was my fault. *Fuck-clown*, indeed. I didn't want to be reminded … of what happened."

Toni gently pushed Mina away. "The show went on. His show. And you know what? It became more popular after he died. Despite what happened, in honor of him, we didn't change the ending. I know that's what he would have wanted. You know the rest. My friends pulled together all their money and used a different ensemble. *The Harlequin* took off in Europe. I only wish he had been alive to see it."

"I'm so sorry, Toni."

She kissed him gently again. He nodded. She turned his head and their lips met. She ran her hand under his T-shirt and felt his belly and chest. She cradled his head in her arms again.

"I'm sorry I made you tell me."

"Whatever is happening," he said, hugging her close, whispering in her ear, "I do believe his spirit visits you. Whether in your mind or as a ghost, I believe the phantom haunts you. I don't think you're crazy. And I wish he'd stop."

"It must be Erik. Thank you for telling me."

Their kisses became more passionate, and they groped each other harder. Mina ran her hand under his shirt, rubbing his belly again. Her hand wandered over his back and along his hip. Then she touched his pants and rubbed over his cock.

"Oh, Mina." He laughed nervously. "I'm just a foolish old man."

"You've been so kind to me. First the part, then the support when Gail died. Why? Why are you so nice to me? I don't deserve you."

"I don't deserve you." He started to smile but then became very serious.

Their eyes were locked.

Her heart raced. "Why did you do this for me? Why have you been so patient with me, Toni?"

"I care about you."

"No," she whispered. She kissed his lips again. "It's more, isn't it? You're not a shy man. What did you say while we danced? Or did I dream that too?"

"What? I don't remember."

"You remember." She brought his lips to hers, hard, again. Then she ran her hand down toward his pants. She reached under the sweatpants and ran her fingers along the skin of his hard cock. He moaned. "What did you say when we danced? Say it. Say it to me again. Please, Toni. I want to hear that too. Do you remember? What did you say?"

She gently pulled down his sweatpants and held the bulge in his underwear.

"Mina, I'm an old man."

"That's not what you said."

"I said I love you. Ti amo. I love you. But ... I haven't been with anyone since Erik. I can't ask anything from anyone anymore."

She shook her head and unbuttoned her blouse. He stared at her bra. Then she helped pull off his shirt.

"Don't blame yourself, Toni. It's not your fault."

There was no more crying. Just the two of them in the quiet room, making out like school kids for the longest time. But it was funny, because neither could go any further. She didn't care. She wanted to kiss forever. Mina figured that they both still feared damaging their friendship. And yet they couldn't disengage.

Then he surprised her. With her eyes closed, kissing his lips, she felt her body being lifted onto the table. She sat on the wooden table while they resumed kissing. She felt wet between her legs. "I think I'm in love with you, Toni. No … I know I am. I love you too."

"We don't have to do this," he said, backing up and looking seriously into her eyes.

She answered him by reaching back and unclasping her bra, throwing it to the side. His eyes stared hungrily at her naked breasts. Then—in the frenzy, she wasn't sure if he took them off or she did— her slacks were unzipped and pulled down. Then came her lace panties. She was naked, sitting on the table in his elegant dining room. He ran his hands along her nude body as she cocked her head back, looking at the to-die-for view of the city.

"Here?" he asked, dipping down and sucking her nipple. "Now?"

"Sure." Then she smiled. "I saw how you looked at me in rehearsal today. Please take me. I said the dining room, remember?"

"You said if I didn't tell you." He laughed between kisses. "I told you."

Then she felt a hand along the curves of her boobs as another touched between her legs. She moaned.

"You are beautiful. So beautiful, Mina."

"Touch me. Yes. Rub me. Do it. Harder."

He obliged. His other hand ran down to her waist; then she arched up and he ran his hand along her ass. He settled between her legs and rubbed her gently like she had once rubbed him in her apartment. His finger ran along her crotch and then entered her.

"Harder," she whispered in his ear. "Yes, Toni. Inside. Please. Fuck me."

He obliged. She felt his finger wander inside and out while they met each other's lips yet again. Her butt was pressed against the cold wooden table as she arched her back and pressed her breasts against his chest. She felt his finger, then two, deeper inside her, and she moaned. She moaned louder, but he stifled her orgasms with his lips and tongue. He rubbed repeatedly, faster, until her whole body lurched up into his hand with her final orgasm.

She closed her eyes for a moment and took a deep breath. Then she looked at him. His eyes were still bloodshot, but hungry, as they gazed at her tits and along her naked body. "That was so good. Oh, God, Toni, that was good … So good … Now take me inside. Fuck me on your table." She said it almost in a whisper. "Please. Fuck me, now."

She closed her eyes. There was a pause, almost a hesitation, where all she felt was his hand caressing her hips and his warm breath. His hands moved along her legs and touched her breasts. His hard cock brushed against her knee. He grasped her waist, and she sucked his tongue, kissing him in rapture.

He entered her and pushed into her as she flexed her butt against the hard table. She ran her hands along his ass and felt the crack as it flexed. He moved in and out of her. He moaned. Then he caressed her breasts again, running his lips down to her hard nipples and sucking them while continuing to thrust hard inside.

As he moved closer, breathing heavily, she heard the door. She looked over as the door cracked open, but it quickly shut.

The interruption didn't stop Toni. But he was careful, so gentle, even now. He ran a finger delicately along her face, as if tracing her, while he closed his eyes and thrust. Mina imagined he was feeling the curves and texture of her so he could recreate it in a painting or a sculpture later. His finger glided over her thin eyebrows and ran along her lips. She touched the hairs along his chest and wrapped her arms around him, embracing him and bringing him closer. She heard the sound of them together, their wetness, while his fingers traced over her sharp nose. Then his fingers brushed her cheek and slipped inside her mouth. She sucked a finger as he continued to thrust.

Then she closed her eyes and glided her fingers along his face, doing the same to him. She ran her fingers over his bushy beard and his eyebrows, then along the soft, feathery hair of his head, which she loved. She opened her eyes, and he was smiling at her as his whole body pushed into her faster. Harder. She groaned with the pleasure she so desired. That seemed to spur him on more. Again and again, he moved inside her until she grabbed him with the sudden animalistic fervor she'd felt when she'd thrown him against the wall of her apartment months before. She pulled him in as close as she could, lifting herself onto him hard, and that's when she felt him quake and orgasm inside her.

"Oh, Toni."

"I love you," he said. He leaned over her, panting. "I love you, so much."

But as he leaned on his side, he opened his eyes wide all of a sudden, seemingly confused, almost afraid.

"What's the matter, babe?" she asked, running her hand along his thin hair.

"There wasn't any protection," he said, shaking his head.

"I don't care." She leaned her head against his and smiled. Then she turned and kissed his lips. "Even if we make a baby, I love you, Toni. I know that now. I wouldn't ever regret it. I love you. I love you so much."

"Yes. I love you, Mina."

21

———

THE YELLOW WALLPAPER

MINA BLINKED HER EYES, GAZING UP AT A SINGLE MAPLE BEAM RUNNING along the center of a vaulted wooden ceiling. She was sunk in the most comfortable mattress she'd ever lain on in her life, digging her head into the softest of pillows. It was quiet. In front of her, through the wall of windows, was an absolutely breathtaking morning view of New York City. She stretched her arms, wearing a soft, white satin camisole. Then she realized she had woken up alone. This was a surprise, for Toni had slept with her every night since their romantic dinner.

The sound of squeaky wheels and the clang of porcelain, or glass, made her turn toward the door to her right. Jacque, wearing what seemed to be the same suit he had worn last night, quietly lifted a silver lid from a plate on a wheeled cart. She stretched and yawned again.

"Oh, mademoiselle, I'm sorry to have woken you."

"Do you know what time it is, Jacque?"

"Around eleven thirty."

"Oh, God, I slept in that long?"

"Don't fret. Mr. Vollini wants you to rest. It's Saturday. He wants you to take the whole day off."

"He's too good to me."

"Me too," Jacque said with a gentle smile.

Then she remembered. Just as he had insisted on her sleeping over, he had insisted she not work this weekend. She imagined the stir this must have caused the crew, particularly her choreographer bitch, Daniella, who had asked for additional practices over the weekend.

"I think I could sleep all day here," she said with a yawn, turning on her side and digging her head back into her pillow.

"Perhaps you should. Don't worry yourself, Miss Daaé. Mr. Vollini said he'd return around five. He only desires that you rest."

And with that, the butler dipped his head, his short hair perfectly groomed, and walked out of the room, closing the door behind him.

Mina eventually removed the covers, crawled out of bed, and enjoyed the feel of the soft, fluffy white carpet under her naked feet. She dug her toes along the floor, its softness and thickness reminding her of a puppy. Then she headed to the window.

She didn't like how high up she was, but the view of the skyscrapers and buildings below was breathtaking. Then she noticed what had gotten her up. It wasn't Jacque's tray; it was the smell of bacon and eggs. All the food at Toni's was pure heaven.

Toni had been so nice to her. He had such a gentle heart. That made him very attractive. Not his features so much. He was a bit overweight, and his beard and eyebrows were a bit too bushy. But it wasn't about looks. It was his smile, his lovely accent, his energy and, more so, his heart. For the first time since they had met, so many years ago, she considered that she could love him. Yes, she could do that.

She stood over the silver tray. Jacque had carefully arranged lovely garnishes around two open porcelain egg jars with coddled eggs. The porcelains were intricately decorated with drawings of two children playing, a boy and a girl. And beside the jars were three strips of bacon and two biscuits.

"You're going to spoil me rotten, Toni." She giggled in delight.

The tray had been placed next to the bed, and there was even a bed tray latched to the side of the cart. Mina didn't use that. She grabbed one of the jars, still hot, and jumped back on the heavenly mattress, staring out at the view. Then she ate her eggs. Of course the eggs were exquisite.

After breakfast, she considered getting dressed, but the lull of the room's comforts, the soft bed, and the silence made her lean back on her side and close her eyes. But she didn't sleep. She kept opening and closing them.

She lay facing the yellow wallpaper. It was darker, almost the color of brass, at night, but now that the sun shone through the window, it was like a bright lemon. She stared at it. It almost tasted sour along her tongue. She peered at all the thin white lines of intricate patterns that looked like webs. The patterns reminded her of the white webbed patterns over the scarlet carpet of the theater. Her eyes grew heavy and she saw that some of the lines overlapped, creating 3D images.

Doing nothing. Maybe this is the quiet I need, Toni. I could do this all day.

In a dreamy state, perhaps asleep, she imagined one of the lines shaped like a wrinkled old man. The upside-down cone-like head had sunken eyes, a warty, pointy nose, and a large toothless grin. Beside the face was a balloon—a yellow balloon, of course—that floated beside the old geezer, on a string, in the wind. And next to that was a stairwell into some sort of circular tunnel.

She refocused her eyes on the stairs. The wall's strange figures seemed to fade back into lines. Replacing them was a vertical uneven crevice, fading in and out, where she had imagined the steps. She might have drifted off for a little bit. Now she blinked her eyes again, trying to make out the figure of the old man. He was gone.

Then she furrowed her brow at the strangest sight. Where she had seen a blurry crevice in the wall, within an arm's distance, there seemed to be a small gap. She reached out to touch the opening in the wall, laughing at herself for being stupid and daydreaming. But then she lost her smile as she watched her hand pass right through.

She snatched her hand back. She jumped up in bed, but she couldn't tear her eyes away from the wall. Slowly, she took her covers off and stood in the small space between the bed and the wall. She ran her hand along the wall again. And once more, her hand passed through a crack. Not only that, now that she was closer, she was able to reach her entire arm inside. It passed through and vanished behind the wall.

Oh, Mina, you're asleep, dreaming … or you're crazy.

She turned back and looked at the room. She saw the tray beside the closed door, the stunning view of Manhattan, and Toni's huge bed. The same lovely bedroom.

She walked through the wall.

She entered a tunnel that descended into an earthen chamber. The dirt walls were glowing the same saffron as the wallpaper. She looked down and saw that she still wore her white camisole and underwear. She pinched her arm, remembering what Erik had done before her adventure at the club. But she didn't wake up in bed.

Her legs moved her toward a brighter light ahead. She squinted then closed her eyes, hoping to open them back in bed. The floor was a little rough, dirty, and cold under her bare feet. Her eyes adjusted to the light, and she found herself at the end of the hall, where the passageway led to a cliff ledge. Below the ledge was a deep chasm surrounded by earthen walls. A valley. The very bottom seemed to move. A thousand snakes slithered under her … no, they were human forms. Muddy, filthy, nude bodies, with their faces dripping tar in that strange blackness again, embracing, kissing, or hugging, and making love with one another. Toward the center was a single concrete pedestal of equal footing to her ledge. It seemed artificial, maybe plastic, in the earthen cave. And upon the concrete platform sat a man—a naked man with legs dangling over the ledge across from her. He was strong with broad shoulders, muscular arms and legs, and ripples along his stomach. And he wore a black ceramic mask and was staring at her with bright-green eyes.

"Where am I, Erik? Is this another dream?"

"Not a dream, mademoiselle," he said, waving a finger. "Real. Your empathic powers call me. Just as we danced in the club. Not a vision, Christine. Real. A real place."

He vanished from the ledge. Then she jumped as she felt fingers run along her cheek. He grasped her shoulder and held her, gesturing to the vast valley below. She tried to escape his grasp, but he locked her in his arms.

"What do you see? Tell me. Lust. Do you see it? Don Juan y Don Juanita? I live an eternity watching all the women and men fuck. Not in fantasy, Christine, but *my* reality. My pleasure." He turned her face, only his mask shading those jade eyes.

She looked down at his naked body.

He followed her glance and smiled. Then he wagged a finger. "But you haven't been guiltless either, have you? Gail. Now Toni. Many more. Love? Or is it lust, Ms. Daaé?"

"What I do is my business."

"Look again," he said, gesturing below. "We are all the same behind the mask. All bodies are a pit of vipers, slithering and sucking. You are Christine, Don Juanita. I am Erik, Don Juan triumphant. None of us ever changes. Neither time nor place alters the base nature of what we truly are. So many bodies below. Come join us and we shall bask in pleasure."

"To die?" she asked, turning from his hungry gaze, furrowing her brow at the bizarre pit below. She tried once more to escape his grasp but she couldn't.

"No," he replied. "Not die. To return to the garden of pleasure."

"Take me away from here," she said, turning her head from him. "Please, Erik. If you truly care for me. What do you want? Why do you keep tormenting me?"

"You visited him. Now I want you to visit me. Here." He smiled as he spoke, his demeanor oddly docile. "With your voice and my fury, I shall show myself one last time to your audience. For them, faker, I shall appear only once. Behold, that will be enough. When they see me one last time on stage opening night, I shall take you down, down with me. Down here. Here we may stay for all eternity."

And he gestured once more.

"But why? All I want is for you to leave me alone." She closed her eyes. "Please let go of me."

"But I am here," he whispered in her ear. "You cannot escape. No matter where you hide, harlequin, you cannot escape. On your opening night, you shall reveal yourself, faker: wear the makeup, don the mask, climb to your pedestal, and fall. You will do this because you and I are the same. As much as you want to turn from me, from my features, one day you shall don your own black mask. Do not judge me, devil, for I am you. You, too, should hide your face from what you have done to bring about your fall. To every man, every cunt, every soul that you presumed to love, as they bear witness to the pit of your fall, you viper, you faker, you harlequin, you fuck-clown."

∾

"Are you done with the tray, madam?" Jacque's voice seemed shrill and made her jump.

She opened her eyes and awoke with a start in Toni's bed.

She turned and just quietly nodded. He collected it, bowed, and wheeled it out. She turned back to the wall and saw a large, dark, earthen tunnel. And then it was gone, revealing only the yellow wallpaper.

22

THE NIGHT

After rehearsing for months, it was very hard for Mina to realize that tonight, right now, was *the night*. The night of *The Harlequin*. Not being in the first act, she looked out from the shadows beside the stage to watch her friends dance or sing.

The acrobat she had befriended, Trist, jumped as much as she twirled, doing amazing contortionist acrobatics, bending her body in half and moving about on her hands. Trist had been in a Cirque du Soleil performance for many years. It had enabled her to work with a bunch of bent white rods that she had fashioned around her body. Wearing white tights and in clown face, she gave a performance that was unique and very strange—very *"Toni."*

Then there were the two strong men—giant men, really—who pushed a cart of five short men to a fire truck that was on fire. And a juggler who juggled with fire beside a fake conflagration. And the tightrope, taken out for the first time before her final number, with four tightrope walkers climbing on top of each other. That made Mina laugh when she thought of her own fears of just singing up on the ledge.

"You better go finish up, Mina," said Henson, gently tapping her shoulder with a smile. "You're up in only another fifteen minutes."

Mina nodded.

"I'm so proud of you," he added. "You're gonna be fantastic."

But she must have looked nervous. Why else would he say that?

Mina tore her eyes away from Toni's circus. His *real* circus. Toni had told her that Act I was really his "macaroni and cheese." The only thing elegant, as of yet, was the orchestra playing Mozart in the background. The rest of the circus was the same as five years before in France.

After Mina changed into her ridiculous heavy gilded scarlet dress and used the restroom in her dressing room a couple of times, she walked to backstage, stage left, and waited painfully as twenty people behind her either stood readying themselves to walk out carrying her tail or inspected the gigantic gauche thing over her shoulder to make sure it was ready for her grand entrance.

As Mina fought with her body, which wanted to use the restroom, yet again, Toni came around backstage with a huge grin. He wore a blue tux, looking out of place among all the circus performers around Mina.

"You make me so happy." He kissed her cheek. "Don't be nervous."

"Why does everyone think I'm nervous?" she asked with an anxious chuckle.

"I've known you for years. And recently, at our home, we've become far closer."

She nodded.

"As usual," he added, "you're less sure of yourself than everyone else."

"I'm not."

"Mina, can you turn to the left," said a stagehand readjusting her costume. "I need to clasp this."

"Good luck." And he hugged her. "You'll do great. I know it."

She turned and felt like a hundred pounds had been added to her left shoulder. *At least he didn't say break a leg.*

Oh, but I am nervous, Toni. I think I'm going to die if they don't let me on stage now.

Why is it always easier once I'm on stage? Just standing here is driving me crazy.

"One more minute, Ms. Daaé."

He had to say that. Like after doing this a thousand times, I don't know my cue to walk on stage?

By now, Toni had masterfully introduced the eighteenth century into the Big Top, and two colonial women in long coats with hoods and hand muffs were singing opera on one side of the stage while a bunch of foolish clowns were juggling or sauntering aimlessly on the other side.

She heard the familiar start of Mozart's Mass in C Minor K. 427 matched with the moving choral of the two singers in colonial attire on stage. Toni's work had masterfully shifted the mood of ridiculousness to a somber note, Mozart's piece asking us to weep for God's mercy in the midst of fools. It was time for Mina's grand entrance. Why had Toni chosen this piece to introduce her? And why was she thinking of that now? But she was. Mina stepped slowly on stage, with twenty people following her, amid gasps from the audience. Jesters stopped juggling to stare at the red serpent walking onstage, and everyone stopped to look at her. Her. How could they not? Her form took up the entire stage.

And then she sang with the most beautiful voice she could muster. And this was it. She was singing on Broadway. She was actually singing on Broadway! And Toni planned the production in such a way that every head in the auditorium—there were over a thousand people in the audience—and every eye looked upon her. She sang "Kyrie Eleison": "Lord have mercy on us." Other voices sang with her.

Stealing from Mozart? Perhaps. But typical of her new lover, Toni also knew the history behind this piece. He smoothly transitioned the orchestral music to "Et Incarnatus Est." When Mozart had first performed this song in Strasbourg, this had been sung by his new wife, Constanze. Coincidence? Doubtful. Toni rarely acted without purpose in his art. Had he planned this for his "new wife"? His new lover?

Whatever the case, Mina sang the piece, happily filling the role. She sang it not only for the play but in celebration of him. And this was easy because she loved him. She sang it with all her soul for him, not only because she wanted to be what the audience aspired for her to be but because she adored the music and the man who had brought it to them.

When it was over, all the lights dimmed, and Mina and her crew left the dark stage. The applause shook the walls and ceiling of the theater as she was crowded backstage with all her helpers.

"Incredible, Mina!" cried Henson.

Daniella placed a hand on her. "Nicely done."

Then they removed the heavy tail. Henson ran to other performers to get ready for the finishing acts. Mina looked around for Toni, but he wasn't there.

"Get in your dance clothes now," said Daniella with her usual smugness. "If you actually move as well as you sing, we might just have the success Toni thinks we'll have."

Mina felt on top of the world in her dressing room. She'd had accolades before but never for an actual performance. She could do this. She knew that now. She could actually make *The Harlequin* a success. She could be a star.

Quickly, she grabbed her white tights and pulled them on. Then she ran to her chair and looked at her face under the bright lights around her vanity mirror. Her face was already powdered white, and there was a hint of red along her nose matching the red on her lips. She carefully ran her hand along the side of her hair, straightening a few curls.

"A wonderful performance, Christine."

"Who's there!" Mina whirled around but saw no one in her dressing room.

She searched the room. Then she faced the mirror. To her horror, a man wearing a Pierrot clown face and white tights just like hers, but with a black mask over his eyes, sat on a stool across the room in the shadows. Mina turned again and he was gone.

"I'm here," he said with a laugh.

She recognized his French accent.

Mina turned back and saw him again in the mirror. This time he was standing, wearing a black cloak and long black cape with his black mask.

"Before I unveil myself to your audience, mademoiselle, I would like to congratulate you. Whatever happens in this fucking freak show, I wanted you to know that you did spectacularly. You sang much better than I ever did. Much better than anyone ever did in your role. Of course the words were Herr Mozart, yes? I take it Toni's message wasn't for me, his long-lost love? Perhaps for Herr Mozart's Constanze?

Or if not Constanze, then perhaps Christine ... for Toni's Christine Daaé?"

"You're not here, Erik," she said, shaking her head. "I'm not seeing you."

"You're not. I'm in the mirror."

"Leave me alone," she pleaded, looking down at the carpet, avoiding the mirror. "If you care for me, Erik, please leave. This is our opening night."

"Now don't upset me." He sounded angry.

She could see his reflection leaning forward and wagging a finger at her.

"The one thing I couldn't do after I fell is what you do next. *Dance.* Don't do that. But you are, aren't you? You are going to try to dance, aren't you? And you know what? You might be a fine singer, bitch, but your cavorting is an embarrassment. It's rather like the way you make love."

"Please, stop. Shut up." And she put her hands to her ears. "Just stop saying anything."

And there was silence. Mina slowly pulled her hands away, and she jumped at the sight of Erik still standing behind her in the mirror. She felt his hand run down her arm. Now he wore white tights with a painted frown behind his mask, exactly as Mina would be dressed for her dance performance in Act II. Mina turned to face him, but he was gone.

"Stop it! God, please stop it, Erik!"

"This shall be the last time I need to show myself," said his voice. "Don't worry. You will see me with everyone when you fall. Your fall shall be glorious. Glory be to you, not God. Such a fall will be in the papers and you will be famous... Ah, but I age myself. What do you use for news nowadays? When you fall, ma chérie, we can be together in pleasure, like I showed you, for an eternity."

Mina got up and straightened her tights. She looked in her mirror, satisfied with her appearance. Erik, still on the periphery, staring at her body, seemed satisfied too.

"You can only pretend I'm not here for so long."

Mina reached over to her purse on the table. She opened it and looked at a medicine bottle, thinking of taking some pills, but she feared they would make her drowsy during her performance.

"And that," he whispered near her ear, "won't get rid of me either."

Mina closed her eyes. "If you love me, Erik, you won't ruin the show. Please. Don't mess this up for me. This is everything to me."

"Everything to you or everything to your fuck-clown? Oh, sweet Ms. Daaé, but it was everything to *me*." He flashed a slithery, sardonic smile. "And who ever said I love you?"

There was a knock on the door.

"Come in!" Mina snapped more loudly than she intended.

Toni walked in with his grand smile.

Erik flashed the nastiest scowl in the mirror but then disappeared.

"Wonderful, Mina! Absolutely wonderful!" He ran over and hugged her. Then he moved her back a little, searching her face. "What's the matter? You look upset."

"God, Toni. I saw him again."

Toni furrowed his brow. Then he lost his smile. "Not now, Mina. Please." His voice was not kind. It was angry.

Mina simply nodded.

"Save your energy for the finale."

"But he's here, he's really here. He said I'm psychic. I must be bringing him to our opening night because of the stress ... Oh, forget it. I'll try to ignore him."

"Just do what you did a minute ago," he said with a sigh. "You stole the show. My God, Mina, we could have just done that one song and the audience would still be at our feet."

"Thanks."

"I'm so proud of you." He kissed her on the lips.

As he did, she could have sworn she saw the reflection of a man in a mask, in the mirror, glaring at them.

"Dance like the wind, Mina," he said quietly. "Sing like an angel. If you do that, this show will be a smash. I know it."

"I know, Toni. I know." Then she forced a smile. "Of course, you know my song was sung by Constanze."

"Che? Constanze? Do not honor me so, my dear," he said with a laugh, putting a hand on her shoulder. "I am not Herr Mozart."

"But I do love you, Toni." She looked up into his eyes. "I do. You've cared about me more than anyone ever has. I sang the piece for you, Toni. I love you."

"I love you too, Mina." He hugged her tightly. "Now, best of luck." He kissed her cheek and whispered, "I love you so much."

CRACK.

They both jumped and turned toward the wall of vanity mirrors. A large line had appeared across a mirror.

2 3

ACT II

Don Giovanni opens with Don Giovanni wooing and raping a woman, then killing the father of the woman he ravaged. Not so in *The Harlequin*. There was no death. If there was any figure of foreboding, it was the mix of grandeur and power exuded by Mina's introduction. No. There was no murder or violence in Toni's play. But there were suitors. Loads of them. And clowns. Lots of them too. And there was Mina Daaé. Mina was what Act II was really about.

After her triumphant entrance, she sat nervously backstage in her white leotard. A pianist played Liszt in the orchestra pit. Then she had her cue, a bit of rouge was brushed on her white-painted cheeks, and she rushed back to center stage.

Male ballet dancers with much thicker white face paint rushed around her. Some pushed each other, others pulled away. All the while, Mina stood frozen. She didn't dance. She was more like a white prop on stage. She was not as grand, but as she was the only dancer not moving, the audience's eyes fell upon her.

Finally, when surrounded by ten of them, she pushed the men from her with a broad, theatrical stroke of her arms. One allowed space for her to twirl and she did her best. She even heard a bit of applause, likely from someone already enamored with her performance in the red dress. Then she did a few leaps and turns, not a stellar grand jeté or glissade—hardly good enough for Daniella, and barely suitable for Broadway—but enough to mark her territory as a dancer. Then came two men. One took her hand and twirled with her as the lights shone over them. He led her, moving her fast to the rhythm of the ebony and ivory playing like waves in the sea, until another ballet dancer in clown face grabbed her other arm. The two spun around her, and the dance became a bizarre competition, vying for her attention.

She took the role of bystander once more. One suitor was knocked down. Mina ran to the fallen man and helped him up. As she lifted him, she raised her head to the other dancer and shamed him by dancing with the fallen man. And so it went on.

Soon came women. They, too, swarmed the stage, twirling and dancing a wonderful waltz with some of the men. And once more a suitor came to take Mina's hand. This time a woman.

Mina had never liked watching female dancers. Their movements were more fluid than hers, reminding her painfully of her failures. But she tried. She danced. The play went on and on like this, with an occasional fool from the Big Top rushing on stage and being splashed by water or stumbling.

Everything went as rehearsed until an unusual suitor in a long, black cape walked onstage. A performer Mina did not recognize. One who wore a shiny black mask and black cape over his leotard. As he took her hand, he said in her ear, "My dear Christine, how are you going to pretend that I'm not here now?"

"I told you to stop, Erik," she hissed by his ear as he raised her hand over her head. She wasn't miked, so she didn't need to worry about the audience hearing them. "Not now!"

He didn't stop. He threw his cape on the stage and, in his white leotard and mask, he danced, following the correct steps for the play.

"Embarrassing pas de bourrée, mon ami," he said beside her. "No, no, no. This will not do. Je n'aime pas ça! Allow me to show you how to dance."

And he stopped, released her hand, and stomped on the ground. Many of the other dancers fled the stage. Then, alone, Erik twirled to center stage as Mina stood and watched. Other dancers gasped as this was not a part of their regular routine. Mina froze. Then Erik did what Toni had said only he could do. He danced as if he were skipping water, or skating, with elegance Mina had never seen before. All the dancers and actors on stage froze, watching him. Many people backstage were staring too. When there were enough sounds coming from the audience, he bowed broadly before Mina and reached out his hand for her.

Mina just stood in shock.

"Move!" Henson said in a forced whisper from backstage. "Mina, dance! Dance!"

She took his hand and they returned to a waltz; this time, Mina was having a difficult time keeping up with her feet. He twirled her around as if she were a prop.

"Erik, you have to slow down. I can't keep up with you."

"I thought I wasn't real?" And he swung Mina right up against his body, his face close enough to kiss her. And then he did. He kissed her with more violence than romance. The audience cheered.

"Why are you here?" Mina asked.

"I'm here to witness your fall," he whispered in her ear, grasping her close. "I've already told you that. Many times."

They held each other. Mina barely noticed their movements, but she was moving. He was lifting her entire body with great strength, and she was simply gliding on her toes.

"But why, Erik? If you care about me? I don't want to go with you. I want—"

"To be with Toni?"

He leaned her down close to the ground, and she could clearly see a scowl through the opening in his black mask. The movements were similar to those in their rehearsal, but far more violent. The audience had no clue, but Mina guessed the producers were going crazy watching the two of them dance off cue.

"Erik, I love him."

"Christine loved Raoul once. Erik didn't grace you with his feet then. Your mind allows this. Your psychic power. Your empathic energy, almost as magical and wondrous as your voice. Christine, you are an angel, but you shall be my fallen angel. Like Don Giovanni, you are a lascivious whore. Your punishment for your lovers shall be your fall. First Gail, now you. That is why we dance. 'Tis a funeral dance. A requiem in celebration of your fall. Relish the splendor!"

"Toni hasn't taken me," Mina said, shaking her head between spins. She came close to his face, but the spin made her dizzy.

Under the mask, he squinted his glowing jade eyes in the darkness and shook his head.

"I'm not taken."

She skipped a step and nearly fell, but Erik caught her. Then he spun her like a top. She felt like his prop, his fan or poi. He was so good that she only had to do her best to move her feet with him.

"I'm not talking about you, stupide bitch! I care nothing for you! You've taken my love. My life. I love Toni. And just like Christine, you shall fall."

Before she could respond, he spun her again. Her feet dragged in circles over the wooden floor, and he let her go. Such was the centripetal force that the whole theater spun around her with the purple light on the ceiling swirling. She heard gasps from the audience. And, for a flash, she saw a bright light shine over one of the top balconies at the back of the theater. There, under the fifth balcony, illuminated by a floodlight above the packed theater, was the naked body of Gail dangling from a rope. Gail was swaying and turning.

"Putain!" Erik violently grabbed her in his arms. Then he pointed up at the balcony and snapped, "Look. Look now! You killed her. Feel love? See what it did to her, poor girl. She took her life, but she died from your rejection. Because of you. Now I reject you! I love Monsieur Vollini. So decide. What shall be your fate, Christine? Rope or ledge?"

The lights were cut. It became pitch black and Erik let Mina go. She fell out of his arms and spun in circles onto the ground in darkness. The applause raged so loudly in the auditorium that it hurt her ears.

When Mina did not get up, people from backstage rushed to help her. She was half carried offstage.

"Incredible!" Daniella exclaimed to Mina. "I don't believe it!"

Mina blinked and caught Daniella's face looking down at her with the strangest thing she had ever seen—a smile.

"I've never seen you move like that." Daniella was still weirdly grinning.

"Get her a bag," said Vince, crouching over her. "She's not well. Something to breathe in. Quick. She's hyperventilating. She fainted, Dani."

"Well, I couldn't expect any better," Daniella replied with a shrug. "I don't think I've ever seen anyone dance like that."

Mina nodded, snatched a bag from a dancer, and breathed deeply inside it. "Can't … breathe." She looked up at Dani as a few dancers helped her up from the floor and onto a chair. "Glad … you liked it," she said, breathing through the bag.

"Liked it?" Daniella shook her head. "Are you kidding? I loved it."

"Great job, Mina!" cried another stagehand, touching her shoulder.

The audience thundered with applause in the dark auditorium, and they wouldn't stop.

"Great job," shouted a dancer in black tights walking by her.

"Incredible," said another.

"*Give her space!*" snapped Henson. "Back away." And they obeyed their director. "Are you okay, Mina? What happened?"

Mina breathed deeply into the plastic bag again. "Where's Toni?"

"We've got another emergency with the lighting," said Henson, running a hand through his thin hair. "I don't know if you happened to notice, but the light shone on one of the balconies. It's always something. But how are you? Are you all right?"

She just nodded.

"You finally saw him," Mina said.

Daniella furrowed her brow. Then she turned to Henson, who also looked confused.

"You finally saw Erik, didn't you? Good. I … I think I finally understand why he's been haunting me. He loves Toni. He doesn't love me. See, Toni loved Erik. Now he's here for revenge over Toni's love for me. He wants to ruin the play because Toni loves me now. And ruin me. He intends to kill me in the last act."

"What's she talking about?" asked Vince.

"Did you take your medicine?" Daniella asked.

"Erik … didn't you see him, Vince?" Mina asked.

Vince shook his head.

She looked up at twenty faces, now hovering over her. Most were just patting her shoulder or waving a jovial thumbs-up.

But a few looked at her like she wasn't well. That gave her the familiar sinking feeling again.

"But … didn't you all see him? He was incredible. He was so grace-

ful. He danced as if he were on ice. Just like Toni said he would. But …
I understand now. I get why the phantom is haunting me. See, it's Toni.
He loves Toni, not me. He doesn't care about me. It's all Toni."

"Fantastic, Mina!" Toni crouched down by the chair and touched
her shoulder. "Incredible." He turned to Daniella. "I told you."

Daniella permitted a nod, but she was finally starting to lose her
smile and look like her old bitchy self again.

"If you can't go on, Mina, we'll stop the show," Vince said.

"Che?" asked Toni. "What did he just say? Can't go on? Stop the
show?"

But he wasn't the only one staring at Vince. All heads, including
members of the stage crew, some actors in colonial clothes, and some
dancers, turned and stared at Vince.

"She's not well," explained Vince. "She looks pale. She fainted after
the dance."

"She's wearing clown makeup," Henson remarked.

Toni said quietly, "Mina, what is it? Are you okay?"

"I don't know if I should do the last act. Erik wants to kill me. He
wants me to fall just like he did. I don't know if I can go up there."

"I thought we were through this," Toni said. "I won't let anything
bad happen to you."

"It's not up to you." Mina shook her head violently. But then she
looked deep into his eyes. She thought of his play. She'd rather die than
stop his play. She took another deep breath in the bag and nodded.

"Mina," Toni said, grabbing her hand. "I'll be up there if anything
happens."

But she wasn't worried Toni wouldn't be there. She was worried the
phantom would be there.

"That was fantastic, Mina!" cried a stagehand, tapping her
shoulder.

"Just give her some space!" snapped Henson.

"Great job, Mina," interrupted another dancer. She was with two
extras and they all nodded excitedly, each putting a hand on her
shoulder.

But then one asked, cocking his head back as they walked away, "Is
she all right?"

"It must be the stress of opening night," Vince said. Then he forced a smile at Mina. "It wouldn't be the first time a performer fainted. All I know is your dance was amazing. It was one of the best performances I've ever seen. It wasn't all scripted but, why not? Who cares? The way you moved. I don't think Daniella thought you could even do those moves."

"I didn't," Daniella admitted.

Vince had asked if they should stop the show. Was he kidding? Everyone had looked at him like he was crazy. Even Mina. She could never do that, especially not with the joyous look now splashed on Toni's face. He was so excited. Even if the critics and the audience hated the show, he'd be overjoyed that his dream had come true.

She took a deep breath into her bag again and looked up at all of them once more. "But did you see the man with the mask dancing with me? He was…"

They hadn't.

"Toni, he said he's going to make me fall to the stage after the net's cut."

"I won't allow it," Toni said, grabbing her hand. "No, I won't. Even if you fall, you'll have the safety wire. And not only that, I'll be up there right with you."

Mina nodded and tried to force a smile.

"Are they practicing?" Daniella asked Henson.

Henson just shrugged.

24

DON GIOVANNI

MINA SAT BACKSTAGE, STAGE RIGHT, ON A STOOL, WATCHING CLOWNS fight one another in a circus scene as a makeup artist wiped the clown makeup from her face. Toni had said he wouldn't have her in clown face in the final act. Her black hair flowed around her now-naked face. Then the artist applied makeup just to accentuate her natural facial features. Meanwhile, others helped throw the heavy, flabby white clown outfit over her shoulders and fasten the wire to it. Another stagehand slipped on the ridiculous large red clown shoes. She had to get ready quickly. Her suitors, more clowns, were already fighting with one another—some actually fighting, others simply dancing—waiting for the Harlequin to arrive.

The fighting stopped. Then she saw what she dreaded. Stagehands in dark camouflage slowly rolled the giant two-tower structure to the back of the stage as the chaos continued up front. Mina knew it came with a tightrope this time, but the tower stood so high that she couldn't see it.

"You're doing amazing," said the makeup artist.

"Thanks, Carl."

Carl was the key makeup artist, an effeminate gay man who Mina loved. He was so sweet. "Gosh, Mina, I don't know how you do this next scene," he said, looking up at the towers. "It's so high up there. I hate heights."

"I don't like heights either," Mina said. "Just don't tell anyone."

"Keep doing what you're doing," he said with a laugh. "You're amazing." Then he saw a cue from someone closer to the stage. "None of the dancers ever danced like that." He brushed her nose and part of her cheek. "That's it. You're up."

Mina had difficulty swallowing. She lifted the legs of her ridiculous frilly outfit; it was so heavy and unwieldy. Then she made her way to the ladder by the steel tower.

Carl stopped her, grabbing her shoulder. "Mina, don't forget the cape."

"Oh, can you help me put it on?"

Carl fastened the black cape over her flabby white suit for her finale. It was hot in all the clothes. Though they were not nearly as stifling as her red dragon dress, now she had to climb the ladder carrying all of it.

"Good luck!" Carl said with a big smile, and he lightly pushed her back from behind.

She walked to the ladder.

In the darkness at the back of the stage, few people could see her. Some actresses by the stage tapped her arm and whispered, "Good luck." The whole time, looking back, she was blinded by the bright lights shining on the stage. And laughter. Clowns were doing the most ridiculous things before she went on.

She touched the metal ladder of the pedestal. It was cold. A few stagehands rushed from behind to help lift her baggy clothes over the first step. Then she started climbing alone.

As she climbed, she heard the orchestra prepare. It was a prelude before *Don Giovanni*, the overture. But in the middle of it all was a distant cacophony of saxophones and drums. Between the fools and the noise, it was madness, something Toni was very good at creating.

Her hands shook. They always shook as she climbed the ladder, but tonight it was far worse. Not only was it opening night; it was the night of her "fall," according to her devil.

Just one step at a time. You can do this. One step. Then another.

He's real. Erik was real. He must be. Though she might be able to squeak by as a dancer on Broadway, her glorious choreographic performance tonight had not been her own. It had been too perfect. He had moved her. Perhaps he would make her fall now. After all, the net was stretched below the pedestal, not the ladder. And she felt his breath beside her. Somehow, she *felt* him. And then she heard him.

"You're really going through with this," Erik whispered by her ear. "Despite all my warnings?"

"I thought you wanted me to fall?" Again, she wasn't miked. She knew that her microphone would only turn on when *Don Giovanni* started thundering.

"It's inevitable. But it really isn't about you."

"You're jealous. You want me to die because I'm in love with Toni?" Her hatred of him, her anger, pushed her legs to climb the steps faster.

"No. I want you to die because he's in love with you. Your fall is glorious vengeance for what he did to me. A fitting revenge. Makes perfect sense, Christine, no?"

"Liar. The only Christine was my great-ancestor in Paris. My name is Mina. Devil, watch me fall. Let it happen. I don't care. It will be the greatest finale. Our show shall be the greatest show on Broadway."

"The greatest show? Indeed. Only … I'm afraid to tell you this, *Mina*, but the net is not the only thing cut. I loosened your wire from the fly tower."

Her legs weakened from those words, but she didn't stop climbing. She did slow a little, though. And yet, even despite this final threat, she made it to the top. She didn't dare look down. Slowly, with her body still shaking, she climbed onto the parapet.

The orchestra thundered. There was no longer time to think. The platform shook. The violins and drums thundered, and she knew that her microphone was now operational. She was surrounded by purple light. A violet floodlight filled the pedestal.

"Don Giovanni …" Her voice rang out strongly in the strange tenor sung by a woman. She was supposed to stand, but she was afraid. This being the first show, half of her involuntarily pushed herself up on her knees, but feeling that particular unpleasant rise in her butt, she couldn't stand as rehearsed. Yet she sang on. She just sat on her knees as her voice rang out her accusations to the theater below. Meanwhile, lights shone on clowns onstage surrounding her, looking up, and pointing at her. They sang the words of Don Giovanni as she played the part of their accuser: the Commendatore.

She forced herself to stand. Then she swept her arm down toward the stage in a broad, threatening gesture, staring with wide-open eyes, accusing all of them. She pointed at the clowns on stage, then the clowns off center stage, and then the crowd, every single one of them, the entire amphitheater guilty of sinful lust and disgrace.

There was no net. She could see that now. There was no net between her and the cold wooden floor. But she didn't stop singing. This was her moment. The moment of her theatrical triumph. And she sang her part as the statue, the judge, and the accuser judging them all.

Yet her triumph was shaken as a light switched on over a balcony, the fifth balcony again. Once more, she saw her best friend dangling from a rope. Gail was more real, more terrible, wearing her fuchsia coat and jeans, her long blonde hair and tranquil closed eyes spotlighted, shifting ever so slightly over the audience. Then the light shut off and Gail disappeared.

Replacing it was another purple floodlight shining on the pedestal across from her. Erik, adorned in his black mask and cape, wearing the same baggy white clown outfit underneath, like her own, accompanied her in a familiar baritone, just as he had done in the audition.

That's when there was a disturbance on stage. Many clowns moved back and stared as a man in a blue tuxedo rushed frantically across the stage. Floodlights shone over him. It was Toni. He was waving his hands desperately at the orchestra for them to stop. But the orchestra played and Mina kept singing.

At the bottom of her ladder, Toni shouted, "She can't jump! The net's cut! She must get down from the ladder! Get her down now!" His words competed with the loud orchestra and her voice, but more lights turned on across the stage. "Get down, Mina! It's not safe. Don't do the final jump!" he cried, looking up at her. Some in the audience stood up in a panic. "Stop the play!" But the orchestra played on. "My God, stop the music!" Toni kept shouting, but it was difficult to hear him. He wasn't miked.

He rushed to the ladder and started to climb.

Mina didn't stop singing. And the orchestra kept playing. All the performers ignored Toni and resumed the opera. Then Mina pointed down at him, wide-eyed once more under the violet light, accusing her lover below.

Every light in the theater turned on.

"Come down, Mina! The net's cut."

From a glance at her periphery, she saw many in the audience stand by their seats. She could see their faces more clearly now, over a thousand, as they stared up at her, some with hands covering their mouths, others signaling for her to go down the ladder. At first, she trembled seeing all of them, so far below, watching her. Then she stood taller, gazing down and accusing all of them, her voice ringing out more strongly than ever.

She saw the phantom, in her periphery, walk across the tightrope. When he was close enough, he started to pull at her arm, back and forth, trying to push her off the parapet. Mina heard screams as she teetered for a moment over the edge. Then, on her other side, Toni appeared at the top of the ledge, grasping for her hand.

"Verrai (You come)," Mina sang.

Toni pleaded for her to take his hand. His eyes looked deep into hers, and she could feel his love. His care moved her so much that she nearly broke character. It was as real to her as her phantom now tugging her other arm. But then she remembered her role as Commendatore. The play would have its fall. She opened her eyes wide and pointed at Toni once more.

"Dammi la mano in pegno (Give me thy hand in token)," Mina sang.

"Eccola (Here)!" Toni cried, reaching again for her to take his hand.

A security guard rushed across the stage and stood under the ladder. "Don't fall! The net is cut!"

"Cos'hai (What's wrong)?" sang Mina, looking down at the guard under the ladder.

The crowd panicked, with many onlookers rushing to the front rows of the auditorium, shouting for Mina to climb down.

Then Toni grabbed her arm to pull her onto the ladder, but Erik snatched her wrist over the tightrope. Mina marveled that Erik could pull her at all while remaining balanced. They tugged her back and forth. Finally, Mina freed her arms from both of them, nearly falling off the ladder. Many in the audience gasped, trying to climb onto the stage.

"*My God, help her down!*" cried a woman's voice.

"Pentiti (Repent)!" Mina cried to Toni.

"No!" Toni said.

"Pentiti!"

"No."

"Sì."

"No."

"Sì."

"No."

"Sì"

"No! No!"

"Ah! Tempo più non v'è (There is no more time)!"

It was her time. Her time on Broadway!

And here is where I soar.

Toni reached out for her once more.

She gazed down at his hand and then the glove of the Phantom. Their reaching hands reminded her of her painting. That painting was still on the easel by her bed. The image somehow gave her comfort in her lonely apartment. She had slept with that hand in darkness, knowing it always reached for her as she slept, just as Toni was reaching for her now. But in the painting, it had been her creation. Now it was Toni and an apparition.

"Tutto a tue colpe é poco (This is nothing, compared to your sins)," sang voices from the auditorium. "Vieni, c'è un mal peggior (Come, there is a worse pain)!"

"Mina!" Toni shouted so loud that his voice echoed in the theater despite not being miked, competing with the music by the orchestra. "Forget the play! Stop the singing and come down. Please! Don't do this!" Toni's eyes were tearing as he desperately reached out for her again.

She stared at his hand once more, gazing at his naked fingers. Each finger a part of a machine that reached out to her like the hand dripping paint on her canvas. How could this muscle, bone, and sinew be of such importance to her? To anyone?

"Tutto a tue colpe é poco (This is nothing, compared to your sins). Vieni, c'è un mal peggior (Come, there is a worse pain)!"

Of far greater elegance was Erik's glove. Even now, as the phantom was attempting to throw her from the precipice, he brushed her fingers with the lovely softness of his glove.

"I don't care about the play!" Toni shouted, violently shaking his head. "I don't. I don't care about it."

Mina looked into Toni's eyes and nodded.

"Take my hand. I only care about you, Mina. *I love you!*"

"Che inferno, che terror (What a hell, what a terror)!"

That was her theatrical cue. She grabbed Toni's hand while yanking her other hand from Erik. The phantom shifted uneasily on the rope by her side. Then he let out a scream heard through the speakers. She watched the fiend fall.

He fell like a sack from the ceiling rafters and pounded the wooden stage below. There was a rush of screams and gasps from the audience, and anyone still on stage scattered.

All turned dark.

Then a single light fell on a body lying at the center of the stage, wrapped in a black cape. And in that moment no one, not one clown on stage or spectator in the auditorium, moved.

The silence was broken when a clown with thick, curly red hair appeared, stage right, wearing a baggy white outfit and twirling a cane. Theater lighting followed him as he sauntered his way across the stage, over to the fallen body. Then he used his wooden cane to poke and prod. He turned to the audience, then looked down at the fallen body. The phantom's pitch-black cape was wrapped so tightly around the body that it reminded Mina of a burial shroud. The clown grabbed the cape and, like a magician pulling a cloth off a table, yanked it from the body with great bravado. There was nothing underneath. The clown swirled the cape around him and draped it over his shoulders. Then he gave a grand bow before the audience.

There was silence. Complete shock. Then applause. A deafening applause.

"I love you," Mina whispered in Toni's arms, both looking down. "I love you so much."

All the lights dimmed. Then a single light delicately shone over Mina and Toni. They held each other tightly in an embrace and kissed.

"We did it, Mina."

2 5

THE MASQUERADE

Mina was nervous. She sat beside Toni before a large table on the brightly lit stage after *The Harlequin*. They wore thick Pierrot clown face and puffy white clown costumes. There were signs everywhere saying No Flash Photography, but that was ignored, and Mina had to keep squinting.

"What's fame like, Ms. Daaé?" asked an older woman with long hair. She was in the front row behind bright lights. Mina's first question. A direct one. And with the rest of the reporters laughing.

"I don't know," she said with a chuckle, looking at Toni. He squeezed her hand. "Not much different from before, I guess."

"But people crowd you. They want your autograph or a picture. Everyone's enamored with you after only one night. It's like instant fame. How do you cope?"

"I help her," said Toni, leaning into the microphone.

They laughed.

"They rush you too, Mr. Vollini. But you two are close, right? There are rumors she's staying at your house. Is that true?"

"Her house."

The reporters laughed.

"So there's something going on between you two? Producer and star?"

"Did you think *The Harlequin* would be such a hit, Toni?" interjected a young male interviewer. He was wearing glasses, but Mina couldn't make out much else behind the bright lights.

"I dreamt it so," Toni said with a nod. "We were very successful in Europe, but that was a different play than in the States. It was more of a circus. Not opera. And we never had success to this degree. Of course, it's mainly because of my star. The musical would have gone nowhere without the voice of Mina Daaé. Her voice touches God."

"Oh, stop," Mina said, hitting his shoulder.

"'Tis true." He looked deeply into her eyes. "If I didn't have you, it would have gone nowhere here."

"So there is something between you two?" asked the woman again.

Toni leaned close to Mina and kissed her on the lips. It was a peck, but the camera flashes went crazy. Mina quickly moved away and shielded her eyes. So did Toni.

Mina knew that this photo was gold. Two clowns sitting together onstage, kissing. It was almost as if they had planned a perfect photo op for a press release. And, knowing Toni, it probably was.

"You played the role in Europe, right?" asked another interviewer. He looked more like a spectator, coming from a row farther back.

"Yeah, yeah. But it wasn't the same. I was trained to sing Herr Mozart, but my voice doesn't touch God like Mina's does."

They laughed but Toni remained quite serious.

"What about—"

"So you two are living together now?" interrupted the woman interviewer. "For the record."

"For the record?" Mina leaned into the microphone. "Yes."

"And the act where—"

"Toni was so kind to give me the role," Mina said. "I didn't expect that." She was surprised to see the whole auditorium quiet down as she spoke. She didn't like the sound of her voice. It sounded a little shaky. She gripped her hand tightly. "I mean, I always wanted to perform … but I never really thought I was good enough. Toni gave me the confidence to stand up here in front of all of you and sing and dance. Performing is a difficult thing, you know. It's like … like being unclothed. Naked. Fragile, breakable. I don't think a lot of people know that. And I'm not trying to be arrogant."

"You could never be arrogant, Ms. Daaé," interjected the woman interviewer.

"Thanks." Then there was more silence as Mina gathered her thoughts. All their eyes were on her. "You really don't know what it's like on stage. I wish you could experience what it's like for me. It's free, but scary. I think that's what Toni is conveying with his ending." Then she put her finger to her chin and said, "There's a power there. A naked, almost primal, power that I feel when I'm showing my raw self and performing before you. It's terrifying, but electrifying. It's free. If I can express that freedom, even for a moment, you know, show the naked raw person behind my mask, then I succeeded in my performance and I'm satisfied. And I get to perform this every night because of Toni. He says he owes the show to me but, no, actually I owe it to him."

"Oh, cara mia," Toni said, rubbing her back, "thank you."

The auditorium became loud. There was a great deal of murmuring, and some of the interviewers talked over each other.

"But really, Toni," Mina added, "I think—" She looked deeply into his eyes.

Toni just smiled sweetly.

"Toni, I think they like your play so much because it's real. I know it's why I do. The pomp is there, the silliness, the clowns, but then it all comes crashing down in the end and becomes real. Very real, you know?"

"Why don't we talk about that last act?" said the interviewer. "At the end, it was terrifying watching you, on opening night, because so many people thought you were actually going to fall, Ms. Daaé. I remember really feeling like you were going to jump. Yes, it was frightening. Just like you said. No one could see your wire. And Toni acted genuinely panicked as he rushed up the ladder. All the lights were on, like now. It was as if the play was over. And Toni wasn't even dressed up in any costume. He just had on the suit for opening night. It was really you two, and there was a desperate sense that it would be over for you, Ms. Daaé—not the show, your life. Yes, it was real. So many of us in the audience were scared."

"I was scared too," Toni said, leaning into the microphone. Many in the audience laughed. "I was. It's a very difficult piece to perform. Many years ago, one of my beloved actors actually fell."

"We've heard that."

"Si ..." Toni took a deep breath and Mina touched his arm. "I've had to live through that memory over and over. It's very hard. But the drama was written by him. Don Giovanni and Mozart with the fall were all written by him. So, as difficult as it is to repeat it, in a way, I perform it in honor of his life. And I know he would not want it any other way."

"So you're going to do it every show? What about safety codes, with everyone rushing the stage? And will the stunt even work when people start expecting it?"

"The play will go on as it did opening night," Toni said dismissively. "I will not dishonor my friend's work. We will play out his fall. You can judge it any way you like. The art is our art."

"But there won't be a net? It's seems so unsafe."

"No, I've assured it is absolutely safe for me and Mina." And he squeezed her hand and gave her a sweet smile. "I wrote the play to draw the audience in. And I think you get that. Anyway, if I changed it, it wouldn't be *The Harlequin.*"

"But what about you, Mina?" asked the lady behind the lights. "Do you intend to perform the same way? Risking your life? Singing and standing high on a pedestal where there's no safety net below?"

"For sure."

"But you said earlier that you were afraid of heights?"

"The harlequin performed it in Paris," she said with a shrug. "So why not me?"

"I love you, Mina," Toni said.

"I love you, too, Toni."

And the two clowns kissed again. There were a lot of camera flashes. And there was applause.

THE END

ALSO BY A.L. HAWKE

PARANORMAL ROMANCE

- THE HAWTHORNE UNIVERSITY WITCH PREQUEL
- THE HAWTHORNE UNIVERSITY WITCH SERIES I-III
- THE HAWTHORNE UNIVERSITY WITCH SERIES 4-6
- THE HAWTHORNE UNIVERSITY WITCH HOLIDAY COLLECTION

- MY EVIL EYE
- THE GUARDIAN
- NECTAR OF AMBROSIA
- CORA

FANTASY: THE AZURE SERIES

- HARMONIA
- CORA: RISE OF THE FALLEN GODDESS
- AZURE BLUE
- CORAL RED
- PRINCESS SOJOURN

SCIENCE FICTION

- CANDY SAVANT SERIES

Books available at https://alhawke.com/books

PARTING WORDS

What did you think of *Phantom Hearts*? By placing a book review, you can inform others of your thoughts and help spread the word about my book.

Want more? Periodically I like to send news regarding current or new projects. If you'd like to be privy, I encourage you to sign up to my email newsletter. Your information will remain private and you can cancel any time.

Sign up at www.alhawke.com or scan the following QR code:

A.L. Hawke is the author of the bestselling Hawthorne University Witch series. The author lives in Southern California torching the midnight candle over lovers against a backdrop of machines, nymphs, magic, spice and mayhem. A.L. Hawke writes fantasy and romance spanning four thousand years, from pre-civilization to contemporary and beyond.

Visit A.L. Hawke at www.alhawke.com

Email: contact@alhawke.com